SNAPS

IAN ST JAMES AWARD WINNERS

AT THE STROKE OF TWELVE (Fontana/Collins, 1989)
David Rose (1st), Judy Forshaw (2nd), Belinda Raine (3rd), Lorna Fergusson, Elizabeth Harris, Clive Lancaster, David Mallett, David Muir, Richard Newton, Hugh Robinson, Denis Sexton, Roland Vernon

SUCCESS STRIKES TWELVE (Fontana/Collins, 1990)
Annie Hedley (1st), William Walker (2nd), Louise Doughty (3rd), Valori Cowie, Phil Feighan, William Harley, Anne McKay, John Moy, Deborah Parker, James Roberts, Linda Sheridan, Gentian Walls

MIDNIGHT OIL (Fontana/HarperCollins, 1991)
Faith Addis (1st), Alan Dunn (2nd), Stephanie Ellyne (3rd), Richard Clarke, Sarah Gracie, Louise Lear, Marian Mathieu, Michael Morris, Patricia Mowbray, Frances Peck, Lesley Tilling, Patricia Tyrrell

BLOOD, SWEAT & TEARS (Fontana/HarperCollins, 1992)
Jeremy Cain (1st), Francesca Clementis (2nd=), Peter Naylor (2nd=), Chuck Anderson, Sylvia Baker, Belinda Caminada, Ellen Eugene, Gerry Fenge, Sarah Goldsmith, Josephine Chia Over, Frances Watt, Adrian Williams

FLYING HIGH (HarperCollins, 1993)
Shorter Category: Kate Atkinson (1st), Juliet McCarthy (2nd), James Maguire (3rd), Cynthia Chapman, Isa Moynihan, Linda Pitt
Longer Category: Philip Sealy (1st), Hilary Waters (2nd), Min Dinning (3rd), Stephanie Egerton, Carey Jane Hardy, Jude Jones, Sheila Kelley, Lorraine Lorimer, Cheryl Nyland-Littig, Leonard Tyler,

BROUGHT TO BOOK (HarperCollins, 1994)
Shorter Category: Anna McGrail (1st), Alison Armstrong (2nd), A S Penne (3rd), Stephanie Ellyne, Clare Stephens Girvan, Kirk O'Connor
Longer Category: Joshua Davidson (1st), Mike McCormack (2nd), Sue Camarados (3rd=), Bronia Kita (3rd=), Peter Caley, David Evans, Vivien Gaynor, Jackie Kohnstamm, Kate Lincoln, Tom Smith

PLEASURE VESSELS (Angela Royal Publishing, 1995)
Shorter Category: Dick Bayne (1st), Hwee Hwee Tan (2nd), Bead Roberts (3rd), Susan Smith Barrie, Fiona Curnow, Justina Hart, Nancy Lindisfarne, Susannah Rickards, Revonne Roth, Kirsty Seymour-Ure, Edward Welti
Longer Category: Kristina Amadeus (1st=), Maria Caruso (1st=), Nick Kelly (3rd), Jeannette AlLée, Heather Doran Barbieri, Jonathan Carr, Tim Connery, Douglas Galbraith, A S Penne, Maxine Rosaler, Tom Saunders

PULSE FICTION (Angela Royal Publishing, 1997 – containing 1996 & 1997 Award winners)
1996: Josephine Corcoran (1st), Indira Debah (2nd), Carrie Worrall (3rd), Julia Darling, Claire Bugler Hewitt, Tobias Hill, Jonathan Leeming, Beverley Strauss, Julia Widdows, Anne Wodehouse
1997: Michel Faber (1st), Kevin Doyle (2nd), David Evans (3rd), Barbara Carnegie, Jean Edmunds, Stephanie Hale, Deirdre Heddon, Wendy McKechnie, Marc Williamson, Mick Wood

COMING SOON – THE 1998 AWARD WINNERS:
Michael Barclay, Lucinda Bowles, Madeleine Dahlem, Lindsay Hawdon, Ann Jolly, Aoi Matsushima, Karen Munro, Amanda Oosthuizen, Barbara Villanova, Frances Watt.

SNAPSHOTS

10 YEARS OF THE IAN ST JAMES AWARDS

ARP
Angela Royal Publishing

Published by ANGELA ROYAL PUBLISHING LTD
PO Box 138, Tunbridge Wells, Kent TN3 0ZT

First published 1999

A CIP catalogue for this book is available from the British Library
ISBN 1-899860-80-0

Typeset by Nick & Fred Hill/Desert♥Hearts
Printed in Great Britain by Biddles Ltd, Guildford

For further information on the Ian St James Awards and *The New Writer*
magazine, write to the New Writers' Club at PO Box 60, Cranbrook,
Kent TN17 2ZR, or telephone 01580 212626.

Contents

Ian St James *Foreword*   7

S N A P S H O T S

Lorna Fergusson *Exposed*   11

Judy Forshaw *Ellie*   25

Elizabeth Harris *Mardy*   44

Denis Sexton *Across the Border*   58

Louise Doughty *A Whore's Vengeance*   72

Faith Addis *Small Beginnings*   82

Alan Dunn *French Kisses*   96

Stephanie Ellyne *Me and Renate*   114

Sylvia Baker *A Dark Circle*   126

Francesca Clementis *Good at Things*   138

Kate Atkinson *Karmic Mothers – Fact or Fiction?*   156

Jude Jones *The Spirit of the Times*   164

Juliet McCarthy *Moira Flaherty*   178

Alison Armstrong *Magdalen*   188

Mike McCormack *A is for Axe*   196

Anna McGrail *The Welfare of the Patient*   211

Dick Bayne *Football in Busanze Camp*   217

Jonathan Carr *Barcelona*   220

Maria Caruso *Strange Weather*   230

SNAPSHOTS

Douglas Galbraith *Officer Shenstone's Nigger*   242

Nick Kelly *Expect Jail*   249

Hwee Hwee Tan *Ground No More*   262

Phil Whitaker *The Window-cleaners of Bjec*   268

Josephine Corcoran *Algebra*   281

Julia Darling *Last Days of the Asylum*   286

Tobias Hill *Losing Track*   291

Carrie Worrall *Gathering*   304

Kevin Doyle *Do You Like Oranges?*   319

David Evans *Dead Man's Shoes*   334

Michel Faber *Some Rain Must Fall*   339

Author Biographies   350

Foreword

RECENTLY, Merric Davidson passed me a letter. With the author's permission, I quote from it now:

> 'You gave me a lot of encouragement three years ago when you highly commended one of my short stories. I entered the Ian St James Awards for a number of years and always considered it a valuable exercise. You must have given a burst of energy and confidence to so many of us and, for me, your comments on that story led to a turning point in my life – I turned it into a novel which was published last year by Hodder Headline.'

How the world has moved on. Eleven years ago, when I was giving talks to writers' circles and conferences up and down the country, the heartfelt cry from audiences was, 'How do I get my first book published?' Many aspiring authors had been trying for years. Of course people are not equally gifted, but since writing is unremitting hard work, for so many to labour for so long without *some* talent is to believe in a world full of masochists. As many of my fellow professionals will freely admit, luck plays a part, but should a career be left solely to chance? Should those who aspire not be encouraged? Surely it was possible to design something better? A showcase for new writers? Which was why and how, ten years ago, the Awards came into being.

Oh dear! 'God knows why you're encouraging them,' moaned a publisher, quaking under the threatened demise of the net book agreement. 'Nobody will be reading books in a few years.' Did I tell him to get off his arse and promote the joys of books instead of relying on price fixing? I hope not, but I probably did. Another publisher sneered, 'Who are you hoping to discover, a new Jackie Collins?' At the time, Jackie Collins was selling by the truckload and the sneer would have become fawning sycophancy within minutes if she'd deigned to let him publish her. Patiently I explained that since books are so subjective, our panel of judges would reflect a wide range of tastes. He was not impressed. Publishers weren't. They'd been in the business since Caxton and needed no help from anyone.

What then of literary agents? Surely they'd welcome a scheme which would bring them new clients of proven talent? 'Of course you're doing everything wrong,' trilled a leading London agent as she quaffed my champagne. 'You should let established writers enter these Awards.' That, I pointed out, would defeat its very purpose. 'Oh, then it's doomed darling, utterly doomed!' Another agent joined in. 'If this is for would-be novelists, why on earth don't you make them submit a full-length novel?' I explained that it takes a very long time to write a novel. 'Yes, I suppose it does,' she agreed, carelessly. Novels also take a long time to read, I said, and our readers would expire under an avalanche of manuscripts. The hope was that a short story of reasonable length would show if a writer had talent – after that it was up to him or her – we were simply in the business of opening doors. 'Hmmm,' she mused as she reached for her glass. She was not impressed. Agents weren't.

What then of those who write and talk about books? 'A cheap publicity stunt!' screamed the media. A stunt it was not. As for cheap, the Awards had already cost me many thousands of pounds. Unwittingly I'd given offence. The British, it seemed, preferred literary awards to be sponsored by a brewer or a grocer, not a working writer. 'Hell does he think he's doing?' they said.

Things were to get even worse. Aspiring authors need feedback; nobody ever learned from a rejection slip. What we want, said our aspirants, is a critique of our work with as much detailed comment as you can give us. So that's what we gave them. Oh dear! *Hell does he think he's doing?* became *Hell does he think he is?* It mattered not that the critiques were produced by our professional readers and not by me. It was of no interest that when I served as a judge I was one of seven with no casting vote. You cannot convince people with facts. *Private Eye* joined the heavyweight press and weighed in with a vengeance.

Hooray for a free press! If you do something in public, you expect to be criticised, but I was unprepared for the hate mail. When I stupidly disclosed my home address in an exchange of letters in *The Bookseller*, the first vitriolic letter arrived within days. Of course it was as anonymous as those that followed, but it displayed *some* knowledge of the publishing world, which I suppose was only to be expected – after all I doubt *The Bookseller* sells big to the National Front. How strange that what we were doing ruffled so many conventional feathers to such a degree. What can you do with hate mail except bin it? And forget it. Except that you never quite forget...

'Snapshots,' said Merric. 'That's what I want to call it. Share a few memories.'

The problem is they're bittersweet. Of course in the early days we made some silly mistakes – there was no blueprint for what we were doing – but if as was claimed, there was no need for such a scheme, surely it would die from neglect? People wouldn't enter. Yet enter they did in their thousands, and thousands more enter each year.

'It will be ten years before this is accepted,' David Frost told me at the first Awards Luncheon in 1989. No wonder he's now Sir David for it was a shrewd assessment of the time it takes to bring about change. That times have changed is now obvious. Publishers and literary agents alike have warmed to the Awards; they now love the Awards, the closing date for which has become an annual red-letter day in the diaries of aspiring authors everywhere. The Awards now reach an international audience. The winning entries are published in book form, currently by Angela Royal, my thanks to her. Also, shortlisted stories are featured in *The New Writer*, the magazine associated with the Awards. Most important of all, over a hundred writers have now received these Awards, and many have achieved their ambition to become professional novelists. They're the ones who've brought about change. Not me, not even Merric who took over the reigns some years ago and whose unstinting efforts reduced chaos to order. So let's hear it for the authors! Here are thirty of them, gathered together to entertain you with their talents. To them, congratulations, and to you as you open this book – enjoy!

Ian St James

Exposed

LORNA FERGUSSON

PART ONE: THE EMPRESS

MISS GOSLING picked up the pen and found herself writing 'Miss Leonie Godling requests...' Really, this won't do, she thought with irritation, hastily scoring out the error and starting again. At the second attempt she wrote, 'Miss Leonie Glosing...'

A week later she was writing her diary and after finishing, with the usual sigh of mixed satisfaction and frustration she began to read it over, as was her wont. She was her own audience: critic, reviewer and fan. To her horror, she found scarcely a line that didn't contain a strange and silly error; mostly spelling mistakes which altered the meanings of words in unexpected and disquieting ways.

It wasn't long before she became worried enough to visit her doctor, to ask him in his authority to explain to her what was going on. He was unable to do so and referred her, through the National Health Service, to a psychoanalyst.

Miss Gosling was not happy at the prospect of having her brains picked over by the tried-and-trusted method. She regarded it as a sort of mental vivisection. Privately, she was convinced, although she didn't know if it could be proved, that she had, after many years of perfect literacy, 'contracted' dyslexia. She herself used the word 'contracted', for she liked to think of dyslexia as some sort of disease; an external force barging into her nice tidy system.

As a child she had always found that words came easily to her. At school, she had won countless essay prizes. Her classmates had disliked this and placed more value on running a good race in the school sports. Spelling had never been a problem, and she had always had a slightly patronizing attitude towards those who found it hard. There was always a bit of the Puritan in her: no doubt if she had been a teacher in an earlier age, she'd have forced sinister pupils to write with their proper dextrous hands.

Later she moved to the city and wandered in the academic groves, entranced and more than daunted. Trees loomed over her, shut out the light. Fruit fell into her hand or was plucked with difficulty. She swayed between a feeling of having reached her home, and of being merely a visitor, a travel-writer with an antagonistic if somewhat jealous attitude towards the natives. Was she, for Heaven's sake, interpreting the rituals properly?

She did well, but – to continue the labouring metaphor – failed to become a tree herself, or a tree-surgeon. She found a minor grove, and settled down to tending the weeds there. She longed to be a sapling of promise.

Occasionally the spirit of her childhood would revisit her and the words would flow once more, as naturally as skipping and jumping waves and having dolls' tea parties in the days of her ignorance. But now, knowing too much, she would sneer at what she had written in her innocence and throw it away. The incipient sapling shrivelled and withered, but her knowledge of gardening techniques improved.

It was at this time that the spelling errors began. At first no more than a minor irritation and inconvenience, but soon a major waste of good paper. She began to phone friends rather than write to them, draw diagrams, gesticulate, anything rather than try to produce the recalcitrant little glyphs.

The psychoanalyst gave her a sage half-hour of his time one Monday, and told her this was merely the beginning. Return next week. Miss Gosling still couldn't see what good could be done. She bracketed psychoanalysis with hypnotism and had always fiercely said her mind was far too independent for her ever to 'go under'. 'They call you "subjects",' she said indignantly, 'but you're nothing but objects, really. I refuse to be an object. I refuse to be patronized.'

The psychoanalyst advised her to write as much as possible, without regard to the errors. 'Let it flow,' he said. No doubt he considered this activity therapeutic. With an ill-will she obeyed, humouring him as she would a child. Rather typically, she bought a special book, with rich pure pages and suitable severe geometric hard covers, in which to pour out what she ironically called her 'scream of consciousness'. She had always loved stationery. So white and tidy, so empty, so full of promise. She got angry when clean white notebooks became tatty and dog-eared, with untidy alterations and deletions, and half-pages scrappily torn out for shopping lists and friends' addresses. She preferred to see the pages left clean than for the wrong words to sit there, like unwanted relatives, jeering at her, saying 'We belong to you.'

The only way was not to let them get a foot in the door, not to open the door at all.

Monday next, she grimly presented the mental vivisectionist with her first 'flow'. No more than a trickle, but he was pleased. He was able to sound out depths in herself that she was unable to fathom. It was only after she had gone that he wondered if the exercise hadn't been *too* perfect. Was she contriving it? Was she mocking him? Ever afterwards, he couldn't be sure.

This is what she wrote:

Scream of conscience stress
I lived the word bard when I was
A chilled loving in my home tin.

He was especially interested in the word 'bard' (she had meant 'bird', she said), with its Celtic overtones of incantation and the mystic role of the poet. 'Chilled' he delighted in, though she insisted she'd had a happy child hood, with no sense of oppression or alienation.

Week after week she returned with pieces like this, which became longer and fuller as time went on. She nodded frequently but distantly, and didn't seem to listen to his comments. She wrote one piece which began:

The jeering condor smiles,
The moaning teaser
Fainting in the groove.

Her smile was indeed enigmatic as she handed it to him. He increasingly felt she was humouring him and this reminded him of his mother's soothing 'Yes, dear' when he was small, just before she forgot to take him to the zoo, or put out the light and left him in that *horrible* darkness, in which he could never find his special comfort blanket to suck. He began to dislike the glacial Miss Gosling.

At the end of the course of half-hour sessions, she presented her final opus:

The Homeprayers knew crows
Wear invincible
To utter fake.

His patient, it seemed, had gone from bad to worse.

A year later the psychoanalyst, whose real name was Smith (he had been mightily offended when she wrote to him as Mr Sniff), was intrigued to find a slim volume of verse by Miss Gosling being reviewed in adulatory terms by all the major literary journals. Critics were stunned by her bold use of adventurous and unconventional language. The first volume, *Scream*, was swiftly followed by *Homeprayers Rail* and *In the Bluff*. Mr Smith watched with fascination the rise of the psycho-symbolic school of poetry. Her reputation well established, Miss Gosling appeared on TV arts programmes and wrote articles for the *TLS*. She talked winningly about the 'new freedom' movement in verse. She staunchly advocated 'letting down defences'. She was asked to edit the works of other modern poets – some of these, not being dead, felt somewhat resentful. They knew that people were buying copies of their slim verses not for their intrinsic merit but for the excellent – albeit occasionally confusing – prefaces by Miss Gosling. One particularly angry young man founded the Go Sling Your Hook Society after discovering that on the dust-jacket of his latest work,

Frankenstein was Innocent, his photograph and biographical blurb were actually smaller than those of Miss Gosling, who had only written a two-page introduction in which she had misspelt his name three different ways. He wrote an angry letter about the orthography to *The Times*, but Miss Gosling briskly retorted that if such a practice had been good enough for Shakespeare, it ought to be good enough for him. (She actually wrote 'ham', but he hoped this was merely a typographical error.)

Meanwhile the first eager American came over to Britain to write a thesis on her work. It was entitled 'Go with the Flow: the psycho-symbolic liberation from the parameters of semantic fundamentalism, as evidenced in the post denotative work of Leonie Gosling.'

Miss Gosling died young, almost as a duty. There was an immediate scurry for possession of the rights to her unpublished diaries and correspondence. An American university put in the largest bid, so presently British scholars had to apply for grants to go to America to study the material in the Free Flow Library, at the University of the New Consciousness, California.

Modern universities in Britain had already put her on the syllabus. Cambridge was more avant-garde in this respect than Oxford. The new school of Freedom critics were extremely prolific, if perhaps a trifle obscure. Marxism and post-structuralism were entirely *passé*.

Her small home town, Little Wittering, became a place of literary pilgrimage. Three days after her death BBC2 had transmitted a programme compiled from her own acerbic opinions, pictures of her when she was twenty, and benign and affectionate comments from benign and affectionate friends and teachers – because after all they had always known she'd be famous. Their carefully memorized accounts were formulaic and tactful, with only one or two good-humouredly bitchy remarks to remind one that the idol had had feet of endearing clay. The programme was a repeat. Perhaps its discretion was due to the fact that she had still been alive when it was made.

Channel Four had in preparation a black women's surrealist theatre group production of *Scream*, which was seen as expressing the female desire to perform autohysterectomy and fly free of the constrictions of womb-oppression. The set was to be all black, with jagged flashes of searing red. The television critics prepared themselves for a lot of primal screaming. Viewers could send for a leaflet which would explain it all to them.

The psychoanalyst read a prime obituary in *The Times*, an admirably balanced effort by one of their best critics, who claimed to have been a close friend of the subject. Cautiously he said it was perhaps too soon for any final evaluation of Miss Gosling's contribution to literature to be made. But he personally felt that once the smoke had cleared, she would ultimately be ranked highly, for she had opened up new avenues for poetry to explore and had communicated art to the intelligentsia and the man in the street alike. The article was accompanied by a rather grainy photograph of the physically deceased. She was smiling.

Mr Smith sniffed.

PART TWO: THE BOY

Little Wittering was a long way from Pasadena, yet it had been the goal of my pilgrimage for a number of years. Ever since I first picked up *Scream* in my local bookstore, and felt the words kind of seize me by the throat. I was still at high school then, and it seemed to me that the words expressed all the misunderstood adolescent *Angst* I was going through: I too was a 'chilled loving' in a 'home tin', and I wanted out.

I got out. Went to College, did well, and still loved Gosling's work. Bought every volume of verse as it was published and it never seemed enough. And that kind of cryptic English quality added a fascinating dimension to it. I guess I was like a lot of Americans; loving the English, respecting their culture, slightly afraid of their chilly distant politeness. They had all those unspoken *rules* and you just didn't know where you were, lumbering around like 'a fool in a tiny ship' as Miss Gosling would have said. We were all loose and hung out and they had their tweeds and their mansions and their rules. We were the gauche descendants of people who knew where they were *at*, in a big way.

What Miss Gosling had, I guess, was the ability to bridge the gap. She had all the prim prissiness of the English; photos of her made her look starched and nanny-ish and I think she was probably that way in real life. But in her poetry, there was that undercurrent, a sense of danger. By breaking the constraints of language she was breaking the rules, and it was dangerous and fun to go with her.

She certainly hit California. I wasn't the only one smitten. I remember my Uncle Jonas telling me about the sixties and how Tolkien's *The Lord of the Rings* hit the campuses, how everybody – in the midst of all that peace and love was wearing badges saying 'Gandalf lives' and 'J. R. R. Tolkien is hobbit-forming'. And back in England there's this old Professor absolutely bemused by his success, wondering what in hell they all *saw* in it? It was the same with her, even though the era of hashish and flower power had long gone, and the era of greed and yuppies and cocaine had arrived.

I was so well into her work that I felt I wanted to devote my life to it. Maybe I had no right to: hell, I wasn't that bright. I knew that over at New Consciousness people were doing the *real* work. Although I went to College, I didn't major in Literature. I suppose that I just had one obsession and that was her. I decided I'd do something that would get me a good income and *then* I could find my own way to her. I ended up as a realtor, and pretty soon I had enough at my back to start planning the visit, what I was going to say to her and how she'd explain it all. I'd decided I wasn't going to be the usual eager Yank, full of respect and polite puppy eagerness – though God knows that's what I was – I was going to be as cool and acid as she was in her interviews. Nobody could get close to the woman, but I was going to change all that.

All the same, it took a few years. Even with an obsession, you get side-tracked by real life. I married, got divorced, had the monthly alimony to pay, so that held me back. Luckily there wasn't a kid – then I'd really have been tied. Meanwhile I just kept track of her and I swear I must have known all her words by heart.

But she died. She died about three months before I was due to go to England. She'd never been to America, so I had had no chance to push my way into her attention. She'd have been such a success too – look at how well Dylan Thomas did way back, with his drunkenness and his angel-goblin looks and that big Welsh voice. I guess, though, that Miss Gosling's cracked-china voice wouldn't have carried in some great hall. Plus, she didn't seem to be into performance art.

What did she have to go and die for? She was only in her late thirties, and it was such an absurd pointless way to go.

For a while, I have to say, the heart just went out of me. I read the articles and I watched the TV – there were a lot of features imported from England and shown on PBS. Some were real weird and I don't know what she'd have thought of them. And sometimes I'd freeze-frame the picture and look at her face, flickering slightly, and those deep-set eyes, and I'd think 'Who *are* you, lady?' And I'd think that she'd have understood me, and I'd get depressed at that, but always there was the question 'Who *are* you, lady?' and that's what did it. Nobody I saw on TV or read in those articles could really tell me; they all had their axes to grind. They all showed a facet of her, or some distortion of it like one of those mirrors in a fairground, but nobody seemed to know the whole picture. So I decided I'd be the one to find out.

Maylene was angry as hell when I threw in my job: she could see her alimony trickling away, I guess. She called me all the time, with that ugly shrillness in her voice I had gotten to dislike so. She was in a panic, and I guess she was right to be: this time, for sure, I was leaving her for another woman.

Then the question arose of whether I should sell the house: it was real pretty, on a rise above the woods, and I knew as an experienced realtor I would have no trouble selling for a good price. But that was a big step, requiring consideration; it meant changing my life for good, not just the semi-break with the past I'd accomplished so far. Maylene was now established in a condo half an hour's ride away. I knew she had her lovers, and money apart, I guess we were still nearly friends. We'd spent a couple of years getting that house just right; it was the focus of all the dreams we'd had, and I'd kept it just as it was even though it was more than a year since we'd split up. It still looked as if she'd just gone out to the shopping mall.

Then one night I was re-reading *Homeprayers Rail* and I came across these lines she wrote:

Pretty Hangland, rape with roses,
Is there money still for me,
Stands the kitsch clock still at twee?

It was just like when Christians shut their eyes and open the Bible, stab the page with their finger, praying to the Lord for guidance, and the verse they open their eyes to tells them what to do. And I was to go to England.

It felt like being born again, to cut away from the past. I guess she'd laugh at that kind of religious expression. But I was so eager, England was the Promised Land. When I thought of England I thought of Queen Victoria and Sherlock Holmes, and Laurence Olivier and Henry Vlll chopping all those heads off and Agincourt and bowler hats. And roses and hollyhocks.

When I reached Little Wittering it was just like some film set. All those cute cottages – I just had to stop the car and it was a real effort not to get the camera out, straight off. There was a village green and a duckpond and a church with a square battlemented tower. It was as if in that poem I'd read, she knew I'd come. The stone was golden in the spring afternoon, and there were daffodils everywhere.

I checked into The Ivy Tree, the only hotel in town – only they called it a guesthouse. As it was early season, everything was still pretty quiet, but I could tell they went all out to catch tourists – particularly people like me. It seemed to me England did nothing but sell its image as this quaint old culture, pickled in the brine of the past. To be honest, even after just a couple of weeks, it was beginning to get on my nerves. To sell itself like a hooker and be so damn superior all the time, a country's got to think it's something special.

The Ivy Tree, as you'd expect, had ivy all over the front, blurring the lines of the building. It was run by a Mr and Mrs Frogmorton – quite a name – who were middle-aged and starchy. 'We pride ourselves...' they always said, collectively, as if they'd created England all by themselves. They prided themselves on the decor of the rooms; all chintz and frills and dark oak wood – so dark it looked as if it had been shined with boot polish. No doubt they prided themselves on the bill too. And the meals – all flabby and fat. Mrs Frogmorton wore a cardigan buttoned to the chin and coyly referred to Miss Gosling as 'our local celebrity'. Mr Frogmorton wore a brown tweed jacket and stood with his legs apart. He should have been a country squire with a gun in the crook of his elbow.

I met Harvey J. Allen in the bar, before we went into dinner, on my first night there. That afternoon, after unpacking my bags, I hadn't had time for more than a stroll around the village, to get the feel of the place. I still felt it was like a film set, only some extras from another lot had strayed into it. Sure there were quaint old inns; The Hare and Hounds, and The Cricketer's Arms, and there was the church – I went in and smelled the cold smell of old stone and lavender polish. There was a little old woman in a floral apron, she was as frail as a bird, polishing the brasses and the wood, and every sound we made echoed round the pillars in a hollow, throbbing way.

I'd rather have been on my own. I sat for a while and looked at the stained glass, with medieval saints in distorted positions, and the worn straw matting and the embroidered altar-cloth, and one old faded knight lying on his tomb, staring up at heaven with his face blurred and flat. When I left, I passed through the market square, which seemed lined with tea-shops and bookshops, as if the English did nothing but read over cups of Earl Grey.

But it wasn't all like that; there were several garish-fronted 'estate-agents': with a professional interest I looked at the prices and the photos of rambling vicarages and thatched cottages. And the price of a slice of English life seemed pretty high. I couldn't believe how many agencies there were for such a small place, probably outnumbering the tea-shops.

There were people of the Frogmorton type and little old Miss Marples chatting on the corner, but there were also groups of teenagers standing around looking bored, and motorbikes roaring up and down with – it seemed – nowhere to go. Several streets had a closed and shuttered look which I couldn't understand until I realized they were weekender homes. There seemed to be few people of middle-age range; either they were young and restive, and obviously what the English call 'working class', or they were old gents in Panama hats and ladies in sensible shoes, like the whole village was some cruise-liner full of the retired.

I began to feel a bit sad and I lost the heart for the English cream tea I'd been promising myself. I felt a long way from home, and unable to understand the attitudes of this society. So when I came into the hotel, and got the 'Here is the colonial, let's educate him in the *proper* way to do things' treatment from the Frogmortons, I was fit to be tied.

They'd just asked me to dress formally for dinner, when I heard the voice of a fellow American over by the bar. I was so relieved I just went straight over, holding out my hand and saying, 'Hey, I'm Carl Bayer from Pasadena, over on a trip. Glad to meet you!'

The stranger turned with a smile, and his grip was firm and friendly as we shook hands. 'Harvey J. Allen. I'm from California too. What'll you have?'

Later, in the lounge, we both discovered we were here because of Leonie Gosling. Well, it was hardly surprising. What other reason would two Americans have for running into each other in a tiny place like this?

Harvey, it turned out, was *Doctor* Allen, of the University of the New Consciousness, and he was here to start on some post-doctoral work. He was full of enthusiasm and I was impressed by the way he could formulate his ideas. When I listened to his academic way of putting things I felt gauche and inarticulate. All my comments on her work sounded emotional; gut feelings vaguely expressed. But he never patronized me – I guess he responded to the sincerity of my feelings.

After dinner we had a few more drinks and quoted Gosling lines at each other in the easy camaraderie brought about by alcohol and by being strangers in a strange land. He put me straight on quite a few things, and I didn't argue; I figured he'd know best. I went off to bed in a haze of goodwill and respect for the guy.

It was different next morning. I came down to breakfast (swimming in grease, on a mean little plate: one rasher of bacon, one sausage, one solid fried egg, one squashed sliver of tomato), and I found Harvey had a companion, a thin intense-looking man in a dark suit.

'Carl!' shouted Harvey, half rising, and beckoning me over with his fork. 'Come on and join us.'

He introduced us while one of Mrs Frogmorton's staff leaned over me to pour some tepid tea. This meant it would be cold before my lukewarm plate of grease arrived. I thought longingly of breakfast out on the deck at our house in Pasadena. Those blueberry muffins that Maylene used to make.

'Carl, let me introduce you to Professor Charles Willoughby; he arrived too late last night to join us. He's from Cambridge University and he's the authority on L. G. over here,' Harvey said, heartily. 'We're lucky to have run into him. If you want to understand Gosling's work, this is the guy whose brains are most worth picking.'

Willoughby barely acknowledged my presence, probably putting me down as the puppy-dog American I was trying so hard not to be, and merely continued his conversation with Harvey, while he delicately pulled a bread roll to pieces.

'Of course, Dr Allen,' he said, 'we at Caedmon College are particularly keen to ensure that the Gosling papers stay in England, which is only right and proper. She was one of the most English of English writers, and she was that *rara avis*, an excellent *female* English poet. The most appropriate sphere for scholarship on such works remains England itself. My College is also proposing to endow a Gosling scholarship as well as the Gosling Library, in order to perpetuate her name.'

'Well, that does sound interesting, Charles, but you know that English Lit. scholars in England are a dying breed. All your Government is interested in right now is technological colleges and such, and even in *that* area things are pretty moribund. In America we have always had a proper respect for English letters – more than the English themselves, I'd say. Now, you know you have to be realistic, Charles – your colleges, even those fine old institutions of Oxford and Cambridge, they may have the clout, but they don't have the *cash*. And, Charles, it's a commercial world.

'I have to tell you, Charles, that the University of the New Consciousness has put in a major bid for those papers, bigger even than Austin put in, and we're so sure of winning that we've already started building a special Library on campus: it's going to be called the Free Flow Library, in respect to the origins of her work.'

Willoughby looked tense and disgruntled during all this; his thin lips tightened, and the bread roll was soon demolished. However, I could see that he wouldn't lose his cool completely; he preserved an icy politeness in the face of what to him must have been a body blow.

'Let us not forget, Dr Allen, the old proverb about counting chickens. Cambridge is not some superannuated house of intellectual dinosaurs: we were the first academic institution to perceive the significance of Miss Gosling's work and we feel we have a special right to be the guardians and interpreters of that work in the future.'

'Now, don't get all tight-lipped, Charles,' smiled Harvey, 'just think of all the time you can spend on the beaches when you come over on exchange to study the papers at New Consciousness.'

There was a silence. Clearly Willoughby found that no compensation.

'You mentioned interpretation,' I said hesitantly, to try to break the impasse. 'It seems to me that more than with any other writer, interpretation is everything with her work. There are so many facets, I mean, you can look at a poem and see something, look again and see something else. It's so rich, so endless. So much fun too.'

Professor Willoughby's eyebrow lifted. 'Are you writing a paper on Miss Gosling's work too?' he asked.

'Well, no, not exactly. I'm just here on my own behalf,' I answered, 'but I'm real interested in what you two have to say.'

Willoughby turned to Harvey: 'But you, Dr Allen – I understand you are writing a post-doctoral thesis on her. May I enquire as to its working title?'

Harvey beamed, eager to oblige. 'It's called 'Go with the Flow: the psycho-symbolic liberation from the parameters of semantic fundamentalism, as evidenced in the post denotative work of Leonie Gosling.''

I could have sworn I saw Willoughby wince.

'Excuse me,' I said, 'but what does all that mean?'

'Well,' said Harvey benignly, 'tell me – when you read her work, what do you get out of it?'

'I get a buzz,' I answered, 'I get a sense of adventure because I don't know where she's going to next, and I get a sense of challenge because I have to work out what she's really saying.'

'Exactly,' said Harvey. 'That's what it's all about: explaining that thrill. Criticism is all about saying *how* you got that thrill, and analysing meanings in the work that you never knew were there. It's an enrichment of the original work.'

'You make it sound creative,' I said.

'I suppose it is, in a way.'

'You see,' said Willoughby, putting the tips of his fingers together, as he rested his elbows on the table. 'Words have two values: denotative and connotative. The denotative value of a word is, more or less, its dictionary meaning, a fairly strict semantic equation between the word and its referent. The connotations of the word are those associations we have with that word, a sort of semantic halo surrounding it. To put it in simple terms, if I say 'nightmare', all sorts of pictures may appear in your mind, not just the translation of it as 'bad dream'. You may imagine all sorts of things: a skeletal horse, werewolves, falling off a cliff, suffocation, fire, rats, vampires – all sorts of things. If I say 'honey', you may associate with it childhood, sweetness, bees, Winnie-the-Pooh, and so on.

'All poets play with connotations; they use them to evoke feelings and an atmosphere – they assume you will have the same associations with certain words as they do.

'Leonie Gosling was a poet who played with semantics more than most. By subtly altering the sounds of words, she achieved a lateral dislocation of understanding, which led to a new perception of reality; a common aim of poets. Our perception of the world is tired and jaded: a poet seeks to revivify that perception by making us look at it in some new way. The metaphysical poets did it by means of astonishing conceits: comparing lovers to a pair of compasses, for instance. Miss Gosling did it by means of adaptation of common phrases: hackneyed rhymes and clichés, or familiar popular images.

'Take, for example, her lines, early in her career:

> *The jeering condor smiles,*
> *The moaning teaser,*
> *Fainting in the groove.*

'If one were to 'translate' those lines back into 'ordinary' English, they would become:

> *The Giaconda smiles,*
> *The Mona Lisa*
> *Painting in the Louvre.*

'This would be a very ordinary and unenlightening description: a mere statement of fact, with no 'attitude' conveyed. Observe however, how by subtle alterations she preserves similarity to the original sounds while guiding our attitudes to the subject. The Mona Lisa herself is famed for her ambiguous half-smile. She is the eternal female mystery. This is conveyed in the poem by means of the words 'jeering' and 'teaser' – is she triumphing, sneering at our perplexity in some way? Is she a predatory 'condor', a literal 'culture vulture'? Or, on the other hand, is she to be seen as vulnerable and unhappy, smiling a brave smile in uncongenial circumstances, trapped, like a fly in amber, in the oppressive atmosphere of the museum: 'moaning' and 'fainting' in the conventional 'groove' all art is slotted into, so that it no longer has any natural interaction with life?'

'Hey,' said Harvey, as Willoughby at last drew breath. 'I'll have to watch my back. Can we take notes?'

'Professor Willoughby, I had no idea there was so much to it. I see now what Harvey meant: that literary criticism can truly be an enriching experience. Although, you know, sometimes it can be kind of fun not to know the meanings – or not too specifically, because then there's no going back. It's all cut and dried. Doesn't that sort of drain the poem, maybe?'

My voice trailed off into uncertainty. Willoughby looked professionally offended, like he was a doctor who'd just told me I had cancer and I'd said 'No I haven't.' I decided it wasn't worth making him hostile. After all, he probably knew better than I did. It was his job.

I tried looking like an eager disciple. 'Tell me, did you ever *meet* Miss Gosling?'

'On several occasions. But do not expect any personal revelations from *me*. Quite simply, the woman was an enigma. It was impossible to get close to her in any way. I've often thought,' he added pensively, 'that she herself reminded me of the Mona Lisa...' There was a moment's silence. 'But,' he said, more briskly, 'perhaps our visit to her house this afternoon will shed more light on her. *Not* that I am one of those critics for whom personal psychology is all. But we shall see.' Harvey and I brightened at the prospect.

In the end, we didn't all go to the house together. After lunch – steak and kidney pie, sherry trifle – Harvey and the Prof. had got into a discussion that was way above my head. I got tired of being the open-mouthed kid, and it seemed to me my ideas were getting more and more confused, the more they explained. So I said I'd see them there at three and set off to stroll through the village and on the mile or so to where her little house sat in neat detachment from all this fuss.

On the way I saw more or less the same cast of characters as yesterday. Somehow it depressed me – I seemed to have lost all that optimism I'd had when I first arrived. The house was going to be a last ditch attempt to recapture the magic.

I tried saying 'Hi' to various people on the main street, with varying degrees of response. One or two gave me an icy stare, several just looked bemused and taken aback, and a couple responded with tense smiles. Finally, just as I was on the outskirts I saw an old man out clipping his hedge. His garden was neat as pie and the hedge severely retarded in its growth, so I couldn't see the need for the clipping, but there he was, methodically trimming invisible millimetres here and there. The sound of the shears was loud but soothing. Once again, I tried 'Hello'. There was a sideways glint of a wary eye and some sort of a grunt, and he went on clipping, sleeves rolled up and bald head gleaming in the sun. I decided to hold out for more interaction than this, and I knew what the British turned to in moments of conversational crisis.

'Nice weather,' I said, hopefully.

''Tain't too bad, I suppose,' he answered.

'I'm an American,' I volunteered. 'Carl Bayer. Pleased to meet you.'

He swivelled round to look at me properly.

'Ah,' he said, cryptically.

'I'm here to visit Miss Gosling's house – you know, the writer – well, of course you know. I guess you're used to lots of visitors travelling through.'

'We get all sorts, that's true. So you're another come to visit her house. Now I ask you, what's the point of that? She's dead, ain't she?'

Suddenly the floodgates were opened and the verbal cataract he unleashed overwhelmed me. He gave me no time to reply. He didn't seem to want a reply; he seemed to have been ruminating over all this for quite a while and he wanted it all off his chest.

'That silly old bat – I ask you, who'd she think she was? Lady Muck, *she* was. Didn't have the time of day for us once her name was in all those stuck-up papers. What'd she do to get famous? I ask you, what'd she *do*? She was as daft as a brush. Just because she got her words mixed up. Good God, lad, there's twenty people in the nuthouse in Effingdean who can do that, no effort at all, and they don't get TV programmes made about them. Daft as a brush, I tell you. Couldn't say anything with any sense in it. Ought to have been locked up.

'I was sick enough of it when she was alive. God knows it was bad enough with film crews and newspapers and all that and those bloody Frogmortons making a fortune out of it all. Then the stupid woman falls downstairs – breaks her neck. I ask you, even a daft way to *die*. So I thought, well, that'll be *that*. Only it wasn't. If anything, it's worse. People parading through here, asking the way to her house the whole time, like some religious pilgrimage or something. Look at you lad – all keen to get there – don't you know, lad, that you've been took in?'

By this time the clipping shears were being held menacingly high. I'd been edging my way past him during the whole onslaught and now I raised my hand in an attempt at a cheery wave and backed away, saying something lame about how nice it had been to meet him. And I went on, feeling more jaded than ever.

Harvey and the Prof. drove up just as I arrived. The house was ordinary, I mean *really* ordinary. The sort of place that even the Little Wittering realtors might have difficulty selling. It was a square little block of dark red brick, set outside the village but right on the verge of the main highway to Effingdean, so it wasn't at all peaceful.

There was a small square garden and a small round woman at the gate to greet us. This was a Miss Dimchurch, the local librarian, who was going to show us round. Indeed, she informed us this little duty was being asked of her so frequently it had almost become a full-time occupation.

What did I expect when we got in there? I don't know, I really don't know. But this was no *literary* house: no book-lined library, no study, no chaos of papers and worn old typewriter. The place was neat as a pin and not very tasteful. Whatever individuality Miss Gosling had had must have been locked up inside her. Even Harvey looked disappointed.

There was a tidy little lounge, with a velour-covered three-piece suite and floral wallpaper. On the glass-topped coffee-table were several leaflets adjuring us to join the Gosling Society. There were few books – some were of course related to her job as a teacher- but there were also historical romances and Agatha Christies. There was a teak-effect unit against one wall, with under-shelf lighting, the shelves bearing various photographs and china ornaments, and a small television. It looked to me like the room of a woman grown old before her time, or who had been pushed so far into conventionality that nothing of her real self showed. She was playing out the role of the soon-to-be old maid.

'And now if you'll follow me,' said Miss Dimchurch in hushed, reverential tones, 'we will mount the very stairs down which Miss Gosling so precipitately descended that fateful morning. Be mindful, gentlemen, of the loose carpet on the third tread from the top. It deprived us of the full bloom of Miss Gosling's literary career – let it not nip yours in the bud!'

I stayed behind in the lounge for a moment, staring at a silver-framed photograph of Leonie Gosling on the wall unit, and hearing Harvey's muffled jovial voice drift down from upstairs. A beam of sunlight, probing into the room through the net curtains, seemed to make the eyes in the photograph more deep-set than ever and the quizzical half smile mocking and sinister.

Suddenly I remembered the first poem in *Homeprayers Rail* and I realized that all along she had been playing a game.

> *The Homeprayers knew crows*
> *Wear invincible*
> *To utter fake.*

More than likely, she played the game with malice. She probably shuffled Scrabble letters around or something and laughed at the pits those academics dug themselves into.

> *'The Emperor's new clothes were invisible to other folk.'*

But nobody dared say so, except a little child.

Hadn't Professor Willoughby, his mind an instrument to prise open meaning, seen this? If he had, or if I tried to blow the whistle, it wouldn't make any difference. The whole Gosling industry would go grinding on. They'd go on pretending to see what wasn't there.

I looked the photograph in the eye. The naked truth was that there wasn't anything there but a smirk. I hated that superior smirk.

I felt a long way from home. A long way from that bookstore, where, full of hope and curiosity, I first picked up a book of her verse and thought she was speaking directly to me.

Ellie

JUDY FORSHAW

WHO DID she think she was, anycase, stood there on the front step, proud as a peacock. All done up in black and red. Large red hat with black feathers hanging down over the brim so you couldn't see her eyes. Black coat. Red dress underneath. Shiny black shoes standing on the steps I'd washed down that afternoon, only half an hour earlier. Such neat little feet, couldn't've been bigger than size three, four at the most. Expensive leather with little gold buckles glinting like the brooch on her collar. A bird's claw curled round a dainty little pearl.

I must've looked a bit too long at that brooch of hers, 'cos she took a step back and covered it with her hand. She was wearing long, fancy, red gloves.

'I've come to see Mother Louis.'

'She's praying.'

'We'll wait then – it's important.'

Her hand came down from the brooch, a rare expensive thing, like the bracelet on her wrist, the string of pearls round her neck. This woman smelt of money. Not phoney, showy, made-in-a-hurry money, but real money. Money that's been about for a bit matures like a malt whiskey. It smells different. You get to recognize it.

'Darling – come on – Mummy's in a hurry.'

She had turned round and was waving one of those red-gloved hands of hers in the direction of this big black car, parked across the drive, near the statue of St Joseph.

'Mother Louis sometimes prays all day on a Sunday.'

Even if it wasn't true, I wanted this proud-peacock woman to know that Mother Louis had more important things to be dealing with than rich women in feather hats and fancy brass buckles on their shoes.

'I'm sure she won't mind sparing us a little of her time.'

A couple of the feathers on her hat blew back and I got to see her eyes. Pale green with little yellow circles round the edges of the pupils.

She was good-looking all right, which meant she probably wasn't all

English. Couldn't've been, seeing as the English are the ugliest race in the world, barring the Chinese and the Irish. And it didn't look like she was mixed up with either of them. Not that I want to get into matters of race, creed and colour right here, seeing as it has no business in this story, although I do have a strong opinion on these things, stronger than a lot of people would realize. As a rule I don't like to say too much but I think a lot, enough thoughts to fill a book, fat as Mother Louis's Bible, fatter. One day maybe I'll write some of them down, mainly for the pleasure of seeing them written on the page. Maybe one day. We'll see.

That Sunday afternoon was the first time I set eyes on little Ellie, as she climbed out the back of that big black car. A Mercedes or something. She skipped, half seemed to fly, like a little elf across the gravel drive and up the steps to her mother's side, where she stood peering up at me. Same green eyes with the yellow circles round the pupils. Only Ellie was fair as her mother was dark, like the opposite sides of the same coin. And tiny. Not much bigger than the average five-year-old child. She was eight years old then.

I can't say now, exactly what was going through my mind then. Call it a sixth sense. I knew straight off that this child was different. Not especially better or worse than all the other little girls I'd seen pass through the school. Just different. And I liked that about her straight away.

'Ellie, don't stare – it's rude.'

I didn't mind being stared at. The little girl could look as long as she liked. It didn't bother me. If it was the first time she'd been this close up to a coloured person, an old black woman at that, she was entitled to take a long look. What these people don't realize is that it's seldom the children that bother me.

'Darling – say hello to the lady.' The peacock woman was prodding her with a long red finger. 'I don't know what's got into her – she's not normally this shy.'

Little Ellie didn't want to say hello. And why should she, when she was too busy staring at me, taking it all in. After she'd had her fill of looking, she crept round and hid her face in the folds of her mother's smart black coat, peering out at me from behind there with one of her big round green eyes, that didn't look to me the slightest bit shy. That little girl wasn't fooling me one bit.

As a rule I don't like to interrupt Mother Louis when she's praying. She's an old, wise woman with a lot of responsibility resting on her shoulders. What with running the school and keeping the other sisters in order, she doesn't get a lot of time on her own to be close to God.

It gets so dark and gloomy in that little chapel in the late afternoons that you need a torch to see your way around. At first I didn't see Mother

Louis and it wasn't until after a bit, and my eyes got adjusted to the dim light, that I spotted her over in the corner at the back praying in front of the statue of the Virgin Mary. The Virgin Mary has always been Mother Louis' favourite. Her special confidante. And I often wonder if she isn't closer to that lady than she is to God.

When things get rough, like the time a little while back, when it looked like they were going to have to close the convent down and there was talk of the sisters having to move to the Mother House in Rome, Mother Louis was up all night with Our Lady. And the other time when Sister Bernadette, who was old enough to know better, ran away for a long weekend with that flash Harry fellow, who pretended he knew all about sewage and nearly caused the sisters a severe bankruptcy problem with his phoney advice, she went and turned to her again. I don't suppose the Old Man minds. He must get enough people knocking on his door to be glad to have some of the responsibility lifted off his shoulders.

You would've thought though, that the sisters could've found a better likeness of the lady. That mean little mouth, close pale eyes and powder-pink face would put me off my praying if I was them. But then the sisters are supposed not to mind about those things. It's the spiritual image of her that they carry around in their hearts that counts. At least, that's how Father Benedict explained it me. And at the time it seemed to make sense. Now I only think so in Mother Louis' case. In my opinion she's one of the holiest women that walked the earth, and if they still went in for saints these days, her name would be top of the list. Pure goodness shines out of that old lady, like a light, like she's lit up on the inside with a special kind of tenderness for the world and all its creatures. And that's a rare thing.

As for most of the other sisters, a lifetime's praying doesn't seem to have got them any closer to God than the day they came in. And in my opinion, which is probably one best kept to myself here, I'd say it's taken them further away. I wonder about it sometimes. I don't know what it is with those poor sisters. But with most of them, like I say, I get the feeling that somewhere, something is nagging away at their souls, gnawing them up like a tapeworm, till they're so starved and thin inside that they don't have anything to give anyone else except the husk of their lost selves. Which sounds like a sort of a strange thing to say. But sometimes I think of them like empty pods with all the goodness taken out. And all the trying in the world to fill that emptiness with prayer only sours them worse. Because when praying's done on an empty heart it does strange things to a person inside. Maybe, I don't know, maybe in some way, they feel God cheated on them. Maybe they expected peace and happiness without having to work for it. Who knows. It's hard for a person to live with their misery. And hardest of all when it's of their own making. I suppose I should feel sorry for them. Some of them I do.

Sister Bernadette for instance, when she ran off with that flash Harry on that long weekend and came back crying. My heart went out to her. A grown woman, over forty years old, acting like a teenage girl over a man that should've had a government health warning stamped all over him. But then how was she supposed to recognize a character like that, shut up for the best years of her life in a place she was never suited to be. It was only natural she was going to want to break out, if she wasn't going to turn inwards, darken and shrivel up inside. She was fighting for her soul. Anyone could see that. I've got time for Sister Bernadette, her and Mother Louis, they're alright...

Back to Mother Louis. As I was saying, that afternoon, when I went into the chapel, she was over in the corner at the back, having words with her favourite person. Mother Louis as a rule is what I'd call a dainty prayer. She likes to kneel very upright, without any of herself resting on the pew, not like some of the sloppy ones I could name, sprawled all over the place like sacks of potatoes. I sneaked up close behind her. I wasn't wanting to spy or anything. And I began thinking maybe I'd got the wrong nun. Maybe it was all a mistake. You know how your mind can play those kind of tricks, when it's trying not to see what you know deep down.

Mother Louis wasn't praying like her normal self that afternoon. She was leant right forward over the pew with her head nearly touching the front. I know it doesn't sound like much. But when you've been used to seeing a woman addressing herself to God with an upright dainty dignity for the past twenty years, and then one afternoon you walk in and find her collapsed in a heap like a sack of potatoes... I got this uncomfortable feeling in the pit of my stomach which wasn't anything to do with what I'd had for lunch that day.

'Mary Mother of God, pray for us sinners, now and at the hour of our death...'

She had a rosary in her hand and her finger had stopped on this one bead. She was whispering the same bit over and over like a record that's got stuck in a groove. Ordinarily I would've waited a bit for Mother Louis to reach a natural break in her praying, but this time I didn't want to wait. I wanted to stop that whispering right away. It spooked me.

'Mother Louis.'

The whispering stopped. Mother Louis lifted her head up from the bench. She didn't turn round. 'What is it, Marsi?'

'There's a lady out in the hall that wants to see you.'

'That'll be Mrs Hollander.'

She sounded so tired, like she had the troubles of the world resting on her shoulders.

'I wouldn't let her in – only she said you were expecting her.'

She slipped the rosary into her pocket and turned to look at me. Her face was filled with a sweet peace, like a young girl in love, like a baby that's just been fed. Looking back now I'll always be happy to remember that expression on Mother Louis' face that afternoon. She reached out and touched my hand, cool and dry as an autumn leaf.

'Has she come with anyone?'

'A little blonde child that's got trouble written all over her.'

'Marsi, would you mind helping me up – my strength seems to have deserted me today.'

It was like holding a skinny little chicken in my arms. There was almost nothing of her under that thick black cloth, nothing but skin and bones.

'What you need is a good rest.'

Mother Louis laughed. 'Rest – whatever for?'

I handed her her stick and Bible, and together we promenaded down the aisle, like a couple of old ladies taking a summer stroll down Brighton Pier.

'You don't eat and you hardly ever sleep. You spend all your time worrying about everyone else – what sort of a way is that to lead a life?'

Mother Louis liked me scolding her. It was our little game we played together, a game we'd played for over twenty years. I was the only one that could manage it with her. The sisters were scared of her. Maybe her special closeness to God made them afraid for themselves. Whatever it was, I had the edge over them as far as Mother Louis was concerned, and they hated me for it. And you can understand it. Their Reverend Mother Louis, who was holier than most saints and closer to God than the lot of them put together, she could've chosen any one of them as her friend. And instead she chose old Marsi, the black cleaning woman, a non-Catholic and a heathen unbeliever at that, who had never been baptized and never would be by the looks of things. I wouldn't've liked it. Not one bit. But then that was their problem, not mine.

Sometimes I think that old lady has a streak of the devil in her. And it's not something I haven't said to her face on a few occasions before now. She may be holy, but she's still human inside. And I've often wondered if she didn't make me into her special friend just to stick a thorn into those poor sisters' sides. I wouldn't put it past her. She's got the cunning of a snake when she wants, which more than likely accounts for her special relationship with God. Something else I've told her on more than one occasion. Anycase, back to the two of us, promenading down the aisle that afternoon.

'What sort've a way is that to lead a life?' I said.

She laughed of course, like she always does. 'That's how I've always lived,' she said.

'And don't you think it's about time you changed?'

'But I like my life.'

'You should be ashamed of yourself at your age.'

There was no reasoning with that old lady, once she'd got the bit between her teeth, which was practically all of the time. All her waking time at least. I wonder sometimes if she ever let go of it. Maybe in her prayers when she was face to face with the Old Man. They must've had some bloody battles, the pair of them. Mother Louis wasn't one to bow down easily, not even to him.

The sin of pride, that's what that old lady had, and sometimes I think she had it pretty bad, worse than I've seen in a lot of headstrong people who are always wanting their own way. And it's my guess, that it would be that proud steely part in her that was going to stop her getting to heaven straight away. But then again she's never been the sort to want things easy for herself, and most probably she would've been pretty disappointed if she'd been taken right there on a conveyor belt along with all the other good souls about. Knowing her, she'd want to fry a bit, enough to feel the heat of the flames on her back and know she'd earned her place up there.

'Stubborn as an old mule – that's what you are,' I said, just loud enough for her to hear.

'What was that?' she said, a wicked gleam coming from the corner of her eye.

'You heard,' I said.

Mother Louis chuckled, tightening her grip on my arm. 'You disapprove of me, Marsi.'

'You know what I think – Sunday's your time – for you and your praying – not for proud women in feather hats who every time they snap their fingers are used to getting their own way.'

Mother Louis sighed. 'Her daughter's a good child.'

'Mother Louis – that little girl is nothing but trouble – she's got it written all over her – how's she ever going to fit in with the other little girls in the school?'

'Maybe you can help her, Marsi.'

'Me?'

'And why not?'

You had to hand it to her. That old lady was slyer than a pack of foxes put together...

'What d'you think you're staring at – never seen an old coloured woman before?'

Little Ellie was sitting at the end of the long table in the kitchen, following every move I made with those big, yellow-green eyes of hers.

Mother Louis and the lady in the feathered hat had left her here with me while they went off to the study at the back of the chapel to discuss things. And since then Little Ellie hadn't spoken a word, which must've been all of ten minutes.

Little Ellie's eyes widened with my question. She took in a sharp breath, puffing out her cheeks like a frog.

'Not one as black as you before.'

'Well, there's plenty like me – and darker – all you have to do is look around.'

I watched her out of the corner of my eye as I lifted the kettle from the hob and poured it into the pot.

'Is the jungle very far from here?' she said.

'Well, let me see,' I said. I carried the pot over and put it down on the table; 'depends which one you mean – I suppose the nearest one is about five thousand miles away – as the crow flies.'

I could see by the look in her eyes she was having difficulty.

'How do you get here?' she said.

'By bus,' I said, 'the number thirty-three.'

Ellie's eyes widened.

Maybe I should've explained that I lived a couple of miles down the road, in a house with a toilet, and a kitchen, and a bathroom and a colour TV set in the living-room. But I figured that was for her to work out in her own time when she'd gotten to know me a bit and realized I wasn't so very different from most of the other people she knew.

After mulling it over for a bit, she let it drop and changed on to something else, in the way children do. I must say though – I wasn't prepared for what came next.

'Are you a heathen unbeliever, like me?' she said.

I lifted the lid of the pot and stirred the tea. It is not something I normally do, but I wanted to be occupied to give me time to think.

'Where'd a little girl like you learn to use such long words?' I said.

'Don't you know what they mean?'

I snapped the lid back down on the pot. I felt a sharp little rush of anger stirring up in me.

'I know what people mean by them all right,' I said, 'ignorant people who should know better than to talk to a child like that.'

Little Ellie peered at me, her green-yellow eyes round as saucers. I don't suppose she'd heard a grown-up person talk that way before, but then I wasn't like all the other grown-ups she knew. She leant back in her chair and folded her arms, keeping those yellow-green eyes of hers fixed on me.

'I'm bad, you know.' She announced like it was a statement of fact, like she was telling me her name, the name she'd been born to and grown up with all her life.

'And who told you that?' I said.

'Nearly everyone – that's why they don't keep me.'

'Who don't keep you?'

'People – places like this.'

'You mean schools?'

Ellie nodded, watching me with those great round-saucer green eyes of hers, with the thin band of yellow circling them. I don't know what she was expecting from me, maybe not as much as I thought, maybe nothing, maybe the look in her eyes was curiosity, it was hard to tell.

'Tea,' I said.

She nodded. I poured her out a cup. 'Milk?' She nodded again. 'Sugar?'

'Two.'

I pushed the cup across the table. 'Watch yourself, it's hot.'

With that over we were silent again.

'How many schools have you been to, Ellie?'

A strange look came over her face, like a worried little old woman, and I wished I hadn't asked the question. But she had already begun to count on her fingers. I watched as she used up the fingers on one hand and moved on to the other. I reached across the table to stop her and touched her tiny little hand with mine.

Ellie looked up. 'If I go on being bad,' she said, 'will I turn out black like you?'

I squeezed her hand tight inside mine.

'Ellie,' I said, 'you're not bad.' She was staring at me. 'And besides, no amount of wickedness ever changed the colour of a person's skin – drink your tea before it gets cold.'

She picked up the cup, peering at me over the top of the rim with a look in her eye that told me she wasn't sure if I was the devil incarnate come to tempt her, or a guardian angel come to smooth all her troubles away.

So – that's how it all began with Little Ellie for me.

She didn't fit, of course. We never expected that. When I say 'we', that's me and Mother Louis I'm talking about. The other sisters, they expected different. But no amount of trying on their part 'til they were blue in the face was ever going to change that child. Little Ellie was a natural-born wild thing. A wild thing that was never going to take taming. She had too much spirit in her for that. A spirit that burnt in her so bright, it seemed sometimes as if it would burst out of her in flames and set her alight. I guess, looking back now, she was what these modern doctors would call a disturbed child. I've heard that word 'disturbed' used a lot these days – and I don't know – I don't like the sound of it. I prefer the word 'troubled'. Ellie was a little girl troubled beyond her years with things from the adult world, that most of the other little girls at the school hadn't even come across in their worst dreams.

I suppose in all the time I knew her, I never got to the bottom of what was eating away at that child. I just remember one time, it was near the beginning of her stay in the convent. I was upstairs in the vestry, washing Father Benedict's chalice down with Dettolled water, and the bell went for morning prayers. I looked up out of the window down into the courtyard, where the school congregates in the summer months, and watched the girls forming into straight lines, the tall seniors at the back, the younger ones in the front. And when everyone was there and in place, and Mother Louis had finished the morning prayer, and they had begun to sing the school hymn, a slow, turgid thing, like a funeral dirge, Sister Dolores' composition, a tiny figure streaked out across the yard fast as lightning, running like she had the wind in her feet. It was Little Ellie, over five minutes late. And I don't know if you've ever encountered a similar sensation before. It's like a bit of you has been taken out of yourself, and everything starts to run slow, like in some movies when the couple are about to kiss and they slow the film to milk the moment for all it's worth. Only in this case, it wasn't anybody kissing, just Little Ellie, running slow, out on her own across that yard, and it seemed to take her ages before she reached the other girls. And it must've been the stink of Father Benedict's Dettol, he's a very germ-conscious man, that brought me back to myself, with a sad feeling that stayed with me for the rest of the day.

Some people, they're just born to hurt, which brings me to my brother Frank.

In Frank you couldn't've found a lovelier, kinder, softer person. Pure innocence shone out of him. An untarnished innocence that hadn't dimmed any, since the day he was born. An innocence that hadn't managed to grow a second skin, that couldn't grow a second skin, because that's how Frank was, he didn't understand the necessity of such things. And I guess it was that not understanding that killed him in the end.

Poor Frank; a day, an hour almost, doesn't go by when my thoughts aren't with him.

With Ellie it wasn't the growing of a skin so much. She had a different kind of innocence, fierce as Frank's was gentle, like a wild animal that hadn't learned to live in captivity. She was always throwing herself against the bars and coming away bruised and cut. And never understanding why. Because the very next day, she'd go and do the same thing all over again.

The poor sisters, they tried their best with her. I suppose they thought if they could get Little Ellie to bend her will to God and learn a little piety, humility they called it, another word I've never liked, she'd calm down and settle in a bit.

Ellie, according to Sister Dolores, was suffering from the sin of pride. One of the worst sins in her book. Well, I don't know about that. People's pride comes in all different shapes and sizes. And Ellie's pride was a skin she wore to protect herself from the things she didn't understand. But I don't suppose Sister Dolores understood that. All she saw was a little girl who was fierce and proud and headstrong, and had to be disciplined, brought into line with all the other little girls under her care. Broken like a wild pony.

Over those first few months of that summer term, Sister Dolores tried everything with Ellie. Every trick in a nun's book designed to tame unruly children. Only in Ellie's case none of them worked.

She was put on a separate table all by herself at mealtimes to stop her incessant talking. Her bed was moved out into the corridor outside one of the sisters' rooms to stop her telling ghost stories which terrified the other children and set them off screaming at the slightest creak in the corridor at night. She was kept back to do detention in the long summer evenings while the other girls were out playing, to stop her dreaming in lesson times and decorating her exercise books with pictures of kings and queens and tall castles and big flying dogs and cats and elephants and things.

But the worst was, when Sister Dolores got Ellie to kneel down in front of the statue of St Joseph in the courtyard and confess her sins in front of the whole school.

During all of Sister Dolores' trials, Ellie never cried, not a single tear, or showed she was the least bit scared. I got the feeling she was used to this sort of thing at the other places she'd been at, and she submitted with a quiet resignation, like it was her due, part of living, and just something she had to get through. And it was that courage in Ellie that seemed to incense Sister Dolores more than anything. Whatever she did, she couldn't win. That brave little girl's spirit eluded her every time. And so she got to be called sly and cunning and deceitful by the nuns. Along with being proud and insolent and stubborn, and a whole load of other things. And it began to seem to me that that little girl had just about all the sins in the book heaped on her shoulders, which in my opinion is a lot for a child to carry, not that Ellie seemed to mind. Like I said, she accepted the blame from the adult world like it was her due, her role in life.

And so the weeks went by with Little Ellie skimming through all the trials and tribulations put in her way by Sister Dolores, staying as fierce and fiery and unruly as the day she arrived.

I suppose everyone must've thought she was unbreakable, forgetting she was a child. And I might've forgotten along with the rest, if I hadn't the memory of Frank to remind me, how things all of a sudden can change and turn it all upside down. With Ellie it happened on the day of her first Holy Communion.

Leading up to that point there was a whole load of controversy stirred up by Sister Dolores. In her opinion Ellie wasn't ready, she still had the stigma of the sin of pride sticking to her and was in no condition to take the light of the Lord Jesus into her heart. Father Benedict, who was Holy Communion mad, even he thought Ellie should wait. But Mother Louis was of a different opinion. She wasn't listening to either of them. She never explained her reasons, but I knew, and Sister Dolores and Father Benedict must've known too. No one ever said as much, but as soon as

Mother Louis made her opinion known, they dropped their objections fast as hot potatoes. After all, what was one little girl's spiritual unworthiness in the face of a grand old lady's dying wish.

Yes, Mother Louis was dying. For the past year we'd watched her fading away in front of our eyes, growing smaller and greyer and thinner, like the flame on a candle slowly sinking. And it wasn't going to be long now, before the light in her finally went out.

I can't remember now, exactly, the last time I spoke to her alone. It must've been about three or four days before Ellie's Holy Communion. She'd called me into her study for a chat.

It was in the late afternoon, around the end of my day's work, sometime between five and six o'clock. She was sitting at that big old desk of hers, with the curtains half drawn to cut out the sunlight. The room was dim and cool and quiet, with a patch of late summer sunshine slanting through a gap in the curtains. I don't know why, but I remember it clearly, like it happened only yesterday. We sat in silence for a long time. There wasn't any need to talk, we both knew what she was going to say. I remember watching that patch of light which slipped across the corner of the desk and dropped down in a fan shape, on to that old Persian carpet of hers, which I'd always had such difficulty making look nice. No amount of hoovering ever seemed to get it clean. I sat watching that piece of bright light, dappled like water from the branches of the sycamore tree outside her window. And although I knew what my old friend was going to say, all I could think of was how much trouble that dirty old bit of carpet had caused me. And how it was just like her to hang on to it all these years, refusing to get a new one. I suppose what I was really thinking was that now it was too late.

Mother Louis was the first to break that long silence. I looked up to see her opening the top drawer of her desk.

'I want to give you something,' she said.

I don't know why that took me by surprise. Maybe because she'd never given me anything before, which isn't as strange as it sounds, when you remember nuns as a general rule have very little that they can call their own. I suppose because I was surprised, more than anything else, I told her she didn't have to do that, which looking back now, sounds like an ungrateful thing to say. Mother Louis smiled; maybe it was my lack of grace that amused her.

'I want you to have it,' she said. 'Come here.'

She had something in her hand. I went over to her. She took hold of my hand and put it in my palm, closing my fingers around it, holding them shut. Then she let go of my hand and sat back in her chair looking at me. I opened my hand. She had given me her mother of pearl rosary. She was smiling. It was her last little joke on me.

'Mother Louis,' I said, 'if you think I'm going to start praying at my age...'

'I'm not expecting anything,' she said.

'Just as long as that's understood between us,' I said. I wanted to square it with her, and let her know I wasn't taking anything under false pretences.

'Of course,' she said and smiled again with a twinkle in her eye. I had to hand it to that old lady, she never gave up trying.

'Marsi,' she said, 'have you thought what you're going to do when I'm gone?'

She spoke so matter-of-factly, like she was taking a trip to the Mother House in Rome.

'Gone?' I said; for a moment I really didn't know what she was talking about.

'I had a word with a dear old friend of mine – Father McBain – it's about time he got himself a housekeeper – I gave him your name – I hope you don't mind...' I stared at her. 'Maybe you've made other plans...'

Other plans, what other plans? It's strange how the expected things are often the ones that take you most by surprise. You spend all your time waiting for them to happen, knowing it's only a matter of months, weeks, days even... And then when they do happen you're knocked back, and you act like it's the last thing you expected in all the world. At least, that's how it was when Frank finally killed himself. And here it was happening in the same way all over again. Only this time Mother Louis was giving me some warning.

'Mother Louis,' I said, 'you're not going anywhere.'

'I'm afraid I am, my dear – and faster than I would like – I do hope I manage to see Little Ellie take her first Holy Communion.'

I don't know what happened then. It was like somebody had pushed a switch in me that I had no control over. I started to cry, great big baby-tears came welling up in me and rolling down my cheeks. I suppose I was crying first and foremost for myself and for Frank. I don't think I was crying for her then, that grief would come later.

'Marsi, I want you to keep an eye out for Little Ellie,' she said, handing me a blue-striped handkerchief that I've still got. I never gave it back.

'That little girl spreads trouble like wildfire,' I said, blowing my nose into Mother Louis' handkerchief. 'What good can I do her?'

Mother Louis smiled. 'I think you like her,' she said.

Like I said, that was the last time I spoke to Mother Louis, but not the last time I saw her alive. That happened on the day of Ellie's first Holy Communion. It's my guess, looking back now, that old Mother Louis held out 'til then, just long enough to see Little Ellie taken into the fold, because that same night she passed away.

Ellie was taking her communion with two other little girls. They looked pretty enough in their white frocks and white veils and little white socks. But Ellie was prettier by far. And she knew it. She had the devil in her that day. The wind in her feet. Running around, shrieking and giggling all over the place.

The two other little girls stood by, pious and prayerful as a pair of toadstools, while Ellie stole all the limelight from under their noses. They had their parents to behave for. Ellie had no one.

Like I explained before, Ellie's way to protect herself from hurting was to act wild. And the more she hurt, the wilder she acted. It's my guess, judging from her behaviour that day, she was hurting pretty bad. Her mother, the proud lady in the feathered hat I described to you, had sent a telegram that morning from somewhere in Italy, where she was acting in a film with a famous actor, saying she couldn't get away on account of bad weather conditions, which sounded like a pretty poor excuse to me.

I think, you know, I might've seen her in something, in a film with Roger Moore, where she was dangled by her little toe over a snake-pit. She had a lot of blue make-up on her eyes and not a hair out of place. But then that could've been someone else. It was a long time ago.

Anycase, that day Little Ellie was wild. I didn't get to see the ceremony, not being a churchgoer, which you will have probably gathered by now; it wouldn't've been right for me to be there. But I did get to see Ellie and the other little girls waiting in the hall outside the chapel for it all to begin. Ellie had calmed down a little by then, but what was strange was as soon as the organ music began to play and people started going in to get their seats, Ellie went quiet as a lamb. She closed her eyes and joined her hands and even managed to look like she was praying. Maybe she was praying. Come to think of it, at that moment I do believe she was.

Just before the organ music came to an end, Sister Dolores came out and told the little girls to come in. I saw them follow her up the aisle. Ellie was the last, with her hands joined and her head bowed in prayer. Then one of the sisters came over and closed the door, and that was all I saw.

Later, when it was all over, the organ music started up. The chapel doors opened up and the people filed out in a long line. Little Ellie was somewhere in the middle of everyone. What happened next all happened so quickly, it's difficult to separate out the stages in my mind, and tell them bit by bit. As I remember it, Ellie seemed to fly out like she had wings on her feet. All that lamblike prayerfulness in her was gone, switched out like a light, and she was back to her old self again. She dived through the crowd of nuns and parents and sped across the hall, right past me. I was standing at the bottom of the stairs, occupying myself with polishing the banisters.

That's when I saw Mother Louis. She was at the top of the stairs on her way down. She must've been in the gallery of the chapel watching it all from up there. It's funny how you remember things. I looked up and saw her hand on the banister. And then Ellie's little feet on the foot of the stairs, and the sound of her laughter. And Mother Louis coming down towards her smiling. And Ellie taking the stairs in leaps, two at a time. It was like she was flying towards her. Mother Louis' hand came away from the banister, and Ellie was getting nearer and nearer, laughing all the time. Mother Louis was still smiling when she started to fall in a black heap like a sack. I remember the sound, a soft thudding that didn't seem real. And little Ellie's eyes open wide, staring. And the sweep of her veil to the back of her head as she turned and ran away. I looked round. No one else had seen her on the stairs but me.

That night Mother Louis died in her sleep. By all accounts quiet as a whisper, having made her peace with God. Happy. Her heart stopped beating and she slipped away to the place where she'd always wanted to be.

And I'll say this now, knowing that old lady like I did, I'll defy anyone to say it was that fall which finished her. Mother Louis had made up her mind she was going that night and the only thing that kept her hanging on so long, was the old lady's stubborn determination to see Ellie right with God. Only as it turned out, she lived just long enough to see the start of something go all wrong.

Well – the very next day at the morning assembly after the Lord's prayer, Sister Dolores climbed up on to the platform. She stood there for a long time with her head bowed and her hands clasped in prayer. Everyone was silent, waiting for her to say something. She looked up, just at the point where it seemed like she was losing their attention, and stared over their heads straight at me. I was standing in the Corner of the courtyard, a bit away from the assembly, washing down St Augustine's statue with soapy water and a little Vim, which helps to get the worst of the pigeons' doings off of him. I don't suppose she liked seeing me getting on with my work while she was up there making an impression on everyone. Well, it wasn't working on me. I bent down and wetted my cloth, getting ready to start on the saint's head, when she began to speak in this loud and sombre sounding voice, like she had it all rehearsed.

'Girls – I have a very sad announcement to make...'

That's when my heart stood still. Mother Louis was dead.

And in my mind, my thoughts flew to Frank and that Sunday afternoon when there was a knock on the door. As soon as I opened it and saw that little bald plain-clothed person standing there with his briefcase tucked under his arm, it was like I'd been waiting for that moment all my life. And I was calm and cold as steel inside, watching as he unzipped his case and brought out the black and white shiny photographs with little white specks on them. Photographs of Frank in the road, with his arms spread out and his head twisted round like he was pinned to a cross.

Frank, with every bone broken in his body, smashed to pieces with the leap he'd taken from the balcony of his thirteenth-floor flat. The plain-clothed person had it written down on his form as an accident. He said he must've tripped on something which sent him over the edge. Well, if that's what he wanted to have down on his piece of paper I wasn't going to put him right. After all, what was the point? He didn't know Frank. None of them knew Frank. He was just a name and a number of a body on a slab as far as they were concerned. Frank's reasons were private. And they were best kept that way.

I didn't hear the rest of Sister Dolores' speech. And by the time I came round, she had everyone kneeling on the ground with their heads bowed and hands joined in silent prayer. Only one little girl was standing up at the front. And as I could only see the back of her head, it took me a while to realize the little girl was Ellie. One moment she was standing there stock-still as a lamp-post and the next moment she was down on the ground. I walked up the side of the courtyard to see what was going on. A group of girls had collected around the place where she fell, and from where I was standing, I thought I saw little Ellie lying on the ground, with her arms spread out and her head twisted back. It was only a brief glimpse, quick as the blink of an eyelid, before one of the sisters came over and cut off my view with a sweep of her long black skirt.

Later that morning I heard little Ellie had been taken to the infirmary to rest. Over that week I didn't see her around, not that I thought much about it, I had troubles of my own to be worrying about.

When the call came to go to see Sister Dolores, I was prepared, ready and waiting, I'd been expecting it all week. Sister Dolores had become Mother Dolores now, and had moved into my old friend's study.

When I went in, she was stood by the window, watching something through a pair of binoculars. She told me to take a seat, without turning round, and went on watching whatever it was occupying her attention, making me wait till she was good and ready to say her piece. Not that I minded. I knew what was coming, and besides, it gave me the opportunity to notice the changes she'd made to Mother Louis' room. The gold curtains were gone, and so was the bit of old carpet, and all of the pictures of Our Lady that used to be hanging on the walls. She'd got Venetian blinds put in, and a rug with the pattern of what looked like a bulldog woven into it, and a calendar with a photograph of three little bulldog puppies on the wall beside the desk. The only other pictures she had were one of St Augustine sitting on a cloud looking glum, and another of an old bulldog balanced on a tightrope on one hindleg. Well, I suppose I learnt something new about Sister Dolores that morning. I never knew she liked bulldogs that much, better than the Virgin Mary by the looks of things.

Sister Dolores was a strange one. Over six feet tall, with great big hands and feet, and a square jaw like a man's with grey whiskers on the chin that she'd never troubled to cut back like some of the other nuns. There was always something about her that put me in mind of John Wayne, out of one of those cowboy films. The way she stood sometimes, with one leg up on a chair and an elbow resting on her knee, like cowboys do when they're having it out with the sheriff, or dallying with dancing girls in smoky saloon-bars. And if it hadn't been for her voice, which was soft and sweet as a young girl's, I think I would've had a difficult time believing that there wasn't a man hidden inside that big black habit of hers.

Anycase, to get back to that morning. Sister Dolores, who had recently become Mother Dolores, which was a change of name I was never going to get used to thinking of her as, put the binoculars in her pocket and came round and leant herself against the front of the desk, with her arms folded and one foot crossed over the other, like a policeman at the start of an interrogation.

'Marsi,' she said, 'I think you know what I'm going to say...'

Well of course I did. As I said, I'd been waiting for it to come all week. But I wasn't going to play ball.

'No,' I said.

'I think you do,' she said, as she took a little nail file from her pocket.

Now if there's one thing I hate it's that sound, it sends shivers all up and down my spine. I'm uncomfortable as a cat dropped in a puddle of water, and I have an intuition Sister Dolores knew that. When you have that sort of antipathy towards another person, like the two of us had, it's a chemistry that binds you both in a strange sort of intimacy, like you can see into the other person's soul. And I suppose that's the thing that makes you hate them, 'cos you don't like what you see, at least I didn't with Sister Dolores, and I guessed she felt the same way about me.

'The time has come,' she said, 'for a parting of the ways.' She looked up, putting the nail file back in her pocket. 'Your position here was never intended to be permanent.' I'd only been in the job for over twenty years. 'And I'm sure you realize that I for one have never shared Mother Louis' opinion of your suitability for the post – and I think you'll know what I'm referring to when I say that you'd be happier and far better off working in a non-religious establishment, where impressionable young Catholic minds weren't at risk.'

'I've always kept my beliefs to myself,' I said.

'That's hardly the point,' she said.

'No, it isn't, is it,' I said, managing to meet her in the eye for the first time since I'd come into the room.

The point was, she and most of the other sisters, apart from Sister Bernadette, who was too preoccupied with matters of the flesh to mind, hated me for my special friendship with Mother Louis. I'd got close where none of them could even get a toe in the door. And her preferring me for myself over the rest of them cut deep. And seeing as the point, at this time, was understood between me and Sister Dolores, I didn't see much sense in pressing on, and I let her get on tying up the loose ends of my dismissal. At the end of it all, in which I was graciously granted one month's notice before I had to quit, she asked me if I had anything I wanted to say.

I asked her if I could go and visit Ellie in the infirmary. She said Ellie wasn't in any fit condition to be seeing anyone. And when I suggested that if Ellie was unhappy, maybe I could help her, that's when a nasty look came into her eye. A sixth sense must've told her it was something discussed between Mother Louis and me.

I saw my mistake straightaway but by then it was too late and Sister Dolores was expressly forbidding me to do something I could otherwise have done without blinking an eyelid, if I hadn't been fool enough to bring it up with her that afternoon.

I suppose these things work two ways. If I'd never asked Sister Dolores' permission to visit Ellie in the infirmary I never would've been forbidden. And if I hadn't been forbidden, I don't think I would've got along there so fast, that same day around lunchtime, which as it turns out it was lucky I did, despite the amount of trouble it caused later.

Twelve thirty is the time the sisters go to their midday prayers, which meant there'd only be old Mrs White in the dispensary up at the end. And seeing as her drinking problem prevented her from noticing much of what was going on around her, I figured I'd be safe to sneak in and get to see little Ellie for myself.

The infirmary around that time of year is usually pretty empty. When I went in there was nobody around, apart from old Mrs White snoozing in a patch of sunshine behind the glass of the dispensary, and a little girl asleep in her bed at the far end. I couldn't see Ellie anywhere, and I began to wonder if they'd taken her away somewhere, when I remembered the isolation room at the back near the bathroom. I went along there. The door was locked. The key for it was kept in the dispensary. Old Mrs White was well away, snoozing with her jaw dropped down and making those little grunting sounds. The smell of whiskey was powerful. It stank like a distillery in there. I reached up and took the key for the isolation room off a rack above her head. She grunted and belched a fresh wave of whiskey fumes, and as my hand came down across her face, holding the key, one of her eyes snapped open and stared straight at me, with an expression in it that was mean and fierce as an old jungle cat. For a moment I thought she had me, then the lid dropped down and the soft grunting snores started up again, sending sharp little twitches down her body, like a fat old dog asleep in front of the fire after mealtime.

I left old Mrs White to her mean whiskey dreams and went to find little Ellie. The curtain behind the bed, which was drawn across the window, billowed out like a full sail, with a pale light shining through. It took a while for my eyes to adjust to the dimness before I saw the dark shape of a child in a long nightdress silhouetted against the pale cream-coloured light. At first I didn't understand. Ellie wasn't in the bed or under it. I felt like I was seeing a ghost. And when I realized, I ran across that room like lightning and pushed back the curtain. Ellie was standing on the window-ledge staring down. I didn't stop to think. I grabbed hold of her by the waist and pushed her back into the room, sitting her down on the bed. I was shaking all over, trembling like a leaf.

She stared up at me, with those round-saucer green eyes of hers, calm as you like.

'I'm bad,' she said.

I sat down on the bed beside her and put my arms around her and held her to me very tight. We stayed like that for a long time. I was thinking of Frank. Frank on the window-ledge, thirteen floors up. Frank lying on the ground with his arms spread out and his head twisted back.

She lay in my arms, limp as a little fish, not moving a muscle. My heart ached, and all I could think about was Frank, over and over, the same thing again and again, on the window-ledge, on the ground, and nothing in between.

After a bit I let go of her. She was looking beyond me, past my shoulder at something in the corner of the room. I turned round to look. There was nothing there. But she kept on staring.

'Ellie – what is it?'

She pointed to the corner of the room. 'Make him go away.'

I forced her head round so that she was looking at me. 'Make who go away?'

She whispered. 'The black man with wings.'

Well, there was no black man with wings that I could see in the room. But I wasn't going to tell her that. To that frightened little girl he was standing there plain as day.

'Who is he, Ellie?' I said.

'You know,' she whispered.

'No – I don't – tell me.'

Keeping her eyes fixed on that spot in the corner of the room, she leant forward and whispered into my ear.

'Mother Louis' friend.'

'What does he want?' I whispered back in her ear.

She was staring over my shoulder into the corner of the room. Her face crumpled up. She started to cry.

'Tell him to go away.'

Well it may sound strange to you, but I knew what I had to do. I got up off that bed, went over to the corner of the room. I raised my hands, jumped up in the air as far as I could and bellowed at the top of my voice. It felt good. I turned round to Ellie.

'Has he gone?' I said.

She pointed to another corner of the room by the basin 'He's up there,' she said. I went over to the basin and repeated the same performance all over again.

'What about now?' I said.

She pointed to the window-ledge. I went over to the window and pulled the curtains back. Now I know this is going to sound even stranger, and you're not going to believe it, but I saw my brother standing on that window ledge clear as day, clear as I'm speaking to you now. And I can assure you I've never been one for imagining things. It was Frank standing there in his old checked shirt I gave him one Christmas and old trousers, and no shoes. Standing there smiling at me.

I turned round and looked at her. She could see him too. I walked over to the bed and picked her up in my arms and carried her over to the window.

'Ellie,' I said, 'I want you to meet my brother Frank.'

She was looking straight at him, seeing what I saw. Her face cleared, like a dark sky after rain. She held out her hand and their fingers touched. She was smiling. And he was smiling. And I was crying like a great big baby, for the first time since he'd been gone.

'Don't cry,' she said. 'Mother Louis sends her love, and says thank you for looking after me, and when she grows wings she'll come and see you for a chat and tea.'

Well, I never did see Mother Louis again, or Frank for that matter. By the time I turned to look around, he was gone.

'Where is he?' I said to Ellie.

She pointed up into the sky. A big white cloud was passing across the sun.

'Home,' she said, 'over there.'

Mardy

ELIZABETH HARRIS

MAY IS Mardy's month.

Tradition holds that May is unlucky. Bad luck will follow a May wedding. May blossom brought inside means a death within the year. The Romans believed that the spirits of the dead came back in May. And maypole dancing, Jack-in-the-green, and all those other May customs that attend the birth of new life also, of course, mark the death of the old.

Was it an unlucky month for me? Have the pain and the longing that followed the joy been May's bad luck for me?

No. For even on the worst days of yearning for her, I've known in my heart that I wouldn't have missed Mardy. Not for the world.

She got off the bus, carrying a cardboard suitcase tied round with string. I heard old Jack Gotobed call out, 'Straight down there, Miss. Big building on the right. They'll help you.' Then he shouted, 'All right, Alf!' and as the bus lurched off he leaned out of the door waving to her. I realized straight away there must be something striking about her – Jack Gotobed is the most morose man I ever met and normally speaks not a word, communicating with his passengers solely by raising or lowering his eyebrows. Usually the latter – he has an impressively thunderous scowl.

I was standing in my front garden. That's the wrong word, for it ceased to be a garden in 1940, when my elderly parents obeyed the exhortation 'Dig for Victory!' and my poor father slipped a disc in his enthusiasm. For six years the erstwhile rose-beds yielded potatoes and cabbages, and now that I was home I was doing my best to follow where my parents had led. I had an egg in my hand – one of the hens favoured the front garden over the hen-yard at the back. It was a large brown speckled egg, and I was going to have it for my tea, if I managed not to ruin it – while it wasn't quite true to say I couldn't even boil an egg, I kept forgetting to note the time they went in. The results varied from bullet-hard to the sort of pappy mess most at home in a prairie oyster. I felt I was being unfair to the hens. But I'd never learned how to cook – from the tender care of my mother I went to boarding school, then to Sandhurst, and out to India as soon as I was commissioned. And throughout the war, although we did without many things, there was always someone to bring me food.

I stood watching Mardy at the crossroads. The bus was a vague shape in the distance and the noise of its passage had died. She stood quite alone, and as I watched she straightened her back and squared her shoulders. That little gesture touched my heart. I moved over to stand at the gate, so that when at last she had gathered sufficient courage to follow Jack Gotobed's instructions, she would have to pass right by me.

She started walking. Her eyes focused on something straight in front of her, and she was frowning. Every few paces she put the suitcase down and picked it up in the other hand. I was brought up to believe that a man never lets a woman carry a weight of which he can relieve her; as she came level with the gate, years of training overcame the diffidence I've always felt with women. Especially young ones, and especially since Veronica.

I stepped out into the lane and said, 'That looks heavy. May I carry it for you?'

She jumped out of her skin. She'd been so intent on whatever it was she was thinking about that she hadn't noticed me.

'I'm sorry. I made you jump.'

'No! Oh, I mean, yes. But it's all right. My fault.'

Her face had changed from an apprehensive pallor to the blush of embarrassment. I thought probably she too was wondering how on earth my making her jump could possibly be her fault.

'Are you going into the village?'

'Er – yes. I think so. The bus conductor said there might be a room, at the pub. The Green Man. He said their son's still away, in the Navy, and that sometimes they let his room.'

She was like a child, reciting a lesson learned by heart. I picked up the suitcase, which wasn't all that heavy. It was her small stature that had made it appear so.

'That's right.' I tried to sound reassuring, and even in my own ears it came out as blustering. Whatever must she think, poor girl. 'Mrs Leavis,' I went on more quietly. 'Her husband's the landlord, but only in that it's his name painted above the pub door. She does all the work. She's not expecting you, then?'

'Oh dear! No, she isn't. Do you think it'll matter?'

I regretted my last remark. She'd brightened at my weak attempt at lightheartedness, and now I'd flung her back into her anxiety.

'No, I'm sure it won't. If you like I'll stay with you, make sure she can take you.'

Silly of me. Too pushy, to have said that. We're trustworthy people, here in the Fens, but she wasn't to know. And here was I, a middle-aged stranger, presuming to adopt a protective role.

But I needn't have worried. She turned to me, and her smile gave an unforeseen beauty to her face. She said, 'Oh, would you? You are kind! My name's Mardy Russett. I've come to search for my parents.'

There was no time then to follow up her extraordinary remark, for we had reached the Green Man and Mrs Leavis herself was outside, briskly sweeping the step. Mardy's charm must have touched its fingers against her, too; on hearing that Mardy wanted a room for a week or so, she put down her broom and led her straight inside. 'I'll take that,' she said to me, taking the suitcase, her tone implying that I was only a man and therefore not to be relied upon to do anything right. I didn't mind; marriage to Nathaniel Leavis would shake any woman's faith in the male sex.

I stood inanely on the step. Mardy, deep in conversation with Mrs Leavis, was being taken upstairs. But halfway up she turned, looking even more fragile framed by the bulk of Mrs Leavis's ascending buttocks behind her. For a moment there was the hint of that lovely smile again.

'Thank you for your help. It–' She glanced over her shoulder, but Mrs Leavis was still panting her way upwards. 'It was so nice, to have a friendly welcome,' she hurried on. 'I hope I'll see you again. Mr...'

'John,' I said. 'John Langland.'

'John,' she echoed, and turned to run upstairs.

I loitered in my front garden all the next morning, despite the rain. But she must have gone out on the first bus, because I missed her. It rained without ceasing the entire morning. By midday I was soaked, and the permanent ache in my left knee had responded, as it always does to damp, with spiteful alacrity. When the sun finally put in a half hearted appearance in the late afternoon, I was good for nothing more industrious than sitting in a deckchair on the lawn doing *The Times* crossword. I was just thinking how sweet the apple-blossom smelt, with the sunshine drying the rain, when the 4.30 p.m. bus from Cambridge pulled up at the crossroads and Mardy got off.

She looked all in. Her steps dragged, and as she approached I saw that she had been crying.

'Mardy!' I struggled to get up, and my knee gave way. She ran in through the gate and came to help me to my feet.

'Oh! Are you hurt?'

'No, no.' I felt very stupid. 'Sitting too long in one position. I was stuck on fourteen down.' I stood up, giving an involuntary wince.

She noticed. Her face winced in syrmpathy. 'You are hurt! What have you been doing?'

'Fighting a war,' I said baldly. 'Me and several million others. My driver skidded my jeep in heavy snow, in the mountains of Northern Italy.' I didn't want to elaborate. January 1945 – over a year since it happened, and still I had nightmares. Of trying to see through a worsening blizzard; of pushing on, on, desperate to keep in view the tail-lights of the vehicle in front. Of the jeep hitting a low stone wall, then cartwheeling into a ravine. I'd been lucky – concussion, neck injuries, and a smashed knee where my leg hit the dashboard. I copped a Blighty one, as they used to say in an earlier war, although until the war ended and we were all driven home up Hitler's autobahns, it got me no nearer Blighty than a Base Hospital.

My driver was killed outright.

She was watching me, her face full of concern. I managed a smile.

'What about a cup of tea?' I didn't want her to go. 'Come inside, I was just going to have one.'

'I don't...' she began. I walked on, along the path that led to the kitchen door. She was a well-mannered girl; not wanting to offend me by simply leaving, she had no option but to follow.

'Did you go into Cambridge?' I asked. I put the kettle on, then turned to look at her. She was standing just inside the door. She didn't look at all happy.

'Yes.'

I was about to make some trite remark about the Backs or the chestnuts. But when it came to the point, I couldn't. She was trying so hard to maintain her party face, and it seemed cruel to make her go on. I put down the tea-caddy and went over to her.

'You said something yesterday about searching for your parents.' Her eyes shot to meet mine, full of pain. I pressed on before I lost my courage. 'No luck?'

'No luck,' she echoed. She tried to smile, but without success. 'There doesn't seem to be any record of my father at all.' Then her face crumpled and she started to cry.

I gave her a large cup of tea, sweet and strong, and a clean handkerchief. She sat down at my table and I perched beside her. I had no idea what to say. I had only been close to two women; my mother, who only cried when she heard *Abide With Me*, and Veronica. Crying was certainly within Veronica's repertoire; once or twice I'd watched her do it to great effect. But I doubt she shed the smallest tear over the letter she wrote to me terminating our engagement. A 'Dear John' indeed. I wonder if every other John who received one felt the extra sting of having such a suitable name? The stuff of music-hall jokes, we jilted Johns. And anyway, I wasn't even sure then that Mardy qualified as a woman. Red-eyed, runny-nosed, she looked more like a child who had fallen off its bicycle.

After a while she stopped. She sat blinking, giving the occasional hiccup. Then she looked shyly at me.

'Sorry,' she said. 'This is awful of me. I don't even know you.'

I wanted to laugh. It was acceptable, then, to break your heart in front of someone you knew? I put out my hand to touch her, but drew back.

'I don't mind.'

She reached into the pocket of her light coat and brought out an envelope. 'Look,' she said, drawing out a sheet of paper. 'My birth certificate.' She placed it down on the table. 'I'm adopted – Mum told me that when I was small. My adopted Mum, I mean. Last October I was twenty-one, and this envelope arrived from a solicitor in Cambridge.'

'May I see?'

'Of course.'

I took it from her.

'Just this? No explanatory letter?' It seemed unnecessarily melodramatic.

'Not really. The solicitor sent a brief note, but it only said that as requested in the last will and testament of the late Georgina Fearon, the enclosed papers were being sent to her daughter on her majority.' Again, she sounded as if she were repeating a lesson. 'And there was this.' She was clutching a photograph, pressing it face-down to her breast. She held it out.

I stared at the two things that made up Mardy's inherit ance.

Margaret Georgina Fearon was her given name. Called, other than the first name, after her mother. Father's name was Theo Arn. I wondered irrelevantly if it could be a spelling mistake – did they make mistakes on birth certificates? – because I'd only ever seen the name Arne spelt with an 'e'. For Father's occupation it said 'student', and for name and address of informant, Georgina's name, with an address in Cambridge. I recognized it; a street where junior dons and other young professionals often had digs. No maiden name of mother was recorded.

I looked at the photograph. A head-and-shoulders study, showing a strong face with a sweep of dark hair drawn back. She wore a plain white blouse under a tailored jacket. Although attractive, an unremarkable face. Until you looked into the eyes.

Dark, heavy-lidded and thick-lashed, they were sensuous eyes, holding a challenge. And for all that their shape was like Mardy's, never in a hundred years could Mardy have imbued her eyes with that knowing, calculating look that glittered in her mother's. For this, I assumed, was Georgina.

'Why 'Mardy'?' I asked. It was unworthy of the moment, but all I could think of.

She smiled, and even so soon after tears the effect was electrifying. 'I have a brother. In my adopted family. He was two when I arrived, and he couldn't manage Margaret. He called me Mardy, and it sort of stuck.'

I wasn't surprised. Margaret was too cool and sophisticated for her. Mardy was far better.

We sat in a silence so prolonged that it started to hurt. I knew I should say something, but I was torn between the awkwardness of pretending nothing had happened and wishing her a polite good-day, and the possibly greater awkwardness of inviting more of her confidences. Not to mention the gossip that would soon start were any intimacy to develop between us.

In the end she decided for me. She was, after all, younger. Less aware, perhaps, of how cruel people can be, of the jeopardy in which we place ourselves by allowing others to become privy to our innermost feelings.

She put her hand on mine, which still held her birth certificate. I heard her draw in her breath, then she said, 'I feel so lost. I thought it'd be all right, that the excitement would keep me going. But I can't bear the thought of going back to eat my supper in the pub kitchen.'

I sympathized; Mrs Leavis as the tyrant of the Green Man was one thing, and doubtless she'd evolved her own brand of martial rule through bitter necessity. But Mrs Leavis with her elbows on the table extracting every last detail of Mardy's life story was something else again.

She was looking at me from beneath her fringe of hair. Theo Arn's hair, perhaps, for it was fair. Not dark, like Georgina's. She asked hesitantly, 'Could I – do you think I could stay here till bedtime?'

My indecision vanished, taking along with it the greater part of my awkwardness. Unto the pure all things are pure. Let them gossip in the village – at least it'd mean they were giving some other unfortunate a few days off.

'Yes,' I said, 'I shall be glad of your company. The fish van's been round today. Do you like haddock?'

That first evening with Mardy was one of the happiest I have ever spent. She was such an optimist, my Mardy, and already she was trying to put the events of the day behind her.

'It doesn't mean I have to give up, does it,' she asked, as we stood together peeling potatoes, 'just because there's no mention of my father in the parish records?'

'No,' I said emphatically. I hoped she wouldn't assume from my tone that I was brimming with helpful suggestions. I wasn't.

'Perhaps he went away, off abroad somewhere,' she mused. 'Perhaps he wasn't born in Cambridge. In England, even. It does sound a bit foreign, doesn't it? Arn.'

Something was bothering me about the name Theo Arn. I frowned, trying to pin it down.

'Yes,' I said vaguely.

She threw the last potato into the pan with a splash. 'There! We've done the messy bit, what shall we do now?'

I wiped my hands. 'We could formulate a plan of action for tomorrow for you, if you like.' I tried not to sound as reluctant as I felt.

'No,' she said surprisingly. 'I'll worry about that in the morning. Let's go outside – I'd love to have a closer look at your apple-blossom. Can we?'

'Of course.' I led the way.

She was an appreciative audience. As we walked through the arch in the rose-brick walls and our feet drowned in the soft grass, I saw the beauty of the old orchard through her eyes. For me, too, it felt like the first time.

'What are they? The trees, I mean.'

'Cox and Bramley.'

'They're ancient, aren't they? The trunks are so wrinkly.'

'I believe so.'

My parents had bought the house from the Church Commissioners, in the late twenties; it had been a vicarage until the parish had dwindled to such an extent that a vicar was no longer necessary. The Church Commissioners hadn't actually provided information about the age of the apple trees.

She was singing, running lightly down the avenues between the trees, occasionally reaching down to pick up handfuls of fallen petals. I felt a moment's keen regret that my parents were no longer alive; they'd both loved the orchard, and would have enjoyed Mardy in it.

Watching her, idly smiling in my pleasure at the picture she made, suddenly I realized what it was that bothered me about 'Theo Arn'.

Without thinking, I shouted, 'Mardy!'

'Yes, John?' She paused and turned, her face alight with happiness, and I couldn't find it in me to tell her. Like her, I'd worry about that in the morning.

I shook my head. 'Nothing. Mind you don't slip,' I said feebly.

Her smile turned to laughter. But all the same, like the obedient child she must have been, she resumed her dancing run at a slower pace.

Turning away, my mind full of warring emotions, I wondered just what it was about her that had this power to reach inside me and find my heart.

She'd said she was going to catch the early bus again, and I set my alarm so that I could get up and see her off. In fact I was awake long before it rang out. A side effect of worry, to rob us of our sleep.

I waited at the gate, and a few minutes before the bus was due I saw her emerge from the back door of the Green Man. She looked excited and happy. I walked to meet her.

'Good morning, John.'

'Hello, Mardy.'

'Come with me,' she said impulsively, tucking her arm through mine. 'Do, it's such a lovely day, and I'm sure I'm going to be lucky because...'

'Mardy, don't waste any more time on Theo Arn,' I said quickly. I couldn't look at her; already I knew so well how her face falling into disappointment affected me.

'What do you mean? I've got to, his name's on my birth certificate, and somebody must have heard of him!'

'No.' I made myself go on. 'Mardy, it's an anagram. I do crosswords, I recognize them. Theo Arn is an anagram of A. N. Other. Your mother...' I had been about to say her mother had thumbed her nose at bureaucracy, had neatly got away with a flat refusal to register the identity of her lover. But I stopped myself.

'A. N. Other,' Mardy whispered. 'My father.'

She hurried on towards the crossroads. The bus was coming round the corner, and she started to run.

'Mardy, wait!'

I set off after her. But it had been over a year since I'd been able to run, and there was no possibility of catching up with her. I stopped in the middle of the road, my weight on my good leg, watching as she boarded the bus and was driven off and wishing there was a way to damp down my increasing misgivings about Georgina Fearon.

She wasn't on the 4.30 bus that afternoon. I drank my tea alone. I went up to the crossroads soon after six, and as soon as I saw her I knew she'd had a good day. She jumped down the steps, handed down by Jack Gotobed, and I swear that as the bus drew off the old misery was actually laughing.

'Oh, John, I've had a marvellous time!' she cried, flinging her arms round me. 'There was this lovely lady in the Registrar's office, she said, why didn't I try the colleges, what with my mother's address being where it was and my father's occupation being put down as student, so I did, and guess what? The second place I went to, someone knew her, they really did! And it's even more extraordinary, because actually she was nothing to do with the college, she worked in the Museum, and this woman just happened to know her. Just think, I've been talking to someone who talked to my mother! Isn't it smashing? Oh, I'm so happy!'

She didn't need to tell me. She was hopping and skipping by my side, her face shining with joy, so intent on telling all she'd done that she didn't even break step when we got to my house but marched straight in.

Later, after we'd eaten – it was poached eggs tonight, hens having obliged – she calmed down. Sitting over a cup of tea, her face turned reflective.

'Penny for them,' I said eventually.

She smiled, looking slightly abashed. 'You'll think me silly.'

'I doubt it.'

She stirred her tea absently. 'I was just thinking about about Mother. Giving me away.' She paused, and for a moment pain flashed across her face as if she too were being made to give a child away. 'I think – I've never been *cross* with her, because Mum always told me it can't have been easy her, having me adopted – but now I... well, it's as if I can understand her better now.' Her eyes had become dreamy. 'I can see her, finding out she's – you know. And being frantic, because all along there's no future for us. Then, after all that, having to part with me.' Her voice shook, 'I think she must have been very brave, doing what was best for me.' Tears ran down her cheeks, and she sniffed. 'I don't think *I* could, do you?'

'No, Mardy love, I thought. I'm quite sure you couldn't. I said briskly, 'Oh, I don't know. I should think most women would act like that, in her position.'

She looked slightly taken aback. I wondered if she resented my comment. Not that I regretted it – her determined romanticism was worrying me.

She stood up. 'I expect you're right. I think I should go now. Thank you for my supper.'

I walked with her to the village, stopping just short of the Green Man. I didn't want to part bad friends, so I said, 'What about tomorrow? Cambridge again?'

She smiled happily. 'Yes. To see the landlady, where Mother used to live. Mrs Armstead, she's called. Rosie Armstead. It should be interesting, don't you think?'

'Yes. Goodnight, Mardy. Sweet dreams.'

She turned briefly to wave, and was gone.

All next day I was uneasy. And the silly thing was, I had no definite cause for my anxiety. Someone else might have admired Georgina for her invention of Theo Arn, applauded her panache in having fooled everyone, but this hypothetical someone else hadn't looked into Georgina's jewel-hard eyes.

And he wasn't feeling in love with her sentimental, vulnerable daughter.

She got back earlier than I'd expected, soon after lunch. Her arrival took me by surprise, and in the first seconds of confusion I didn't know whether this was a good omen or a bad one. She seemed bright enough, but I noticed she was restless.

'How did it go?' I asked, pulling out a chair for her which she appeared not to notice.

'Oh, fine! It was a lovely house, in a road by a sort of meadow, with a little stream through the middle. Mrs Armstead's a keen gardener – she showed me her herbaceous borders.'

She stood with her back to me, staring out of the window.

'Did she remember your mother?'

'What? Oh, yes, she said Mother was very lively, that the house was much quieter since... since she'd gone.'

She didn't want to talk, for some reason. I wondered if it was because she was only now feeling sorrow that Georgina was dead. All the time Georgina had been a distant, unknown figure, it probably hadn't mattered. Now that she was materializing into a real person whom others remembered and described, perhaps Mardy was beginning to grieve for her.

I tried to steer her away from thoughts of Georgina's death.

'It's a nice compliment, isn't it, that Mrs Armstead remembered her as lively?' I said cheerfully. 'I like lively women!'

She kept her back to me. 'Yes! Mrs Armstead said there used to be lots of parties, and always people visiting, and that Mother often used to ask her in for a drink and a chat.'

'It must have been interesting for her, meeting you.'

She didn't answer. As I watched she seemed to sag. I had a feeling I knew what was coming. I stood up and went to her.

'Mardy?' I put a hand on her arm.

She lifted her head, still staring out of the window, and she moved slightly so that my hand fell away.

'Oh, I didn't tell her, actually. She – er, she was quite frank about Mother, and I thought it might embarrass her if I said who I was.'

My heart went out to her. But I had to ask. 'What do you mean, frank?'

She forced a laugh. 'Oh, it seems Mother had a lot of friends. You know.'

'Men friends?'

She turned on me. 'Of course! Why not? She was pretty, wasn't she, and lively, and I bet they all wanted to take her out! So what if sometimes they stayed rather late, it doesn't mean anything. Does it?'

The thought struck me that she was the wrong age for this. Younger, and she wouldn't have understood the implications. Older, and some of that innocent idealism would have had time to be eroded by the reality of life. I could think of no comforting words. I went back to the table.

But she wasn't satisfied.

'Does it?' she repeated. 'Or are you like Mrs Armstead, full of winks and nods and suggestive nudges?'

I was, of course. But I fell before the idea of explaining to her.

'No,' I said. 'No, Mardy, I'm not. You're right, I'm sure it doesn't mean anything.' I don't think she was convinced, but I couldn't bring myself to tell her any more lies. 'What are you going to do now?' I asked, trying to sound as if the previous matter had been finished with and I was merely going on to something else.

She looked at me for a long moment. I couldn't read her expression; she was standing in the corner by the door, and her face was in shadow.

She said very quietly, 'I think I'll go for a walk.'

She went out, closing the door behind her. I got up and hurried after her, thinking to ask her to come back for supper, but when I got outside she was running off up the lane, sprinting as fast as she could. Even if I'd called out to her, she wouldn't have heard.

She went into Cambridge once more. She hadn't told me, but Mrs Armstead had given her another contact, the name of another woman who had known Georgina. I wish she'd told me. Whatever it took, however overbearing I'd have had to be, if I'd suspected where she was going I wouldn't have let her go alone.

But I didn't know.

She was very late. The last bus had come and gone without her, and I was frantic with worry. She was so young, so unworldly. I didn't know where she'd been brought up, but I had a fair idea of by what sort of people. Good people, gentle and kindly, but without the least idea of the wickedness that is in the world.

I'd been waiting at the crossroads, thinking that she might have caught a bus to the nearest point and walked the rest of the way. I'd been there on and off for three hours, but at last I had to give in; my knee was hurting in a way it hadn't done since just after the accident. I stumbled home.

She was sitting in the kitchen.

We didn't speak: she stood up and almost fell into my arms, and before the pain in my leg made me shout out I collapsed with her into my armchair. Her whole body was trembling, and she was making awful coughing sounds in her throat. Her arms round my neck were almost choking me, and I could feel her hot tears against my cheek. I let her cry.

After a while I said gently, 'I'm sorry, so sorry, I wasn't here when you came. I was waiting for you at the crossroads.'

'W-w-were you?' Her words were uneven. 'Th-thank you. I-I thought you'd left.'

'Now why would I do that?' I tried to sound soothing. 'I wouldn't go without telling you. And anyway, I live here!'

She was too far gone to respond to my feeble attempt at humour. I should have realized. But the calm words themselves seemed to be having an effect; she was breathing more slowly and she'd stopped crying.

I stroked her hair, and it was as smooth as a young animal's coat. I laid my cheek on the top of her head, smelling the sweet scent of her. Gradually she relaxed. It was time to ask what I had to ask her.

'Mardy, what happened?'

She gave a great sigh, and it seemed wrong that such a defeated sound should come from one so young.

'I shouldn't have come,' she said. 'I should have left well alone, and gone on living with my dreams.'

'Ah.' Poor Mardy, poor love. 'Do you want to talk about it?'

She hesitated. Then she untangled herself from me and stood up, moving round the table and sitting down on a chair opposite to me. She sat as if collecting herself; as I watched the softness and trust in her face resolve into resignation, it seemed that in those few moments she put childhood and innocence behind.

'Today I saw a lady called Mrs Renwick,' she began distantly. 'Mrs Armstead gave me her name – she said she'd helped Mother, and that if I was interested in the same sort of help, I should go and see her. I had no idea what she was talking about, but I thought I'd go anyway, as this Mrs Renwick had been a friend of Mother's.'

She paused, looking down at her hands clasped tightly on the table-top.

'Mrs Renwick was a bit odd, at first. She asked me who had given me her name, and I told her. She was still reluctant to let me in, so I said I was Georgina Fearon's daughter, and that I'd come to Cambridge to find out about her. Then she did a funny thing – she apologized! She said, 'My dear, I do beg your pardon.' Then she said of course I must go in, and we went inside and she made a pot of tea.'

She looked up, but not at me. Her eyes were unfocused, as if she were staring inside at her memories of the day.

'She started talking about Mother. She said she'd had no hesitation in helping her the second time, because it had all gone so smoothly on the first occasion. Then she said she was so sorry, so very sorry, but these things did happen sometimes, and that she suspected Georgina hadn't taken good enough care of herself. She said, 'Mrs Campbell would have given her detailed instructions, you know. She always does. But of course she can't be held responsible if people choose not to follow them.' I must have looked a bit blank – I still hadn't a clue what she was talking about – because she came over and held my hand, and said we mustn't forget this was my mother we were speaking of, must we? So I explained about never having known her, about having been given away, and imagining how sad she must have been. And then – and then Mrs Renwick put her hand up to her mouth and said, 'Oh, my God. What have I done?''

She stopped again, for longer this time as if it were becoming increasingly hard to gather her courage and go on. But eventually she managed it.

'She didn't want to tell me,' she went on, her voice tight, 'she said she had no right. But I begged her, and she must have realized that by now she'd gone too far, that it would hardly be any worse for me to know the whole truth. She can't have realized how stupid and naive I was – I don't think she appreciated that I still hadn't the least inkling.' She gave a bitter laugh. 'I was so stupid! It's obvious, isn't it? I felt such a fool when she told me. All that rot about being loved, about it being a dreadful wrench for Georgina to part with me. Well, it can't have been all that bad, because it didn't stop her getting pregnant again, twice more, only those later babies didn't even get the chance to see the light of day. She had them aborted.'

There was silence in my kitchen apart from Mardy's fast breathing. She had poured out her angry words with hardly a pause, her voice rising higher until it was almost a wail.

I sat staring at her. It didn't matter, she was no more aware of me than of the cobwebs in the corners. Her face was hard, and she didn't look like Mardy. Fleetingly, she looked like Georgina.

Then, very slowly, the mask began to crack. Her lower lip started almost imperceptibly to tremble, and after a moment she could no longer control the downward curve of her mouth. She seemed to be holding her breath. But it was no good – grief was overcoming her faster than she could run away from it. Mourning for her mother, her dreams and her innocence, her face collapsed into anguish. In the last moment before she dropped her head on to her folded arms, Mardy came back to herself.

It was a long night. I knew I ought to return her to her room at the Green Man, but I couldn't abandon her. I thought vaguely that she could tell them in the morning she'd stayed the night in Cambridge. What the hell, it wasn't important. What mattered was that she stayed with me, that she had the small comfort of being with someone who loved her. Even though she didn't know it.

There wasn't much I could do. What can you do, for someone who had just had to say goodbye to the myth that had sustained her all her life? There was no comfort. There rarely is, in the brutal truth. We sat together in my calm old living-room, side by side on the sofa. She leaned against me, and after a while put her head down on a cushion on my lap. I think she went to sleep.

I stayed awake throughout the night.

I couldn't even hate Georgina. She'd never asked for Mardy's love; in fact she'd done the best thing, given her nature, by keeping right out of Mardy's life. She'd probably have hated it had she known that somewhere she had a daughter who entertained such fond and inaccurate thoughts about her. She'd have taken it as an insult.

Why, then, arrange for Mardy to be sent the birth certificate and the photograph? Had it been the gesture of a woman knowing she was dying and wanting somehow to be remembered? No one else would have grieved for her, for she took no husband and left no other children. Was she, I wondered, quite alone when she died? I preferred to think that one of her lovers came back to hold her hand. But perhaps by then I'd caught some of Mardy's romanticism.

In the morning she quietly slipped out of the house and went back to the Green Man. I couldn't, wouldn't believe that she would leave without saying goodbye, and she didn't. This time I had no need to haunt my front garden for fear of missing her; she came striding up the lane with her battered suitcase and turned without hesitation into my drive.

She walked up to me, putting the case down beside her. I leaned back against the warm brick wall of the house; suddenly my legs felt weak. I wanted to look at her, fix the sight of her into my head, because I knew it was the last time.

'You know I have to go, don't you?'

I nodded. 'Yes.'

'It's a dead end, this enticing trail that led me here. I've got to go back to real life, and make myself forget this dream. Haven't I?'

I wished she hadn't appealed to me like that. I wasn't sure that I could agree with her, when my whole body ached because she was leaving.

'Yes, Mardy.'

Her eyes were very bright.

'John, if I manage to forget everything else, I won't forget you. I wanted to die, yesterday. You brought me back.'

Swiftly she took a step towards me and kissed my cheek, her lips as soft as a falling petal. Then she picked up her case and ran, through the gate and away up to the crossroads. I didn't try to follow. I didn't even wait to watch her board the bus. Some things are unbearable.

I went back into the house and sat down at my table. There was her chair, where she used to sit, and all around the lonely room was the promise of a gaiety that only she could have brought.

I had no idea how I was going to cope with living without her.

May is almost here again. Lucky and unlucky month. The summer is beginning, and as always it's an optimistic time. It's five years since Mardy went, five Mays I've waited hopefully to see if she'll come back.

I planted roses, the year before last. I was sick of potatoes and cabbages, and I thought it was time we had something pretty out there again. Fragrant, too – the roses come into their own just as the last of the apple-blossom fades away. They're thriving, especially Peace. They remind me of Mardy, those ones, in that peace is what I wish for her.

I have turned my energies to writing. There are few enough jobs hereabouts, and none at all for a man with a stiff leg. I live comfortably; the house is mine, and as well as leaving me that my parents left also a fair amount of capital. It provides a small income, augmented by my Army pension. Extra, of course, for disabilities.

I write not so much to put bread in my mouth as to keep my thoughts occupied. Although, naturally, I'm gratified to have concrete, monetary proof that someone else besides me finds my articles and stories entertaining. But I find I need to have something to think about. A humorous story to tell, an informative piece about Italian wines, anything will do.

Sometimes I work in the orchard, at a little table that is light to carry, sitting under the trees that Mardy loved. I shall do so today. The blossom is glorious this year, better than I've ever seen it.

I'm glad.

For five years I've waited, and five times I've been disappointed. This year, I'm waiting with a greater optimism. The blossom, I think, is a good omen.

This January, just into the new year, I received a card. Quite plain, and unsigned. It said simply: 'I hope the blossom will be good this year.'

May, I'm quite sure, will be Mardy's month.

Across the Border

DENIS SEXTON

'WHAT TIME is it now?'

Pauline's mouth immediately tightened. Too late. The words had shot out of their own accord. She stared fixedly through the windscreen as if mesmerized by the line that glistened whitely down the centre of the wet road. Without looking at him she sensed Liam's reaction to her question; a slight crouch over the steering-wheel, chin pushing forward another fraction.

Outside, the gloom of the evening was cut by a flash of lightning. Pauline could feel the back of her neck press hard against the head rest. She heard Liam's breath escape in a whistle of admiration.

'One thing about Northern Ireland,' he said cheerfully, 'their weather isn't any better than ours.'

'What's the time?'

'Nearly four. We should be home before six. We've saved over an hour by cutting through the North,' said he, pleased with himself.

A hazard of the profession, she thought; sooner or later all teachers develop a tone of smug certainty. One thing for sure, the next time they drove home from Letterkenny she wouldn't be persuaded so easily to take a short cut through the North. Going round by Sligo might be longer and the road surface might not be as good but at least she'd know where she was. She looked back at the carry-cot stretched along the seat.

'How is he?' asked Liam.

'Fine.'

'Good to see that someone is enjoying the drive. He's hardly moved since we left Letterkenny.'

Pauline ignored the teasing. She noticed the tiny beads of perspiration on Ronan's upper lip and loosened the blanket.

'Could you turn down the heater,' she asked, 'it's getting muggy.' She wiped away the perspiration with a tissue. The chubby face crinkled momentarily and the pink mouth sucked at a non-existent teat. 'Wonder why he always sleeps best in the car?' she mumbled half to herself.

'Must be the bottles of Scotch at his feet.'

'Oh Liam, that was a daft idea.'

'Why?' he replied with mock innocence. 'At least he'll be able to keep a straight face when we get to the customs.'

He grinned to himself as he rehearsed in his mind the imminent question-and-answer session with the customs officer. He was sorry now he hadn't bought another bottle. Ronan wouldn't object to having a litre of Teachers under his pillow for a few miles until they crossed over the Border.

Pauline tucked in the quilt and then turned to gaze ahead. Despite the thickening blobs of rain on the glass there was still enough light outside for her to distinguish the main features of the Tyrone landscape. The countryside was much like that around Navan, rich and rolling with regular stands of mature trees. Good farming land, she surmised, and well used. Yet it all looked strange, as if it was another country, as if she was a foreigner. I'm the one who's daft, she thought. Sure, Navan is only down the road.

'Are we far from the Border?' She tried to keep her voice casual.

'About ten miles, I'd say. Ballygawley Cross should be next on the map.'

'God, I'll be glad when we cross into the Republic.'

Liam chuckled. 'Relax, Pauline. I promised you there'd be no problems. Let's see now. After Ballygawley we should be heading into Aughnacloy. Then...'

His voice carried on, listing the names of the towns and villages en route, those they'd passed through, those that lay ahead. When it came to maps his memory was photographic. It was only natural that Geography should be one of his subjects. Place names. Places Pauline had no memory of ever seeing but the names sprang out at her: Ballygawley, Kilgreen, Omagh, Newtownstewart, Sion Mills, Strabane, Lifford, Letterkenny. Unfamiliar places, but the names resonated in Pauline's mind. So many other names; names she had seen on clear, well-positioned sign-posts... Pomeroy, Enniskillen, Cookstown, Benburb. They came easily to her: Portadown, Scotstown, Clogher, Dungannon. She mouthed them silently, the list of names. She had heard them so often, on the radio, the television, in the newspapers. They echoed in her mind like a litany; a litany of horror; bombings, shootings, killings, murder, slaughter. All those familiar place names.

'Do you want it on or don't you?' Liam's question startled her.

'What?' she said, coming out of the spell.

'The radio, it's four o'clock.' His voice had an edge to it.

'Oh yes, yes.'

'You didn't fall asleep, did you?' he teased.

'You must be joking.'

Smug bastard, she thought, you never lose a chance to send me up. Before she could think of something sarcastic to say he had turned up the radio. The continuity announcer was introducing the news headlines in Irish. Pauline reached over and pushed a long-wave button.

'BBC, what's that for?' Again the mock innocent tone.

'You know bloody well I can't follow the news in Irish.'

Of course he knew, knew that her fluency in Irish was almost nil. Why should it be otherwise? She had hardly spoken a word of the language since leaving school. Not that she had anything against it, but well... She said no more about it; it was Liam's second subject to teach. The voice of the BBC newsreader was crisp and detached.

'In Dungannon this morning a part-time member of the UDR was shot by two men armed with revolvers.'

Dungannon! The word made Pauline shiver. The newsreader continued, voice as impersonal as ever, though dropping a half-tone in recognition of the atrocity. The same story, thought Pauline. The gunmen escape in a stolen car which is later found abandoned and a man lies in hospital in a critical condition, bullet wounds in his head. Meanwhile there is a possibility that the politicians may consider having talks about talks, about talks... She switched off the radio, cutting the newsreader in mid-sentence.

'What's the matter?' Liam took his eyes off the road to look at her.

'These bloody roads,' she muttered.

'What?' he asked, confused. 'I think they're marvellous; a pleasure to drive on.'

'They're so quiet,' Pauline murmured; 'you'd know you were in the North.'

'No potholes, you mean. Take it easy, Pauline. When you see the Gaelic on the signposts and hear the loose chips flying off the windscreen then you'll know you're over the Border.'

Liam smiled to himself. One of these days he was going to write that letter to the Meath County Council about the condition of the roads. It was hard enough trying to keep a home and run a car on a teacher's salary, without having to negotiate a hundred bottomless pits on every mile of road. The smile became grim. He was going to have the council's guts for garters, one day soon.

Pauline looked back at Ronan. 'I hope he doesn't wake up before we get home,' she said.

'Haven't you a feed made up?'

'How am I supposed to heat the bottle?' she retorted.

'If he gets thirsty he can help himself to some of the whiskey in the carry-cot. That'll warm him.'

'Daft,' was all Pauline trusted herself to say. When they did get to the customs post she was going to let Liam do the talking. It might serve him right if the Customs Officer saw through his line of bullshit.

'By the way,' Liam remarked casually, 'remind me to fill up the petrol tank at Aughnacloy.'

'Do you have to?'

'I'd be mad not to. It's a pound a gallon cheaper than in the South.'

Pauline was unimpressed. 'Haven't we lost enough time?'

'What time?' he countered.

'You spent long enough in the off-licence.'

Liam laughed. 'Did you not see me nip into the chemist next door?'

'The chemist?' said Pauline.

The grin on Liam's face widened into a smirk. 'Supplies,' he said, 'supplies,' and as he spoke he sounded the car horn.

'Supplies?... Oh.' In spite of her irritation she laughed. 'Well done, Liam, you're not the worst.'

'I thought we'd better wean Ronan off the Scotch first before going into production again.'

'No, he's not the worst, she thought. Not many other husbands would have remembered. Even now she could feel the flush coming to her face as she recalled the scene. Old Hogan looking at her stonily as she stuttered her way to asking for a packet of Durex. 'No, Mrs Walsh, we do not stock those items in this shop,' had been Hogan's reply, spoken in the disembodied voice of a man in deep shock.

Pauline squirmed at the memory. The stupidity of it. Why hadn't she waited a few more days? She had gone to Dublin that weekend and every chemist's shop she'd gone into had been awash with condoms.

'About an hour and a half.' His voice broke in on her thoughts.

'What?'

'We'll soon be home.'

'Well, don't get any ideas,' she snapped.

Men! It had been all hours by the time they got to bed last night. Even then the post-wedding hooley was still in full flight. Her brother's wedding had turned out to be a great success. But it had been a long day. Maybe that was why she was so jumpy.

The rain outside was sheeting against the car. Liam put the wipers to full speed. A car approached them, headlights on full. The driver dimmed as it came near and the car sloshed by.

'Orange bastard,' said Liam.

'What do you mean?'

'He took his time about dimming the lights.'

Pauline stared ahead. Why waste her breath... There was little to see. The dark rain deepened the November gloom. Liam whistled quietly to himself as he concentrated on his driving. She admired him for that; his driving. His conversation wasn't always the kind that she liked to share but when he was behind the wheel she felt safer.

Ronan whimpered. She looked around. He was sleeping peacefully, his breathing inaudible over the rhythmical whirring of the wipers and the swish of wet tyres. She hoped he wouldn't waken. 'Where are we now?'

'Coming into Aughnacloy.' She repeated the name soundlessly. 'Last chance for petrol, booze and true blue videos.'

Aughnacloy, Aughnacloy? It had been on the news recently. Was it an ambush, gun battle or just a lone killing? She couldn't remember.

'Like to stop for a cheap pint?' said Liam.

'Piss off, would you.' He glanced at her in surprise. What had he said now? How was it women had no sense of humour? 'Liam, stop, stop the car!'

'What?'

'Jesus, Liam, what is it?'

Liam squinted through the clouded windscreen. 'I think it's probably...'

'For God's sake stop, slow down... stop the bloody car!' She wanted to grab the steering-wheel but she was frozen in her seat.

'Relax, Pauline, it's a checkpoint, an army checkpoint, nothing for you to worry about... just relax, okay, relax.' His words calmed her; she released her breath. Coolly he moved down through the gears and approached the barrier at a steady twenty miles per hour. A soldier stood on the centre line of the road, his arm upraised. Halt! In the crook of the other arm he nestled a submachine-gun. As Liam cruised up to the barrier he noticed other soldiers. Without turning his head he could see them along either side of the road. Some crouched along the ditch, others lay full-length in the wet grass. Their battle fatigues and dirtied faces merged with the undergrowth but Liam detected the slight head movements as he slowly cruised by them. I hope the rain freezes the balls off them, he thought as he brought the car to a halt.

'What do they want?' Pauline could feel her heart thumping. There seemed to be no air inside the car.

'Routine patrol,' said Liam. 'They'll check us out and wave us through.'

'Are you sure?'

'Pauline, they're not here to arrest us for having an extra bottle or two of Scotch. Just relax.'

She sat back in the passenger seat. Liam was right, of course. They had nothing to worry about. She rolled down the window a little to clear the mist on the glass. Pulled into the lay-by she could make out the shape of a large van or portable building of some kind. A door opened in the van and a soldier came out. For an instant the light from the interior spilled over him. He stood there in a cocoon of golden light. Pauline saw that he carried a mug in his hand. The door snapped shut.

'God, I'd love a hot drink,' she blurted.

'Yeah... do you want me to order you a hot whiskey?' His voice was heavy with sarcasm.

Twenty yards ahead of them was another car with three men in it. Some troops stood close by and watched as the driver spoke to the soldier at the window. Another soldier shone a torch on some papers. He shielded them from the drizzle as best he could. Pauline looked at the soldiers all around her, on the road, in the ditch, on the verge. They were like statues, impervious to the rain. Only the movement of a head indicated that they were alive.

'They look so miserable,' she said.

'Who?'

She ignored the truculence expressed in the one word. 'The soldiers, most of them are just kids.'

'Yeah, look at the artillery your kids are carrying.'

She made no reply. Liam's attitude to British troops in Northern Ireland was something he did not disguise. The last thing she wanted was an argument. She'd keep her mouth shut until they were over the Border. It couldn't be more than a few miles away.

She looked at her baby. He was still sleeping. Please God they'll get moving soon before he wakes up. She pulled the quilt closer to his sleeping face.

'What the hell is keeping them?' Liam's fingers drummed on the steering-wheel. 'Are we supposed to sit here and freeze?'

Pauline looked out again. The men in the car in front were still being questioned. Nobody made an attempt to approach their own car. What was delaying them, she wondered. Jeez! This is a right place to be stuck on a wet November evening.

She noticed that two soldiers in particular were keeping a steady eye on them. Again she was struck by how young they were. Teenagers. Maybe that's why they put dirt on their faces, she thought, to convince people that they were full-grown men, or to convince themselves. One of the two chewed gum methodically. Like a cow in a field, thought Pauline, looking at the morose figure standing there in the drizzle, large innocent eyes staring at them out of a blackened face. The soldier shifted the position of his submachine-gun. Pauline saw the water gleam on the short, squat barrel.

'Those guns terrify me.' Again the words were out before she could stop them.

Liam latched on to the slip. 'Half a chance and they'll show you what their tommy-guns are for.' Her lips tightened. But Liam was now on his way. 'Arrogant bastards. Wait until you hear the fake politeness.'

Pauline tried to keep her voice even. 'I wish you wouldn't take the whole thing so personally, Liam.'

'Huh!' The scorn was unmistakable.

'Every time we see a British Army uniform I can feel you getting tense,' she accused.

'Christ Almighty!' he exploded, 'You're one to talk. Every two minutes you want to know how far we are from the Border. You can't wait to be over it. You never even wanted to set foot in Northern Ireland!' He snorted at the incredulity of her criticism.

Pauline looked away. The gum-chewing soldier chewed on with the same slow rhythm. His gaze never left their car.

'It's the guns that frighten me, not the uniform,' said Pauline. 'I wouldn't know a British soldier from an Irish one.'

Liam toyed with her remark for a few seconds before squashing it. 'Let me tell you girl, there's one hell of a difference,' said he with finality.

Pauline said nothing. In his carry-cot Ronan stirred grumpily. His lips smacked together as he shifted his head on the pillow. Gently Pauline wiped the saliva that dribbled from the half-open mouth. The sucking stopped; his breathing was quiet and even.

'Liam, please don't argue with them,' she said as she put the tissue into her handbag. He didn't seem to hear her. She went on: 'Have identification ready and answer their questions and there'll be no hassle. Please.'

'Look again would you, and see if the driving licence is in the glove compartment,' he asked. She snapped her handbag shut and dropped it on the floor. She was glad to oblige him, glad to see that his anger was gone.

'Why are they taking so long with the car in front?' she enquired as she rummaged in the glove compartment. How did it get into such a mess?

'After the shooting this morning, I suppose,' said Liam in his deliberate teacher-offering-the-solution manner.

'Yes, that must be it, the shooting,' agreed Pauline. The UDR man shot on his doorstep.

'Dungannon's not too far from here.' He went on to speculate on the number of miles and on the direction in which Dungannon lay.

She didn't listen. Dungannon. The word echoed in her head. The sound seemed to draw her in, as if it wanted to reveal to her the atrocity that lay behind the name. She resisted. She didn't want to imagine a human being with part of his face blown off. She refused to picture it in her head. She attacked the glove compartment.

Oh shit,' she hissed. 'I can't find the bloody licence.'

Liam shrugged. 'Not to worry,' he said, 'my credit card will do. In fact, a Visa card is quite appropriate.' He chuckled to himself.

At the sound of a car engine spluttering into life Pauline lifted her head. The car in front was moving off. The driver smiled and waved to the soldiers.

'Good little Prods,' said Liam, noticing the smile.

Pauline saw the soldier who had been asking the questions turn towards them. His companion noted the number plate. They spoke to one another. She grabbed at the contents of the glove compartment and dumped them in her lap. The licence must be in here someplace, she thought.

'Relax, Pauline, relax.' Liam spoke soothingly, as though he were calming a hot-headed pupil. 'Just relax.'

'I'm sorry we didn't bring our passports,' she said.

'Passports!' His mouth was open in disbelief.

'We should have brought them,' she said firmly.

'Jeez, are you gone soft in the head?' His eyes blazed with a mixture of shock and scorn.

'There's no need to raise your voice. You'll wake the baby.'

He ignored her diversionary tactic and spelled it out for her.

'We're less than sixty miles from home, on our own island, in our own country and you want us to carry passports. Maybe we should swear an oath of allegiance while we're at it.' The fists clenching the steering-wheel had turned white at the knuckles.

'I just don't want any hassle, that's all,' she pleaded quietly.

'Sure,' he said, 'no hassle.'

She flicked through the service manuals angrily. What possessed her to mention passports? A half-wit could have predicted his reaction. When was she going to learn?

She was shoving the service manuals back into the glove compartment when a shadow at the car window made her look up. Almost immediately came a sharp rapping on the glass at Liam's side. What was he up to now, she thought, why hadn't he rolled down the window?

'UDR man,' said Liam calmly.

'What?'

'The badge; UDR.'

'Liam, no trouble please, roll down the window.'

'Sure,' he replied agreeably, and just as the hand outside was raised to rap again he rolled down the glass.

'Good afternoon, sir.' Liam was right. The soldier's accent had a sharp Northern Ireland lilt. Everything else about him seemed rough and unfinished, uniform, face and his heavy moustache.

'Afternoon,' said Liam.

'Did you not hear me tapping on the glass?'

'Yes,' replied Liam.

'Or maybe you didn't notice me standing here?' The soldier's impatience was barely controlled.

Pauline glared into the glove compartment. Why did she have to mention those bloody passports? If she'd kept her big mouth shut Liam wouldn't now be acting so thick.

'As a matter of fact, Sergeant,' said Liam sweetly, 'my wife, my child and myself are almost frozen stiff from sitting here for the past fifteen minutes.'

'Doesn't the car have a heater?'

'It does,' said Liam, 'but it's not functioning at the moment.'

Liar! thought Pauline. Then she relaxed. Maybe now that he's had his little victory he'll co-operate. He's won the point.

The sergeant paused, as if to get his voice under full control. He then proceeded with the standard questions. Who were they? Where were they coming from? What was their destination? What was the purpose of the trip? Pauline leaned across Liam and embarked on a full account of Shane's wedding and why it took place in Letterkenny and... The sergeant thanked her curtly. 'We're just passing through,' she added.

'That's right, Sergeant, just passing through,' said Liam pointedly.

The repetition was for her benefit; to let her know that her apologetic tone had been noted, marked and would require a further explanation.

'Could I see your driver's licence, sir?'

Liam had his answer prepared. 'I can't find it at the moment. Here's my Visa card.' He took it from his wallet and handed it to the sergeant. 'My signature's on the back,' he said, pointing, 'William Walsh.'

The sergeant studied the card dispassionately. The pause seemed to last an age. Liam whistled cheerfully under his breath. Pauline saw that other soldiers had moved into position around the car. They were watching, but when she looked at their faces their eyes slid away.

'Have you any further means of identification, sir?'

Liam opened his wallet again and produced his teachers' union card. As the sergeant inspected it Liam added, 'I'm a teacher,' in case the bedraggled soldier failed to make the connection. Pauline bent to take a tissue from her handbag. Half-hidden by the bag she saw the maroon cover.

'Something with your address on it, sir, would be helpful.' The delivery was casual, like a poker player careful not to tip his hand.

'I think I've got it,' shouted Pauline.

She opened the cover to check. It was Liam's all right. She reached across Liam to hand it to the sergeant. Liam fingered his wallet; a grin came to his face. Dourly the sergeant inspected the document. Pauline wondered what took him so long. Surely there was no need to read the fine print; the name and address was what mattered.

'It's two years out of date,' said the sergeant gruffly.

'Is it?' said Liam, eyebrows raised in surprise.

'Is this your signature, Mr Walsh?'

'Yes,' Liam replied firmly.

Again the sergeant paused before speaking. 'It doesn't correspond with that on your credit card, sir.' He was the poker player spreading his hand. Pauline wondered was it a note of triumph or could it just be the Northern accent She could feel her heart beginning to pound. Liam gawked at the driving licence. Then he laughed.

'I signed it in Irish, Sergeant. Liam Breathnach.' He underlined the two words with his finger as if to clarify matters for a rather stupid pupil.

Pauline searched the weather-beaten face for a reaction, a face that seemed to fill the window, its dourness emphasized by the moustache that drooped unevenly past both corners of his mouth. She decided it was time for her to explain.

'Liam teaches Irish, Irish and Geography. Years ago he used to sign his name in Irish. Now he signs in English. Isn't that right, Liam?'

Liam had resumed his under-the-breath whistling. He nodded in agreement. The sergeant looked Pauline in the eye. She saw the raindrops glisten on the bushy eyebrows.

'I'm sorry madam, but I can't read Gaelic. At school I could never master foreign languages.' He continued before Liam could make a reply. 'Perhaps you could pull your car over to the side there, sir.'

'What's the problem? We've told you who we are,' retorted Liam. The poker player collected his winnings.

'Your two identities don't seem to correspond, sir. Now if you'll start up the motor and pull over beside the truck.' He moved away.

Liam swore savagely. Such a stupid waste of time! Pauline grabbed at her handbag. She wanted to tell the soldier she had more identification, letters, bankcard, children's allowance book, as much as he wanted, but his back was to them. Then he turned and waved them into the lay-by. She clung to her handbag hopefully. Liam turned the key in the ignition; the engine stalled. He pressed the accelerator hard. The motor attempted to splutter into life but the mixture was too rich. Liam cursed through his teeth as he turned the key again.

'Go easy, Liam,' Pauline said softly.

'It's not my shagging fault, is it?'

This time the engine fired; he revved it loudly to clear the carburettor. The blue smoke of the exhaust was immediately swallowed up in the drizzle. Liam released the hand brake and the car lurched into movement. The soldiers alongside kept pace as they moved towards where the sergeant stood waiting. One of the escort then peeled off and trotted towards the large van which was now closer.

'Lousy bastard,' said Liam, his indignation growing. He clenched the steering-wheel with both hands as he glared at the arrogant figure of the sergeant who dared Liam to run him down. Liam spat noisily.

The soldier reached the van door and knocked urgently. Pauline saw him being admitted into the pool of light. They're lucky to have someplace to get out of the rain, she thought, someplace to get a hot drink.

At that moment Ronan began to cry. First a whimper, but as Pauline turned towards him, it became a full-throated wail.

'Oh blast! That's all we need.'

'Stop shouting, Liam,' hissed Pauline, 'he might settle.' But Ronan had found his voice and was crying with purpose. The wailing filled every corner of the cramped interior.

'That bloody Brit!' said Liam, spitting the words out. 'Just because I had my name in Irish.' He drove up to the sergeant's upraised hand and braked violently. The rasp of the handbrake brought a howl from Ronan.

Pauline turned her body as best she could in order to get closer to the carry-cot. She loosened the coverings and wiped away the dribbles and the tears from Ronan's face. His plump cheeks glowed brightly, the rest of his face was contorted with the effort of crying. It would be impossible to get him back to sleep, she thought. On top of everything he was probably hungry. She spoke his name soothingly in an effort to stifle the shuddering wails that permeated the enclosed space.

The sergeant spoke briskly. 'That's fine, sir.' He came to the window. 'Would you mind opening the boot, please.' Liam took the key from the ignition and offered it through the window. 'I'd prefer if you'd open it, sir,' was the sergeant's reply.

'I haven't got a raincoat,' protested Liam.

'You'll have to open it, sir.'

Pauline was about to lift Ronan from the cot when she sensed the deadlock. 'Liam, I can't get the baby to settle; hurry up and open the boot.' He contemplated her request; his left eyelid twitched involuntarily. 'Please, Liam, please.'

There was silence while Ronan gathered his breath. Pauline's pleading eyes tried to catch Liam's but he was staring out the windscreen. Ronan started to cry again. This time it was a full-bodied roar. As Pauline swivelled to calm him Liam pulled abruptly at the door handle. He got out, slammed the door after him and marched round to the boot. The sergeant stood beside him as he flung the boot lid open. He invited the sergeant to inspect the contents.

The two men were hidden from Pauline's view by the upraised lid. Their muffled voices came through to her but she concentrated on getting the baby out of the carry-cot and on to her lap without aggravating him further. She managed the manoeuvre and cuddled his rigid body close to her, all the time talking softly to him. She saw from the way he sucked his lips that he was hungry. Holding him with one arm she fished around at the bottom of the cot with her free hand. There was a clinking of glass and then she located his feeding-bottle. She recognized its shape by feel, same as she did at night when she left off the bedside light so as not to disturb Liam.

The howling eased into a persistent moan. As she drew the bottle from under the cot blankets Pauline knew that there was only a slim hope of satisfying him with a cold bottle. It was worth a try.

Holding the bottle to his mouth she talked to him in a mixture of encouragement and desperation. He responded eagerly to the teat. If even he takes a few mouthfuls, she hoped, it might calm him down until we get moving again.

As she pressed the bottle firmly into her baby's mouth she was aware of the voices from behind the car. An argument was clearly developing. She looked down at Ronan and launched into her usual routine of baby-talk, rhymes, jingles and high-flown praise. But the voices of the two men would not be shut out. Blunt questions, truculent answers. What was in the cases? More questions. Where had they stopped? What was in that bag, the other bag and that bag under the case, the Stewart's Pharmacy bag? She could near her husband's voice raised in anger and embarrassment as he showed the packets of condoms to the sergeant.

For God's sake, thought Pauline, won't they ever get sense? Standing out there in the rain squabbling like children. She looked in the driving mirror but the boot lid blocked her view. To her side the light from the van caught her eye as the door opened. A soldier stepped out into the rain; he pushed a fresh wad of chewing-gum into his mouth as he walked towards them. Pauline swallowed; her own throat was dry.

Suddenly Ronan wriggled in the crook of her arm. With legs kicking, body twisting and face frowning he dislodged the bottle from his mouth. He paused, took a breath and roared with all the might of his five-month-old lungs. Pauline felt an urge to ram the bottle down his throat. As she hesitated the unseen voices from behind the car came to her in snarls of mutual hostility. She looked down at the struggling child in her lap. She shook her head. What am I blaming you for, you poor little mite, she said aloud, all you want is a feed you can enjoy, but those two! Ronan stopped crying. His red-rimmed eyes looked up at her expectantly. It seemed as if his mouth was about to shape into a smile when the slamming of the boot lid made the car shudder. The tentative smile turned into a scream of terror.

'That's it,' said Pauline.

She turned and bundled the child back into the carry-cot. With the feeding bottle in her hand she ran towards the van, leaving the car door flung open behind her. Her rubber sneakers slithered on the grass but she checked her fall with her free arm. The first shout to reach her ears was from the sergeant; a clear-cut order to halt. She slowed. As she wavered, she heard her husband's voice. It ordered her to get back to the car. The command made up her mind. She rushed across the last stretch of tarmacadam to the van and pounded on the door with the heel of the bottle. It opened almost immediately. A soldier with a rifle in his hand looked down at her. Surprise showed on his face. His part-time training had not prepared him for the sight in front of him; a young woman, gasping for breath, was holding a baby's bottle towards him.

'What do you want?' he shouted, swinging the barrel of the gun towards her.

'Some hot water.' Pauline's breath came in a rush. The young soldier peered at her. Was she crazy? 'Some hot water, to warm the baby's bottle, please.'

Her voice was under control. The soldier gazed down at her from the step. He lowered the rifle; it was just a harmless lunatic arriving out of the darkness.

'Listen, ma'am,' he said slowly, 'this is an army checkpoint. We do not...'

'What is it, Mac?' a woman's voice from within interrupted his patient explanations. Before he could reply the woman came to the door. Despite her sober uniform she looked younger than Pauline.

'This lady,' said Mac, 'wants hot water.' He waited for the girl-soldier's laughter.

'Well bring her in then,' replied the girl. 'Mac,' she said as he hesitated, 'we can spare some hot water.' She turned to Pauline. The Northern accent was brisk but friendly. 'Come in out of the rain,' she said, 'come on in,' and reaching down her hand she helped Pauline to clamber on to the step. The door clanged shut behind them. Pauline stood and gathered her breath. It was warm and dry inside the van. The girl smiled at her. 'C'mon this way,' she said, 'I think it's very possible we might have some hot water on the premises.' Pauline grinned back and followed the girl-soldier towards the electric kettle.

Minutes later Pauline returned to the car. She thanked the soldier for the loan of the cape and sat into her seat. Liam handed her the whimpering child. As soon as Ronan was sucking on the warm feed Liam started up the engine. A soldier beckoned the car on to the road. The Border was three miles away.

Pauline spoke first. 'Sorry for the delay, luckily the kettle was on the boil.'

'I thought we were in a hurry,' said Liam quietly.

'We won't have to stop now. This feed should do him until we get home,' she assured him. Ronan was sucking contentedly.

'I meant in a hurry to get over the Border,' pursued Liam. She wiped the dribbling milk from Ronan's chin.

'I hope you didn't get soaked standing out in the rain.' She could smell the dampness from his clothes.

'Nope,' he said, 'I didn't get wet.'

They drove in silence. There was no other traffic on the road. Pauline knew she had to say something. Otherwise the cold silence might last until they reached Navan.

'They offered me a mug of tea.' They were the first words that came to her mind.

'What?'

'While we were waiting for the bottle to heat up.'

'You didn't drink it, did you?' He spoke with low politeness.

'Of course I drank it.' She savoured the lingering taste of the hot, sweet tea. 'I was dying for a hot drink.'

'You stupid bitch!' His eyes never left the road as he shot the words at her. 'Stupid treacherous bitch!'

'What do you mean?' said Pauline. His sudden ferocity was more frightening than the rifle pointed at her earlier.

'That Orange bastard enjoyed humiliating me. He had me out in the rain just to make a fool of me, to degrade me; then you march off and have tea with them. I hope you had a lovely tea-party!' A cyclist appeared on the road in front of them and Liam blasted him with the car horn.

Pauline clenched her lips. She looked at the feeding child in her arms. I might as well talk to the baby, she thought. If I told him that the soldiers were looking for killers, that the man gunned down this morning had died leaving a widow and two children, if I told Ronan all that and more he'd probably understand better than my husband.

The lights of the car lit up a signpost; the Border was a mile away. The Border, she thought, a line on a map doesn't make much difference... not when it comes to hatred and bigotry.

They drove south without talking. Liam switched on the radio. As soon as he heard the BBC voice, he pressed another button. The music was country-style, a waltz tune. Pauline was glad of it; anything was better than cold silence. She felt tears coming to her eyes. Oh no, she thought, as she held them back. She wasn't going to let him see her cry, not him, that figure hunched over the wheel, his jaw jutting over it, his mind replaying, reinventing the battle with the Orange sergeant. No tears. She would not give him that satisfaction.

Ronan wriggled in her arms; his legs stiffened. She lifted him to her shoulder and rubbed his back with her open palm. When it came, the burp was like a rifle shot, loud and sudden. For an instant the sound of it filled the car.

Why shouldn't she? Why shouldn't she cry? Not because of the slushy ballad, or for her marriage to a thick husband or for the man gunned down in Dungannon. But for Ronan. Would he grow up to be like them, chasing small victories, cursing trivial defeats? Was there anything she could do, anything that would save her son? She'd bloody-well cry if she wanted to.

Through her tears Pauline looked at him. He was again noisily sucking on the feeding-bottle, unaware of her desperation and her defiance.

A Whore's Vengeance

LOUISE DOUGHTY

'There is a promise made in any bed.
Spoke or silent, a promise is surely made.'
—*The Crucible*, Arthur Miller

MY MOTHER and father used to fight and he would end up beating her. Then he would sob his heart out as she lay on the floor. 'Why do you make me do it?' he would cry at her. Then, looking up at the ceiling, he would give a great shout, '*Why?*'

They died in 1680, when I was five. The Indians came in the night. Later, I used to tell the other kids I had seen the braves smash their heads against the farmhouse wall. It wasn't true. I was nowhere near at the time. I only made it up to scare them. My mother had been due to give birth again and was ill with it so I had been sent to stay with my aunt and uncle in Salem, until her time came. When I first heard the phrase 'big with child', I thought it meant that grown-ups looked tall when they stood next to children. I used to think all adults were big with child.

I hated living with my aunt and uncle. They had to keep me, of course, after my parents were killed. They stuck a mop in my hands the minute I was big enough to hold it. They treated me like a skivvy. Wash this, scrub that, clean over there and don't speak 'til you're spoken to – oh, and while you're at it, take that sullen look off your face. Sullen? I was furious. How dare my parents dump me here? For every sweeping movement of that brush, I imagined I was prodding a pin into my aunt's face or my uncle's pious arse. He was a reverend, my uncle. *The* reverend, to be precise. Reverend Paris of Salem, and I, his niece, valued about as much as his black slave, Tituba. They made me sick.

As soon as I grew old enough, I was farmed out, to be a slave in other people's houses and earn my keep. That was how I ended up there, at the Proctors'. They had a small farm, some way out of Salem. I begged my uncle to send me to a family who lived in town. I couldn't stand the thought of being stuck out there with some fat old wife and husband and screaming, red-faced farmhouse brats. I sulked from the moment they told me I was going till the moment I arrived. My uncle drove me over in the cart. He said he was doing it to curb my wild nature. Ha. As I climbed down, clutching my small bag, Goody Proctor came forward to meet me. She smiled, the way those good women can when they know they are being nicer to you than you probably deserve. 'Welcome to our home, Abigail', she said, magnanimously. I smiled back with my mouth. My uncle came inside with us but didn't stay. More important things to do. He kissed the top of my head, bidding me farewell, but I said nothing. I wasn't going to let him off the hook. Goody Proctor walked back outside with him and I heard their voices murmuring. He was telling her to beat me, no doubt, if I gave her any trouble. When she came back in, she looked a little nervous, as if I was a stray she had been landed with unexpectedly. This one's a pushover, I thought.

She took me upstairs to my room, the usual poky little cupboard, clean and unforgiving, designed to make you look forward to leaping out of bed in the mornings and scrubbing the floors before sunrise. 'I'll leave you alone for a while. Come down when you're ready,' she said. After the door shut behind her, I burst into tears. To be stuck here, out here, miles from anywhere, until my hands were raw with housework and my face cracked by peering into dusty corners. I couldn't stand it. Damn my uncle, damn my aunt, damn the Proctors, damn them all. I'd run away. I'd run away to Boston. After I had finished, I straightened my apron and my bonnet and went downstairs. I knew as soon as I looked at Goody Proctor that she had heard me crying. She came forward and put her hands on my shoulders, giving me a look of such agonizing pity it made me want to stick something up her nose. 'It must be very difficult for you, a young girl like you,' she said. I decided to play on her sympathies and sniffed. 'Leaving your family. You must miss them very much.' Miss my uncle? It was the only good thing about being sent out to this hole. I nodded. 'Well I'm sure you'll do fine here,' she continued. 'I'll not lie to you, the work is hard, but we have a fair farm, my husband and I. The land is good'. She took her hands from my shoulders and wandered over to the window, gazing out across the fields. 'It is a good land,' she repeated, 'good, and beautiful, a great gift.' That's all I need, I thought, some half-wit sentimental rubbish about how great this mother earth is. It's farming that does it, and the loneliness. Turns their wits. The men are just as bad. She showed me round the building and the outhouses and then we went inside and started on a small supper. 'It'll be just the two of us tonight,' she said, stirring a pot with some brown muck in it. 'My husband has taken our boys out round the farm. They'll not be back till late.'

Perhaps it was just hindsight. I don't know. But I'll swear I had some sort of premonition when she said it. My *husband*. She spoke of him delicately, as if she was discussing a mole on her face or some ailment it wasn't quite polite to mention. They don't get on these two, I thought. They don't get on at all.

Later she bundled me upstairs, muttering something about how tired I must be. Not too tired, all the same, to be given a list of duties to be started in the morning. There was a basin and a jug of water by my bed, cold of course. I couldn't bear to wash. At least at my uncle's we had Tituba to heat some water for us. The blankets were coarse and the straw in the mattress packed so tight it might as well have been a slab of stone. I lay awake for a long time. After a while, there was the sound of doors opening and shutting downstairs and the murmur of voices.

In the morning, I splashed my face and dressed myself quickly. The room was so cold. It had just grown light. I went and looked out of the small square window. Goody Proctor was standing in the yard, filling a bucket at the pump. I saw her look towards the house and speak to someone I couldn't see. Then she came forward and disappeared from view. I went to my bedroom door and opened it a crack. From downstairs, I could hear voices.

'I am sorry, John, but we need wood.'

'I have a day's farming ahead of me, Elizabeth.'

'I didn't notice how low we were until after dark.'

A door slammed.

I went back to the window and looked out into the yard. From the house emerged John Proctor, striding, axe in hand. He marched over to a log pile by the fence and took a large log from it. He stood it on one end and then lifted the axe, high, high up above his head. For a moment, he was poised there, his arms uplifted and his face taut. His shirt had ridden up above his belt and a flat, brown stomach was revealed. His legs were wide apart, his feet planted solidly on the solid brown earth. The axe glinted, and fell.

There was a light tap at my door. I turned quickly and began smoothing the blanket on my bed.

'Good morning, Abigail. Did you sleep well?'

'Yes, very well, Goody Proctor.'

Downstairs, we laid the table together and I was introduced to the boys, one thin and sensitive looking and the other, the younger, tearing round from wall to wall and jumping and talking about farming. Goody Proctor smiled indulgently. 'Matthew takes after his father.' She laid out five bowls on the table. 'We all eat together as a family here, Abigail.' Well that's something, I thought. She told me to sit down while she ladled porridge into the bowls. I was starving. It was all I could do not to seize my spoon and wolf it down there and then. I noticed she put very little in her own bowl, even less than in the children's. She saw me watching her and smiled nervously. 'I do not eat well in the mornings.' Then she went to the door and called her husband.

John Proctor was not as tall as I had expected. He came in standing straight, his shoulders square. Brownish hair curled against his forehead and thick eyebrows hung over a lowering gaze. He was wearing a tough cotton shirt and dark breeches. He was glaring. Sweat from his exertions stood out on his forehead despite the morning chill. He had the axe in one hand, holding it half way down the shaft, and a bundle of wood cuttings cradled in the other arm. His hands were rough and heavy. Our eyes met.

'Thank you, John.' His wife came forward and took the axe from his hand and hung it up on the wall behind him. He walked over to a large wicker basket to the left of the fire and let the wood cuttings drop into it. Then he came and took his seat at the table. Goody Proctor chivvied the boys to sit down before sitting herself and saying a short grace. We all muttered amen, and began to eat. For a minute or so, the only sounds were the spoons scraping against the wooden bowls.

The first thing John ever said to me was, 'Well now, Abigail, do you miss the great goings-on in the town?'

I looked down at my bowl, then back up at him. 'Well, Mr Proctor, I don't know really.'

'Abigail is bound to be a little homesick to begin with,' said Goody Proctor.

'Well then,' replied her husband, 'we must do all we can to make sure she feels at home.'

We were lovers within a month.

I wasn't the first housemaid to be dismissed by Goody Proctor. They had had quite a turnover, that household. Rumour in the town said she was a slave-driver and dismissed so many because none satisfied her in their work. I remember Mercy Lewis telling me about Sarah Hall, the clerk's daughter, who got sent back after two weeks. A month later, she left Salem altogether to go and live with an aunt in Andover, for her health, her family said.

My uncle beat me senseless for getting the sack. I'll never forget it, as long as I live. Afterwards, I lay face down on my bed sobbing, digging my nails into the pillow. All the same, every one of them, all the same. Always. From my room, I had overheard John confess his wickedness. I knew what was coming. Goody Proctor's feet pounded up the stairs. She dragged me down by my hair and pushed me out of the door. She was strong, for such a virtuous woman. She flung my things out after me calling, 'Harlot! Whore!' All the usual stuff. I landed on my knees in the yard, grazing my hands. My bonnet was hanging from my neck and my hair was loose. John was standing in the doorway watching, completely helpless. His cheeks were damp with tears. Just like my father. Exactly like my father. These men. What good would it have done if I had begged for her forgiveness? None. Somebody has to be the bad one. Besides which, I wasn't sorry and I wasn't going to pretend I was. She pushed him back inside and slammed the door. I picked myself up, and my things, and brushed the dirt off my apron. Then I began the walk back to Salem, five miles in the dark. I knew what would happen when I got back. I knew I would be beaten. All the same, trudging along the road, all I could think about was John. John. I couldn't believe that he had confessed to her out of shame and guilt. I couldn't believe that he was just like all the others, my uncle, my father. He couldn't be. Not my John. He had held my face when we made love, in the shed, on the ground. He held my face so tightly, gazing at me with eyes that burnt holes in mine, looking, looking. As if he would die if he didn't look. Elizabeth and he hadn't made love since their youngest was born and he said even before that, when they did, she would never look at him. She would look at the ceiling, at the walls, never at him. He bruised me sometimes. I couldn't believe he had gone back to her, not after all the things he'd said and done to me. It must be part of a plan, I thought, as I trudged along. He must have told her deliberately, so that he can be with me. He's worked it all out somehow. He'll come after me on his horse. After a while I had to stop. She had thrown me out in my slippers. My boots were still in their kitchen corner. I kept stumbling in the dark and catching my toes. It was freezing cold but I was completely numb. I sat down and rubbed my feet and listened for the sound of horse's hoofs tumbling along the dirt track. It was impossible that he would not come after me. Quite impossible. There was a strong wind blowing. I strained my ears to listen. So many sounds. It's amazing how many noises can sound like the far-off clatter of hoofs. I knew he would come after me. He had to come. It was all part of his plan. We would go to Boston. Nobody would be able to find us there. We would have our own house and make love in a bed and fall asleep and wake up together. Putting my slippers back on, I began to cry, but I didn't stop believing he would come after me. I didn't stop believing it until I was on my uncle's doorstep, banging on the door to wake up Tituba. It was a stupid thing to do, in retrospect. I should have hidden in the barn or in the church 'til daybreak and then tidied myself up first. I had lost my senses by then. I was dirty and tired and freezing cold. The grazes on my hands and knees were stinging and my feet were bleeding. My head ached where she had pulled my hair. I wanted to be bathed by Tituba and put to bed, the way she would when I was little, scrubbing my back until it tingled and glowed, humming a Negro song.

It wasn't her who answered the door. It was my uncle, in his nightshirt, peering out into the darkness and calling fearfully, 'Who's there?'

'It's me, uncle,' my voice was quite steady. I had stopped crying and

was steeling myself for what was about to come. I stepped into the light.
'Abigail.'

'Abigail?'

Well of course the whole house had to be raised to hear of my
wickedness. I didn't tell him why she'd thrown me out but I had to tell
him I'd been dismissed. He only would have found out later and then I
would have been beaten for lying as well. He must have known it was
something bad, to be hurled out in the middle of the night. He started
raging about how he had brought me up, put clothes on my back,
educated me, and so on and so on. I stood in front of him, swaying from
exhaustion, while my aunt clucked around like a hen and Tituba stood
shaking in the corner. I think she half expected to be beaten as well. She
often was when my uncle was in one of his tempers. Get on with it I
thought, looking up at him while he shouted and quoted scriptures about
ingratitude. We all know what you're going to do. Get on with it.

Later, Tituba came to me in my room with a mug of hot milk,
mumbling soothing noises. I was in pain and could only be cross with her
for not getting to the door before my uncle did, not that it would have
made much difference in the end. Whilst she dabbed at my back with a
damp cloth, she told me about what had been going on while I had been
away. Apparently, there was some move to oust my uncle from his
position. There had even been a meeting when he had been called to
explain some irregularities in the parish accounts. She had listened outside
the door and heard a lot of shouting. Good, I thought, not really
considering that if my uncle was replaced we would all have to leave this
house. Things were bad all round, she said. One of the farmers was
bringing another suit against a neighbour in the county court and there
was talk that if he succeeded he would be bringing them against others,
including my uncle. 'These bad times, Miss Abigail,' she said, curling her
bottom lip and rocking back and forth, 'bad times, bad times.'

Funny how right she turned out to be, stupid old Tituba. Everyone in
that town hated each other. They had done for years. Everyone thought
they were being persecuted. They all had axes to grind. They were just
waiting, waiting, waiting for it all to explode. My uncle once said in
church, 'Remember, when you point a finger at someone...' (raising a
hand, making the gesture) 'there are always three of your own fingers
pointing back at you.' It was one of the few intelligent things I ever heard
him say. Shame no one listened really.

I didn't start, it you know, all that witchcraft stuff. They started it, my
uncle and the others. I just joined in at the appropriate moment. Even
then I only did it because they were pointing their fingers at me. It didn't
occur to me to get my own back on John until well after it had all begun.
'A whore's vengeance,' he said in court – which is one way of looking at it
I suppose.

We had to run away when things got out of hand. I took Mercy Lewis with me. She had been as much involved as me and, anyway, I needed her help to get to Boston. I wasn't sure we would make it. They probably set up blockades on the roads behind us but we had a day's advantage over them and managed to slip through. I knew we would be all right once we made it to the city. Anyone can disappear in Boston. Especially a whore. I didn't have any illusions about how we would have to earn a living. We had to go somewhere where there would be no questions asked. It was either that or thieving, and I preferred to earn an honest living.

At first, we were turned away. We were filthy. Skinny, seventeen and desperate. We hadn't eaten for over two days. Mercy was coming out in red blotches all over her face and I had a sore growing on my neck. Then, at the fourth place we tried, just as we were moving on, the madam called us back.

'Come here a minute,' she said, 'you.' She was looking at me. Mercy was near collapse, clinging to my arm. I tried to make her stand up straight. The madam took my chin in her hands. A wave of violet scent hit me and I nearly fell over. I had never smelt it before. She looked at me closely. I couldn't tell whether she was being hostile or just curious.

'You...' she said. 'Two girls. I've heard about two girls on the run from up-country, all that hullabaloo up there.' Mercy panicked. 'It isn't us, it isn't us,' she babbled, and began to cry. The madam dropped my chin and sighed theatrically, 'Oh for God's sake get her in here, off the street.' I pushed Mercy forward and followed.

Madam led us through into the kitchen where she made a sullen-looking girl in petticoats serve us soup from a huge dark stove. Back in Salem, they were still cooking soup over fires. I stared at the stove while we ate. A real stove. The girl in petticoats flounced out, pulling a face. I suppose we smell, I thought. 'Don't mind Mary,' Madam said, 'she's always a bit uppity when it's her turn to cook.' I stared at her. She laughed. 'Oh yes, missie, you cook as well in here. We take it in turns. We have a woman in for the evening meal but we all muck in together for the rest of it. Fairs's fair.' Mercy had fallen asleep with her head on the table. Madam came and sat next to me on the bench and covered my hand with hers. 'Now look here, missie, whatever you want to call yourself. You're all right underneath that mud, you'll clean up OK and I can tell you know what goes on and you'll be good. But I'm not sure about your friend here.' I looked at Mercy and then back up at her. She had very round blue eyes and huge powdered cheeks. She reminded me of a poppet doll I sewed once back in Salem. I gave it dimples with a cross-stitch either side of its mouth. 'Abigail,' I said, 'my name's Abigail. And you take me and Mercy or neither of us.' A broad grin spread across her face. 'I knew it. I knew it.' She gave out a laugh and slapped her thigh. 'I knew it was you I'd heard about. I could tell by your eyes. You showed that Salem lot, my girl, by God you showed them. Pious fools. You showed them.' I couldn't help smiling as well. She made it seem like an enormous joke. For the first time, it all seemed like one enormous, breathtaking joke. 'OK, you're in.'

'And Mercy?' Madam looked at her, then back at me, sighing, 'Well, well, Mercy too, then. See she pulls her weight, mind. And if you go, she goes with you.' Then she went over to a cupboard and pulled out a pewter jug and two large mugs. 'Cider!' she declared with relish. 'Cider to celebrate! I hope you don't mind only cider but I never drink anything too strong at this hour.' Only the men were allowed to drink in Salem. We clunked our mugs together and drained them. Madam turned and went to the door and shouted out, 'Mary, go and see if that back room at the top is fit.'

She told me later that she turned back to see that my head was on the table next to Mercy's.

That was three years since. I've stayed with Madam. I could have moved on, even set up a place of my own, but I like it here. It wasn't easy at first. I hadn't really thought about what it would be like, lying back for some grunting animal, knowing he would pray for forgiveness on Sunday, turning and smiling at his wife and worshipping her for her ignorance. My first customer turned out to be called John. That helped in a way. As he lay there, panting and groaning like a stuck pig, all I could think was, my God, if only you could see how stupid you look. If only you could see. 'Oh my darling,' I whispered in his ear, 'Oh my love.' Madam gets good reports of me from the regulars. 'It's the way you lie to them, Abby,' she said to me the other day, 'nobody lies to them like you. It's those eyes, the way you look at them.' It was John that taught me that. He was the first man who ever touched me. He taught me how to look and look and see – how to lie with glances and finger-tips.

I'm Madam's favourite now. She's grooming me to take over the business when she gets too old, although that won't be for years yet. It caused some jealousy when I first got here but everything is fine now. At dawn, we all get together in the parlour to swap stories and relax. The customers are thrown out into a Massachusetts sunrise, massaging their eyes and consciences. Madam locks the door and breaks open a bottle. We have a bit of a party. I like entertaining the others with my stories of the bad old days. They're always asking me. 'Then of course there was that day in the courtroom, when John finally decides to discredit me as a witness by telling the judge him and me had done the business. I deny it, of course, so the judge summons his wife to give evidence. She doesn't know that John has come clean already and says her covenanted husband is as pure as a new born baby. I am vindicated and he is branded a liar as well as a devil-worshipper.' Madam loves that bit of my story. She slaps her thigh and roars with laughter, that deep rich belly laugh she has. 'The best thing about Christians,' she says, spluttering cider, 'is you can always rely on them to pretend they're better than the rest of us. Leaves them wide open. Never fails.' Before I came, apparently, some of the good townspeople tried to close Madam down. She went to see a few judges with whom she was very well acquainted and begged for their assistance in continuing a service to wayward men with less self-control than their good selves. She promised to make a donation to the church and put a Bible in each room. We stayed open.

'Tell us about how your uncle used to watch you in the bath,' says Ann. 'Well, when I was little...' I begin. They've all heard it before but they listen eagerly, waiting for the punchline. When it comes they throw themselves backwards and scream with mirth. Even Mary and Elizabeth smile, lying on the sofa, wrapped in one another's arms. Mercy crouches next to me, rubbing her latest bruise. She always gets them. I never do. It's odd really. I don't know why she should attract those types but she does. For the first six months or so, she kept having nightmares. She used to cry out in her sleep. Once she even said we should go back. We would only be whipped she said. 'Don't be stupid, Mercy,' I told her, 'people died because of what we said. They'd hang us soon as see us.' She knew I was right. Virtuous people have long memories. Most of the girls here are on the run from something. Occasionally we get visits from a constable but no one tells him anything. We all stick together here. If he gets too nosy, Madam gets on to one of his superiors. Apparently, I have achieved some degree of infamy. Rumours of my whereabouts are rife.

After a couple of hours of chat, it's someone's turn to go out and buy fresh bread and cheeses, or make soup. We eat until we're stuffed, then slope off to sleep until early evening. Only Madam stays up. She must catch a few hours somewhere but she never seems to rest. She's never tired either. She is always there, beaming through her powder. Not that she's soft. Last month, she threw out a girl called Beth who made herself ugly and stupid with drink. She'd get rid of Mercy if it wasn't for me. If I ever do get my own place, I'll take Mercy off the game and let her do all the cooking and cleaning. You need a full-time housekeeper in a place like this. I don't know how Madam does it sometimes, running somewhere this size on her own. I couldn't do it. She can't delegate, that's her problem. She'll have a job handing over to me when the time comes. I ought to get my own house really, but it's difficult when you start up. You have to build up the customers' trust. You have to nurture them. It would be much easier to take over Madam's clients.

I think about it upstairs, lying awake in the room I share with Mercy. It always takes me a while to get off. White beams slip through the wooden slats of the shutters, into the darkened space around me. Traders are shouting in the street outside. Mercy whimpers in her sleep. Downstairs, Madam will be sitting at the table going through the books.

What I'd really like is the biggest place in the country, open twenty-four hours a day, with the girls working in shifts. Mind you it would mean employing a lot of other people apart from the girls, to keep it running. I might have to employ some men. My mind is churning it over as I grow drowsy. Keep it small to start off with. Several small houses. I don't dream of Salem, well, not like Mercy anyway. I dream of John sometimes, out in the yard, when I first saw him. He is standing there, the axe raised up in his two fists, his face taut and haunted. A bolt of sunlight hits him as the axe falls down and down and down and I, underneath, watch it hurtling slowly towards me. I wept no tears when they hanged him. He could have saved himself. If he had confessed, it would have bought him enough time. They released the people still in prison after I ran away. By then they had realized the whole thing was a dreadful mistake. Still they never prosecuted the other accusers. Everybody had accused everybody else by then and it would have meant prosecuting the whole town. When they looked around for someone to blame, I was handy. They conveniently forgot it wasn't me who started it. Ah, well. Enough of that. It brought down a few learned men, reverends and judges. John would move back and forth inside me, so slowly, looking at me, gazing, holding my face so steady. My eyes would stare back, wide open. Boston is growing every day. New immigrants flood in. 'Look at me,' he would say, moving back and forth and holding my face, 'look at me.' There's no shortage of customers, and the new silks are coming in from Europe. His eyes promised such volumes. Vengeance means nothing next to survival, but it's helpful when the two coincide.

Small Beginnings

FAITH ADDIS

DAVID WANDERED along the pavement looking for feathers. His mother had told him to play in the garden until tea but she didn't know about the hole in the fence. Anyway he'd only be gone for a little while. The man in the next-door-but one house kept chickens in his front garden and sometimes you could find a feather or two lodged in his privet hedge.

'What's up, Sunshine? Lost a tanner?' It was the chicken man.

'No. I want to be a Red Indian but I haven't got any feathers.'

'Oh dear, that's not very good is it? Got any war-paint?'

David said firmly: 'I don't want any war-paint, thank you. I'm going to use peace-paint.' It was 1942 and although David had been born before the war he couldn't remember that time at all. His world, like that of many London children, was narrow. His mother defined 'Is Your Journey Really Necessary?' to mean no further than the local Co-op, so apart from a twice-yearly duty visit to some ancient aunt, David's life was strictly confined to house, garden and school.

Peace-paint indeed. Poor little devil, said the chicken man to himself, and to David: 'Help yourself to feathers, mate.' He opened a wire-mesh gate and David slipped into the chicken run. Six fat hens, mildly disturbed, stood up and shook themselves. David laughed at them and inhaled the lovely smell of their enclosure – sun-baked dung and dust, mingled with poultry-feed spices. He said 'Excuse me' to a hen sitting in one of the nest boxes and grasped her tail. With a squawk of outrage one very cross hen took off in a flurry of sawdust.

'Oh, I'm sorry.' David looked helplessly at the bunch of feathers in his hand. 'I only wanted one.' The chicken man shook with laughter and said next time David must collect feathers from the ground not from someone who was still using them. 'You'd better run along now, son, or there'll be fireworks from your mum. Does she know you're out on your own without your gas-mask?'

'What's a firework?' asked David.

'Sodding, sodding Hitler,' said the chicken man, from which David guessed that a firework was something like a banana or chocolate, something you couldn't have because of sodding Hitler. Of the war itself he knew that the Allies were good and the Jerries bad. Daddy was somewhere in Europe. Messerschmitts sounded exactly like wasps but Spitfires sounded kind, like bees, so obviously they were on our side. Spitfires had Merlin engines and the Brylcreem boys said wizard when they meant nice. Uncle Mac, Stuart Hibberd and Mr Churchill were the most important men in the world.

'Where have you been? I've been calling you for ages. And what's that awful smell? Honestly David, you look like a gypsy. I don't know what people must think.' His mother attacked the grime on his hands and face with a damp flannel. David screwed up his eyes tightly and pretended he was a lion cub being rasped clean by the mother lion's tongue...

'... moving in next door tomorrow so I want you to be extra nice to her little girl.' With an effort David brought himself back from the jungle, half glad half sorry that his mother's furry paws had become her familiar pink capable hands. 'Poor woman,' his mother continued. 'Bad enough to have her husband a POW but this business with the grandmother going off has left her homeless so she's rented next door for the duration.'

David thought the business with the grandmother going off sounded interesting. Had the old lady exploded? He filed the promising picture away to be brought out and savoured later. Meanwhile he concentrated on his tea, spam, potatoes and greens. He hated greens but finished them nonetheless because the starving children in Europe were mysteriously made happier by people who ate up nicely.

The next morning Big Chief Reindeer was hard at work in the garden composing a rain spell when a small girl appeared in front of him. David stared. Although he had implicit faith in the powers of magic he couldn't think where he had gone wrong. 'I asked for rain,' he said accusingly, 'and you're um, you're a person.'

'Your mother sent me,' said the person and David remembered that his mother had said he must be extra nice to someone's little girl because her grandmother had exploded. He said politely and not without a degree of morbid curiosity: 'Did you see your granny go off?'

'No,' said the newcomer. 'Mummy says it's disgusting at her age. She's fifty-six and her boyfriend's sixty.'

'Disgusting,' agreed David. 'I expect all the gizzards and things fell out. Come and help me with my rain spell. I'm Reindeer so you'll have to choose another name and you can have a feather to wear.'

'Reindeer's a very good name for making rain,' said the girl. 'I'll be Big Chief Spaniel.' She took the proffered feather and stuck it in her hair. 'Shall we make thunder and lightning while we're at it?'

Common sense told David that while a summer shower was one thing, a full-blown storm was quite another. 'We'd get into trouble,' he said with a certainty based on experience.

'Then we'd have to get married.'

'Married? Why?'

'People who get into trouble have to get married. Didn't you know?'

'Gosh,' said David, impressed at his companion's depth of knowledge. Then he had an idea. 'If we got married,' he said hesitantly, 'if we got married *before* we make our thunder and lightning, would it keep us out of trouble?'

'I don't know. We could try. What's your name?'

'David.'

'I'm Liz – Elizabeth, same as the princess but Liz for short.'

David said: 'Have I got to give you a ring?' and his fiancée, sensing his inexperience, decided to forgo the ring. 'You can build me a house instead,' she said.

'Then what?'

'Then we exchange vowels.'

'What's a vowel?'

'I don't know,' Liz admitted. 'I'll go and ask.' She ran indoors where the two mothers were getting acquainted over a cup of tea and reappeared a few minutes later clutching a scrap of paper. 'It's five letters out of the alphabet,' she reported. They studied the document closely. 'It's nice and short,' said David.

Their marriage ceremony was equally nice and short. Each in turn chanted 'a-e-i-o-u' followed by 'I give thee my vowels' (the 'thee' being insisted upon by David who liked archaic words in his rituals) followed by a formal handshake which they both felt was appropriate to the occasion.

'Are you six yet?' asked Liz. 'I'm six and two months.'

'Six and a week,' said David, 'but I'm taller than you.'

'And very handsome. Do you think I'm pretty?'

David examined her face. 'No,' he said and added kindly: 'But people change. I like your yellow dungarees. Mummy won't let me wear things that show the dirt.'

'Shall we let our children wear what they like?'

'*Children*?' Fleetingly David had second thoughts about his marriage.

'Why, would you rather have puppies?'

'Yes, I would. But we'll have children too if you like.' David was acutely aware of the age gap between them and was determined not to be thought too young for his responsibilities. 'How many would you like?'

'Ten, please. You can choose their names.'

David thought for a moment. 'Jack,' he said, 'we'll call them Jack.'

'What, all of them?'

'All of them,' said David firmly. 'It'll save having to remember ten different names. When their lunch is ready we can shout Jack and they'll all come in...'

'. . . and eat condensed milk out of the tin with their fingers,' added Liz with relish.

And so the ten Jacks were born, androgynous and of indeterminate ages. Housing for such a large family could have proved difficult but David, inspired by his new status, found the answer. 'They can live in a raspberry house. I've often made one for myself – it's easy. We'll make a really big one.'

Their mothers called them in for lunch. Before going indoors they swore an oath of secrecy, a hybrid oath, part Arthurian, part Enid Blyton.

'Seems a dear little boy from what I could see of him through the window,' said Liz's mother. 'Were you playing Lexicon with those letters?'

'Mm,' said Liz through a mouthful of sausage.

'That's nice. I think I'll put our garden down to vegetables and fruit, same as theirs. You must have David back here to play next time – fair's fair.'

'He's dark,' said Liz.

'Touch of the tarbrush somewhere back probably. I always think curls are wasted on a boy.'

David was jubilant when Liz told him they now had the run of both gardens. 'Smashing,' he grinned. 'Oh Liz, I am glad to have you next door.' Liz felt a wriggle of pleasure at this, short-lived when it turned out that it was her garden tap that was the attraction. 'We can canoe up the Nile to the Canadian Lakes,' he said gleefully – his own house did not possess an outside tap – 'Shoot the rapids with savage crocodiles coming out of the swamps–'

'What about our house?' Liz reminded him.

'I haven't forgotten. We'll make a house today and tomorrow we'll canoe up the Nile. OK? Now we need some big stones or bricks.'

They collected some stones and laid them in a row parallel to the row of raspberry bushes which David's mother had planted the previous year. By bending the tip of each raspberry cane down to the ground and anchoring it with a stone they soon had a snug tunnel literally dripping with ripe fruit. For the rest of her life Liz never forgot the enchantment of their first home; the smell of earth, the dappled sunlight, and best of all the roof, so cleverly designed to provide both food and shelter. Lost for words she picked a fistful of raspberries and crammed them into her mouth. The purple juice ran down her chin. 'A bearded lady.' David giggled and soon they were both helpless with laughter as they painted each other's faces with squashed raspberries.

All too soon they discovered that marriage was not after all an insurance policy against calamity. But it certainly helped – a trouble shared, etc. Lying in bed that night, still smarting from the smacking he had received, David relived the glorious afternoon. Having a wife and children next door was a lot more fun than being single. He drifted off to sleep, well pleased with the change in his fortunes.

For the rest of the summer David and Liz managed to stay more or less out of trouble. There were a few setbacks – like the night they forgot to turn off Niagara Falls, an oversight which transformed Liz's mother's brassica bed into a paddy field – but on the whole they climbed Everest and swam the Channel and scored centuries at Lords without too much adult hindrance. But when winter drove them indoors to play it was a different story. The mothers found out about the ten Jacks and forbade any more of 'that nonsense'. With nerves already stretched to breaking point by air-raids, rationing and absent soldier husbands, they simply could not cope with a houseful of invisible children, each of whom had by now acquired a puppy of its own, not to mention mannerisms and catch-phrases.

Liz and David dug their heels in; they refused to get rid of their precious Jacks. 'Want them to be refugees, do you?' David stormed at his mother. 'Living on Red Cross parcels?'

'But David, they're not *real*,' his mother pleaded. 'It's just a silly game and it's time you grew out of it.'

'If they're not real why do you keep tripping over them?' said David. His mother looked at him uneasily. To her, being 'different' was practically a capital offence. She decided to seek professional guidance.

The doctor at the clinic listened patiently to her outpourings: 'Ten of them, Doctor... there's never an empty chair to sit on... these blasted puppies now... it's not healthy, is it?'

'That depends,' said the doctor, who privately thought it sounded extremely healthy for a lonely child to create for himself a large cheerful band of companions. 'I'll see David on his own now.'

If he was surprised to learn that his young patient was a married man with ten children and ten puppies to support, the doctor was careful not to show it. 'The puppies were a mistake,' David admitted at the conclusion of his story. 'They bark a lot.'

'Good God,' said the doctor with a momentary pang of sympathy for David's mother. 'Look David, it seems to me that it's high time some of your elder children started to earn their own livings.' He consulted his notes. 'Big Jack for instance. Isn't he old enough to go in the navy?'

'Big Jack is going to be a circus acrobat. It's Jack Tar who wants to go in the navy. I did tell you.'

'Sorry. But surely acrobats are small and thin? How about sending Smallest Jack to circus school to learn how to be an acrobat?'

David said witheringly: 'You didn't listen. Smallest Jack is a cripple. We have to carry him everywhere.'

'No problem,' said the doctor. 'Bring him to the clinic and we'll make him better.'

'He's here now,' said David. 'He's sitting on your foot.'

Liz liked the idea of sending the Jacks out to work. 'We can give them going-away parties,' she said. 'Dress them up and play Pass the Parcel and things.'

'But we'd miss them,' David objected.

'They'll write to us and they'll come home on leave sometimes.'

The mothers proved surprisingly cooperative with the going-away parties. Preciously hoarded tins of pineapple chunks appeared, sacrificial offerings to speed things up. David and Liz rationed the parties to one a fortnight. Their mothers thought the time would never pass. Eventually Smallest Jack (now miraculously cured) was waved off, his puppy at his heels, to start his circus training.

'Goodbye, Smallest Jack. Please write to your old mother.' Liz sobbed happily and melodramatically.

'Don't cry, Liz.' David put his arms round her. 'He'll come back one day. Listen, do you like cobras and pythons? I've had a good idea what we can do tomorrow...'

When the war ended the children's fathers returned, not the hoped for conquering heroes but khaki strangers, ill at ease in their own homes and unprepared for domestic life. Liz's family moved house, only a bike-ride away but it meant the children saw less of each other. David's mother was relieved. 'That Liz was a bad influence,' she said, and tried to describe the difficulties of bringing up a boy who lived in a world of books and fantasy. Her husband, who had spent five years trying to avoid getting killed, was less than sympathetic. He was bitterly disappointed in David who, he predicted glumly, would turn into a pansy if Something Wasn't Done. Fortunately for David the hardships of the austerity years left his father little time or energy to do whatever it was that prevented people turning into pansies. Apart from being exhorted almost daily to get his hair cut David was able to make the transition from boy to youth – teenagers had not yet been invented – without undue influence from his jaundiced parent.

Secondary school came next, boys' grammar for David, girls' grammar for Liz. Being at separate schools was not the great divide that both sets of parents had hoped for and the youngsters continued to meet, sometimes just the two of them but more often in a crowd. Everyone had bikes, and expeditions were the fashion with tennis whenever they had enough money to get a court and swimming when it was hot enough. *The Goon Show* was required listening.

The Festival of Britain with its Skylon, fireworks, music and crazy buildings proved to be a turning point in Liz's and David's lives. The first time they went they had to stay with their respective school parties – the boys' headmaster being convinced that his pupils would all turn into raging sex-maniacs if they were let loose among girls – but despite this restriction they and most of their friends were poleaxed by the South Bank wonderland. For a generation which had been brought up to regard drabness as the norm (bottle-green and brown indoors, grey public buildings, beige dassrooms) the colours alone were intoxicating. Geranium-red railings, poppy-red seats, blue stairs, cascades of jewel-bright flowers in hanging baskets, this was more like a dream than a school outing.

David started his week's essay on the subject of the Festival: 'A fanfare of trumpets has sounded in my head', which did not please his English master ('I thought you were taken to Battersea not the Albert Hall'). Liz, similarly affected but of a more practical nature, went to the Post Office and drew £3 out of her savings. 'We're going again,' she informed David.

For the second visit they sought out Battersea's infant Mafia. Coppers changed hands and they were shown how to bunk in through some bent railings thus saving several precious shillings. Hours later, money spent, they flopped down on some grass, bewitched and transformed.

'Liz,' said David at last, 'did you ever read Plato's *Republic*?'

'Mm, of course. Why?'

'Well, I think I'm just beginning to understand things. This place – the colours, the architectural anarchy – it makes my mind giddy. I could ravish the universe.'

Liz made a mental note to put herself first in the queue if any ravishing was on the agenda. 'I know,' she said. 'It's as though we've been at the bottom of a murky pond and now we've come up into the real world.'

'That's it. We've had a mystical experience. Do you feel converted?'

'I feel different. Not converted, more sort of privileged. When we were watching that colour film in three dimensions – you remember we had to wear those funny little goggles – I felt privileged that whoever had thought up the idea was prepared to share it with me. The same feeling you get when you read a good book.'

'I felt that about the Skylon. Someone with the vision to break the rules invented that.'

'Smallest Jack would have loved this place, wouldn't he?' said Liz. They often referred to their old 'family' casually and without inhibition. 'He was the one for colour and noise.' They giggled and went home on the bus quoting from Smallest Jack's repertoire of catch-phrases; side-splitting to them but mildly irritating to their fellow passengers who were not accustomed to being greeted: 'Hello, Humans.'

At David's school he was not the only one to have seen the light at the Festival and by the time they entered the Upper Sixth half the class were wearing green corduroy trousers and saving hard for velvet jackets. Their fathers reacted in various ways, from apoplexy to ridicule – pointed references to Oscar Wilde. David's mother, still fighting her own private war against dirt and what the neighbours might say, kept her head down.

She washed David's fuchsia shirt separately from the family laundry and dried it indoors safely out of sight. Meanwhile Liz had locked horns with her parents over the matter of her future. They wanted her to go to secretarial college, she wanted to go to art school. Stalemate.

'We need money of our own,' said David when they met at their favourite coffee house to discuss their problem parents. He handed Liz a pencil and paper and asked her to write down all the ways of earning money she could think of. He would do the same. They sipped their coffee. Liz wrote: Saturday jobs, baby-sitting, bank robbery, football pools, while David stared into space. Eventually he wrote one word on his paper and pushed it across the table.

'Ideas,' she read. 'What on earth does Ideas mean?'

'Well, it's all I can think of that I've got to sell. My call-up will come as soon as I'm eighteen so I can't get a normal job until after my National Service. But they're not calling up my mind – they only want my lovely body – so I'll use the two years to sell ideas.'

'Such as?'

'Such as the one I had at breakfast this morning. Have you noticed how boring cereal packets are?'

'Can't say I have. I read the *News Chronicle* at breakfast.'

'Precisely. You don't notice the cereal packet because *there's nothing interesting on it.*'

'Christ!' Liz was immediately on his wavelength. 'You mean games and puzzles and–'

'Little cut-out figures for kids to collect and swap. What do you think?'

'I think you're a genius. Let's make a prototype game and send it off to one of the cereal manufacturers.'

Next day their first idea, a cut-out puppet theatre, neatly drawn up on white card and with a typed (laboriously with one finger) letter was on its way. They never had so much as an acknowledgement but not long afterwards they were incensed to see their idea adopted and reproduced on the cereal packets. It was a hard lesson to learn. David, vowing he would never be caught out like that again, spent a morning in the library boning up on copyright laws, a useful morning's work. The next time he had an idea to sell he took it in person to the firm of his choice and asked for a receipt. To his astonishment he was given not only a receipt but a cheque for £25.

'Twenty-five pounds?' said Liz, open-mouthed. 'But David, it was only a weeny idea – something to do with perforations wasn't it?'

'Yes, I showed them how they could save acres and acres of cardboard just by redesigning their boxes. They seemed awfully pleased. All I had to do was sign something promising not to tell anyone else about it.'

Fired by the success of their first sale the young entrepreneurs set themselves a firm objective: to earn enough money to buy Liz her independence. After A-levels they had just eight weeks to achieve their goal, September being the month when David would have to go into the army and also the start of the secretarial college term. By mid-August they had amassed £61.1s.0d, the odd guinea coming from a friend of theirs called Michael who had bought the idea of setting up an agency to provide single shoes to disabled ex-servicemen. Michael flatly refused their offer of a free name for his agency. He felt Hoppalong Happily did not convey a caring image at all.

Then came an unexpected stroke of luck. David categorized his ideas into first, second and third class and it was one of his thirds that hit the jackpot. The cheque came by the same post that had brought him two rejections (special mazes for hamsters and garden dog loos were anticipating the market by some twenty years but David was not to know this) and he opened the envelope without optimism. He stared. Two hundred pounds? For what Liz called one of his weeny ones? He stared again and nearly fainted. He had missed a nought off. Stuffing the cheque into his pocket he leapt on his bike, flew round to Liz's house and hammered on the door until Liz's father opened it. 'Bugger off, you young lunatic, filling her head with your rubbish.' David pushed past him calling hoarsely for Liz. She was having a bath but hearing the commotion downstairs got out and peered over the banisters. David took the stairs three at a time, grabbed her wrist and dragged her back into the bathroom. 'David – my parents,' Liz protested.

'Fuck your parents. Look.' He showed her the cheque – 'Two thousand pounds.' They hugged each other and Liz deliberately pulled David fully clothed back into the bath with her. Alternately laughing and crying they were making such a noise they didn't hear Liz's parents. Her father's rage gave him the strength to haul David out of the water, box his ears and march him out of the house. 'I'll get you certified,' he snarled, and slammed the front door. David retrieved his bike and rode to the bank, leaving a spoor of bath water behind him.

They bought a secondhand Pickfords removal lorry with some of the money and a course of HGV driving lessons for Liz. Two of David's friends converted the interior to living and sleeping areas, a galley kitchen and a tiny shower room with a chemical closet. Now they had a mobile home which could be parked anywhere at any time without attracting attention. As long as Liz was careful to park unobtrusively each evening she could live rent- and rate-free for the whole of her time at art school. In September she drove David to Norfolk where he was to begin his army training and then made her way back to London. Parking was easy, relatively little traffic and traffic wardens not yet even a gleam in a bureaucrat's eye. She began a game of spending one night in each district on the Monopoly board starting with Park Lane and Mayfair. Art school was wonderful, everything she had hoped it would be.

David headed his letters 'Somewhere in England'. He didn't much care for army life at first, all that shouting and marching about in rows bored him, but after the initial six weeks' training the new recruits were given more interesting things to do and life became quite tolerable. He made some new friends and had one or two mild flirtations with the local girls.

Liz too had a few flings, medical students from the London Hospital (this was when she got up to Whitechapel on the Monopoly board) whom she found fun but immature compared to David. They called her Mary Pickford and stole a park bench for her with 'LCC' carved in the back rest. She had no use for a park bench but it proved a devil of a job to get rid of. As she wrote to David: 'Every time I try to leave it on the pavement some well-meaning person bangs on the cab door to tell me I've forgotten some furniture. It has become my albatross.' David replied: 'Change the L to an M and *deliver it openly* to Lords. If the groundsmen stop you all you need to say is that it's a present from an anonymous cricket lover.' The ruse worked so smoothly it made Liz wonder why all criminals didn't take to removal lorries since, like milk floats, their appearance never aroused suspicion.

The lorry once saved her from the unwelcome attentions of an admirer. He was a French student called Gerard, an intense lad who shared her table one lunchtime and then pestered her for a date. Liz didn't like to hurt his feelings so she told him in her atrocious French that she had to stay in and wash her hair. What she actually said was 'wash my horse' which Gerard took to be a joke until he followed her home and watched her climb into what looked to him like a horse-box. Mon Dieu! Mama had always said English girls only ever fell in love with their horses...

David came out of the army fit, hard and a dab hand at sticking bayonets into straw victims. There were very few vacancies for trained killers in central London at the time so he and Liz decided a debriefing holiday was called for. They drove across France and camped in the Pyrenees for a month, after which time Liz was pregnant and David's ability to daydream their livelihood restored to normal.

Returning to London they parked in Soho and David sold fabric designs (painted by Liz) to Heals, Habitat and Selfridges. On the proceeds they hitch-hiked to India, returning this time mind-blown by all the new sights and scents. Until they saw Goa they had not known that sea could be so blue or sand so white or people so beautiful. Carnaby Street shops beat a path to their door – or strictly speaking, tailboard – to buy their ideas. Liz would draw or paint impressions of India then they would both think out how best to use the work. Sometimes a simple line like a single flower on a whiter than white background would suggest its own solution, and that one would be earmarked for high-class bone china. Or tendrils of jungle foliage pierced here and there with brilliant flashes of humming-bird colours would make them think it would look great as curtains or wallpaper. They experimented with cane, raffia, leather, wood, clay and silk. Curiously neither of them ever had an interest in plastics. They used Sellotape and polythene bags, finding these new inventions useful and hygienic but for their own creative work they stuck to natural materials. Not all their ideas found favour, even in Carnaby Street and the King's Road. The world was not yet ready for leather shoes in primary colours or reusable containers of any sort. Britain's youth wanted the freedom to throw things away – the Save It generation could Stuff It.

Their home became a bit crowded now that it was doubling as a workshop so just before the baby was due David and Liz bought a tall house in the then still slummy Camden Town. It had a large garden gone wild and plenty of room in the street to park their much-loved lorry.

Liz went into labour and David sat in the hospital waiting room with two other expectant fathers. Five hours passed. Ashtrays overflowed. The other two were called out, leaving David to pace up and down in traditional fashion. There was a health poster on the wall advising people to eat a balanced diet. Little pyramids of meat, fish and eggs sat under the word protein, likewise vegetables under vitamins, bread under carbohydrates and butter under fats. David added a bottle of gin and a packet of cigarettes and labelled them 'Essentials'. More hours dragged by. He gave the Queen a monocle and a pipe, then his patience ran out. Finding his way to the labour ward he opened the door and walked in. There was a gasp from the attendants round Liz's bed and a nurse bustled over. 'Are you the father?' David said he would kill the milkman if he wasn't and could he please see Liz? The nurse hesitated: 'It isn't really allowed, but in the circumstances–'

David's heart thumped. 'What do you mean? What circumstances?'

The nurse made him put on a sterile gown. Then she said, 'Your wife's having twins.'

David was at Liz's side in a flash. 'Twins – oh Liz, how *marvellous*, how efficient. We never thought of more than one at a time, did we? Could you manage a few more while you're at it? Have a litter?'

Liz looked up at him, her face pinched with exhaustion. 'Hi.' She smiled weakly. 'I wish we'd settled for puppies instead.' Then David had to leave because this was going to be a forceps job.

Both sets of parents, who had steadfastly refused to speak to Liz or David ever since they left home to live in the lorry, now wanted to bury the hatchet. The lure of grandchildren was powerful, the babies themselves perfect. At ten days old they were huge, healthy and beautiful. David's mother said tearfully, 'At least you got something right' as she cuddled the boy twin close. (The fact that David earned more in a month than his father did in a year was never mentioned.) Liz's mother, similarly clutching the baby girl, asked, 'What are you going to call them?'

'Felix and Daisy,' said Liz.

'*Felix and Daisy*?' chorused all four grandparents in horror. David's father said, 'Felix is a cat's name.'

'There's an actor called Felix something,' said his wife, hoping to defuse the situation and realizing too late that she had put her foot in it.

'Daisy's quite nice,' said Liz's mother. 'I used to know a Daisy before the war. Housemaid she was, had a hare lip, poor thing.'

'Mum,' Liz groaned.

'I don't care if they have got horrible names,' said David's mother. 'They're Granny's little cherubs and that's all that matters.' Liz and David escaped to the kitchen where they collapsed in giggles while the coffee percolated. 'Oh Christ – Granny's little cherubs.' Liz mopped her eyes. David said, 'Did you see my father's face when Mum said actor?' This set them off again and Liz was still dabbing her face with her hanky when they carried the tray of coffee back to the family. 'Post-natal depression I daresay,' whispered Liz's mother. 'After all, you did have a Bad Time, didn't you?'

The twins thrived but, sadly, although Liz and David were fond of them they didn't enjoy them as they had expected to. As babies they were not very lively and seldom laughed. They didn't throw their food about or scribble on the walls; at a year old they were toilet trained without any effort on Liz's part and by the time they were three they had never quarrelled. It was unnerving. It was also very hurtful to hear them referred to by friends as 'your bourgeois babies'.

But it was true, David and Liz had to admit one evening after they had been ferreting around in the twins' playroom to see if they could find some clues as to the children's remarkably boring personalities. The playroom was painfully tidy. Teddy bears and golliwogs segregated like South Africans sat on one shelf, with miscellaneous soft toys on a shelf below. Down on the farm all the animals had been tightly penned-in according to species. David groaned and released a herd of Friesians into a green felt field. Liz let the pigs out. David, getting carried away, laid a milkmaid tenderly under a tree and placed the farmer on top of her. 'We won't tell,' he whispered. They opened Lego boxes which contained Lego and domino boxes which contained dominoes, ditto Plasticine and marbles. There was a bridal doll still in her gift tissue paper- she was immediately taken out and set to work grooming the rocking horse, while sailor dolls were issued with rum from the plywood shop and left to sleep it off in the streets of Toytown. David and Liz felt a lot better after the revolution. But this was only the start.

'Something will have to be done,' said David. 'Good God, they'll end up working in a bank if they carry on like this.'

So for the next few years they took the twins camping, rock climbing, sailing and swimming. (On their travels they looked up Liz's exploding granny, an old lady now, blissfully painting at Newlyn with her boyfriend.) They showed them the sky at night, sunsets, sunrises, minnows in ponds, elephants at the zoo. But it was as though Felix and Daisy had been blinkered at birth; to them autumn leaves were autumn leaves, not fairy gold or something to run through shouting at the top of your voice.

When David found they had discarded Mozart and the Beatles in favour of Max Bygraves singing 'I'm a Blue Toothbrush' he took them to the Child Guidance clinic. The psychologist there said he did not think Max Bygraves was an aberration. David had one more try, this time with the twins' headmistress.

'Look.' He waved their reports in front of her. They never varied: cooperative, polite, punctual, neat, a credit to the school. Never creative, amusing, original or wayward. The headmistress, who had not quite recovered from a spate of fourth-form arson, suggested coldly that if David wasn't satisfied with her standards he should send his children to Dartington.

In their teens, hope flickered briefly when all the boys in the neighbourhood developed a craze for Ben Sherman shirts in pastel colours. All except Felix. He stayed loyal to the school outfitter's white nylon regulation garment. Daisy half-heartedly bought herself some platform-soled shoes because her friends were wearing them to parties but she managed to lose them on a bus and didn't replace them.

David and Liz tried hard not to show their disappointment. They accepted philosophically that you really can't make a silk purse out of a sow's ear. They worked hard and saved hard, planning to travel round the world once the children were grown up. Meanwhile they took short camping holidays leaving the twins (at their own request) with one or other of the grandparents. The only serious row that ever occurred was when David asked Felix to fetch his and Liz's passports from the desk. Felix handed them to him and asked why they didn't have a joint passport. David said, 'You have to be married to get a joint one.'

Felix went white. 'You mean – you mean you're not married?'

'Not officially. Why? Does it matter?'

'Matter? Of course it matters you, you *artist*,' Felix shouted. 'What does that make *us*, I'd like to know?'

'Bastards,' said David mildly. Daisy sided with her brother and the row raged for two days. David and Liz were quite glad to get away to France for a bit of peace.

Ten years passed. Felix became a vicar and Daisy married a branch manager of Freeman Hardy and Willis. David and Liz rented out their house and took off to hitch-hike round the world.

They were exploring the foothills of the Himalayas when the letter came telling them that Daisy had had a baby boy and was going to call him Charles after Prince Charles. As everything had gone smoothly they saw no reason to cut their Grand Tour short, so they sent congratulations and a lovely bolt of silk and carried on travelling for another three years. Daisy wrote to them regularly *poste restante* of whatever place they were visiting, keeping them up to date in the matter of the baby's weight and her husband's golf handicap.

Eventually it was time to go home. Daisy wrote to say they had rented a holiday cottage in Berkshire (*'Berkshire?'* said David) for two weeks and would be so pleased if David and Liz would come and stay. The letter went on: 'It seems a nice place from the brochure, four bedrooms and all mod cons even though it is rather old. And something I'm sure will interest you – a mulberry tree in the garden that's reputed to be 150 years old!! I expect we shall have to watch out that Charles doesn't get them in his mouth!!'

'Better than sticking them up his arse,' muttered Liz, who didn't like the sound of the mod cons or Charles or the golfing husband.

They landed at Heathrow and took a taxi to the address Daisy had given them. Opening a wicket gate they walked up a brick path towards the cottage which they could see was of lovely mellow old brick like the path. A huge gnarled tree with crusty bark dominated the garden. 'This must be the mulberry tree. What a lovely–' They stopped, blinked and looked again. The genes of Liz's exploding granny mingled in with Liz's and David's own were only too apparent in the little figure before them. He had painted his naked body with mulberry juice from head to toe and now swung upside down from a low branch whooping like a monkey. 'Hello Humans,' he shouted. 'You're upside down. Are you from Australia?'

'We're from Mars,' said David, stepping towards his grandson with outstretched arms.

Liz's eyes filled with tears. It had been a long wait. 'Hello, Jack,' she said.

French Kisses

ALAN DUNN

EACH TRUCK spat hot air at me, hit me with dust and diesel fumes, whipped my hair into my eyes, sandpapered my skin. It was useless hitching. I wouldn't have stopped to give myself a lift. That bastard Jatte! I was angry with him, with me, with the guy in the blue Citroen who put his hand on my knee. I wouldn't have minded if he'd let it rest there, given me a few miles before his fingers started sliming their way up my thigh, but no, he was into fifth and doing one-sixty down the outside lane, fast as they come. There was one of those child seats in the back, and a doll lying on the floor.

'You've got good legs,' he said. His hand seemed intent on exploring territory beyond what would normally be defined as leg.

I told him quietly, politely, that he'd made a mistake.

'Me? Oh no, cherie, you dressed like that and I'm the one who's made a mistake? I'm not that naïve! Don't get me wrong, please, I don't mind paying, providing I get my money's worth. And I'll give you a lift as far as Arles just to show I'm a decent type. But don't play the innocent virgin with me, it doesn't turn me on and it doesn't suit you.'

He had a point. I wasn't dressed for a stroll. Short black Lycra skirt, really short, and skintight too, as if I'm offering the goods for approval before sale. No stockings (like he said, I had good legs), heels, off-the-shoulder cotton blouse, no bra (no need), plenty of eye make-up, dark red lipstick. I looked like the whore he'd taken me to be, and part of me said give in, play the part, you need the money, you need to be south, you need him. Roll with the punches, bend in the wind. Perhaps it was the fear of relying on someone that made me fight back. Perhaps it was the fact that he was reasonably young, reasonably good-looking, and it would have been easy to let go. I might even have enjoyed myself. But his index finger went too far too soon, moved from skin to cotton, knuckles grazing aside the fabric of my skirt. If he'd only waited a few more minutes he might have had me, no fee at all.

My reactions got the better of me. I wrenched his hand away and punched him in the groin (wishing I'd had the knife which must have been hundreds of kilometres ahead of me down the autoroute), reached for the door handle at the same time. It wouldn't open of course, air pressure too great, but the shock of sudden movement and pain (not too intense, I didn't make very good contact) made him pull the wheel to one side. He lurched across the lanes, missed a Mercedes in the centre, made a tanker driver realize how fragile he was, perched on a few thousand litres of instant hell fire. We spent a few seconds on the hard shoulder, a few more digging up the grass beyond, and eventually stopped. I thought he was going to chase me, he would have caught me if he'd tried, me in my heels lurching down the side of the road.

I'd gone a few hundred metres before I saw movement. Perhaps I'd hit him harder than I'd originally thought; if so he must have been a damn good driver, or very lucky. The car started slowly. I suddenly remembered that film, the first one by Spielberg or Lucas, the one where the big black truck tries to kill the hero. Dennis Hopper? I forget. Anyway, I ran up the slope so he couldn't get me. He didn't even look as he drove away.

I sat down, waited a while to calm my nerves, lay back to let the air dry the sweat under my arms. I normally let the hair grow but Jatte had said I looked better without, that men preferred naked armpits these days. He should know. He'd wanted me to shave my pubic hair as well but I said no, the regrowth is itchy as hell. There was a bird, a hawk of some type, hovering then swooping, hovering again then darting down to pick something out of the grass down below me. Twice it caught nothing, or insects too small for me to see. The third time it had a small mousey creature in its claws. It was still twitching when the bird began to eat it. I began my litany.

Screw you, Jatte.

Screw you, Jatte!

SCREW YOU, JATTE! SCREW YOU, YOU FUCKER, I'LL GET YOU! Then I started to laugh. I was shaking. I needed a drink.

My concierge had locked me out of my apartment. Sounds good, 'apartment'. A damp room, window jammed half open, half closed. Sharing a toilet with a bunch of druggies, the smell of piss and puke and shit in the hall. Cooking on a camping stove because the gas had been cut off. It was cheap, but I couldn't even find the 300 francs a week I needed. All of my clothes, my address book, my make-up and perfumes, my glass animals, the little food I had, two bottles of damn good whisky, my stiletto, they were all inside and I was outside. 'I'm sorry, mademoiselle,' she'd said, 'I'm only carrying out my instructions. If you pay the overdue rent you'll get your things back. If not' – a Gallic shrug of the shoulders – 'well, they might fetch a little money.' I walked out. Begging wouldn't have helped. Besides, I knew her son very well. If I could find him he'd be sure to let me in when it was dark, might even let me stay one more night if I promised to be away early and offered him a little favour. But it would be another few hours before he came in, might even be after midnight. Besides, he didn't wash often enough. I went out into the street.

I had my purse with me and I opened it in vain, my fingers already too familiar with its contents. Twenty francs and some shrapnel, three condoms (one red, one black, one green; life had been quiet of late), an old photograph of a young woman holding a baby. Some receipts and fluff, the scrawled telephone number of a forgotten admirer. Two credit cards, out of date. Nothing. An old man playing boules alone in the dirt across the road whistled and leered. I whistled and leered back. 'Allo, Anglaise! Not going out tonight?' he shouted. 'I thought everyone was heading for Petitpois's party! If you're not going you can always come round to my place and keep me warm!' I declined gracefully.

I knew Petitpois. Well, I knew of him. Local hoodlum, fresh out of gaol for the sixth time, celebrating freedom. I knew where he lived. At least there'd be food there, a drink, no questions, a floor to sleep on. Perhaps a wallet to finger if I was lucky. Just enough to pay what I owed. I stopped to look at my reflection in a window. Not bad for thirty, not bad given the life I'd been leading. I patted a hair into place, smoothed down my skirt and blouse. I felt lucky.

It was easy getting in. Wait for someone looking like an American thirties spiv to drive up in a Jag, follow him and his party in, smile sweetly at the fists on the door. There was food and there was booze and from the smell in the air I knew that someone was passing joints around. I poured a triple Glenmorangie (someone knew their whiskies), then another, and didn't get as far as the food. There was no one I recognized. One spotty youth, drunk, no more than fifteen I swear, came up to me with the usual chat-up lines and seemed genuinely offended when I told him to stop stroking my backside. 'Don't you know who I am?' he slurred. Before I could think of some sarcastic reply (whisky affects me like that) he provided his own answer.

'Jean is my brother. He's very fond of me. He likes to make sure that I get everything I want. I want you.'

I could see the family resemblance but I'd been wrong about his age, he was sixteen. Where his brother was doltish but friendly and therefore well liked, this one was cold and bad. He specialized in carving his initials on his women.

I panted out the old lines, how I'd love him to screw me, I was getting hot and wet at the thought. But I couldn't, hadn't got the all-clear yet, still taking the antibiotics, hence the booze making me hazy, some reaction, sorry and all that.

'Doesn't worry me,' he replied. 'What I want from you only involves your mouth and your hands.'

I considered fainting; the alcohol or the prospect of sex with him, either could have made the pretence realistic. I swear I was on the verge of collapsing when Jatte appeared at his side and whispered in his ear. The boy blanched and left.

'I told him,' Jatte said, 'that you were a friend of a friend of mine, that you were a transvestite, homosexual, that you had open sores on your gums, and that your doctor hadn't yet told you that you were HIV positive.' His grin was disarming. 'May I get you something to eat?'

We left early with a bag full of food and two bottles, me leaning on Jatte's arm. I'd met him before, he informed me, when I'd auditioned in a club four or five years ago.

'The Blue Parrot I recall, alas no more. You didn't get the job. Good mover, no doubt about that, but it was the time breasts were in fashion. And I seem to remember you wouldn't help the punters in any way other than taking your clothes off for them. Look but don't touch. Still the same?'

I nodded. It wasn't, of course. I'd turned a few tricks since then, but I didn't see any reason to tell him. And I could remember him now. Jatte had been a pimp. Girls, boys, men, women, queers, dykes, AC/DC, twosomes, threesomes, s/m, you name it he'd supply it. So I was wary, despite being drunk. I knew I was safe, short-term; Jatte didn't go with women. But I owed him, and I wasn't sure how or when he might want paying.

His apartment wasn't much bigger than mine, but it had class. Its own shower and toilet and bidet; a balcony with a view over a small but green garden; separate kitchen; cupboards to hang clothes in. It was clean and smelled of honeysuckle and expensive soap. I grabbed one of the whisky bottles and flopped on to the bed, a huge bed, kingsize and soft and sweet. He pulled off my shoes as I lay and took the bottle from me. He was strong, in his mid-forties perhaps, possibly older, his hair white and long at the back. It was beginning to get dark so he pulled the shutters closed and switched on two or three table lights.

'I am a reformed character,' he said, smiled when I began to giggle.

'I am no longer a pimp. I no longer trifle with the bodies and souls of innocents. I prefer to steal from those whose morals prevent them from seeking assistance from upholders of the law. I am, I suppose, a gentleman blackmailer. A swindler of the unprincipled classes. An unarmed Robin Hood. I earn a living from the indiscretions of others. I am however, suffering from a severe cash-flow problem, as, I suspect, are you. We may be able to help each other. Allow me to explain.'

And so he told me, at great length. He was fond of his own voice was Jatte, almost put me to sleep. Turns out he'd found it easier to make money from blackmailing his whores' clients than from acting as their agent. He'd stung two or three of the rich ones and they'd provided a steady income. This allowed him to live well and indulge in his other vice, poker. Just recently he'd had a bad streak. Two of his bankers had died, the third was in gaol. He'd lost steadily at cards. And Petitpois, newly released, had asked, in return for a long forgotten favour, for a 'loan'. Requests such as that could not be refused; Jatte's protestations of poverty had brought only smiles and a demand for further funds.

'I can raise money easily, but not quickly. I need a million francs before the weekend.' It was Tuesday. I giggled again, reached for the whiskey in his hand but missed.

'There's a poker game in Nice on Friday, a high-stakes game and my luck's changing. But I need the entry. I need, at least fifty thousand before then. And you can help me get it, and there'll be the same amount in it for you. No risk. No trouble. All you have to do is listen. Are you interested? Or perhaps you'd like to spend some time with Petitpois Junior?'

'Tell me more, tell me more,' I sang at him. For a brief moment a look of disgust plucked at his face, a look which killed my humour immediately.

'Stand up,' he ordered. I did so.

'Take off your clothes.' I did so, unquestioningly.

'You stink of sweat. Take a shower. And while you're in there tidy yourself up, you'll find a razor in the second drawer down in the cabinet. I'll find some clothes for you.'

The sweat and worry of the day were easily cleaned from my body. I found time to ask what I was doing, but no answer was forthcoming. The prospect of money, fifty thousand at that, was far more tantalizing than giving the concierge's son a blow job. I was halfway sober by the time I stepped out of the shower, wrapped in a huge warm towel. Jatte was arranging some clothes on a chair, feeling each garment, nodding his approval. Without looking up he reached to one side and threw a nightdress at me. It was long, cotton with a floral print. I started to tell him that I slept naked but he wouldn't allow me to finish.

'You and I are sleeping in that bed tonight, together. We both need to sleep, and you will wear that nightdress. I shall explain the plan. Come here.'

He sat down, sat me down on the floor in front of him, dried my hair with a towel as he spoke. It was quite straightforward. I was to dress up as a hooker. I was to take my john to a hotel room. We would undress. Then in would come Jatte the high-ranking police officer. He would explain that the hotel was shortly to be raided, that my john, because of his position in society, would suffer more than was fair; his family would suffer, he would lose everything. In return for a large sum of money, however, he could be spirited away before the raid took place. What if he doesn't have enough money? I asked. We pick someone who does. What if it's someone who isn't married, doesn't have kids? We pick someone who does. What if the someone turns rough? We pick someone who won't.

Jatte seemed very certain. I elected to follow. What did I have to lose? My virginity?

He finished my hair and I watched him undress. He took off his clothes carefully, explaining that they were all handmade and expensive. The cut was certainly flattering; naked he was far less impressive than dressed. He seemed shorter and fatter than a few hours before, his body wrinkled, his flesh pale like that of a plucked chicken. He came to bed wearing silk pyjamas. He breathed heavily in his sleep but didn't snore.

The sun was hot and I could feel my skin reacting. If I stayed on the verge much longer I'd begin to burn. Ahead of me was a bridge and slip road, as good a place as any to consider my options. After only ten metres sweat began to pool again in my armpits, trickle down my chest. My feet and legs were clouded with dust. The need for a drink was overwhelming. The bridge approached slowly, the road leading to it a slab of shivering, molten tar. I reached the crest and saw on the downward slope a bright red rucksack, a Union Jack fluttering from a thin wooden stake pushed into its frame. Shit! Competition! Above the traffic's growl I could hear music, a recorder or flute playing a tune familiar to that part of my memory which still belonged to England. Then the music stopped. A young man (I nearly said a boy, he was fresh-faced with blond hair and an innocent air about him) stood up. He wore a white shirt. That much at least was normal. His trousers were black and stopped just above the knee. He had on one knee-length blue sock and one green one. Around his waist was a red sash. A blue ribbon, about seven centimetres across, was looped from one shoulder to his waist; a similar ribbon in green traversed the other shoulder. On his head sat a straw hat laced with plastic flowers and badges. In his hand was a battered tin whistle – my uncle used to play one at New Year just before singing the Internationale, molesting Aunt Maisie, and falling down drunk.

'Bonjour, Mademoiselle, j'espère que...'

I pointed out with my usual impeccable manners that there was no need to embarrass himself with his bad French, that I was, for all my sins, as English as he was.

'Oh! I'm sorry, it's just that you don't look, well, you don't look very English.'

I merely glanced at his costume.

'Oh. Yes. I see what you mean. It's a traditional English dancing costume you see, and it certainly helps...'

...when it comes to hitching lifts. Yes, I knew. That's how I explained my outfit. Except some bastard stole my case with all the rest of my clothes. I glossed over the details, asked if he happened to have a drink in his bag.

The Coke was warm but wet, helped the burning in my, throat but not in my head. The situation seemed to demand a different approach, so I switched into please help me mode, heard words falling ever so sweetly from my honeyed lips. Look, I know you were here before me but I'm desperate to get a lift down to Nice, I've got some rather pressing business, so would you mind if...?

'Nice? Me too, there's a folk festival on, I'm meeting some friends of mine, we're part of a dance-team, sword-dancing, clog, morris, you know the sort of thing.' I couldn't hide my look of frustration. He hummed to himself, cleared his throat. 'But you look as though your need's greater than mine. Yeah, go on then, if someone stops you've got first claim.'

No one stopped. My new friend started talking. He told me his name was Malcolm, that he was a civil engineering student in Leeds, third year, that he was engaged to a Melanie and that this trip was his final solo fling. That I could stand. It was his questions that annoyed me. A name, yes, I could make that up. Michelle I chose. Background, I told him I was a dancer. In the past I've often tended to mix lies with facts, then usually forget what I've said and give the game away. I thought I'd be rid of him quickly, so this time I decided to tell the truth. Mostly. How seven years ago I'd seen my husband off to work, dropped my kid round at my mother's, taken nearly two thousand pounds out of the bank (we'd been saving for a house) and left. No note. No message. Since then I'd been living in Paris, making a living most of the time. Dance to start with. Then topless. Then stripping. Sleeping around. Lucky to get away with a dose of clap. Beaten up once. Almost on to prostitution. I'm not sure if he believed me or not, it was a fragmented story anyway, what with one or both of us hurtling towards the road every time a car or truck went by. Eventually he interrupted me.

'Look, I hope you won't be offended. I think you look great, but that outfit might be a bit offputting to lots of people. Someone might even call the police. I've got some spare clothes in my bag, you could borrow them if you want.' He had a point. I messed around in the bag, pulled out a baggy T-shirt and some Bermuda shorts. He went a touch red when I wriggled out of my skirt, licked his lips when I pulled my top over my head. I had to laugh, there I was standing by the side of the autoroute dressed in nothing but a G-string, being ogled by a bumpkin, with murder on my mind. The T-shirt was nice though, cool. I knotted a red handkerchief round my neck, struck a pose. He actually applauded. A car stopped.

It was an Espace, seven seats and only one occupant, German. Where were we going? Well, what a coincidence, he too was heading for Nice. He could take us all the way. Promenade des Anglais good enough, ha ha? His French was poor, his English worse, which left Malcolm and me to converse. He didn't say much about himself, his life had been so commonplace in comparison to mine. I suppose I was flattered. At the first stop he disappeared for a while, came back with a half bottle of vodka. I sipped it gratefully, kept on passing it back to him; he held it to his mouth but didn't drink any. It began to get dark. I confided in him. I told him about Jatte.

We'd got up early. It was the first time I'd slept with a queer, about the only time I'd slept with a man and had an uninterrupted night's sleep. He told me in the morning that I'd been curled up around him, but that doesn't sound like the type of thing I'd do. I had croissants and black coffee for breakfast; he chose Weetabix and milk, then toast and tea. He watched me dress, gave me instructions in how to apply make-up (which I ignored), then wrapped me in a huge gabardine. We walked to the nearest Metro. His car had packed in. I thought we'd head for Montmartre but he said that was too poor these days, for tourists only. Instead he took me centre-ville. Business areas, he said, full of out-of-town executives. The hotel he chose was above a bar but had a separate entrance. Once we had the keys we could come and go without being observed. The room itself was clean, sparsely furnished, a bed, drawers and desk combined, seat, wardrobe. Jatte fussed about, turned back the sheets, closed the curtains. He switched the bedside light on, stepped back to look at it, switched it off again. He was making me nervous, I threatened to leave unless I got my first fix of the day. We went back downstairs and sat in the bar and he bought me a double. It steadied my nerves, the second relaxed me even more. I began to look forward to the adventure. I was swathed in grey cotton, but inside the skirt was riding up my thighs, the G-string was beginning to feel like a knot between my legs, the cotton blouse was arcing electricity across my nipples. Jatte nudged me. I looked up. Number one.

He was in his mid-fifties I'd say, balding, fat, heading for a heart-attack in a year or two. He was standing outside the bar, briefcase in one hand, jacket draped over his arm, other hand mopping at his shiny forehead with a handkerchief. It was hot outside, but not that hot. He could have been a salesman, but Jatte had noticed his alligator shoes, the cut of his suit, the Patek Phillipe watch, the gold bracelet and cufflinks and tie-pin. I didn't need any prompting, I felt like a bitch on heat. By the time I'd reached him the buttons of my coat were undone. With my heels on I could look down on the top of his head. His eyes couldn't decide where to rest their gaze, oscillated from breasts to stomach to groin to legs and back up again. He was hooked.

I can't remember the exact lines I used, something about me feeling as hot as he looked but the thirst I had wouldn't be cured by a Pernod with ice. I wiggled my arse as he followed me up the stairs, took it very slowly to give Jatte time to catch up. I was also worried that my new friend might collapse before we got to the room. I made sure the door wasn't locked, took his briefcase and jacket from him, began to undress him.

First his tie, then, oh so slowly, the buttons of his shirt. He was wearing a vest! Next his belt, his zip, his trousers lowered gently to the floor. I left him like that – Jatte told me that a man is never as weak as when he's caught with his trousers round his ankles and his socks and shoes still on. To fill in time (come on, Jatte, where the hell are you?) I started my own strip, top first, then skirt, much playing with nipples and grabbing of crotch, gyrating hips, little pants and groans. If I'd been allowed to keep going I might have begun to enjoy myself, but Jatte made his entry on cue, identification card in hand, uniform (where did he get it? I swear he was in civvies only a moment before!) pressed and neat and smart. He had his lines off pat. Mr Short and Fat was leaned against the wall and frisked, his wallet examined and lightened, his jewellery lifted, a credit card or two fingered. He was crying when Jatte gave him the get-out, searched through his trouser pockets for more money to hand over. We accepted, bundled him downstairs into a pre-paid taxi whose driver had had instructions to lose him in the suburbs.

We played variations on the same theme for the rest of the day. Lunchtime was best, from midday to three, then it went quiet but picked up again about six. By ten I was exhausted, by midnight and fourteen punters even Jatte had had enough. We stayed in the hotel room counting, it came to just over forty thousand. Jatte then gathered up the other items we'd collected, let me sit the cash while he went to find a fence he knew. He tossed me a present, something he found in the pocket of number ten, I think, a flick-knife. He said it was to replace the one I'd had locked in my flat. I somehow felt reassured by this, as though he was trusting me with some thing which could be potentially harmful to him. I played with it for a few minutes then put it in my handbag.

It was after four when he got back with another twenty-five thousand. Five thousand for expenses he said, leaves sixty, thirty each. It wasn't enough, really, but it would have to do. He gave me my share. Thirty thousand francs! In cash! It was more money than I'd ever had in my life! But it wasn't enough for Jatte. I thought he'd want to stay on, try for some more the next day. I even suggested to him that we could do that, but he said it was too dangerous, we were operating on someone else's territory, and he or the police might object. It was then he suggested I come away with him to Nice, just to stay safe, lie low for a while. We could even try the same trick again down there, take our time coming back, work Marseilles as well. We were a good team.

We taxied to Charles de Gaulle, hired a car (I think he used one of the cards he'd kept back) then headed south. We pulled off the autoroute for a few hours' sleep in a service area. When we woke up we had something to eat and he bought two of those little instant cameras in the shop, one each. We were in the car, about to leave, when he suggested we take photographs of each other. He took one of me first, lounging over the bonnet flashing my tits and looking sexy. Then he asked me to take one of him at the wheel. It seemed a natural request so I backed away, further and further, he said he wanted the car and the background. When I was ten metres from the car he let out the clutch and roared away. I threw the camera but it missed. He didn't even look back.

My right hand was still holding the vodka bottle; I lifted it to my lips and drained it; Malcolm was half leaning, half lying across me, sound asleep. So much for a thrilling story.

It was well past midnight when we were woken by our driver. Nice. The cool breeze coming in from the Med was a relief after the gluey air of Paris. I'd been able to think a little during the journey; the stereo had been loaded with unrecognizable classical tapes which did little to tax the mind. I had no money; no clothes; I knew no one in Nice. It made sense that I stay, until I could hustle some cash with or from him, with Malcolm. I'd just have to make sure he conformed to my plan. After thank yous, mercis and dankes we found ourselves alone on the Promenade des Anglais, palms dancing to muted soft jazz, cliffs of brightly lit hotels our backdrop. Malcolm, bless his heart, rose to the occasion like the gentleman he was.

'I don't want to be presumptive,' he said in a professorial voice, 'but you appear to have little chance of finding somewhere to stay tonight. You're very welcome to come with me to the hotel where my friends are staying, there'll be a bed there which you're welcome to use, no strings attached, I'll sleep on the sofa or on the floor. You can stay until the end of the week or till you get yourself sorted out, it's not a problem at all. In fact,' he blushed, 'I'd consider it something of an honour.' I didn't need to reply. I just linked my arm in his and said a small prayer of thanks to whoever was looking after me.

The hotel wasn't too far away. It was smart without being stylish, a couple of marbled colonnades, rotating doors, comfortable sofas on view in the foyer. Malcolm took off his rucksack put it down on the ground, reached inside for his wallet.

'Nice place, eh? All paid for by the organizers of the festival! In return for a dance or two they feed you and keep you for five days. Now all I have to do is find out which rooms they've allocated to us and... I think it might be best if you waited outside you know, they're expecting one person, not a couple, and they might get the wrong idea, if you see what I mean. You don't mind, do you?'

I did, but had to acknowledge that he was probably right. So I watched the bag and peeped round the corner as he spoke earnestly to the man behind the desk. I ignored two men who passed by and, noticing the Union Jack in the rucksack and thinking I wouldn't understand their guttural French, suggested loudly to each other what they'd like to do to me. Then Malcolm reappeared. He was wearing that resigned 'I'm sorry' look, the one you use at funerals where you don't know the corpse very well.

'They aren't there. None of them. Just a message saying that Jack and Mojo had an accident, broke a leg each. Nothing serious, but there was no point in coming when two-fifths of the team was out of action. They couldn't get hold of me to tell me. I've come all this way for nothing. Shit! And the organizers have cancelled the rooms.' If he was pissed off, I was devastated! My mind had been in that soft hotel bed, my body had already succumbed to that hot shower, my tired legs were being soothed by that warm, mellow feeling three or four whiskies bring. He'd asked about renting a room, but he didn't have enough money.

'What do we do now?' We? I was already thinking back to the two men who would be only a block away, in fact I think I'd already taken a step or two in that direction. But there was something helpless in his voice, something sad. I don't think it was being without a place to sleep, and it wasn't that his friends weren't there. I think it was more that he'd promised to help me and had, through no fault of his own, broken that promise. What could I do?

It was uncomfortable on the beach, cold even though I was wrapped up in his tracksuit and anorak. We ended up cuddling each other and dozing fitfully, ignoring interruptions from dealers and drunks, the pervert who thought he'd caught us screwing and wanted in on the action, even, towards dawn, a gendarme who seemed as tired as we did. Searching for sleep we talked, worked out what we would do next day. Apparently this folk festival was one of the biggest in Europe, dance-teams from nearly forty countries. Malcolm had his whistle, I could dance; he said he'd teach me one or two of the easier solo dances and we could busk, see what we could collect. I agreed, more to please him than for anything else. So far as money-making went it wasn't on the Jatte scale of things, but it was legitimate and harmless. Give it half a day, I thought, you can always sneak off to find a strip-joint somewhere. And the idea of dancing in front of people interested in what you're doing rather than what you're not wearing was refreshing. That's why 8 a.m. found us outside the nearest toilets, washed and groomed and ready to go. The problem of suitable shoes was easy to overcome. I told Malcolm my size, he put on his tracksuit and jogged into the foyer of the nearest large hotel, looking suitably sweaty. Smile at the girl on the desk then straight up the stairs, along the corridors, find a pair of shoes my size, newly polished. Then back out of the service exit with shoes and, bless his cotton socks, a breakfast tray with croissants, jam, orange juice. When I told him he'd make a good con-man he laughed.

After half an hour I had two routines off pat, a step-dance from Cumbria and some sort of freeform American stuff that was as much my invention as his instruction. With a couple of tunes from him we had a fifteen-minute programme that we repeated all morning. At first he did the introductions, but once I realized how bad his French was and took over, the people couldn't keep away. We drew crowds along the promenade, sure, but the best were in the shopping centre and down by the harbour. I was really enjoying myself! I was enjoying myself enjoying myself! We broke just before noon, collapsed into a café and had coffee and cakes and watched the world go by. I didn't even feel the temptation to ask for a whisky. The barman agreed to swap our loose change for notes and watched as we counted up the piles of coins. A thousand francs for a morning's work. I felt good. Malcolm said as much. 'You look new, rejuvenated, as if all your worries have disappeared.' They had, for the moment. I leaned over and kissed him on the cheek. He blushed.

We applied a little logic to our afternoon. Those with the most money gave most money; where in Nice were those with most money? The casino! Where should we go? That's right. But first we thought ahead to tonight. We needed somewhere to stay, nothing more than a room with a bed. Or two. I hadn't quite decided what my relationship with Malcolm would be, and he wasn't forcing himself on me, so I preferred to take things as they came. We wandered into the narrow streets and alleys well away from the tourist areas, found a hotel which was cheap enough. I did all of the negotiating this time; I felt a strange mastery at asking Malcolm to wait outside while I spoke to the proprietor and inspected the room. It was first-floor, small with two beds, a double and a single, a washbasin and chest of drawers; toilet and bathroom were just down the hall. I paid for two nights and took Malcolm's bag in with me, left it there while we continued our attempts to make an honest living. We bought quiches and baguettes, some salade Nicoise, two or three different types of cheese, some pate, a bottle of cheap wine. A skirt and blouse and underwear for me, a proper pair of comfortable shoes, a toothbrush; and still money left for the evening meal even if we didn't collect any more all day. But we did. The casino was a good hunting ground, twice as much in two hours there as we'd collected in the whole of the morning!

We decided to take the rest of the afternoon off, busk again in the evening. More essential purchases. A bikini and sun-tan oil, some mats and towels. Malcolm said he'd sunbathe in his underpants but I sneaked into a shop and bought him some trunks, nothing more than a thong really. At first he was too embarrassed to put them on, but when he saw that there were others dressed exactly the same he gave in. He looked quite nice really, sun-tanned, thin but muscled. A pity he was so young. I went topless of course. We swam and then sunbathed, he rubbed oil on my back and arms and legs, humming one of his little tunes. It felt so good, being looked after like that, being with someone who was content to be with me, to do things for me rather than have me do things for him. Life seemed worth living.

At about six we ceased our lives of inactivity to freshen up for our evening performance. On the way back to our room we passed a shop selling fishing rods and lures, guns and green knitted sweaters, all horrendously expensive. Malcolm seemed attracted by something in the corner of one of the windows, he called me back to look.

'Why not get one?' he asked. 'Replace the one you had stolen.' He'd seen a display of knives and remembered my saying that Jatte had taken the one he'd given me.

'It can be a present from me. Go on, go and pick one. I'll wait out here. Here's some money.' He pushed some notes into my hand and I found myself inside the shop, pointing at a small stiletto with a pearl handle. My frequent mention of knives was bravado; I'd never actually used one for anything other than peeling potatoes, but to tell him that would have been wrong. He'd wanted me to have something I'd said I needed, not a present which reflected his view of me. I came out of the shop to see him smiling and could only smile weakly back. I said thank you, realized I'd nowhere to put the knife, gave it to him to keep in his bag.

He sang us back to our room, and I made him sneak in without being noticed by the clerk. It wasn't difficult, the youth was engrossed in a Metal Hurlant, eyes wide open at a Bilial nude. We showered (separately). I felt ill at ease, unused to the way he treated me, unsure of the way he saw me. He started a playful argument about who was sleeping where. We both claimed the double bed, and what started as a pillow fight ended up with him astride my stomach, holding me down, holding my arms down, pushing me down into the mattress, both of us breathing heavily in the sudden surprise at our efforts. I went limp, submitted, looked him in the eyes. He returned the gaze. If he'd kissed me – dammit he should have reached down to kiss me, it's in the rules, I've seen it happen in so many films – I wouldn't have objected, wouldn't have fought back. I wanted him, then and there, wanted him to make love to me. It's not a term I use very often. Fuck, yes, screw, hump, fornicate even. I do all of those, perhaps too often. But not making love. Not love. Love.

But he didn't kiss me. He wanted to, I could feel that much, feel it in his eyes, feel it in the pressure of his body against mine. Instead he rolled off me, left me lying there, wanting him.

'Come on,' he'd said, 'we've got the whole evening ahead of us.' He looked at me, over his shoulder, as he gathered his stuff together. He seemed sad.

It was not too far to the casino. Malcolm played his whistle as he walked. I lost myself in thoughts about him. What must his thoughts be of me? That I was an easy lay? Good God, from what I'd said he could easily see that I was the whore I denied being even to myself! A thief? A blackmailer? Certainly both of those. And I was surprised he didn't kiss me? He was probably worried that he might catch something. And he'd wanted me to buy a knife. Not kinky underwear, or a box of chocolates, or a vibrator even, not perfume or jewellery. A knife. Jesus Christ!

The crowds at the casino were good, and generous, even if my dancing was, to begin with, rather more wooden than earlier on that day, and my patter uninspiring. A constant stream of visitors passed by, some serious gamblers, others sightseers, some leaving happy (one old dear gave us a 500-franc note), others with heads bent in anger or despair. My feet looked after themselves as I watched my audience come and go: the man with the blue fedora, the woman with the gold inlaid walking stick, the little boys with ice-creams, the young couple holding hands, the older couple kissing, tongues searching each other's mouths. Money fell from heaven that evening, from the tall blond Swedish man who stared at me then left abruptly with his boyfriend, from the young girl who couldn't take her eyes off my feet, from the drunks who began to mimic me then applauded as my steps grew more and more complex. I was unstoppable, I could hear Malcolm's breathing grow hoarse, could feel him labouring for each high note and trill, yet could only move on, faster and harder and with more control, full of the selfishness which comes from doing something well and knowing it. I was leaving him behind, he wasn't necessary, I was becoming the dance.

I stopped. Sweat was running down my back and I could barely see through clouded eyes. My chest was rising and falling, I felt in danger of collapsing. Malcolm was by my side, supporting me as the crowd cheered and clapped and threw money.

'You were going some there, love,' he whispered. 'You want to watch out, you're not used to these temperatures.'

It wasn't that. I'd just seen Jatte.

He had been climbing the steps to the casino, slowly, elegantly, as befits a man who has no worries. He even glanced in my direction to see what the crowd was doing, to find out what the noise was about. He'd seen a mad woman dancing. It was of no interest to him. He continued his pilgrimage into the cool of the temple.

'OK, OK, keep calm.' It was Malcolm speaking, bringing me back.

'What do you want to do?' I must have looked puzzled; he repeated himself.

'What do you want to do? He's stolen your money. You can try to get it back if you want. Or you can forget him and we can go on as we've been doing, for the rest of the week. It's up to you.' I still didn't say anything. My brain was in neutral.

'If you want the money back, if you want to take him, I'll help you. I swear I'll do everything I can to help you.' I nodded.

It was still early evening, the tuxedos and haute couture gowns weren't yet on display. Jatte was easy enough to find; he'd always said that cards were his love, and if poker wasn't available then vingt-et-un certainly was. I pointed him out to Malcolm who pulled me to one side.

'Right then. If he sees you he'll run. He doesn't know me. So you go back to the hotel room and wait for me, I'll follow him and find out where he's staying. Then I'll come and tell you and we can figure out what to do next.' It was then I remembered what day it was. I counted back the nights, Tuesday at Jatte's, Wednesday the sting and Jatte's car, Thursday on the beach. It was Friday, the day of Jatte's poker game!

'That really doesn't change things, unless he manages to lose all of his money. Look at him, he's just killing time. When he leaves he'll either go straight to his game or back to hls hotel room. I'd bet on the latter, but we'd better cover everything. Look, when he leaves, have a word with the dealer on the table he's playing. Ask if Jatte mentioned anything, just in case I lose him. Here, take some money, you might have to offer him a bribe. He's off now! Don't forget, stay put in the room and wait for me to come back. See you later!' He blew me a kiss as he left.

The dealer was a sweet little man. He said he knew nothing of what the man was intending to do and, when I offered him some money, still said he knew nothing and gave me the money back. I asked him about poker games in town; he still knew nothing. I believed him. I went back to our room, stopped on the way to buy two bottles of whisky. I felt in need. The clock on the entrance lobby wall whispered 8.30 as I walked in. The desk clerk winked at me and I could feel his eyes on me as I trod each laborious stair.

Just after ten-thirty, when I was two-thirds of a bottle down, there was a light knock on the door.

'*Mademoiselle? Mademoiselle?*' I opened the door a fraction to meet the leering face of the clerk.

'*Ah, mademoiselle, tu ne dors pas.*' I took an immediate dislike to his use of the personal.

'*Le téléphone, c'est pour toi. C'est un homme, je ne sais pas le nom.*'

I ran past him down the stairs to the booth in the hall. It smelt of tobacco and disinfectant.

'Listen, I don't have much change, so do exactly as I say.' It was Malcolm.

'I followed Jatte to his hotel, it's not far from you, it's called the Hôtel de la Reine and it's in the Place Victor Hugo. Have you got that?' I repeated the name and address.

'OK, get all of our stuff together, pay the bill, then get yourself round there. I've already booked a room for us in the name 'Michelle Dubois'. I reckon it's going to be easier to get your money back if we're in the same building as him. He's playing cards now in the backroom of a jazz club. I'll wait till he comes out. Now tell me again what you have to do.' I whispered back the name of the hotel, the name in which the booking was made. 'Have you been drinking?' came the voice from the mouthpiece, then 'Damn, my money's running out, be careful, I...' Love you? I added.

The desk clerk wasn't pleased that I was leaving, even if I didn't demand a refund. I didn't tip him; he didn't offer to carry my bag, Malcolm's rucksack, out into the street. I soon found the Hôtel de la Reine, and the giggle I felt as I walked up the stairs to my, Michelle Dubois's room, was due both to the alcohol in my stomach and to the appropriateness of the hotel's name to Jatte's nature. The room was hot, I opened the windows wide but closed the shutters, listened to the noise from the street. Somewhere, not too far away, a band was playing something German or Scandinavian, lots of violins and close harmonies. I raided the fridge (it was a good hotel, drinks, coffee and tea, television set, the works) for some ice and a glass, poured in the last of the first whisky bottle and felt better after two mouthfuls. The nervous, almost painful apprehension, the ache in the pit of the stomach which forces you to clench your fists and think of punching the wall, was replaced with a calmness, a willingness to accept what would happen in the knowledge that Malcolm would win through wherever he was and whatever he was doing. I took my drink into the bathroom and we had a cool shower together. We danced round the room naked to dry off, the radio playing Gershwin and Porter and Carmichael.

I can remember waking up to see Malcolm standing at the end of the bed, looking at me. I hadn't bothered dressing before lying down. Only the light at the side of the bed was on, so his face was half in silhouette, but there was a gleam in his eyes. I reached up to him and he came to me, lay beside me on one elbow, his hand smoothing my hair then diving to run fingernails harsh down my back. He smelled of smoke and sweat and beer and he kissed me, his tongue tracing the shape of my lips in hot acid, forcing my teeth apart to hunt me down in the dark, sweet warmth beyond. I pushed myself at him, I wanted to feel him against me down the whole length of our bodies. He pulled away.

'Listen, listen! Good God, I'll do this more often if I get a welcome like that every time. Are you listening?'

I purred a yes and reached for his shirt, began to undo the buttons. Did I mention that he had no hairs on his chest?

'For Christ's sake, woman!' he said, almost angry. 'Stop behaving like a bitch on heat and listen.' That hurt, and we both knew it.

'Look, I'm sorry, but this is important. It's three in the morning. Jatte's back in his room, happy and smiling. I think he had a good game, one of the bouncers escorted him back to the hotel! Then he tipped the night porter with a 500-franc note. I managed to hear why as well, he was asking if he knew where he might find a boy to come to his room, give him a massage. I followed Jatte up and listened outside his door, he'd left it open. The porter tried but couldn't get any one for another hour, so Jatte said to ring him when the boy arrived, he was going to have a sleep. At least I think that's what he said, you know what my French is like. After he spoke on the phone he shut the door but he didn't lock it, I waited a couple of minutes and tried turning the handle. It's still open. All I need do is go back now, sneak in, find the money, and come back. Nothing to it. I'll be back soon, don't worry. Now where's my rucksack? There was a torch in it, I might just need it.' He was a little boy playing a new game. He found his bag, rummaged around inside it and left. He'd called me bitch. Sometime in the night I'd opened the second bottle and I reached to it again now in desperate consolation.

I don't think he'd been away too long, but I'm a fast drinker. He held open a handbag, my handbag, the one Jatte had stolen. It was full of money! I raised myself up on to my elbows, blinking, trying to hold on as the room turned Picasso and melted on me.

'Go on then,' he said, 'count it.' So I did, very roughly, watching him at the same time. By the time I got to a hundred thousand he was undressed and heading for the shower. Four hundred thousand and he was back out again (I'd had to stop and start again round about two-seventy, I dropped a bundle on the floor), towelling himself and dripping all over the carpet. He came over to the bed and sat down beside me – I knew I was drunk, I knew that I'd missed some notes and counted others twice and even misread the denomination, but my final count was still just under eight hundred thousand.

'When I was putting that stuff into your bag I noticed this,' said Malcolm, pushing fingers into the side pocket and bringing out a condom, the green one, green for go. 'I thought it would be a pity to waste it. But I'm not quite sure how to use one.' His smile told the lie. 'Perhaps you'd give me a hand?'

I don't normally like making love when I'm drunk, although there've been times in the past when I've been forced to combine the two just to survive. But this time, this time the alcohol seemed to rid me of the few repressions I still had, to make each nerve-ending fire at the touch of a finger or brush of tongue or lips, my head turning from side to side in the agony of pleasure. I wanted to sing, to write poetry, to become the song itself. I reached for him but was pushed back on to the bed.

'No, this one's for you, I want you to remember this for the rest of your life.' And so I lay while he made love to me, his hands and lips moving over me and inside me, spiralling me into orgasm again and again. His shadow was leaning over me, hands on my arms, eyes closed and mouth clenched, moving into and against me, holding me, rising and falling, loving me, loving me. I think I screamed as I came for the last time.

I was almost asleep.

'Your skin is dry, so dry. You've been lying in the sun for too long. Let me help you.'

He helped me over, laid me on my back. I didn't feel dry, my skin felt slick and moist.

'This is all I have to give you,' he said. The condom was flaccid, red, a deflated balloon. I giggled at the thought, how clever, I knew they came in different flavours but I'd never seen one before that changed colour. Red for stop. He pulled at the rubber ripped it, allowed the semen to drip on to my stomach and up on to my breasts. It smelt of newly-mown lawns. It was cool. Or perhaps I was very hot. He began to rub slowly and lightly, then more firmly, up to my breasts then down over my stomach, up then down, up, down, down, down. I think I love you, I slurred. I swear I heard him say the same thing.

First they questioned me, wouldn't even let me get dressed. Then a doctor inspected me, internally and externally. Then they charged me with Jatte's murder.

The evidence was all against me. The knife in the stomach had my fingerprints on it. The man in the shop remembered me buying it.

They found Jatte's camera. The only photograph on the film was of me at the service area in Paris.

From their examination they determined that I'd had sexual intercourse no more than a few hours before my arrest. They found traces of Jatte's semen on my body.

My room had been booked by phone by Mr Jatte himself, according to the hotel receptionist. He'd asked specifically that it be close to his own.

They checked my story, of course. I told them everything.

There was no English dance-team at the festival that year, no rooms booked for them at any hotel. There were lots of buskers in town; no one seemed to remember me in particular, and Malcolm had always stayed in the background. At our first room, the one I'd booked, the desk-clerk had seen no one but me. He could, however, remember the telephone call just before I left; yes, it had been a man; and he had spoken impeccable French with a Parisian accent. It sounded more like Jatte than Malcolm.

At first I thought that Malcolm and Jatte might have been in league, but that didn't last long. Then I tried to persuade myself that Malcolm had been attacked by Jatte and had killed him in self-defence. Then I considered the evidence and figured out that Malcolm knew all along what he was doing. Me.

They found no trace of anyone else having been in the room. I don't think they searched very hard, after all, they had me, the perfect suspect. I'm accepting things as they are, they say I'll get a short sentence if I plead guilty and claim it was a crime of passion. The more I think of that last night the more I'm sure he said he loved me.

I'm sorry Jatte's dead, he didn't deserve it, he was only being greedy. And I suppose we had something in common which even his death couldn't take away.

Malcolm had fucked both of us.

Me and Renate

STEPHANIE ELLYNE

ME AND RENATE are waiting by the side of the road. She sticks out her thumb every so often, never when we're in danger of getting picked up, just so as to let me know she's trying. I kick up some dust, shift my chew to the other side of my cheek, spit a while before I give her the eye. She knows not to go on aggravating me too long. I trained her real good.

'Honey,' she says. She got one of those butter-slick voices, soft and yellow and none too good for you if you swallow too much of it. I squint at her, push my hat back, raise my forehead to the sun. 'Something I can do for you, sweetheart?' I ask her after a while. If I respond too quick she might get cocky. She gives me one of them slow smiles her mammy taught her. It don't work as well as it use to, maybe on account of the fact she lost her knapsack in Santa Fe and ain't had the use of a toothbrush regular. 'Why don't we skip El Paso and just go straight on to New Orleans?'

I trained her good, my baby. I can see that. She almost got me saying yeah before I saw what she was up to.

'You know what's in El Paso,' I say to her, low but making sure there's enough iron in the voice to make it weigh on her. 'Yeah but,' she says, almost a whine but a bit too sure of herself for that, 'there's no need to go there for it. We can get the same thing most any place.'

This gets me interested. Maybe she's learned a thing or two on these rides while I caught myself a nap. Before I can question her any closer an old Pontiac screeches up, driver looking us over real good. Renate pouts a bit but does her stuff, eyelashes whipping back and forth like a crow caught on barbed wire while I yank off my hat and flash my poor half-bald head, more GI than prison issue to soothe the heart of preachers and patriots everywhere.

'Why hello, sir,' little Rennie breathes out. 'My mama told me to say my prayers regular and they'd be answered and I guess she was right 'cause we need a ride more'n a baby needs a tit.'

This stops me in my tracks, but she read him right, Renate, 'cause he lets out a scream of laughter that fairly rocks his rusty heap. 'Git in, git in,' he calls out, one of them high, cracked voices like a hog caller at the county fair. 'I got a ways to go and I need some company.'

Rennie flounces into the front seat, hiking up her skirt over her pretty legs and I ease myself into the back where I can keep an eye on him. He catches my eye in the mirror, gives me a wink through his little round glasses. 'Bo's the name,' he says to me and pulls away before I can get the door shut. My head cracks back against the window but I come up smiling. I like to know what I'm dealing with right from the off.

'This here's Rennie and I'm known as Link,' I say, grinning like a yokel.

'Link short for Lincoln, boy? – 'cause I'll let you know for free I don't hold with niggers taking over,' he sings out, taking a swig from his flask, whisky by the smell of him.

'Naw, Link is on account of he's always missing,' Rennie says, taking a pull from his bottle. This is a bit high-toned for old Bo, 'cause he shuts his mouth for a good five minutes and concentrates on trying to get the car up to 80.

Bo commences humming to himself. I'm expecting some Jesus wept kind of thing by the look of him, but sounds more like one of them corny songs city kids learn at tennis camp – Froggy Went A Courting, If I Had a Hammer. 'I'm heading to Memphis,' he announces presently. 'Can I drop you two anywheres in particular?'

'Well, we was in mind of New Orleans, but most anywhere that would be convenient for you would be fine with us –'

'El Paso,' I break in, closing my hand affectionate-like on Rennie's shoulder. 'Any chance you might be dropping by there?'

Bo makes a show of sucking in his breath, confused and dismayed. 'Sounds to me like you children don't know exactly where you headed! If you don't mind me saying so' – he cuts his eyes at me in the mirror – 'you look like you got some dirt under your nails, son, but this little girl ain't hardly more than a child. How old are you, darlin?'

Rennie giggles and squirms in her seat. 'I ain't no baby! Link's always bossing me around but I reckon that's what big brothers are for.'

Bo seems mighty touched by this revelation. 'Brother and sister! I should have guessed it. I thought he was a mite old for you.' He gives Rennie a paternal pat on the head that slides like a sick eel down her neck on to her shoulder.

She beams up at him. 'How old d'you think I am, mister?'

They love this part.

'We-ell.' Bo gives her a good old eyeballing, lingering so long round about the chest area I expect he's calculating inches instead of years. 'You're certainly a woman now, ain't you, sweetheart? Though I don't suppose' – he checks in his mirror to see me staring bored out the window, lowers his voice anyhow – 'no one's been at you yet, have they, honey? So in most ways' – a shift in his seat – 'you're still an innocent young girl.'

Renate gazes demurely into her lap. 'I'm not so innocent,' she murmurs.

A speculative silence.

'Oh, I don't know,' drawls Bo, kind of serious for him. 'I 'spect there's a thing or two you could be taught.'

High time I hit the road.

'Sir –' I venture.

'Bo, son!'

'Uh, Bo – I was wondering if it might be possible to ask you a favour?'

He purses his lips, gives a flick of his little piss-brown eyes towards his wallet pocket.

'Such as?' His voice goes all sour.

I promised my Daddy I'd see Rennie safe to New Orleans. She's starting a new school there, staying with my Daddy's sister to make sure she stays out of mischief and goes to Church regular – but it's taking a lot longer than I thought it would. We ain't getting the kinds of rides I expected. That is, we get offered lots of rides on account of Rennie here, but them boys expect something for their trouble.' I lean forward and whisper into his fleshy ear. 'It would most likely shock an upstanding citizen like yourself, sir, to hear some of the notions they got about what they can get up to, and with her very own brother in the same car.'

'I got an imagination,' Bo grunts, with a sidelong look at Renate.

'Well, sir, let me lay my cards on the table. It's getting time I was in El Paso and we ain't much closer to New Orleans than when we started.'

'What's waiting for you in El Paso, boy?'

I smile, gone all bashful. 'I thought you would have guessed 'cause of my hair, sir. I'm due back at the base in two days' time.'

He regards me suspiciously. 'Now I know – and if you love this fine country then I would hope that you know there's no army base in El Paso.'

I guffaw at this. ''Course there ain't, sir. Just not many old officers like yourself pick us up, and that's the nearest town a civilian is likely to know.'

He likes this. 'Hell, I was a private for the duration and proud of it. Hard work's sweeter than glory to a man, son!'

Things are almost getting tearful for a minute, till thought steps in to cloud his brow.

'Let's see if I can second-guess you, boy. You want me to escort little Rennie here to New Orleans?'

'Link!' squeals Renate, fairly writhing in her seat. 'You can't expect poor Bo to go out of his way and drive me halfway cross the country like some kind of movie star! What would Daddy say?'

'It would be an honour, little lady,' intones Bo, a respectful look trying to make itself felt on his ratlike features. 'And I feel like I can speak for your Daddy as well as your brother here in saying a well-brought-up girl needs a man to protect her from the filth that stalks these roads. Just the other day there was a crime that turned my stomach. It seems a feller was driving –'

'No, please, we heard about it,' gasps Renate, clutching her little handbag to her heart. Then she smiles and gives him a playful punch on the shoulder, sweet face all flushed. 'I guess I'll let the two of you boys convince me.'

'Why, this is fine!' I say. The three of us commence to grinning at each other, a right picture of the happy family old Bo'd like to think he had. 'This means I can get the next bus to Fort Bliss. Sir, I'm eternally grateful to you. I don't know what I would have done if –'

'Now, now, son, any red-blooded man would have done the same! That is, anyone who calls himself a gentleman.' The Pontiac jerks to a halt and the back door's yanked open. I find myself in the dirt and right happy to be there.

'I want you to know, boy, that I mean to take care of your baby sister like she was my very own,' vows Bo.

'I knew I could depend on you, sir.' I shake his hand, one gent to another. 'It's a funny thing,' I confide. 'I probably shouldn't worry about this little girl here. She looks so delicate but she can take real good care of herself.'

And anyone who gets in her way.

'Well, Renate.' I clear my throat manfully. 'Be a good girl now, you hear? Make your family proud of you.'

'You be good, big brother, and make them sergeants proud of you!' she calls out in her clear little voice. 'Remember, Jesus loves you!' They rattle away in his sorry contraption, Rennie taking turns sticking her tongue out and blowing me kisses till I can't see them no more.

I decide to stretch my legs a bit. It'll be a good hour 'fore I see my baby again and I might as well use the time for some exercise. It takes some doing to keep up with Renate and I don't aim to disappoint her.

Trouble is there ain't enough energy in this tired old world. I don't need no book to convince me there's nothing that's pure good and nothing that's pure bad. I've had my fill of preachers, and when it comes right down to it I don't care what made us or created us. Got no time for that talk. All I know's what is, what you see when you open your eyes and look around you. It's hot or it's cold, sometimes so dry all the crops shrivel up, others when it's so wet everything just slldes off into ruination. But weather ain't bad or good, it's just there and that's what's real about it. A cat ain't evil for ripping a mouse apart. It's just obeying its nature.

Most people got no idea of who they are. They crawl out of bed into a car, go hunch over a desk all day taking crap from someone maybe half as alive as them, then crawl on home and goggle at a box just waiting to die. They got no suspicion of their true nature.

Now me and Renate are trying to discover what we can do, just exactly what we are and aren't capable of. We got ourselves a game plan and that plan's this. Once we've tested all the possibilities, experimented with just about everything we can think of, then we'll decide what it is we got a hankering for without too much worrying we might have left something out. One thing's for certain. We'll try anything more than once.

I reckon one of these days our true nature is going to shout out and reveal itself.

I set myself down after a spell. Don't want to go so far she can't find me again. I scoot back well off the road and sit up against a fence post, tilt my hat over my eyes. I must have fell asleep, 'cause before I know it, here she comes straight at me. She pulls up with an almighty screech, dirt and pebbles flying up in my face like bees.

'Hop in, soldier boy,' coos Renate. She peers at me over Bo's little spectacles, perched crookedly on her pretty nose. One of the lenses is cracked.

'Why, little lady, you sure you're old enough to be driving that thing?' I yodel and climb on in. His corduroy shirt is draped round her thin shoulders. Underneath all she's got on is her panties. As usual they're black with blood.

'Damn it, Renate, you're getting the seat all filthy! Lift up.' She sighs and raises her bottom while I scrub at the imitation white leather upholstery with what must be Bo's hanky, hoping I have a nice day in red, white and blue embroidery.

'How'd it go?'

'Pretty much the same.' She yawns, squinting half hopefully out the back for a cop car. Rennie'll do anything for a little excitement.

'He put up a struggle?'

'Honey, he didn't get time,' she drawls, then busts out laughing. 'That old boy was so quick he almost went off before Pearl did.'

She calls her gun Pearl 'cause of what the handle's supposed to be made of. Like so many things these days, it's imitation. I been telling her once we hit El Paso I can afford to buy her the real thing but she keeps dragging her feet.

'That's just fine, Renate,' I say, real sarcastic. 'All we need is an itty-bitty version of Bo running around to make our lives pure perfection.'

'Bodine, if you please,' she snaps. 'I already got me a little boy, if you care to recall. Matter of fact, seems I got two.' She glares at me, steering the car with one hand and helping herself to one of my cigarettes with the other.

'You want to light this for me or do I got to do everything for myself?'

I light her up and shut my trap. It's best to give her some time to settle down after her bit of excitement.

Every so often Rennie gets worried about her baby. It's staying with her sister in Crockett, been there for over a year now and I personally feel that it would confuse the kid if some pretty piece comes tripping in and makes him call her mama. The only ma that kid knows is sturdy and solid in puke-stained polyester and it might as well stay that way. She has a court order keeping Rennie away, and if I got to go back inside it'll be for something more drastic than swiping a snot-nosed kid and its diaper collection. When she gets tearful about it I give her a slap or two, wake her up and give her something real to cry about. I'm glad to say I ain't had to do that for awhile though. Fact is it don't seem to trouble her so much no more. She hardly never mentions him.

It ain't mine, of course. My kid would be with me all day and night and first SOB tried to take him off to school would have buckshot for breakfast.

Rennie swerves to avoid a gopher and does some cussing. I give her a good hard look. She seems awful wound up for this time of morning. 'What's the matter, cupcake?'

'Lincoln, we got ourself a problem,' says Rennie.

'Didn't he have nothing?'

She tosses his wallet down on the seat. I'm amazed to find it stuffed full of hundred-dollar bills.

'Lord have mercy! Why didn't he buy a better car?'

'He couldn't exactly get rid of this one yet.' She jerks her head towards the back. 'Take a guess what's in the trunk.'

'Drugs?' I say doubtfully. It don't seem likely but it's one of the few things gets Rennie real upset, her preferring other kinds of stimulation.

'Let's just say I ain't the first sweet thing he been messing with.' Her lips twist and all of a sudden she's crying. 'There's a little girl in the trunk, maybe eight years old.'

'Damn it, Rennie, stop the car!' I make sure no one's in sight, then hurry round the back to check it's shut up tight with nothing leaking. This ain't exactly the place to take a look. I push her aside and take the wheel, starting up nice and slow. She's still snivelling to herself.

'What's got into you, Renate?' I ask, soon as she quiets down enough to hear me. 'Why didn't you leave her with him?'

'She's just a baby, Link, and he done ripped her apart! I couldn't just dump her by the road like trash.' She brightens up a touch. 'I'll tell you something, sugar, I'm right proud to have blown him away.' She chews thoughtfully on her gum. 'I feel something like the Lone Ranger.'

I don't say nothing, keep cruising down the road easy while I try to think. At least now I'm driving. To say it ain't wise to have a body in the back won't mean much to you unless you've had a taste of Rennie at the wheel. If driving was ice-cream speed would be her favourite flavour. She flashes by and the cops are on our tail like dogs on a bitch in heat. She always outdrives them, but then we always been in a newer car. This thing couldn't outrace a go-kart.

We got to be practical right now, a word that don't mean much to Renate. It was me taught her to shoot and to give her credit, she's had so much practice she's got to be a damn sight better than me. But you can love a thing too much. She gets so carried away she uses all her bullets when with her aim one would do. You could say it's a fault in her.

It weren't like this when we started. We'd set 'em up the same but never go the whole hog. Didn't seem no point in it. We knew they wouldn't risk reporting us on account of what they'd got up to with a minor. Far as we know no one ever did. We'd relieve them of their wallets and their wheels and leave them near the road, boiling mad but breathing. The gun was just for show. Lord, Rennie loved waving that thing around! She kept hold of it in case things got out of hand.

And then she did.

The first time she emptied her pistol it surprised me. Way after he stopped twitching she kept plugging. I hollered at her to let go, finally had to knock the gun from her hand once the chamber was empty. She just kept firing like she was mesmerized. Hell, she'd be there now if I hadn't stepped in.

I take full responsibility if she goes astray. It's only right. I taught her everything she knows.

I ain't told her this 'cause some things should stay private. But I never feel so excited as when I see that little girl getting her own back. I usually arrive round about the time one of these old boys crush her to the ground, her pinned and wriggling beneath his flabby body like a bug. Then wham-bam, before you know it they're jerked backwards by the shot and she's the one on top doing the pumping.

Ain't no need to talk about it. She ought to know. Seems any more that's the only time I get romantic, and she's so fired up she's ready for anything. I can't remember the last time we done it regular.

Once you got a taste for danger, normal things go stale.

These last few rides she's had a hankering to do the whole thing herself. She's still a kid most ways, and you know how they love to feel independent. She pestered and pestered me till finally I indulged her. And look where it's got us.

I've come to know her real good and I understand the problem. My baby's a born enthusiast. Once she starts a thing seems she gets so caught up she don't know how to stop. I scold her about it. There's no sense in wasting ammunition. Plus it's so damn sloppy when they splatter. Seems I got to buy her a new dress most every day. Come to think of it, that could be why she does it. Like your average woman, she loves keeping fresh and pretty.

I can't complain about her feminine side. It's her good looks that keeps us in rides and her charm that cons the good old boys out of their cars and into their graves. But that same female part of her's got us crawling down the road with a Girl Scout in the trunk. Trust a woman to be too sentimental to dump a stiff 'cause they ain't had their grown-up teeth.

Lucky for us I ain't afflicted by such squeamishness.

As we creep along I'm scrutinizing the surroundings for camouflage. You got to have the eyes of a tracker for this type of work, everything's up to the territory and the weather. Rain's good on account of the mud. Usually we cover them with mesquite or brush, maybe some leaves if he's took her into the woods and the time of year's right. Once we come across a ditch chock-full of baling wire and that worked out fine. Most anything will do if you use your imagination. You'd be surprised the things that work.

Unless you're driving down a road like this. Smooth, flat and level, us gliding across like syrup on a pancake. On this kind of terrain you can bet any little bump sure shows.

'Teenage avenger,' says Renate.

'You mind keeping quiet, Rennie? I got to concentrate.'

'We're teenage avengers, Lincoln. This time the thing we done is pure good and no one could blame us for it. We was simply being good citizens and disposing of filth!' She blows a bubble and pops it, real excited. 'We can't just go off and bury her. Think how her mama and daddy'll feel never knowing what become of her. Why don't we leave the car somewheres the cops can find it? Even a cop hates a baby-raper. They'll be mighty grateful we took him off their hands.'

'And just how are they going to know anything about him, Miss Teenager? The smell of asphalt done gone and fried your brain.'

There's a short silence.

'Link, there just weren't no place to hide him...'

'For Christ's sweet sake, Renate! You don't mean there's two of them back there!'

She knows me well enough to duck.

'Honey, what else could I do? I knew it weren't right keeping them together after what he done but I could hardly put him in the back seat, now could I? The trunk was all there was.'

She waits a couple minutes for me to cool down, then starts stroking my arm. Backwards the way I like it, so all the little hairs go the wrong way and give you the shivers.

'It ain't no catastrophe, is it, punkin?' she asks real soft. 'No one's gonna stop us in this car 'cept an out-of-stock junk dealer. I went all peculiar when I found that child. I was running out of time and I got so scared I just couldn't figure what to do!' She gives me a little kiss side of the head. 'I knew *you'd* be able to think of something.'

She ain't going to get off that easy.

'You been on the road too long, Rennie. We ain't Bonnie and Clyde.'

She jerks her hand off my arm and sits up all stiff.

'Hell,' she spits out, 'if you was a hunk like Warren you wouldn't need me for bait.'

'There ain't a thing coming out of that head of yours but that pretty blonde hair and that ain't real. Don't you realize what they'll do to us if they catch us? They ain't going to believe you were defending your honour and then decided to take them for a Sunday drive! I'll be lucky to get out in time for my own funeral. And just 'cause you're not legal age don't think you'd get off so light.'

This don't faze her at all.

'Don't be too sure. I can tell a story about how you corrupted me so pitiful I could make them two cry.' She takes a long pull from Bo's bottle. 'Don't you know me by now, Lincoln? There ain't no judge drawing breath I can't sweet talk. He's a man, ain't he? Who'd ever take your word over mine? Not only are you big, mean-looking and almost twenty-one, you done time.'

'Could be the judge is a woman!'

'That'd suit me fine! A lady judge could appreciate how easy a girl goes astray without the ever-loving arms of her mama to steer her straight.' She winks. 'And I wouldn't have to spend time with her later.'

I got to admit she's got me licked. Before I know it she's caught me grinning. She starts in giggling and wraps her arms round my neck so tight I got to push her off to breathe. She's strong for a little one.

'Ain't this something, sugar? Seems lately we got so good at what we're doing all the fun's gone out of it. Like soda pop when you want a big, juicy steak. Sweet and easy but nothing to chew on.' She bounces up and down on the seat. 'But driving along knowing any moment they could get us and something bad might happen – why, it makes electricity shoot up my spine right through the sky!' Her voice goes all husky. 'Baby, I'm excited.'

I steer one-handed and give her a big sloppy kiss. Suddenly I'm feeling fine myself. Rennie makes every day a picnic. Times like this I feel so good I think about us settling down, having our own kid and raising it right. But you take two folks like us, accustomed to the smell of excitement. How long could we stay in one place before Rennie's trigger finger starts itching?

No, chances are we'll always be ramblers. Leastways till Rennie hits eighteen.

'What do you say, sweet thing?' she croons. 'We ain't done it in the car for a while.'

'Soon as we get these two in the ground I'm all yours, baby. Damned if I can see any place to turn off.'

She scowls, all sulky. 'But I like having them back there, Lincoln, I just told you! It's more spicy.' She lowers her voice. 'If I asked you for something extra, extra special, would you do it just for me?'

'What's that, precious?'

'Let's at least keep 'em till we get to New Orleans.'

I keep my temper on account of her asking so nice. 'That ain't exactly possible, Rennie. First thing is we got to ditch this car 'cause there ain't enough room for what we're carrying once we hit El Paso. And even if it was big enough, which it ain't, it's full up with grandpop and his little sweetie. That answer your question?'

Of course she decides to sass me.

'Lincoln, I been studying on this and it plain don't seem fair how you always get your own way.'

I glare at her. 'I don't see no other man in this car, do you?'

'Oh I'm not denying that, honey. You're the natural-born master round here, of course! But it's important to me to think I got some say. I mean, we don't get rides 'cause of what you got on offer. Seems only natural since it's my talents being noticed that I should decide where them rides are going to take us.'

'Rennie, once we hit El Paso, you can set your sights on the moon and I'll be right beside you.'

'We ain't going to El Paso.' She sticks her chin out like a mule. 'If you're so set on going you can go by your own self.'

I pound the steering wheel. 'And just what is it you got against El Paso all of a sudden?'

She takes a deep breath and screams at me. 'I ain't living off your drug money, Lincoln ! You done that before you met me and I don't hold it against you. But we're a team now and if you can't survive on what we do together and like it you go back to prowling playgrounds! But do it on your own.'

No wonder they don't want too many women in the army. A lick or two of shooting and they think they rule the roost.

'Where do you get off telling me what to do ?' I holler back. 'And since when are you such a do-gooder? Don't act all pure and holy with me, Renate, we been travelling together too long. I seen some things in my time but I have never seen anyone enjoy a thing as much as you love watching 'em breathe their last.'

'Damn right!' she says. 'I got every reason to be proud of what I do, and it ain't hooking innocent babies for profit. Every last man I wasted was begging for it. How dare they think they can stick their thing in some girl young enough to be their daughter, grandkid even! They should have found their own sweetness instead of trying to drink mine dry. Don't aim to make me feel bad, Lincoln. They was just dirty old men that paid the price for their filthy stinking lust.'

She stops for breath. 'They had plenty of time to repent what they were doing. But did they see the error of their ways ? The hell they did! They went on sinning and sinning till I come along like the Lord's own angel to strike them down.'

I had no idea she held such strong opinions.

'And just what in hell are you going to do if I go to El Paso? Go back to high school? Start knocking off football players?'

Rennie just grins. 'I'll do what I'm doing now only a damn sight better. I'd get a lot more rides without you tagging along to cramp my style.' She muses on this. 'Maybe I should get my baby back. It would be impossible to drive past a helpless young mother and her innocent child.' She giggles. 'I can train J.T. to use a pistol. Lord, just think of their faces!'

It's time to knock her down a peg or two. 'Just 'cause you got familiar with Pearl don't mean you're dangerous, darling. Not to me you ain't. Before you met me you couldn't load a BB gun.'

'That's a fact, Lincoln, and I thank you kindly. You're one fine teacher.' She shrugs. 'I do believe it's time to graduate.'

I try reasoning with her. 'So you don't want no part of drug-dealing. You're plain not interested in having a big new car all our own, lots of pretty clothes, plus any little thing you set your heart on in the store windows? There's big money to be had, baby, and it's all ours if we want it.'

'What do I need with fancy clothes? Mostly someone's taking them off me. And I like different cars all the time.' She tosses Bo's bulging wallet into my lap. 'Besides, we ain't doing bad for cash right now.'

'What about a real nice place to live, with a pool table and a barbecue and our very own swimming pool?'

She snorts at this. 'A wall-to-wall grave called home sweet home! At least in motels you don't have to clean up. I'm sorry, sugar, but I can't live like that. I got to keep moving.'

The car goes quiet while I think things through. My heart's been set on going back to El Paso and picking up the pieces of my old life. But I got to admit half the fun was going to be showing Rennie off to my buddies. They never seen anything like her and that's before she opens her mouth. Without her there, don't seem much point.

I sneak a look at Renate. She's staring out the window and humming to herself, acting real unconcerned. I clear my throat. 'Rennie, I'll make a deal with you. I'm not saying this'll be for ever, mind. But if you want to skip El Paso for the time being that's OK by me.' She whoops but I put my hand up before she can start in hugging and kissing. 'On one condition. That we dump these stiffs before we go to New Orleans.'

'It's a deal, cowboy!' she squeals, flinging her arms around me. 'You won't be sorry, Link. I'll make it up to you.'

'Just let me know one thing. Why is it you're so all-fired anxious to get to New Orleans?'

She rubs her cheek against mine. 'Don't you know nothing, silly? It's almost Mardi Gras!' Her voice gets dreamy. 'My mama said it's the biggest party in the US of A, even more spectacular than the 4th of July! I aim to see it before I'm too old to enjoy it. People don't do enough celebrating.'

The Lord himself must be riding with us because just then I spot a little turn-off, a bumpy tractor trail heading off towards what looks like, in the distance, a stand of big, leafy trees. The kind that grow out of wet, rich earth.

We turn off down the track and, sure enough, after fifteen minutes of rattling along come to the perfect place. The trees are growed in so thick it's dark as a chapel inside. Ain't no one around, but even if they was they couldn't see what we're about to do.

'He's got a shovel in the trunk,' says Renate. She's real cheerful now she's made up her mind to be. 'I reckon he was planning to use it himself.'

I strip off my shirt and get to it. Each time I stop to rest Rennie grabs the shovel and works on a little hole some ways from mine. She feels quite strong about keeping them apart. With both of us working, seems like we're through in no time.

I drag him by the ankles and drop him in. Renate leans over and spits, then starts kicking dirt and sticks down on him like a wild thing. I pull her away when her breathing gets ragged.

'Let me do this, honey. Why don't you take care of the kid?'

The little girl is a sight. I got to admit it ain't pleasant to look at her. Rennie lifts her out real gentle, smoothing her little pink dress together where it's been torn. 'It's a shame to lay her to rest with her dress all nasty. I wish we got something else to put her in.'

'Well, we ain't.' I'm itching to get out of here. I ain't had a thing to eat since breakfast.

Renate carries her over and lowers her in as smooth as though she was tucking her in for the night. I get the shovel but she grabs my arm before I can use it.

'Just one more second, Lincoln.' She opens her handbag and takes out her beat-up rubber doll. Petunia, she calls it. Rennie stands looking into the grave for a minute. Then she drops it in.

I'm real surprised. 'Are you sure you want to do that, sweetheart?' I know that doll means a lot to her. It's one of the few things her mammy ever give her.

''Course I'm sure.' She smiles kind of shaky and for a minute I think she's going to cry again. She don't. 'It's high time I gave up baby stuff.'

I go to put my arms around her. She lays herself down on the moist earth and smiles at me, lifting up Bo's shirt. 'Tell the truth now, Lincoln. Wouldn't you say I'm pretty near a woman?'

I pull her apart and in I go. I'm the only man still living that's felt this heat in her, and I like keeping that thought inside as I feel my way through. No matter how deep I go I never feel more'n halfway there.

I use her eyes as beacons. I press her forehead to mine and try to tunnel through her but sooner or later I got to give up and still her life's a secret to me. She lends out her control, never loses it, spins it out in a thread too even and tight to be more than plucked.

I'd consider it an honour to have someone kill me if I was so occupied. That's why I get a sweet warm feeling in my heart when I think of the men we've done. We're the best friends those mothers ever had.

A Dark Circle

SYLVIA BAKER

I WAS really surprised to see that strip of wallpaper hanging down from the ceiling just above the coroner's head. I thought the court would be like a palace. Mind you, Montgomery Duvall could have been a king sitting high up behind that enormous desk, with his bow tie and suntan. People with suntans at this time of year always look so important. The man they called the clerk bowed to him and I heard one of the policemen call him sir. Every time my stomach tightened with fear, I made myself look up, right over his head, and concentrate on that bit of wallpaper.

Yesterday, when the doctor said I was fit enough to attend the inquest, I was terrified and I couldn't sleep thinking about it. And I was worried about the sight of my legs. They don't hurt so much now but I can't bear people seeing them

The nurse said I should wear trousers, so I did because I was acting like a zombie, hardly able to think anything out for myself. When my mother came to fetch me, she asked what the hell was I doing dressed like that which made me all the more scared, but there wasn't any time to change. And in the end it didn't seem to matter, what with the peeling wallpaper and the state of some of the other witnesses. The man who'd found me in the street was dressed in jeans and a leather jacket. I looked up as he took the oath because I recognized his voice although I couldn't remember his face. The only thing I remembered was how he wrapped his coat round my legs and held me until I stopped screaming. And how I didn't say a word to him.

The smartest witness was a lady doctor. She had a foreign-sounding name and swingy dark hair that kept falling across her face. When I realized what she was there for I kept thinking how could someone so pretty do such a job. Once, at the end of a sentence, she looked straight at me, her lips slightly apart, and I could see the word 'sorry' all over her face. But everybody was sorry; I'm used to those pitying looks. I stared back for a moment, thinking how I'd rather be me than have to do what she did.

After she'd given her evidence, the coroner beckoned the clerk to his desk and said to him: 'I don't think it's necessary for the family to see these.' He lowered his voice but I was in the front row and could hear every word. Even when I was staring at the ceiling I was still listening. He had hold of some photographs and was fanning them out like a pack of cards. Then he leant forward and spoke to my mother.

'Is that all right, Mrs Poole?' His voice was still very quiet and he didn't even look in my direction. That's it, I thought, treat me like all the others. Is that all right, Mrs Poole, I mimicked inside my head. Why didn't he ask *me* if it was all right? My mother nodded and then fumbled about in her handbag which she'd put between us on the bench when we sat down. I could hear her sniffing and realized I'd never heard her cry before.

When they called my name I didn't know who they meant for a moment. I still thought I was Lizzie Poole, and then the clerk came over and tapped me lightly on my shoulder.

'You needn't go into the box, you can stand beside Mr Duvall if you like,' he said. 'But he must ask you some questions about the accident.'

'She won't speak, I know she won't.' My mother had stopped crying but her voice still sounded snuffly. 'She's been like it since she was five – can't get the words out. She shouldn't be here.' I wished she hadn't tried to explain; it only made me worse.

'Perhaps you'd like to take her,' the clerk said to my mother. But I didn't want her to 'take me' so I stood up and went to the witness box on my own.

My mother used to take me to school every day, right into the classroom, otherwise I'd creep back home after she'd gone to work. I couldn't get indoors but I used to sit in the porch and wait for her even though it meant a good hiding when she got back. Sometimes my brother Vince took me to school. He'd grip hold of my wrist so tight and if I struggled he gave me what he called a Chinese puzzle which was like being strangled. I was always crying when he finally pushed me inside the classroom door. But I never told the teacher what was wrong because he said if I told tales I'd get worms like our cat and that they'd eat up all my food and grow huge inside me until I died of starvation. It was his fault about the roundabout.

Before I started school, before my mother went to work, we'd go down to the recreation ground when Vince was on holiday. While us kids were busy swinging and climbing about, our mothers sat on the benches by the cricket pavilion and talked and smoked and took off their tights to get their legs brown. It was the only time my mother seemed happy, laughing and joking with the other women. One day there was a terrible storm. It was the first storm I remember and I'll never, ever forget it. The sky got so dark it was like night-time and some of the kids said the end of the world was coming. I didn't know what that meant and I only got frightened when it started to rain and all the others ran for cover and left me clinging to the roundabout. It was going too fast for me to jump off; I wasn't quite five and very small for my age. Then Vince shouted that I'd be struck by lightning because I was holding on to the metal bars. I called for my mother but she was round the side of the pavilion talking to the man who cut the grass and didn't take any notice. When the first flash of lightning came I leapt off but the bar caught me in the stomach, knocking every bit of air out of me. I couldn't move. I just lay there in the pouring rain struggling to get my breath, every gasp hurting my ribs so much I nearly stopped trying. When my mother finally came to pick me up she kept shouting at me, what was wrong, but I couldn't answer. Then she started shaking me and saying, look at the state of my dress and why was I always such a nuisance. She swung me round until one of the other women stopped her. I can't remember whether Vince got told off; probably not – he had a father who used to come and take him out on Saturdays and that's why my mother liked him best. I only remember the pain and not being able to speak and wishing and wishing that she was not so angry with me.

When I started school I was worried that she might not be there when I got home; that's why I didn't want to go. Well, that was part of the reason, the other thing was the way all the class laughed when I couldn't speak. Sometimes I was all right but just the slightest bit of anxiety and my breath just seemed to grip in my throat and I couldn't say a word.

It was better at the special school, the teacher was really kind and helped me to read aloud, two or three words at a time. Most of the others couldn't read at all. I didn't mind so much if they laughed because they were always laughing at nothing anyway. I was the cleverest in my class and probably the only one who got a job all on their own. I saw the notice in the window of the Burger Bar at Waterloo Station when I went to get my mother's cigarettes from the kiosk. At the interview they didn't seem bothered that most of my sentences consisted of only two words. As long as I was prepared to work late on Saturdays, they said the job was mine.

I was so excited the first time I put on my uniform. I'd ironed it twice, spending ages on those little creases that gather at the edge of a collar as though they've nowhere to go, when everything has to go somewhere. Then I tied up my hair and put on my cap, which took much longer than you'd think because I have such a lot of hair and it's very frizzy and springy. My mother used to plait it for school. That was agony because she brushed so hard and I didn't dare yell or she'd do it harder.

Even when I had secured the cap with all the grips I could find, some hair still hung round my face, so I chopped it off with nail scissors and had just flushed it down the toilet when I heard my mother's key in the front door. I rushed downstairs certain that for once she'd be pleased with me; smile and say how smart I looked the way she had when Vince first appeared in his army gear. But she just looked at me and sighed, her lips pressed together in a crinkly line. Then she said: 'Pop up the station and get me some fags... and take that lot off before you go.'

Every week I gave her half my wages and put the rest in the Post Office. Seeing my savings grow gave me more pleasure than spending the money because I couldn't think of anything to buy. I never went anywhere or did anything apart from work.

I liked my job even though I was always the one who had to do things like unblocking the sinks or scraping the fat from behind the fryers. They just asked me and I did it. Nobody bothered me and I kept really busy gathering up the dirty plates, emptying the ashtrays and filling up the cutlery and sugar. Sometimes I slipped some of the packets of sugar into my overall pocket to take home. Lots of customers did it, even well-to-do looking old ladies who should have known better. They'd take half a dozen, put one in their tea and the rest in their bags. I used to wrap them in a serviette and give them to my mother as a present but all she ever said was: 'So that's the kind of thing you're learning at that place, is it?' Once I took home a bag of rolls that the manageress had given me but my mother said they were stale and threw them in the bin. There was no pleasing her. I should have learnt that after trying for nearly seventeen years.

And then Joe came to work at the Burger Bar. On his first day he smiled at me and called me darling and for the first time in my life I felt as though someone really liked me.

Everybody liked Joe; he was always singing and telling jokes. Even when things got dropped and he had to mop the floor or when customers complained, which they did all the time, he was always good tempered. And he never ignored me like most of the others did. Sometimes, when a group of them were gathered round laughing and talking in the break, he'd pull me forward and stand with his arm round my shoulders so I didn't get left out. And he never got impatient when I couldn't speak.

He reminded me of the only friend I'd had at school because his hair was very black and shiny and his face was covered in small holes. Sabina had got the marks on her face from having smallpox when she was a baby in Pakistan; I don't know how Joe got his.

He also had something wrong with his eye. The lid hung down like he was winking but he wore dark glasses most of the time. But now and again when he was standing over the smoky fryers, he took his glasses off to wipe them. When he caught me staring at him, he just winked at me with his good eye.

In a way, I was glad that Joe wasn't perfect; it made me think that perhaps I stood a chance with him. I'd never had a boyfriend and sometimes I wondered if I ever would.

When he began to take out some of the other girls who worked at the Burger Bar, I was quite disappointed and I tried not to think about him, only I just couldn't help it. I'd stand in front of the mirror at night and hate myself for being so skinny. In fact I hated everything about myself. If I had big tits and sleek blonde hair and pale skin that I could dab with powder and blusher, I knew he'd take me out.

Then one day as I was wiping the trays he came up behind me and slipped his arms round my waist and pressed his lips against my ear. I just giggled, it was nothing unusual, he did it to all the girls.

'Well, Lizzie, are you coming out with me tonight?'

I kept on wiping away at the trays and giggling because I thought he was only teasing me.

'Come on, you can answer me, it's only yes or no,' he laughed and tickled me and blew against my neck and then I was sure he meant it and I said yes so loud he put his fingers on my lips. My heart felt as though it were jumping up and down all day and I nearly forgot to collect my pay packet.

My mother was waiting when I came downstairs in the new T-shirt I had bought on the way home from work. It was bright red and very tight. I had tried on so many but only this one had made me look less skinny.

'Where the hell are you going in that?'

'With Joe.'

'Joe from work?' She sounded as though she didn't believe me and I knew she didn't like the T-shirt.

'Where are you going with him ?'

I didn't answer. It wasn't the disapproval in her voice working its old trick of keeping me silent, I didn't know.

That's it, play dumb. Well, my girl, just make sure you can say the word 'no'. I've had enough trouble with you already without worrying what you're getting up to with some randy little Eyetie.'

Normally when she got angry I was filled with panic because I couldn't answer her and I was afraid I'd never speak again, but tonight it was different. The excitement I'd been feeling all day was still there, swimming around in my stomach, tickling about deep inside me, freeing me from the anxieties that had chained me down for so long. I just didn't care what she said any longer. The realization spread through me until I couldn't help laughing with the sheer joy of it. She gave one of her disgusted looks and told me to clear off.

Sitting in the pub in Kennington Park Road, I watched Joe laughing and talking at the bar while he got our drinks and I thought, what if he doesn't ask me out again, if he takes someone else out tomorrow? From the back, when you couldn't see his pitted face, he looked so handsome. His hair curved round his neck like the feathers of a sleek dark bird making me want to reach out and stroke it. I was consumed with longing to keep him and gripped with fear that I wouldn't be able to.

Later, back at his flat, when he pulled the red T-shirt over my head, pressing his lips against my neck and saying he loved me, I couldn't believe how easy it was to please him. And once I got the hang of all the things he asked me to do, there was no stopping me.

'You've got hidden talents, you know that?' We were lying naked in front of the gas fire and Joe was trying to light a cigarette from the flame. We couldn't go in the bedroom because Joe's mate and his girlfriend were in there and the flat only had the two rooms. It was quite tidy compared to our house but there wasn't a lot to get untidy; you'd call it bare I suppose, not squalid – it all depends what you're used to, which in my case wasn't much. But that evening I wouldn't have swapped places with anyone. Once, when I was at the special school, we had to draw a picture of our mothers and I was allowed to take mine home because it was so good. My teacher said I was like a dog with two tails. That evening with Joe a thousand tails wouldn't have been enough.

I went to his flat every night that first week and on the Friday, which was his thirtieth birthday, I drew out eighty pounds from the Post Office and bought him a watch.

'Hey, it's wonderful! How much did it cost you?' He looked really pleased.

'A lot.'

He put it on and held his wrist towards me. 'Can you tell the time?'

'Course.' I didn't offer to read the hands because sometimes I got it wrong and I didn't want Joe to think I was stupid.

'It must have cost you a week's wages,' he said.

'My savings,' I replied, despite the fact that my mother had made me promise never to tell anyone about my money.

'Savings?' He looked surprised, then grinned. 'I've never known anyone with savings.'

I showed him my Post Office book. It was wrapped in a brown paper bag as I'd had to smuggle it out of the house. My mother would have gone mad if she'd known I'd bought Joe the watch.

'My God, Lizzie, you've got nearly a thousand pounds!'

'For the future,' I told him. That's what my mother had said when she made me open the account.

The future came three months later, the day after I married Joe, when we went and drew out half my money. Part of it went to repay my mother for the wedding expenses: the licence, Joe's suit, my dress from the secondhand shop and the drinks at the pub for our friends – or rather Joe's friends; he didn't have any relations but a lot of friends. The rest went on a video.

Verity, one of the girls at the Burger Bar, was really nasty to me. She was the first one that Joe had taken out and she caught me alone in the cloakroom one day. She said that I was a slag and that my baby would be retarded because I was backward and Joe was diseased. I wanted to say she was a liar or tell her that Joe said she had ice in her knickers – it had sounded really funny when he said it, only I didn't feel like laughing now. But as usual, when anybody was aggressive towards me, the words stuck in my throat. I just stood there holding my breath with the awful feeling that something was tied tight round my neck. Even when she reached out and pulled my cap off I didn't move. Anyone else would have stuck up for themselves, maybe even hit her, but I had never hurt anyone in my life.

Most of the others were kind to me. The manageress even knitted some jackets and bootees for the baby, which was more than my mother did. She also reminded me of the days I was supposed to go to the clinic, although I was soon skipping my appointments because they asked so many questions.

Apart from the antenatal clinic, I loved being pregnant. For the first time in my life I got plump – I had the sort of figure I'd always wanted and I looked healthy. Even my skin seemed to get brighter. When I got ready for work, I spent a long time looking at myself in the mirror, putting on eye-shadow and lipstick and thinking I wasn't so bad after all. Two months before the baby was due I changed to part-time hours. I should have packed up altogether – all that standing – but I was fit and we needed the money. The Post Office book showed a balance of one pound and Joe had been sacked for bad attendance. Once I had to ask my mother for a loan. You'd think I'd asked for one of her kidneys. I decided I'd rather starve than ask her again.

Luckily Joe went back to work two weeks before I had the baby, so we managed to get a few things together. The old man who sorted out the waste food at the Burger Bar died and they offered Joe the job. He was quite pleased at first because they seldom took back people they had sacked, but I didn't think the work would suit him and I was right – he walked out the day I went into hospital. It was a shame because we really ate well that fortnight; six burgers each for dinner and mountains of chips – you'd never believe what makes its way into the waste bins!

Giving birth to Tommy made me feel like a star. Joe visited with armfuls of flowers, took me home in a taxi and made plans for our son to be heavyweight champion of the world. He'd started to decorate the flat – that was like painting the whole street for Joe – and he'd bought the biggest teddy bear he could find. I don't know where he got the money; I didn't give it a second thought. And I didn't care that the fridge was empty, the rent in arrears and we'd received a summons for not having a television licence. The only thing that mattered was that Joe and I had this perfect baby. For the first time in my life I felt special, like I'd performed some sort of mirade. Most of our belongings were either secondhand or rented but Tommy was brand new, darkly beautiful and he was mine. And Joe adored him.

Even my mother was impressed with Joe's devotion to Tommy. She called in each day to help us when I came home from hospital and she and Joe hardly had a cross word. Once I saw her smiling while she watched Joe holding him and she said to me, if only your father had cared so much about you. I wanted her to say more but she just looked at me and said, no use now. I expect she'd noticed that her words had made my eyes fill with tears; she hated people crying.

When Joe went off down the snooker club, he told her he was looking for work, so that pleased her as well. Every day I was happy.

At the end of the week she took the dirty washing to the launderette, cleared up the mess from the takeaways we'd been living on and said she had to get back to work. The same day Joe went off to light a candle for his son in the church and didn't come back until three the next morning. When he did finally come home the first thing he did was lift Tommy out of his cot and hold him so close I thought he would suffocate him. But then he laid him down again as gently as if he were made of glass and I knew he could never do anything to hurt Tommy in a million years. It made my heart hurt to see how much he loved him.

My mother sometimes popped in after work. She made a fuss of Tommy but began to pick fault with me so much that I wished she wouldn't come. She was worse than the health visitor with her nagging. They seemed to think I couldn't manage. But looking after Tommy was easy. At first he slept a lot and so did I, and when he got bigger we spent hours curled on the settee with the comics Joe brought home. If he cried I cuddled him until he stopped. And Joe was with us quite a lot of the time.

When his giro came he went down the snooker club every day, but I didn't mind because when the money ran out he stayed with us.

We'd walk down to the river taking it in turns to carry Tommy because the wheel of his pram was broken. In the good weather the office workers sat outside with their sandwiches and we fed the ducks with the stuff they threw away. Sometimes on the way home we stopped in the car park at the back of the supermarket and gave Tommy a ride in one of the trolleys. If the coast was clear, we wheeled him right the way home in it then left it in the street for the kids to play their racing games with.

On really hot days we just sat in the park. There was always something going on and it was quite crowded in the school holidays. Tommy loved watching the dogs. They weren't really allowed in there, but someone had scribbled over the notice and no one ever came to turn them out. Tommy squealed at them and reached out his hands but we had to be careful, some of them looked really fierce. Joe said the drug dealers used them for protection and they were trained to kill, but if one of them hurt his son then they'd be dead themselves!

When Tommy learnt to crawl we had to keep a watch out for the mess they made. The health visitor told me it could blind a child if they got it in their mouths and she said I ought not to let him on the grass. Joe said she was talking a load of crap and I couldn't stop laughing because he hadn't meant to say it like that.

Tommy learnt to crawl in the park. He was sitting on the grass, good as gold as usual, when he noticed the flowers in the border. I think it was the colours that caught his eye, he loved anything really bright and there wasn't much like that in our flat. He moved quite fast, his black eyes big and surprised as though he couldn't believe what he was doing. Then he caught his knee on a stone and toppled over. He started to howl but Joe picked him up and covered his little knee with kisses and carried him over to the flowers. He soon stopped crying and pulled the head off one, cramming the petals into his mouth before Joe could stop him. We let him pick a few more but made sure he didn't get them in his mouth this time. Then a posh-looking woman came over and called us vandals. Joe just laughed and broke off the biggest flower he could find and gave it to her with a bow. I giggled about it all the way home, the way her snooty old face had puckered up trying to make us feel ashamed and we just didn't care.

Sometimes we stopped at the Burger Bar hoping our old friends would be on the till. I was getting used to handouts and the feeling that people felt sorry for me, but I wasn't bothered because I'd never been happier.

It was my mother who said I had to take Tommy to the doctors. He'd been sick twice and I knew it was my fault because I'd let him eat a cake that an old lady had given him. She was one of those who beg for money outside the station and I remember her when she used to come in the Burger Bar and get turned out because she was so filthy. But I didn't want to say no, she was only trying to be friendly and anyway Tommy had seen the cake and had his hand out for it.

The doctor said he doubted if the cake had harmed Tommy so that was a relief, but he did keep me quite a while and ask me lots of questions and it was getting dark when I left the surgery. I was a bit scared about walking home because of going through the underpass; so I called in the snooker club for Joe.

I looked through one of the windows but I couldn't see him, so I wedged Tommy's pram against the wall – we'd fixed the wheel but now the brake didn't work – and went inside. Joe was in the bar and didn't see me put my head round the door because he had his face pressed against a woman's neck. She had blonde hair and it was all mingled up with Joe's black hair and looked so beautiful that I just stood there staring at them for a moment. Then I got this bad pain in my stomach and couldn't get my breath. I pressed my lips together and backed out into the passageway because the gasping noises were in my throat. I crouched behind the door with my hands over my mouth until someone stopped to ask if I was all right and was it my baby crying outside. I just nodded and ran out to Tommy and forgot all about being scared even though a man was peeing up against the wall in the underpass.

Joe came home really late. He smelt of beer and cigarettes like he always did, but there was another smell on him. It was thick and sweet like the perfume counters in expensive shops and it reminded me of everything beautiful like flowers and silk – and blonde hair. In the morning he gave me two bars of chocolate but I didn't feel like eating mine and after he'd gone out I gave them both to Tommy.

He was still eating it when the health visitor came. She fetched a flannel and started to clean the chocolate from Tommy's hands and face. Then she told me a social worker would be coming to see us and she said I must take better care of Tommy or he might not be able to stay with us. I thought she was fussing about the mess he was in, but then she started telling me lots of other things, only I couldn't hear what she was saying properly because I had the pain in my stomach again and I kept hearing a noise like a train. It got louder and louder until I had to put my hands over my ears, but when she asked me what was wrong, I just smiled and said, nothing, nothing. When she left all I could remember was that I mustn't give Tommy any more chips.

Joe went to their office that afternoon and when he came home he was swearing and laughing all at once. But it wasn't happy laughter. I thought he'd be able to make everything all right – like he'd made my life all right – then I thought of the woman with the blonde hair.

Tommy had fallen asleep on the floor. The washing-up liquid container that he'd been playing with was squashed beneath him and it let out a sigh as Joe picked him up. He put him gently on the settee and covered him with his cot blanket. Then he picked up a piece of plastic which Tommy had chewed off the top of the container and waved it in my face.

'You incapable dummy!' The words wouldn't have hurt so much if he hadn't pulled that face – just like my mother when I had tried so hard to please her and failed. I felt like hurting Joe back – but I didn't know how.

He threw the bit of plastic at me and then bent and kissed Tommy's forehead. For some reason seeing his lips brush so softly against his son's head made me want to hurt him even more and I was glad when he went out.

I went to the window and listened to the sound of his footsteps until they had faded away up the street and still the desire to hurt him was there, right inside me.

He'd left two cigarettes for me that morning along with the chocolate. He often did that. I didn't smoke much; it was something to do more than anything else. I lit the first, inhaling deeply for a change and trying to blow smoke rings just as Joe used to do when he taught me to smoke. At last I made one. Perfect. It drifted upwards without breaking, hovering over my sleeping baby's head like a tiny halo. He was a beautiful little angel, I thought, the only beautiful thing left in my life. His lashes were thick and dark like Joe's and now and again they fluttered against his cheeks as though he were about to wake, but he didn't.

I finished the cigarette and lit the second one from its glowing end, wanting to keep the fog of warmth that was filling my head. But halfway through it I began to feel sick and my throat was prickly and dry with smoke. I propped the cigarette in the ashtray and went for a drink of water. When I came back it had fallen on to the arm of the settee and there was a small black hole smouldering away in the vinyl. I stood there sipping my water and watched as the hole grew bigger. It was like a living, growing thing, a dark circle full of life, and I couldn't take my eyes off it. Curls of smoke started to climb out of the middle and for a few seconds it glowed quite brightly. Then it died down, back to that smoking black hole, spreading and spreading like all dark things do.

How long I stood there I don't know. I watched the vinyl curl open, the edges splitting and turning black right down to the cushions. My eyes were stinging and I couldn't help coughing with the smoke even though I kept drinking the water. I watched as the pile of comics beside the settee began to smoulder and then I reached out and pushed them and they burst into flames. I knew exactly what I was doing but I felt nothing except the certainty that Joe would be hurt beyond all the pain he had caused me.

Even when the flames caught the hem of my skirt, I didn't move. I wanted to stay, more than anything I wanted to stay, but then it felt like my legs were on fire and I just lost control and ran outside screaming for help.

And now I had to tell them. As I repeated the oath after the clerk, I was surprised how easy the words came – only two at a time – but easy, sort of mechanical. I looked round the room as I spoke. There were just rows of blurred faces, people I didn't know. Then, as I repeated the last 'truth', I looked at Joe. He was sitting the other side of my mother staring at me and for a moment I thought how ugly he had become, his pitted face stamped with misery, his black eyes dull and sunk in shadow. I tried to think of him laughing and gentle, coaxing me to talk, making me read the comics aloud to give me confidence. I tried to remember his smile of pride in the hospital when I had Tommy and the roses and carnations he'd brought me and all those beautiful flowers in the park. I tried to put them right there at the front of my mind but I couldn't; I had no control over my memories, just like I had no control over my life.

The clerk tapped my shoulder and I realized that the coroner was speaking to me.

'... but I must ask you just a few questions.'

I nodded. The questions were simple. All about Joe and me. All I had to say was yes or no.

'And tell me what happened after you smoked the cigarette.'

I looked down, trying to escape all the eyes that were on me. He beckoned me out of the box and let me stand by his desk. There was a large yellow folder in front of him and I read the name across it – Montgomery Duvall – with a name like that and the suntan, it was certain he'd feel sorry for me, just like all the others. He'd be thinking, she couldn't help it, poor, stupid girl – forgets her words, forgets she's left a cigarette burning... I'd never said it was an accident, never. The police had filled in the gaps when I couldn't talk and I just let them because I couldn't bear what I'd done and anyway when did I ever decide what I did?

Joe thought it was an accident. He'd visited me in hospital with flowers, just like before. But I wouldn't say anything and after he'd gone I crushed them, scattering the petals all over the floor, and the doctor came and gave me another injection. Standing by Montgomery Duvall's desk, staring at the yellow folder, I wished I'd ripped the flowers to pieces in front of Joe.

'I did it.' The words came out quite loudly and I felt as though I'd torn apart a thousand bouquets.

'What do you mean, Lizzie?' The coroner leant back in his chair and I caught the familiar edge of impatience in his voice.

'I let the cigarette burn – I made the comics burn.' I spoke easily because I was suddenly very sure of what I wanted to say.

'You mean it wasn't an accident?'

'No, no!' I was crying now and he was telling me to stop. Talking or crying I didn't know and I didn't care. I could hear a jumble of voices but mine seemed louder than any of them. 'I'm not stupid – I didn't do it by accident.'

I looked across at Joe. He had his head in his hands. My mother was clutching her bag against her chest, her lips moving silently as though she were trying to speak but couldn't. I felt like I was bigger than them, that no one could use me or laugh at me again. Even Montgomery Duvall had lost that look of pity and his brown forehead was all creased up and shiny with sweat. He called the clerk over and started whispering to him.

They were probably discussing what to do with me. Oh, I knew that I'd be punished but it wasn't important. I'd already paid a terrible price and nothing they could do or say could possibly hurt me anymore. Joe would be hurting for a long time but that didn't seem important either now. I stopped crying and went back to the witness box and sat down. I felt calm and I wasn't frightened anymore because I was completely in control for the first time in my life.

Good at Things

FRANCESCA CLEMENTIS

CATHERINE: '5... 4... 3... 2... 1... Happy new year!' Party poppers and kisses came at me from all corners of the room as we all sang *Auld Lang Syne* out of time to the scratched record accompanying us. My husband, Alex, was about four drunks away from me trying not to look down his sister-in-law's dress. The circle of linked arms evolved into a conga line and Alex danced over towards me.

'Happy new year, sweetie.' He kissed me with an exaggerated smacking sound. 'How long do you want to stay?'

I looked at my watch. I don't know why I did this but perhaps time was too abstract a concept to grapple with so late at night, and I needed a clock face to help visualize the possibilities.

'That's funny, my watch has stopped.' I shook my wrist, which had about as much effect as shouting into a dead phone.

'Maybe now you'll get rid of that old thing and let me buy you a proper one.' He hated this watch because I'd bought it for myself when I returned to work after having David. I loved it for the same reason.

I ignored him rather than start 1993 with a row. 'It seems to have stopped dead on midnight. Don't you think that's funny?'

'Hilarious. So how long do you want to stay?'

'You could read all sorts of things into this, couldn't you?'

'All sorts of things. It could mean that the battery has gone, perhaps leaking corrosive acid into the mechanism if we're lucky. It could mean death of old age or perhaps my threats and insults have crushed its will to live.'

'But it could be a sign, couldn't it?' I've liked the idea of signs since getting married on the hottest day in recorded history. I once wrote an article entitled 'Why Portent is Important' but I didn't know what to do with it. Nevertheless, coincidences should always be acknowledged, taken seriously and acted upon for there are few in one's life and they must mean something.

'Hello in there. Is there anyone at home?' Alex was knocking on my head and shouting into my ear. He knew what I was thinking and was getting ready to deliver his particle physics speech on how coincidences can be explained statistically. It was at times like these that I wished my husband was a poet or a footballer and not a research chemist. I resorted to the distraction of a sweet smile and a smoochy dance before he could start his lecture.

We got home at about one o'clock although, according to my watch, it was still midnight. The kids were spending the night with my parents so the house was empty. I called from the kitchen to ask Alex if he wanted some hot chocolate but he was already asleep on the sofa. I sat on the cold radiator and licked the creamy froth from the top of my drink. My kitchen was a haven that I had not allowed to become a family gathering place. Even the Waltons had enough respect for their saintly mother to save their confessions and problems for the dinner table. No wonder Ma Walton was always baking, it was probably the only chance she had to escape from her twenty-seven children. I refused to have seats in the kitchen in case it encouraged people to linger and talk to me.

I looked at my watch again. Because the hands had stopped moving, I felt as if time had also stopped for me. They say that some people can't wear watches, that watches always keep bad time on certain individuals, which suggests to me that a watch is actually responding to some force in the person wearing it. At midnight tonight, that force in me stopped being. I felt different, which was further proof that something had happened to me and I needed to deal with it.

1.30 a.m. is probably not the ideal time to make long-term resolutions. The blue silence can concentrate the mind a little too effectively and change seems simple. You really need the dilution that daytime noise imposes on the background if you want a lifelike setting when picturing new dreams. Still, by the morning, Jenny and David would be back, the television would be switched on for the day and there would be no private moments for a mother.

I thought about my hormones and wondered if I had them. They're supposed to spend their time coursing around my body like suicidal test pilots inducing mood swings and manic cravings. Mine seemed to have treated the whole journey like a vintage car rally, chugging along at a steady twenty miles per hour. I suppose I could have waited for the certain madness of menopause to make life interesting but I was only thirty-seven.

I was actually thirty-six when I started the juggling lessons which could be seen as the start of all this, but I only took up juggling because Callanetics was full. It provoked a gratifying response. My work colleagues were suspicious of any non-vocational activity and casually left leaflets on my desk with details of evening classes in Hospital Administration (Management). My husband thought I might be having an affair, a situation he considered more suitable for people like us than a course in clowning. Jenny was vaguely interested and David thought it was cool. My mother remarked that a tendency to early menopause ran in our family.

After a lifetime of amusing others with my clumsiness, I displayed an unexpected aptitude for juggling and basic acrobatics. Even more surprising was my new-found capacity for fun. Having it, that is, rather than providing it for my kids when children's television ended each afternoon.

My teacher's name was Toto. It was actually Trevor but he liked us to call him Toto in class for reasons of inspiration that I sort of understood. Anyway, Toto always called me out to the front when he'd taught us a new trick because I seemed to pick things up before the others. Once he said to me: 'Catherine, if you carry on improving like this, I'll have to watch out because you could be stealing my audiences!'

I wonder if my watch began to stop working at that moment.

ALEX: Her mother reckons that it's an early menopause. You can get pills for that now apparently. I know I never wanted her to go back to full-time work but I understood that she needed some kind of fulfilment outside of the home. And yes, I have to admit, the money has made our life a lot easier. So now she wants to throw it all in and become a busker. It's obviously all my fault for not paying her enough attention. What am I supposed to do now? I've already taken her to see *Phantom Of The Opera*. What more does she want?

CATHERINE: 'Have you spoken to the doctor about this?' Alex asked me.

'There's nothing wrong with me. I'm just changing my career before it's too late.'

'Catherine, becoming a secretary would be changing your career. Learning to teach would be changing your career. Becoming a juggler is the act of a crazed, irrational woman who has lost touch with reality.' I thanked him. I'd always wanted to be perceived as crazed and irrational and to achieve this goal without the assistance of oestrogen gave me immense satisfaction.

'What about the money?' he asked reasonably. I was earning almost as much as Alex when I filled in forms for a living. It afforded us two cars, two holidays a year, private education for our two children and about two hours each month to ourselves.

'I'll still be earning, it just won't be so regular, that's all.'

'That's all? How are we supposed to pay school fees with pennies and buttons tossed into a hat by passers-by who pity you?'

'Toto says he can take over £50 a session some days.'

'That's in Covent Garden which is not quite the same as Southend Railway Terminus.'

'Hundreds, if not thousands, of stressed, weary commuters pass through the station every morning and evening. If only a fraction of them give me 50p, I could be generating a good daily income.'

January was a cold dry month. The IRA terror campaign continued with a series of incendiary devices placed at selected railway stations in the South East. McDonald's launched MacEscargot's to celebrate the opening of the Channel Tunnel.

JENNY: Nan says that mum must be having her menopause and she needs hormones. I think she's just gone barmy and it's a bit embarrassing. Tamsin's mum is pregnant and that's bad enough but at least she stays at home so she doesn't show Tamsin up. Everyone will see mum at the station and Stephen Fletcher will never fancy me now.

DAVID: I've got a great new computer game called 'Revenge of the Killer Croissants'. Mum's chucked in her boring job at the hospital and she's going to be a busker. I think it's brilliant. She's really good at juggling. She can do five things at once which is amazingly hard to do. Mum says all mothers learn how to do five things at once but no one else I know has a mum who can juggle like she can.

CATHERINE: You think I'm pathetic, don't you? A ridiculous woman making a fool of herself out of some kind of frustration. Well, there's something you need to know. I'm good. Really good. This is no false arrogance either. I've never been good at anything before now so the discovery of my one talent is all the more rewarding and I'm not going to waste it. Nor am I stupid. I recognize the risk I am taking, not just of failing financially and bringing hardship on to my family, but of facing personal failure, finding that the one thing I am good at, I am not good *enough* at.

I worked my notice in January but started busking on January 31st out of a superstitious feeling that a new year's resolution should be carried out while the year is still just new.

DAVID: Now that mum is home in the day, she's started cooking again. That's a shame because she's not very good at it. We never get Chicken Drummers or oven chips any more.

ALEX: Catherine has always been the one to take care of the money. We both preferred it that way. She liked to think of me as an absent-minded professor, out of step with the material demands of the modern world. The truth is, I let her organize the household because she needed to feel needed. It's hard to say whether she has been any good at it but I've never seen a red bill come through the door. Maybe I was wrong and the pressures were too much.

CATHERINE: On my first day I took £6.27 despite dropping my Indian clubs a few times. It was the greatest achievement of my life, earning money by my own skills, every penny a willing payment for my personal efforts. As it was my first day, I blew the lot in Sainsbury's on steaks and a frozen gateau. That evening when we sat around the dinner table, I actually felt part of a family instead of a socio-economic unit. The food was earned by me, prepared by me and cooked by me. I was more than a mother, I was a provider and a good one.

David was the most excited by it all. 'Everyone at school was jealous. They've all got really boring mums. And they said you were brilliant and that you should go on *Opportunity Knocks*.' Alex deliberately ignored this suggestion. While limited embarrassment in Essex was a tolerable burden, national network humiliation was unthinkable.

'You don't think your skirt was a bit short?' Jenny asked anxiously. At fifteen, any pride in my unconventional behaviour was tempered by a strong yearning for a mother a little more like Jane Asher.

February was bitterly cold and there was heavy snow across Great Britain during the second half of the month. The Post Office went on strike the day before St Valentine's day. Fifteen passengers were killed by a bomb placed on a busy commuter train in Kent. The Channel Tunnel was closed when the new snow-sweeping trains from British Rail swept 250 tons of snow into Boulogne, knocking down an electric pylon and causing a national power cut.

CATHERINE: Summer will be easier. I'm taking a steady £15 a day but it's hard. It takes me all day to thaw out from the cold morning and, by the time I feel warm again, I have to go back for the evening session. But I'm getting better all the time, not just technically but also in the way I communicate with the audience. Usually I only have their attention for a couple of minutes because their timetable is so strict, so I can't waste any time building up a rapport. It's immediate impact or you've lost them. I'm having to make up the money with my savings but Alex doesn't know about that. He sees bills being paid and believes he has nothing to worry about.

ALEX: I think my rash is stress-related.

JENNY: I've got a new boyfriend. His name is Spunk and mum will hate him but I don't care.

March was cold and dry. The Princess of Wales had a baby girl with red hair. Questions were asked in the House. The public finally took notice of police warnings to be alert and suspicious and became paranoid. While the police were kept busy dealing with the sevenfold increase in reports, crime rose by 23 per cent. The Channel Tunnel reopened.

CATHERINE: March wasn't a bad month to get arrested. It wasn't so cold that the magistrate was short-tempered, and the promise of spring was close enough to make him generous. Of course I knew that I should have sorted out some kind of permit before starting my new career but I'd made this decision to get away from bureaucracy and I resented the pull of paperwork so soon in my bohemian life. I was fined £200. I earned £176.77 this month. Alex hasn't spoken to me for two days. Jenny has a new boyfriend. He seems very nice despite his haircut.

April was dominated by a mini heatwave over Easter and a series of bomb scares that brought the capital to a standstill. The Channel Tunnel closed for three days when English Animal Rights protesters occupied a stretch of tunnel where a family of moles were nesting.

JENNY: I could have died. The headmistress called me to her office and gave me a letter for mum and dad. Then she asked me all kinds of weird questions about home. I opened the letter in the toilets because the stupid old bag hadn't stuck it down. It said that the cheque for my summer term school fees had bounced, 'returned to drawer' it said, and that this was the third reminder that payment was seriously overdue. I could have died. I mean, Jennifer Tinsworth's mum works in the school secretary's office so she'll know about this, she might even have typed it herself, and she's bound to tell Jennifer and then everyone will know we're poor. I hate mum.

DAVID: Only three weeks until my birthday. I'm getting a new computer with colour monitor, digital graphics and CD sound unit. I hope mum buys a cake from Selfridges like last year. She's not very good at making them.

CATHERINE: The April sun felt different to the March sun. The light was more insistent, the temperature more intrusive. The pavements chattered with the click-clack of flimsy sandals and people smiled. Business was not good because the police didn't like me standing on the station concourse. Security, they said. Bloody IRA. I've got no more savings left, not enough money to pay the mortgage and three red bills stuffed in the desk drawer. Oh yes, and David's birthday coming up. There's a boot sale on Sunday. Perhaps I'll see something there for him. You can find amazing bargains at boot sales.

ALEX: I went to the bank to cash a cheque today and was told we were overdrawn. We've never been overdrawn before now. I don't know what to do about this. Every time I mention money, Catherine gets tetchy and accuses me of not trusting her. Trust is one of those loaded words she lobs at me which she feels I am unworthy to return.

May temperatures soared into the eighties. The Channel Tunnel closed when the railway tracks buckled under the heat. The IRA considered taking responsibility for the well-publicized series of disasters befalling the Tunnel but obviously decided to wait until the first trainload of English football fans finished off the task properly.

JENNY: I'll get pregnant. That'll teach them.

ALEX: 'I suppose you're doing this because I refused to fire Sara.' She didn't say anything to this. 'Well, I don't know how many times I have to explain myself. She's the best lab technician we've got and I can't fire her. That would have to be a group decision and I would have to give the group a good reason for firing her.'

'I haven't even thought of Sara in the last few months.' She didn't look up from the mixing bowl, just reached past me for the rolling pin, tutting slightly as if I were in her way.

'She means absolutely nothing to me. It was a stupid mistake...'

'Once is a stupid mistake. Eighteen months is a long series of very clever mistakes. Eighteen months is not a stupid mistake.'

'I knew this was what it was all about. You're trying to get back at me by ruining all our lives. Well, what about the children? What happens to their education when all the money has gone? What about the house? Is it worth losing our home just to punish me?'

'Believe it or not, Alex, there are whole parts of my life that have nothing to do with you or anyone in this family. You've just got on and done whatever you wanted to while I have watched my life being shaped by everyone else's needs. Now it's my turn. I'm still your wife and the kids' mother but, first and foremost, I'm a thirty-seven year-old woman who has not lived for herself since she got married.'

DAVID: Sometimes my Dad is stupid. He had a row with Mum in the kitchen today. It was bound to end in a row in there. Mum hates us going in the kitchen when she's cooking. Once she dropped a leg of lamb on the floor and I went in while she was rinsing it under the tap and sticking bits of parsley into the holes. I think that sort of thing happens quite a lot and she naturally doesn't want us to see what she's doing to the food. Frankly I'm happier not knowing. I'll have a word with Dad if he doesn't work it out for himself. My birthday tomorrow!

CATHERINE: Today I was happy just to be out in the open, under the sun, doing what I'm good at, making people smile, earning a living. I never noticed the reluctant handover of spring to summer before. Just when you get used to the heat of the day, a prickly breeze blows in with the evening to remind you that it is only May. In my former life it was either hot or cold, Christmas or Easter, Monday or Friday. There were no wriggly intangibles to guide me firmly from one faceless day to another.

My earnings are increasing all the time. I've just about made enough to begin paying off some of the mortgage arrears. I don't know what to do about the other bills yet. I'm going on a talentsearch night next week at the Ritzy. Top prize is £1000 and a regular spot. I really need to win that. I really need to.

The weather turned in June. The heaviest rainfall was in the South where residents welcomed the end of the hosepipe bans after five years. Twenty-three people were killed after an explosion in a West End theatre. Madonna got married for the third time. The Channel Tunnel was open for the entire month but only 673 cars and 342 rail passengers used it because nobody else realized it was open.

JENNY: I'd rather be pregnant than just fat. The doctor gave me a diet sheet. I ate four Mars bars while I read it.

ALEX: Christ, that woman doesn't care who she hurts. She didn't tell me that David was expecting a new computer. His face when he opened that box of secondhand children's encyclopaedias... I could have killed her. Why didn't she tell me? Not that I could have done anything since my salary appears to be doing little more than nibbling away at our spiralling overdraft. But I think she might have told me what *my* son wanted for his birthday. Or even told me that it was his birthday at all. Christ.

DAVID: I'm going to sell my old computer then wash cars and do errands until I have enough money to get a new one. I felt really sorry for mum. I know she's got money problems but she's getting really good at juggling. She should have won that contest. That other woman only won because her dress didn't fit properly. Anyway, after the first shock that it wasn't the computer, I was quite pleased. I'd always said that I'd like a set of encyclopaedias of my own and these were brilliant. I'm doing a project on natural and unnatural disasters and I've found loads of great examples. Dad was late home as usual and lost his temper when he realized that he'd missed the birthday dinner. We did save him a piece of cake but Jenny ate it.

CATHERINE: There are talent contests all over the place if you know where to look. I buy *The Stage* every week and there are pages filled with announcements of Starsearch nights. There's big money involved too. I only need to win one and we'd be on our way to solving the money problems.

Not that it's my fault it rained all month. I'm self-employed in a job where the elements have a major impact on my turnover and earning potential. I pawned my engagement ring to pay for groceries. David's birthday was a success even if Alex forgot about it and turned up smelling of toothpaste and talc at half past nine. I made a birthday cake decorated like a computer to compensate for not being able to afford a real one. I think David was pleased. A homemade cake is always more appreciated than a shop-bought one. Jenny had four slices. It's nice to see her eating so well.

It was a glorious July day for the marriage of HRH Prince Edward to Kylie Smith. The former Page Three girl looked elegant in a catsuit. The Abbey was not as full as expected since most of the European guests were stuck on the royal train which broke down in the Channel Tunnel. The terror campaign ceased for two weeks while IRA masterminds were on holiday in Camber Sands.

CATHERINE: I came second! £250 and a rosette! Mind you I deserved it. It was the best performance of my life. I finally found my gimmick. I decided to learn from the success of female alternative comedians who have played up their femininity instead of competing with men on men's terms. I juggled a doll, a foodmixer, a bra, a copy of *Delia Smith's Cookery Course* and a tampon with *I Will Survive* playing in the background and the audience loved me. Now that I have my niche, I should be able to supplement my income from busking with prize money and get the phone switched back on again.

ALEX: I don't care what she thinks of me. Seven months is more than enough to stretch the tolerance of a reasonable man. I opened a new bank account and had my salary paid directly into it. I'm being more than fair. I give her £200 a month which pays for all the groceries and I pay the bills when I find them screwed up in a drawer somewhere. I told the building society that my wife had had a nervous breakdown, hence the neglect of our monthly commitments to them. They seemed to understand and were happy to accept my offer to pay instalments until the arrears were cleared then increased payments for the remaining fifteen years on the mortgage. And I told Catherine that if she didn't get a job within the next month I would leave her.

JENNY: I don't think mum even noticed that I'd shaved my head. Anyway she'll notice when I lose weight. I'll get anorexia and then she'll be sorry.

DAVID: Mum won £250 last night. She was fantastic! She juggled all sorts of weird things and people laughed. Anyway, she came second and won all that money. We'll be rich again now and dad will probably come home more. I wish he could have seen mum last night. He said he'd try and get there but he didn't try very hard. Still I don't think mum minded too much. At least she had me there.

'Phew, what a scorcher!' The traditional August headline of The Sun *made its appearance on the day England lost the Ashes. The Ashes were being sent by train to France to be exhibited as part of an Anglo-French Cultural Exchange. British Rail blew them up thinking the box to be a bomb planted by the IRA in a fiendish plot to destabilize the Channel Tunnel which had just completed three weeks' unbroken service.*

DAVID: I think mum and dad are going to get a divorce. Dad sometimes doesn't come home all night. And now that we've had the phone reconnected, there's no excuse for not ringing to let mum know. When he is home, they argue all the time. I had a word with dad about not trying to talk to mum in the kitchen but he ignored me. But that's nothing new. Anyway when dad's not around, mum's really happy. She's won three more of those contests. I didn't get to see them because they were in Manchester or somewhere. She gave me £25 to go towards my new computer. That was really nice of her. Only another £173 and I'll have enough. We're going to Butlins for our holiday. I can't wait! Free funfair and a fantastic waterslide and go-karts and activities all day and night. It's all free. We've always had to go to France before. Boring.

CATHERINE: I'm going to make it. I've started telling jokes during my act and suddenly I'm a star. Well, not exactly a star but a Starsearch winner. And they're not even jokes, just stories about Alex's and my marriage, the kids, that sort of thing. It's just like talking to a friend and audiences seem to love it. I won the big £1000 prize last week, plus the £600 from the beginning of the month. I paid all the bills and had enough to put away for new clothes for Jenny and David. Apparently they can wear what they like at Southend Comprehensive but I'd like them to have some new things to make them feel better about their new school.

I still do a bit of busking but only to try out new routines. I've also applied for a pitch in Covent Garden. I'm taking the kids to Butlins for a week. They have a weekly talent contest with an overall prize of £2000. I've booked a chalet for four but I don't know if Alex will be coming. He says he has a course that week.

JENNY: Southend Comprehensive. I'm going to Southend Comprehensive. They'll all be drug addicts and have tattoos. I'll never see any of my friends again and I won't make any new friends. Who's going to talk about Sylvia Plath and Virginia Woolf with me? And I'll probably be the fattest girl in the class. I'm not doing very well on the anorexia front. And Butlins. I'm too embarrassed to tell anyone where I'm going. It will be the worst holiday of my life. I wish I could go away with dad wherever he's going. I wish I could just talk to dad.

ALEX: All right, so she's had some luck. At least we've still got a house, a phone and electricity. But what sort of life have we got? We've had to take the children out of private school and abandon them to the public sector. My children at a comprehensive. I hope no one here finds out. It's competitive enough in the research establishment without having to include family status in the equation. Christ, it all comes down to money. And of course I can't discuss money with Saint Catherine. Ever since she found out about the flat I got for Sara, she's carried her superiority with her like a halo. Well it was my money, my trust fund. And I said I was sorry about Sara, didn't I? And it's all over now. As good as.

The leaves decided not to fall in September this year. Since British rail had already attached new untested leaf sweepers to their trains, the absence of leaves was ignored and the sweepers promptly scraped most of the coating from the rails causing wheels to stick and jam on the surface. The Channel Tunnel was closed while French and English engineers redefined the seasons.

CATHERINE: I could easily live in a hot country where it was sunny all the year round. Even though I now have a regular cabaret spot at the Circus Tavern and don't need any extra income, I still enjoy my mornings outside the station. I look forward to recognizing the pale faces that started the year gradually turning biscuity as the year relaxes its hold on them. I'll never know the role I play in their life. Do they talk about me to their friends and families? Do they laugh at me? Or envy me? Do they care about me? I suppose an eyes-down smile and a coin is as much acknowledgement as I can expect from a stranger.

I saw Alex at the station today. I suppose he lost the company car when he got fired. I should feel sorry for him but it's a long time since I've found naivety a sympathetic quality. Actually naivety is too kind a word. Stupidity is closer to the truth. Did he really think Sara wanted him back after he dumped her so coldly last year?

'You just can't believe that anyone could want me when you so clearly have no interest in me yourself. Sara never stopped loving me. I should have left you when she first asked me. But no, I let you talk me into the famous 'one last chance'. Fat chance, more like. I give up the promise of a new life with a beautiful, young, intelligent... young... young...'

'You've said 'young' already,' I pointed out reasonably.

'... successful young woman who loves me. And for what?'

'A successful eighteen-year marriage and two surprisingly nice kids who would rather have two parents than one?'

'You see, you're doing it again, making me out to be the villain. Well, I did my duty, stayed with my family, carried on providing so that you could all continue to do exactly what you wanted. And none of you ever thought about what I wanted.'

It was like arguing with Jenny so I didn't bother. He moved into Sara's flat and a week later she stole all the papers from his briefcase documenting his confidential work and sold them to a rival company for the price of a new job. Alex was fired the next day. Apparently Sara had written to his boss but Alex doesn't know what she wrote. Still it did the trick. The woman in me admired the effectiveness of her revenge and the wife in me hated her.

JENNY: It was the most wonderful holiday ever. I met a gorgeous boy called Steve and he lives in Basildon so I get to see him at weekends. We spent every minute of the holiday together, swimming, dancing, playing crazy golf, going on the funfair, everything. It was just so wonderful. And mum won her competition which was a bit embarrassing but it means we all get a free week's holiday at Butlins Skegness in December for the Grand Final. And Mum said Steve can come if I still want him to in December. Of course I will. Dad's living in a grotty bedsit on the seafront. His girlfriend got him fired and then chucked him out. Serves him right.

DAVID: I won a computer for taking part in the most activities over the week. I did everything, entered all the contests, played all the sports, joined all the clubs. As soon as I saw that there was a computer to win, I just set out to win it. Mum cheered really loudly when I went up to get the prize. She cried a bit which was really silly because it was the happiest day of my life and not a bit sad. I cheered when she won her contest too. I can't wait to come back here another year. Dad didn't come which was great because it meant we could have chips every night. I think they're definitely going to get a divorce because he doesn't live at home any more.

ALEX: I thought it would be a good idea to move into a flat by myself for a while to think things through. This time last year I had it all – house, career, girlfriend, wife, kids, pension plan, six numbers in the Readers Digest Prize Draw. Sorry, that's the drink talking. I'll try and be serious. After all this is serious, isn't it? I'm forty-one years old. I've got no home, no job, the girl friend turned out to be a bitch, the wife turned out to be Miss Juggling England 1993, the kids will probably become juvenile delinquents, I can't touch the pension until I'm fifty... and it's all Catherine's fault. She couldn't let things be. We were fine, just fine, until she decided to change all our lives. And look at her now. Making a fool of herself all over the country. Making money too, I agree, but if it was money she wanted she could have got her old job back just like that. Or even a better one if she insisted on being ambitious.

Well, she's not the only one with ambitions. Does she think I'm living out my deepest dreams? Does she never think that perhaps I might have liked to be a tap dancer? Or a bus conductor? Or anything but a chemist? It's easy for a woman. Ultimately she knows that the man will always provide the financial safety net so that she can go off and fulfil herself whenever and however she chooses. Want a baby? No problem. Just take five years off work and let your husband work out how you'll manage. Want to become a juggler? Easy. Just become a juggler and let your husband renegotiate the mortgage. Becoming a husband was the most poorly thought out career move I ever made.

DAVID: I forgot to mention that Jen and I started a new school. It's got a computer club every lunchtime.

Terrorist attacks fought for front-page supremacy throughout October. There was so much death that the weather wasn't even mentioned until page three in most of the tabloids. It was hot, really hot, not just 'warm for the time of year' but 80° hot at any time hot. If there had been nothing better to write about, a journalist would have checked the records and come up with some dull statistics about this being the hottest summer on record. British Rail ignored the temperature since they had officially redefined the seasons and it was now winter. The Channel Tunnel closed when British Rail staff went on strike in protest against the compulsory wearing of woollen balaclavas and donkey jackets from October 1st.

CATHERINE: Have you ever smelled October? Or watched it? October was the only month when my eyes were so dazzled by the intensity of the sunlight that I preferred to work in the shade. It's strange to think of sunshine as disabling but I am beginning to prefer the more consistent atmosphere of the gaudy clubs where I make my living. The Covent Garden crowds are great though, a patchwork quilt of ages and nationalities enjoying the language-free entertainment that a good street performer delivers. I sometimes take a couple of hundred pounds in a day but I think I'll stop when my TV contract comes through.

I'm very worried about Jenny. She hasn't settled into her new school at all. I try to talk to her about it but she just clams up.

I wonder if this heat is a sign.

DAVID: Mum's going to be on the Paul Daniels show every week. And she says that I can go along and meet him and get his autograph and that he might even let me take part in one of his tricks. So I might be on telly.

Mum's won millions of competitions since Butlins and she bought me a computer table. We had an unbirthday party like Alice in Wonderland with a cake from Selfridges and Chicken Drummers. It was the best party ever. Even Jenny enjoyed it now that she's not on a stupid diet any more and she's not going out with that stupid Spunk. Mum invited dad and he bought me a game for the new computer. It was a really good laugh and dad didn't go into the kitchen and have a row with mum so that was even better. I reckon they might get back together.

JENNY: Mum's going to be famous. I expect David and me will have to go on *Whose Baby?* and *This is Your Life* and mum'll have to give us a hug even though no one has hugged anyone in this family since David was a toddler. I think mum and dad are going to get a divorce. Rebecca Potts says you can tell when they start buying you presents. Well, mum hasn't stopped buying presents since she got rich and dad bought us presents for the first time ever. They had this unbirthday party for David because he didn't have much of a real birthday party this year. I thought it was going to be boring but it was quite good fun really.

The new school is fantastic, much better than my old one. But I'm not going to tell mum that after all the fuss I made about leaving St Saviour's. When I got to Southend Comp, everyone had heard of me. They all thought it was really cool to have a mother like mine. I've got loads of friends and they all want to come home with me and meet my mum. They obviously haven't tasted her cooking.

ALEX: I know I should be gracious about this and congratulate her on her success but it's all so unfair. How lucky can you get? Just when the world of entertainment decides that the one fish missing from its vast ocean of mediocrity is an alternative juggling feminist, along comes my wife, *my* wife, who casually dips her toe into the water and drowns in celebrity. But look at what it's done to the children. David is a computer junkie, so miserable that he's cut himself off from us all and lives in a blinking, beeping world where mutant turnips do battle with avenging matchboxes. As for Jenny, she could be on drugs for all we know. She won't talk to either of us. At least she's eating normally and has got rid of that ghastly freak she was hanging around with. I can't say I approve of this new one though. She met him at Butlins and you can just imagine the sort of boy that goes there. Catherine has asked me if I want to go with them to the grand final of the talent contest in December. Pretty ridiculous when she has a TV contract and fame oozing from her pores right now, but she has this obsession with seeing things through. I suppose it wouldn't do any harm to go. We're getting on quite well at the moment. The good thing about being self-employed is that you can take holidays whenever you like.

*

November crept up on the British just when they were becoming complacent about the warmth. A winter curfew descended as doors closed firmly during the evenings to be opened only reluctantly the following day. Stewing beef was in demand and diets joyfully abandoned as three layers of thick clothes provided perfect excuses for getting fat. Heating on the Channel Tunnel trains was so efficient that fifteen people were taken to hospital suffering from heat exhaustion. Prince Edward's wife gave birth to a baby boy. Buckingham Palace confirmed that the baby was five months premature but at 9lbs 6ozs was doing fine. The baby, who appears to be very dark skinned, will be named Prince Rasta George Edward Ziggy. Her Majesty The Queen has just begun a six-month tour of the Australian Outback. She is unavailable for comment.

ALEX: I went to Mafco Pharmaceuticals today to tie up a sponsorship contract and they told me that my old team had all been made redundant. They can't all have been sleeping with Sara so obviously firing me was just a strategic move towards breaking the whole team up. I'm not really interested any more. Mafco are setting me up in my own lab and giving me a free hand in choosing a project from their wide range of research commitments.

'I'll be hiring a couple of assistants,' I told Catherine as she sat in the bath. I've learned my lesson about the kitchen.

'You could always give Sara a call. Just joking.' Sometimes I feel that my wife's sense of humour is more highly evolved than my own.

We talk every night while she's in the bath. Sometimes I get in with her. I only do that when Jenny and David are both out because I'm sure they'd be horrified to learn that their parents still fancied each other.

She took the disappointment really well, better than I did actually. I was furious with them for treating her like that, leading her to believe that a TV contract was practically hers when really they couldn't even guarantee her an audition. She doesn't seem to mind. She's back busking outside the station again as well as playing at the Circus Tavern and travelling all over England for talent contests. She's still making more money than me. She's still my wife.

JENNY: Yuk, it's so grotesque. They're all over each other. I hope this is just a temporary phase, a second honeymoon like Philippa Sanderson said, and they stop all the kissing soon. And they've started kissing me too and asking me caring questions around the dinner table. And that's another thing. We all have dinner together every night. If one of us is going out, we eat earlier or later, but always together. It's like Little House on the Prairie only with Marks & Spencer food. That's the good part about mum's money, the Marks & Spencer food.

CATHERINE: Working for himself has changed him. I knew it would because I've been through the process myself this year. I don't think he resents my earning more than he does because he knows how shaky my earning potential can be. I may have made a lot of money in the last few months but juggling feminists could be replaced in fashion by plate-spinning Croats next week.

Our marriage is a new place. He's stopped provoking me in the kitchen and switched to seducing me in the bath. He's never been like that, not even when we were first married and a relationship only really changes when both the people involved change. I know I've changed but although Alex is behaving differently, I don't see any real transformation in his character. Perhaps if I did, I wouldn't trust it. One thing that did surprise me was his attitude to the audition fiasco. He hadn't shown much enthusiasm for the idea in the beginning but when it fell through he became an avenging knight seething with indignation on my behalf. I didn't like to show how disappointed I was about being let down in case Alex was incensed enough to do more than write to *The Times*.

JENNY: Steve came to stay this weekend. Although he's the most good-looking boy I've ever seen, he doesn't wash very often.

ALEX: 'Have you spoken to Jenny about... things?' I couldn't say the word.

'They learn all about that in school. There's nothing left for a modern mother to say.'

I've never thought of Catherine as a modern mother. Juggling apart she has always been the most conformist of women.

CATHERINE: Alex thinks Jenny is getting up to 'things' with Steve. Why do men know so little about the women around them?

DAVID I'm president of Southend Comp Computer Club. It means I get to try out new games first and print newsletters from the new desktop publishing programme. I'm going to be a publisher when I grow up.

A bomb went off on Platform 3 at Southend Central railway station at 8.17 on Tuesday December 7th killing nineteen people. One of those killed was a wanted IRA terrorist who is believed to be responsible for the spate of bombings on the mainland over the last eighteen months. Flann O'Gerraghty had reserved a seat on the 11.45 Dover/Paris train giving rise to suspicions that the bomb was aimed at the Channel Tunnel just when tabloid coverage of its inefficiency was at a tolerable low.

*

ALEX: Butlins was a revelation. It was the best holiday I can remember and I think the whole family would agree with me. Thank God Jenny decided not to invite that yobbish boyfriend at the last moment although I was quite prepared to be civil to the lad. Catherine was busy with rehearsals and photo sessions for the first couple of days before the first heats began. Jenny got in with a nice enough gang from London and we only saw her at breakfast and when she ran out of money in the evening. I spent the time getting to know my son. I don't know how he ever turned out so well adjusted but it certainly wasn't my doing. He showed me some of the computer games in the amusement arcade and I was soon hooked. It's a bit irksome to be humiliated so conclusively by one's son in competition but I like to think that I taught him something about gracious defeat.

'Why did we go to France?' I asked Catherine in the shower on our third night. 'Because you wanted to.' 'I thought you wanted to.' 'Well, the kids certainly never wanted to, they were always bored by the third day. What do you think of this new concept of having fun with your family?'

'I wish someone could have shown me that life could be like this fifteen years ago. Is there room in the shower for two?'

JENNY: I've met this really lush boy called Philip. He's from London and he looks just like Marty Pellow from Wet Wet Wet. His sister won them this holiday. She's in the junior talent section singing 'Honeybun'. She's revolting, all highlights and eyeshadow which looks gross on a seven-year-old. I'm praying she gets through to the final on Friday night otherwise the whole family is going back early so that Honeybun doesn't have to suffer the indignity of early public failure. The family all talk like that. I think they watch *LA Law* too much.

DAVID: Dad's rubbish on the games but he's trying really hard and he pays for all the turns. Every morning we play crazy golf then we go to the amusements. Dad gets £10 worth of 10 and 20 pence pieces which last us the rest of the morning. He keeps on with the same game Dirtsmackers – and he says he's not going to give up until he gets his name on the High Score board. I like playing all the games and if I don't get a high score after five turns I give up. It's just a waste of time to keep on if you know you're not ever going to be very good at something.

CATHERINE: I thought I'd get through the preliminary heats at the very least. I lost to a teenager singing 'What I Did For Love'. Alex, David and Jenny were all in the audience cheering me on and I felt guilty for letting them down.

'Sweetheart, perhaps feminism hasn't reached Butlins yet.' Alex was more upset than I was. He was too kind to mention that I'd stumbled at least three times raising laughs where there were supposed to be gasps. The truth was that I hadn't been able to concentrate since hearing of the bomb on Tuesday. 8.17. I knew exactly who'd be there at that time. There would be the man who never smiled but gave me 50p every Thursday, the woman who always wore mini skirts even though her legs begged to be covered, the weary woman who cleaned the station, the paperseller who knew which paper all his regulars preferred, the girls going to St Saviour's in Laindon where Jenny used to go. I wrote down the telephone number you could call for details of friends and relatives you suspected could be involved but I couldn't phone because I didn't know the names of any of the faces. The papers printed the names the next day but none were familiar.

JENNY: No one I know was in the bomb blast. It could have been me. This made me feel a bit funny but Philip was very understanding. His sister's through to the Grand Final so he's staying. Mum got knocked out but we're staying anyway because this is the best holiday of all time.

DAVID: I cried when mum lost. She dropped things and people laughed. I hated them and hoped everyone laughed at them the next time they dropped anything. I think we made her feel better. Now she's got the rest of the week free to play with me and dad.

CATHERINE: Alex was dragged into a Lambada competition by one of the redcoats and won first prize. I've never seen him less inhibited or more pleased with himself.

'She said I was a natural dancer. I just picked up the steps and then added something personal. That's what made me stand out to the judges apparently. I was always good at dancing if you remember.' He was good at everything and it had brought him the rewards a man in his position craved. The recent setbacks only served to reinforce his skill at survival and made his achievement more substantial. I was a good juggler and it had brought me to a holiday camp in Skegness in December.

ALEX: Catherine has signed up for a hospital management course starting in January. She has come to regard the whole year as a sort of madness. Her mother was probably right all along, it was probably something female that a gynaecologist could have sorted out. Still it's over now and we've paid off all the debts she accrued in those first seven months so nothing's been lost. Since she's decided to take a more positive, productive approach to the coming new year, I'm going to do the same. There are no commercial skills I need to acquire so I'm going to pay attention to making myself a more well rounded person. On January 2nd I begin tap dancing lessons.

Karmic Mothers
– Fact or Fiction?

KATE ATKINSON

THE CHOICE of reading matter on the suicide ward was eclectic – Volume Four of the *Encyclopaedia Britannica* ('Delusion to Frenssen'), a copy of *Jackie*, a book called *Fact or Fiction?*, the Penguin edition of Chekhov's plays and a Hare Krishna book about reincarnation. Agnes dipped into them all at random.

She was particularly engaged by 'Liza's Dilemma' in the *Jackie* – would Liza realize that Matt Greene was just a chancer, despite his surfboard looks? Or would she recognize the good qualities of Robbie Davidson who was nice to his little sister and spent his Saturday afternoons playing football? Agnes suspected she would, but had no way of knowing as the *Jackie* was two years old. The book on reincarnation was considerably less confusing.

The ceiling of the suicide ward was a long way off when you lay flat on your back on the bed. It was just a room really, painted in apple-green gloss and ivory – Agnes liked the names of colours. The floor was covered in a speckled linoleum made from minced-up mushrooms and magnolia blossoms.

With an effort, Agnes lifted her head. Her chins concertina'd uncomfortably. She waved the book on reincarnation in the air. 'Did you know,' she said to Jeannie, lying on the bed opposite, 'that according to the Swami Prabhupada, you get the body of your choice?'

Jeannie snorted dismissively. 'I widnae have chosen mine.' (Agnes had to agree it did seem an unlikely theory.) Jeannie was the first Glaswegian that Agnes had ever met and she liked the way her voice was laced attractively with nicotine – it made everything Jeannie said sound emotional. Jeannie put the Chekhov down on her bedspread with a sigh (she'd run out of romances). 'I don't know about this Chekhov guy,' she said, shaking her head. 'They're an awfy miserable bunch of folk. I mean, I like a happy ending – you know? What kind of an ending is that – "If only we knew"?'

'It's the mysterious nature of the meaning of existence,' Agnes said, transferring a wad of gum from one side of her mouth to the other.

'That'll be right,' Jeannie said glumly. 'De youz wanna cuppa tea?' She swung herself off the bed and put her feet into a pair of powder-puff-blue, fluffy mules. In another life, Jeannie would have been a dancer – she had a dancer's legs, all muscle and tight, spare flesh, their shape distinct beneath her black nylon night dress.

Agnes was Jeannie's counterbalance – plump like satin cushions, with rosy cherub skin and flesh like ripe apricots – Agnes weighed fourteen stone, one for every year of her life.

'No, ta – I've got juice,' Agnes replied, letting her head fall back down on the pillow with relief.

Agnes had been on the suicide ward for nearly two weeks now. There were two things that could be said in its favour – 1) It was better than school, and 2) It was better than home. It was nothing like the hospital afterlife she'd expected. She had imagined waking to the soft faces of concerned nurses and the terse, urgent conversations of doctors as they engaged in the dramatic struggle to bring her back to life. (There had actually been quite a lot of drama in the Accident and Emergency ward when Agnes was brought in, but she'd missed most of it because she was unconscious.) Nor was there any sign of the experienced, kindly psychiatrist she'd anticipated, an understanding man who would unravel the tangle of her life and give it back to her as a clean skein, free of snags. Or better still, explain that a terrible mistake had been made and she'd accidentally been given the life of Agnes Ballinger for the last fourteen years, when in fact she was really...

There were twenty-six and a half polystyrene tiles on the ceiling one way, eighteen the other, all painted – in bold defiance of Health and Safety regulations – in the apple-green gloss paint that, if there was a fire, would fall in great flaming, melting lumps on to Jeannie and Agnes, lying below on their salmon-pink cotton bedspreads and lily-white sheets. Agnes heaved herself up on to one elbow and searched in her locker. It smelled of old plywood and other people's things. With some difficulty she trawled a half-empty bag of liquorice allsorts from it.

The red-haired nurse flew in, looking for Jeannie. 'She's not away to the toilet, is she?' she asked, a wild look in her eye.

'The hair and nails continue to grow after death – fact or fiction?' Agnes quizzed her.

The red-haired nurse stopped to consider for a moment. 'Fact,' she said decisively.

'Fiction!' Agnes said triumphantly.

She offered the bag of liquorice allsorts to the red-haired nurse who chose one of the ones that are covered in little blue dots, the colour of heaven, before rushing out again. Mostly the red-haired nurse bustled –

she was born bustling. Agnes imagined her bustling from the womb, tiny arms and legs angling furiously.

Jeannie and Agnes were the only patients on the suicide ward. This was due not to a shortage of suicides, but the relocation of the old suicide ward to the new hospital. Jeannie and Agnes remained, leftover suicides, in an old side ward of the maternity wing (the maternity department wasn't due to move for another month yet although the occasional baby got sent on ahead by mistake). Agnes couldn't work out whether she and Jeannie had been left due to an administrative oversight or because they weren't regarded as true suicides. The suicide staff had, naturally, moved to the new hospital along with the suicides, so Agnes and Jeannie were looked after by midwives.

Agnes parked her gum on the side of her bedside locker and ate the rest of the liquorice allsorts quickly.

Jeannie came back carrying two thick, white mugs of tea. 'I brought youz wan anyway.' Agnes put the mug on the glass top of her locker, placing it carefully so that it would overlap the previous circle stain. She was building a pattern, like a slow Spirograph, of milk, orange squash, tea, Ribena, hot chocolate. No one even bothered to clean any more in their neglected little ward. 'I understand now how Gregor Samsa felt,' Agnes said to Jeannie.

'Who was he?'

'A giant insect.'

'Oh, aye – I've got a cousin like that.'

Jeannie thought it was jammy on the suicide ward for one reason – 1) It was better than prison. Jeannie was doing time in the local open prison for fraud. ('Life is an open prison,' Agnes said, comfortingly.) Jeannie didn't admit to being a suicide, she claimed that she'd been in the sewing room of the prison, pinning up a hem, when she'd laughed so much that she'd accidentally swallowed the pins and needles she was holding in her mouth. Now the nurses were waiting for the pins and needles to 'pass' as they politely put it (hence the red-haired nurse's interest in Jeannie's toilet activities). Jeannie herself seemed blithely unconcerned about the whereabouts of so many sharp objects in the vulnerable interior of her body. Agnes was reminded of the martyrs of the early church, she thought of Jeannie as a kind of inside-out St Sebastian. It would account for the expression of dreadful anguish that convulsed her haggard good looks occasionally.

Agnes tried to re-enact the prison sewing room scenario, using the contents of a box of matches, but couldn't get it to work. They were allowed anything – matches, razors, nooses – further proof that no one took their suicides seriously.

Jeannie delicately peeled away the cellophane on a packet of Player's Number Six. They were allowed to smoke. They were allowed to lie on their beds all day, smoke, eat chocolate – do anything they wanted in fact.

Nobody seemed to care. 'Regular holiday in here,' Jeannie said with a sigh of satisfaction and dragged so hard on her cigarette that her lips retracted, showing pointed yellow teeth, a shade somewhere between crocus and mustard on Agnes's private paint chart. Jeannie was forty but her teeth were older.

'Catgut is made from the guts of cats – fact or fiction?'

Thoughtfully, Jeannie removed a flake of tobacco from her lower lip. 'So,' she said, coming over and sitting on Agnes's bed and picking up the book on reincarnation, 'I could come back as a cat?'

'Correct. What about the catgut?'

'Fiction.'

'Correct.'

'That widnae be so bad, eh? Cats have an OK life. What would you come back as, wee Agnes?'

Agnes shrugged her shoulders. 'Anybody but me, really,' she said after some thought.

Jeannie stubbed out her cigarette in a bedpan. 'Come on, let's go look at the weans.'

The babies, or the 'weans' as Jeannie insisted on calling them in her foreign language, were next door.

There were twenty-two babies and two suicides (or accidents, depending on how you looked at it), creating a temporary imbalance between birth and death.

'Typical of the marginalization of rites of passage in our society,' Duncan, Agnes's boyfriend said earnestly, looking round and sniffing the heady cocktail of baby urine, cooked vegetables and disinfectant. 'How are you?'

'Did you bring the crisps?' Agnes asked, allowing him to peck at her cheek.

Agnes didn't know why Duncan wanted to be her boyfriend, and presumed he must like fat, clever girls, which wasn't really the kind of boy she wanted. She wanted someone who'd just climbed off a surfboard, but she occasionally let him run his hands over her flesh just to see his pot-holed face assume that weird, tranced look that boys got at times like that. And at least having Duncan as a boyfriend meant she had a visitor, bringing relief supplies and schoolwork and news of the unreal, outside world. And nicer than her mother, which wasn't difficult.

Agnes's mother – Vera – didn't come every day to the hospital because she was busy in other places, she had a 'little part-time job' and (really frightening this) she was a hospice visitor. Agnes imagined the chill of fear that must descend on the terminally ill when her mother's icy wings wafted over them. 'Pull yourself together,' she could hear her whispering in their dying ears.

Agnes knew that was what her mother said to the dying because it was what she had said to her, the accidentally suicidal child, when she'd discovered her. Agnes was just entering the peaceful passing-out stage (ignorant that this was a temporary lull before entering the triple-Technicolor ride on the rollercoaster from hell), lying on the burnt umber and caramel of the autumn leaves living-room carpet, when she saw Vera's legs, like cartoon legs, moving across the carpet, crunching underfoot Agnes's leftover pills that looked like sweets spewed up by a rainbow ('Rowntrees Of York Give Best In Value'). Agnes wondered what Vera told them in Accident and Emergency, 'My daughter's accidentally swallowed the entire contents of the medicine cabinet'? Yeah, that sounded like Vera.

Jeannie had a lot of visitors – the prison chaplain, the governor, the wardens, even a couple of fellow prisoners. They brought her sweets, flowers, cigarettes, magazines. They pulled up their visitors' chairs eagerly and chatted and threw back their heads and laughed. Jeannie's visitors always made a point of including Agnes in their get-togethers and Agnes began to think that prison didn't look like such a bad place at all and she wouldn't mind ending up there, because, 'After all,' she said to Duncan, indicating the suicide ward, the hospital, the town, the country, the planet and slightly beyond, 'if this is freedom, I'm not impressed.'

Agnes followed Jeannie on her rounds of the babies. Jeannie's already hoarse voice got all chokey when she saw the babies. She claimed to have 'twa weans' of her own, although their whereabouts was mysterious. There were two wards of mothers and babies. The babies all looked remarkably similar; swaddled in their white cellular-cotton blankets they seemed, Agnes thought, like cocoons, all waiting to turn into something.

They must look at the ceiling too, she realized, storing up their first shadowy memories of glossed polystyrene tiles, seventy-two one way, thirty-six the other (their ward was bigger). Agnes wanted to paint them a different ceiling, a celestial view of azure skies and golden, fiery-edged clouds.

The mothers, beached on their beds, weren't very interesting – plump and smug in their cotton nighties with frills and ribbons. They spent a lot of time putting on their make-up and talking about how 'orful' they looked and how they longed for a curry or a visit to the hairdresser. They made Agnes feel sick when they went on like that.

One of the mothers reminded Agnes of Vera – like Vera she thought she knew everything. She was called Dolly, which Agnes thought was a stupid name for a grown woman, and had permed hair, dyed a cough-drop yellow with coal-black roots. Her baby girl had much nicer hair, it was like sooty kitten fur and Agnes would have liked to touch it. Dolly was always knitting, she was knitting her baby's future in the colours of sugared almonds.

There was only one mother that Agnes liked, a girl called Mary with big, soft doe-eyes who was in love with her baby in a way that made the rest of the mothers uneasy.

The babies were nearly all being bottle-fed because the mothers felt breast-feeding was 'disgusting'. Jeannie explained this was because breasts were sexual objects, so it didn't seem right to stuff them into babies' mouths. Agnes looked down at her own large wobbling bosom which seemed to give such pleasure to Duncan. What were they like? Turkish Delight – a thin layer of pale milk-chocolate skin covering a solid, rosy jelly?

The babies were learning about time because the mothers liked to feed them by the clock, reasoning that if they got fed when they were hungry they would become spoilt and demanding. (The generally held belief was that the babies were in a conspiracy against the mothers.) So the babies were left to scream until they were exhausted. The ceremonial feeding ritual was then rigidly adhered to. First they were fed, then they were winded, then they were changed, then they were laid down like little parcels and ignored. Agnes wondered what would happen if they got mixed up by mistake – what if, say, all the little baby parcels were put in a big bran tub – would the mothers be able to pick out the right one?

Agnes herself had been taken home from the maternity hospital by the wrong mother. Of this, if nothing else, she was certain. The Hare Krishna book said that people were given the mother they needed for a particular incarnation, but Agnes couldn't even bring herself to think about why she might need Vera. Somewhere, in the parallel universe where things went right, roamed Agnes's real mother, ladling out milk the colour of Cornish cream. Her real mother was a fierce, hot breathed lioness padding around the hospital grounds. Her real mother was the Queen of the Night, a huge galactic figure who trod the Milky Way in search of her lost child. Her real mother had been one of the ones who dropped garnet red blood on to linen-white snow and picked up shiny jet-black raven feathers and wished her heart out for the perfect baby girl and –

The little blonde midwife with mature acne stood at the door of the ward and shouted to Agnes, 'Your mum's here!' and two startled babies woke up and started crying. 'Bloody hell,' the mother of one muttered under her breath.

Vera ! 'Mum' she was not. Centuries ago she had been 'Mummy' – Agnes had the diary entries to prove this: 'Mummy met me from school and we went and got my hair cut.' 'Mums' were what other children had, Agnes had Vera, so unlabelled as a mother, so lacking a maternal noun (mum, mummy, mother, mam, ma, mama, mom) that Agnes was never able to address her directly.

'You've lost weight,' Vera said, sitting down cautiously on an orange vinyl armchair in the maternity ward day-room.

Agnes looked down doubtfully. She couldn't actually see her feet.

'You're skin and bone,' Vera said.

It was Vera that was skin and bone. Vera's arteries were flat grey electric cables, binding the skin and bone together. She was so thin that when she turned sideways she disappeared. 'You can come home soon,' she said.

'But I haven't had any treatment,' Agnes protested.

'There's nothing wrong with you.'

'I tried to kill myself,' Agnes pointed out.

'Don't exaggerate,' Vera said dismissively. Out of a plastic carrier bag she produced lemon barley water, salted peanuts and banana sandwiches made with sliced white bread. ('Sandwiches were named after the Earl of Sandwich – fact or fiction?' The book was unusally dismissive on the subject of sandwiches, 'It seems unlikely that no one before 1762 had thought of wrapping a couple of slices of bread around a piece of meat.')

'I have to go,' Vera said, getting up, 'I'm needed some where else.'

Jeannie put her head round the door, 'Time for Baby Bath Demonstration!'

Agnes had seen it all before, but it was something to do, so she went through to the maternity ward anyway and observed politely. After all, it might come in useful one day, if she survived long enough to have babies. A baby started crying and someone identified it as Dolly's. 'What does the little bugger want?' Dolly asked no one in particular, her head wobbling rather like a budgerigar's. 'She's been fed, she's been changed. She hasn't got wind,' her voice became threatening, 'but she will have if she goes on like that.' Agnes looked daggers at the back of Dolly's nodding skull, thin silver stilettos that went – Thunk! Thunk! Thunk!

Everyone murmured their sympathy for Dolly. Why babies cried was a mystery, there was no doubt about *that*. The blonde midwife looked up from the soapy-wet baby she was demonstrating on and glared at Dolly's baby. 'It's having a temper tantrum,' she declared.

'You're going home tomorrow,' the red-haired nurse said to Agnes when she wheeled in the supper trolley.

Jeannie jumped off her bed, screeching, 'Aaw – al miss yew, hen!' and pulled Agnes to her scrawny bosom.

'Who says?' Agnes asked, pulling herself free.

'The gynaecologist,' the red-haired nurse said.

'I want to see a psychiatrist,' Agnes said reasonably.

'Wouldn't we all?' the red-haired nurse laughed and bustled out of the ward.

Agnes tiptoed into the nursery where the babies were kept at night. They were taken away from the ward like flowers, perhaps in case they used up all the mothers' oxygen ('fiction'). The babies were all sound asleep, their little mouths half open, their top lips puckered. Sleep rose off them like the vapour of a milky drug. ('Cats suck the breath from sleeping babies – fact or fiction?' Fact.)

Very carefully, Agnes lifted Mary's baby, cradling its head in her hand like the midwife had shown them in Baby Bath Demonstration. The peaceful rhythm of its breathing didn't change as she carried it across to the other side of the room and placed it gently in a spare cot. Then she took Dolly's baby and placed it in Mary's baby's cot. Then she took Mary's baby out of the spare cot and put it in Dolly's baby's cot. *Voilà!*

The reasoning behind this sleight of hand was logical – Mary's baby had already been given a good start in life, whereas Dolly's baby hadn't a chance in hell.

Agnes's father came the next day to take her home. She'd only reached 'Doge' in the encyclopaedia. Liza was left suspended in her dilemma forever. She had a tearful farewell with Jeannie, who kissed her wetly on the cheek and told her she was like 'wan of her ain weans'. Agnes missed the drama later in the day when the prison social worker visited Jeannie and told her, regretfully, that her ain weans had been taken away from her for good.

Agnes walked through the front door of the mock-Tudor semi. At the end of the hallway she could see into the kitchen where her mother was sipping a 'tiny sherry'. Vera turned and said, 'You're back then.' Agnes wondered if this was the real world. Agnes herself didn't feel at all real. She floated along the hallway, the house smelt of roast chicken. 'I'm cooking you a chicken,' she heard Vera say. Beyond her, the back door stood open and Agnes could see the garden – the neatly clipped lawns, the carefully controlled beds of pansies, busy lizzies and nasturtiums. Behind them was the vegetable patch, then the fruit bushes.

But further away was a wood and then a whole forest of birch trees. Agnes floated towards this landscape, buoyant with hope. The vista went on forever rolling on towards steppes, foothills, mountains – wherever it was, it looked a lot like home to Agnes. In an azure sky, fat cherubs bounced on white, woolly clouds. Vera shut the back door quickly. 'And a rice pudding,' she said. 'You like that, don't you?'

They found Jeannie in the hospital grounds the next morning – not such a fraud at all, it turned out. They discovered her hanging from an apple-green tree, one fluffy mule had fallen off and lay on the ground, the other somehow dangled precariously from one toe. Her unslippered toe pointed gracefully towards the ground, you could almost have imagined her in a mid-air jeté as she jumped off into another life.

Mary gazed at her baby, sound asleep in her cot. She picked her up and held her to her breast. The baby purred and smiled the smile of a very lucky baby.

'Look – she's smiling,' Mary said to the blonde midwife who'd just come in.

'Wind,' she replied dismissively.

Mary's real baby began to scream in her cot, noisily protesting at her new life. The red-haired nurse bustled in and picked it up. 'Why do they do that?' she asked the blonde midwife, a look of exasperation on her face.

'If only we knew,' the blonde midwife said, shaking her head, mystified. 'If only we knew.'

The Spirit of the Times

JUDE JONES

MY MUM never knows when I skive now since I met the old girl up at Hob's Lane. Makes me laugh the things I get to do these days and mostly everyone leaves me be which is dead ace. I'd say bugger them all but I ain't allowed to. The old girl stop me from swearing, see? Though I does when she ain't around.

You have to go past the old mill to get to Hob's Lane. It ain't a proper road though. It's a kind of track with this stream by it and you get the cars go along it every now and then but only if they're coming up to the cottages there. It's a 'No Through Road' and it don't even go where it was supposed to go now they built the big motorway past it. No Through is right. There's this high fence at the end and then you turns and has to go back so the folks what walk their dogs there goes mainly round by the woods now and leave the Hob to me.

The old girl told me her name once but it was funny. I mean it weren't the kind of old-fashioned name your mum might have or your gran even. So I lets it go. I calls her Missis and she calls me Nipper and that's OK. We don't like fuss, me and her.

We does chatting mostly. She knows how to gab, she does. Not that she's particular lonesome for all she lives in the water. She got her mates same as me. I know most of them. There's Foreman, he's a slippery old sod. Pretends he's a fish. And Longman, he's the big oak. Then there's Ringman and I tell you about him in a bit.

The old girl says he's shy. I ain't seen Littleman yet. Littleman's whatsit – invisible.

My mum used to bawl me out when I went up the Hob but she's quieter now because we done the change.

When I first seen the Missis I thought it was some bored old wrinkly what topped herself in the stream. I went close to look because I ain't never seen no corpse. Then she sits up, like she was finishing off a sunbathe and I wet me knickers. 'Course she ain't real old. Not underneath. Not like my mum.

*

'What them chaps doing over there?'

'They're building the new motorway, Missis.'

'A road? They're building a bloody road near my stream?'

'Yeah. Why you lying in the water?'

'A bloody road! If that don't beat all!'

'I thought you was dead.'

'Well, I ain't. A bleeding road! You know how noisy them things are?'

'Yeah. You'll get rheumatics, sitting in there. My gran has rheumatics every time she goes out in the rain.'

'Your gran's a wanker, Nipper, and no mistake. Why'd they build here? Why can't they go and mess up some other place?'

'My mum says it'll make getting over to Langley real quick.'

'Your mum's a wanker. Why'd she want to go to Langley to start off with? Bloody awful town.'

'Everyone's a wanker to you, Missis. I reckons as you're a wanker yourself.'

'You hold your tongue, smart arse. And don't swear. 'S'not becoming in a young girl.'

'You swear. You're swearing like buggery.'

'I'm allowed. You're not. You hear me?'

'Why?'

''Cause I says so.'

'I'm fourteen. I'm big enough to swear now. And smoke. My mum don't mind.'

'Your mum ain't brought you up right. What's your dad say?'

''E don't say bloody nothing, do he? I ain't got no dad.'

'Don't bleeding swear, girl. I told you once and I won't tell you again.'

'What'll you do if I does?'

'This.'

'... Oh!... Christ almighty, Missis, how'd you do that?'

'With practice, Nipper. I had lots of practice.'

'Could you show me how to do it?'

'Might. Depends.'

I got ordinary mates too, like I said. Not as many as when I was a kid but that's sort of how things go, ain't it? I got this bloke, Ian. He's leaving school soon but he ain't training for anything except thieving. No jobs round here, see?

I let him do it to me once when we was out down the Rec. I makes him get a thing, you know, a condom thing, because of the HIVs and he didn't know how to put it on. So I done it for him.

It was quite nice but it hurt a bit.

My best mate is Marie. I took her down Hob's a couple of times but the old girl didn't show up. Marie said I was a nutter and I got cross. Then the silly bitch told her mum about what I said about the old girl. Marie didn't say what her mum said back. I was real narked so I stole her trainers and slashed them with my Stanley. She keep her mouth shut now.

I didn't tell Ian about the Hob. Ian thinks he's tough. He'd think I was soft and I ain't. I told Dixey though. Dix is my mum's mate when they ain't slagging each other off. She lives two doors down with her brats. Dix is all right. She just nods and says, 'What, the old cow's still up Hob's Lane?' and carries on frying chips. She don't know nothing about Foreman and Longman though, so I scored there.

My mum give me some grief. Shit, she was a pain. Always going on about what time I come home at night just because some silly little prat has got herself done in over on the Park estate. She wanted me to be a nurse! A nurse, I ask you! And tight. God, tight as a duck's arse. Mind you, I don't have to bother with that lot nowadays. The old girl saw to it. She's got some sense, I'll give her that.

Mind you, the Missis come over mean when I tell her I seen Foreman down in the square drinking with the alkies. She tells me to hold my tongue and gives me a shiv when I cheeks her. I don't mind though. I'm going to learn how to do it back. Stands to reason, don't it? Like we was saying in Community Studies last term, it's everybody for theirselves, ain't it? Because there ain't nothing else to do. Nobody else cares about you but you. That's what the old boss, that Thatcher woman said and I agrees. The Missis calls it survival of the fittest which is what she said she'd done. Yeah, well, I'm pretty fit. And I don't take no crap.

Anyway here's how I first went up the Ridge.

The old girl says one day she's off on her travels, yeah? Could have knocked me over – I was gobsmacked. I never seen her walk about much, see? Most of the time she sits around in her stream like it was a chair in front of the telly. Every now and again she'll come and squat down besides me on the bank and wave at the cars when they goes past. But I never seen her walk about before. So I says, 'Where you going then?'

'Why? You want to come along, Nipper?' she says.

I caught the old bus and got off at Yalderton. Stupid bloody place – not even a shop. Mainly farmhouses and snotty kids riding horses. I walked up the big hill like she said and threshed around in the wood at the top for a bit. Full of sodding stingers it was. And wet and muddy in spite of it being late June and dry everywhere else.

She was halfway down the other side under this great yew tree sitting in a kind of pond thing like it was her own personal swimming pool. I suppose there must've been a spring coming out up above somewhere. Mind you, I wasn't going to mess my tights up finding out. Too many spiky trees around. Too many bloody bushes. I was cut to pieces, you can believe it. When I comes down to her I sees the old tree she's underneath is all hung up with bits of rag and scraps of cloth like it's some kind of mad washing line. Dead weird it looked.

She was making a kind of singing, droning noise too when I comes down. It had words to it. They goes:

> *'Dance, Ringman, dance,*
> *Dance, my good men, every one,*
> *For Ringman, he can dance alone,*
> *Ringman, he can dance alone.'*

Out of her barrel, I thinks. Always was loopy but gone and ripped her hairnet now.

'You been doing your washing, Missis?'
'What? Quiet, kiddo, or I'll smash you good.'
'You finished singing yet?'
'Yeah, I finished now.'
'What you doing up here?'
'Visiting.'
'Who you visiting? I don't see no one.'
'See that stone there?'
'What, the big one?'
'That's Ringman.'
'That's Ringman? Where is he then?'
'Told you before, girl. He's shy.'
'He won't come out like Longman does, you mean?'
'Might do.'
'Them blokes, Longman and Foreman. They ghosts?'
'Ghosts? Nah, Nipper. They're real. Same as you and me. They ain't dead, you know.'
'What's Ringman doing in that stone?'
'Waiting.'
'What's he waiting for?'
'Tonight.'
'What's happening tonight?'
'Depends.'
'Oh, come off it, Missis. Tell us. I ain't come all this way in that stupid bus just to fuck about.'
'You watch your language, girl. Or...'
'Or what, then?'
'Or Ringman might decide he don't like you, after all.'
'What d'you mean?'
'He's good looking, Ringman is. A sight better looking'n that wanker Ian you mess with.'

'So what?'

'If you was to play your cards right Ringman might make you his girl.'

'What if I don't want to be his girl?'

'I reckon you will. Oh yes, Nipper, there ain't much doubt about that.'

'What's he like?'

'Oh, he's nice, Ringman is. And he's good. Very, very good.'

My mum made one hell of a stink when I didn't come back that night. There were pigs out all over the place looking for me. God, the fuss they made. Where was I? Who did I talk to. Did I get raped?

Raped! Took most of my cool, but I kept a straight face. I mean, who'd tell the fuzz about the old girl and the bloke? Bloody fascists, the lot of them. And my mum, she raved so much I reckoned it was funny-farm time for her. Tried to ground me, she did. Locks me up in my room. But I got to go to the bathroom now and then, ain't I? And when I goes, it ain't my fault if the window's just above the extension roof. And it sure ain't my fault if I just tests it to see if I can climb down. Which I done nice and quick. Then I borrows old Dixey's bike and cycled the six mile up to Yalderton Ridge for another visit with the bloke.

It was all them social bloody workers what made me do it. If she'd have left them out I might have let her be. But she always had to be in charge, did my mum. I suppose I didn't mind when I was a kid but now I tells her I'm a grown woman she just laughs at me. And I won't have that.

I thought maybe the old girl could do something about it. And I thought right. Mind you, the old girl give me one hell of a time joshing me but I sticks to my guns.

'How'd you like it,' I says, 'if you had some prying old cow asking you questions night and day about everything you does and getting a pack of half-arsed women coming around too? Bloody nosy bl– idiots. Would I like to change school? Am I happy? Happy? 'Course I'm ruddy happy long as they leave me alone.'

The old girl had a little brood and she says she'll fix it for me. Which she done.

I got to roar each time I think about it. She got made up as one of them social workers, see? She come visiting my mum. They shuts theirselves in the kitchen and I hears Mum making her a brew and later they comes out and the old girl goes off. Didn't even look at me, she didn't, but she grab my hand niftyish and squeezes it and I knows she's pulled a stunt.

Mum went all pale after that like she'd had the spunk taken out of her and she stop fussing and telling me off and trying to keep me home. It was as easy as peasy. It was wicked. Excellent.

Dixey come round next day. 'What's the matter with Lynda?' she asks me. 'Why's she gone so quiet?'

'Dunno. Got a cold, probably,' I says.

Dix give me a nasty look and I gives her one back. And that worked too. She goes off like a little white mouse and don't even give me no grief for cheeking her while she's going.

It was more or less the same the rest of term. What's more I got bloody good at cycling.

In August Mum says Uncle Mick's given her some dosh and she wants to go to Majorca with Dix and her brats. I says that's well OK by me just as long as I don't have to go. And that was OK with them. So I nicked Dix's tent and went up to the Ridge. I was there all August with the bloke and he weren't shy at all.

In September he goes back to sleep so I comes down again and gets back in harness. I don't mind school too much, see? They learnt to treat me right now. In fact, I got school taped.

'What you done to all them creeps, Missis?'

'What creeps?'

'All them folks at school and my Mum and Dixey. All them people.'

'I ain't done nothing to them.'

'You must've. They don't mind what I do. They don't even mind me thieving and smashing things.'

'I ain't done nothing to them. I done something to you.'

'What you done, then?'

'That'd be telling, Nipper. You just be grateful I done it.'

'It ain't wrong, is it, what you done?'

'You slimy little squirt! I never heard such hypocrisy in all my born. You really take the cake, you do! You beat the rest of them hands down.'

'What you mean? What rest of them?'

'You think you're the only little tart I've ever talked to?'

'Yeah, I did... You ever talked to Dixey Foster?'

'Might have. Yeah, I remember. Snotty so and so she was. She weren't no good.'

'No good for what?'

'No good for nothing.'

'What about me, then? I'm good, am I?'

'Ringman says you are.'

'How long's Ringman going to kip for?'

'You missing it? I could get you some more, you know.'

'He woken up then?'

'Not Ringman. Someone else.'

'Who?'

'Longman's good at it. He's even better than Ringman.'

'I don't fancy Longman though.'

'Oh, you will, love, you will.'

*

In October I missed my third period and I got dead worried. I went to see the old girl and she thought it was a right joke, she did. I goes on about an abortion but she really let rip. I'd got to have the kid according to her. Abortions wasn't right. I told her it was all right for her to say that. She wasn't in the club.

She took me to see Longman. He was down by the copse over near the motorway works. He wanted to touch me but I told him to bugger off. He weren't nothing like as smashing as Ringman. I wasn't having him but the old girl said he knew how to fix it so it wouldn't show until it was time to get the bloody thing out and if I did it with him she might look after the brat herself when it come. So I let him and after that I didn't mind what he looked like just so's he didn't stop.

The old girl was a soft touch then so I got her to show me how to do the shiv.

I practised on everybody. My mum, Dix, the brats at school, creeps in the street. I got the Head. I even got Ian's dudes one time when they was feeling the mean Fridays and was all tanked up. I got them real good and nowadays they don't call me those names no more.

When it was Christmas I asked my mum for everything I could think of. Make-up, clothes, Nike trainers, a Walkman, a music centre with a CD player, you name it I wanted it and she come up sweet. Don't know where she found the juice to pay for all them things because you don't get big money working at the Co-op but I wasn't going to argue. Dixey give me lots too. Best Christmas I ever had and I made Mum let Longman stay nights with me. Up to then we'd been doing it outside but I never did enjoy getting my arse frozen off, though he didn't seem to mind the frigging frost. She didn't say much about Longman being there, except on Christmas Day when she bawled a bit when we stayed in bed. But then, she was getting proper grey round the gills. I reckoned she weren't long for this world, see?

I stopped going down the Hob when the weather turned nasty. I ain't good in the rain and after Christmas Longman just stayed in with us, fiddling with my CD and screwing me and that was like all I wanted. Besides the old girl had shown me how to do the shiv so sod her, I thought.

Past the New Year though, that bugger Longman ups and leaves. One minute he was listening to some old Motown crap of Mum's on the music centre – the next he's halfway down the garden path. I went after him yelling but he just gets over the fence into the field next door and disappears. I swears fit to bust. Who cares about the odd swear? The old girl ain't there.

Sneaky bastard, that Longman. After all I done for him!

I waits for him to come back that night but he didn't and I got mad. So I went round town doing the shiv to any creep what asked for it. Then I met some geyser coming out a pub and I let him do it to me round the back. He weren't much cop but he give me a tenner and that paid for a few drinks.

Up at the Ridge there weren't no sign of Ringman neither and I laddered my best tights climbing about round them bastard bushes looking for him.

'There ain't nothing for it,' I says to myself, 'I'll have to go and see the old girl.'

But you wouldn't credit it, when I goes up Hob's she taken a bloody powder too.

I got right moody that January, see?

'*Missis! Where you been?*'

'*Around, girl. Where you been?*'

'*Looking for you.*'

'*You're a bare-faced liar, Nipper. I hope you passed a merry Christmas.*'

'*Yeah, it was great. Look, where the hell's Longman?*'

'*He had to go.*'

'*Where? When's he coming back?*'

'*Stone me, I never seen a girl so desperate for sex as you, love. Proper little nymphomaniac, you is.*'

'*Oh shut it, Missis. Just tell me where Longman's hiding out.*'

'*Don't you tell me to shut it, Nipper. You try and remember I don't take no cheek.*'

'*I ain't frightened of you, Missis. I knows what I knows. I can hurt you too now.*'

'*Oh no, dear. No, no, no. You can't pull no tricks on me. I ain't made quite the same as other folks and you never knows what I might do next if you was to try it, hey? It don't make sense to make me mad, do it?*'

'*Nah, well, all right. Just as long as you tell me where Longman is.*'

'*Ah yes, Longman. Well, Nipper, Longman's having his kip.*'

'*Like Ringman?*'

'*Yeah, just like Ringman. But don't you fret. They'll wake up in time.*'

'*In time for what?*'

'*For the baby, sweetheart. For the birth. And afterwards.* '

'*But what about... ?*'

'*I can arrange that too, girl. I arranged the rest, didn't I? Look at you! No unsightly lump. No morning sickness. No backaches. No funny cravings. A fifteen-year old sylph, you is. And so pretty. It'd make Foreman's heart melt to look at you.*'

'*Foreman! I ain't going with Foreman!*'

'*Foreman's better even than Longman.*'

'*Oh, come on, Missis. Foreman's a nasty old sod. I seen him down the square, evenings. He's dirty and he smells. The lads throw their cans at him when he's pissed. I seen him throw up all over the bus shelter. He's well out of order.*'

'*Never judge by the outside, Nipper. If I'd have judged by your outside you would never have got where you is now.*'

'*What d'you mean?*'

'You ever look in the mirror? You look incredible clean, girl, like some kid's Barbie Doll. You're so pretty, you're boring. But I thinks hard when I sees you and I waits till I sees your insides. Then I knows.'

'What? What you know?'

'You're the spirit of the age, see? The times. What you are is what this place is. You're what they calls an epitome. See, I likes to take what I can and I likes to get it right. I likes an accurate reflection and I likes to enter into the spirit of the thing, you get me?'

'What you mean, Missis? Can't you talk straight?'

'Oh sure, little Gemma. I can talk straight. Yeah, I can do that. So. You want a man, right?'

'I want Longman.'

'Ah no, ducks, you want Foreman. I can get you Foreman. Come on, now. Let's have a little sing. Join in. You know this one...

> 'Dance, Foreman, dance.
> Dance, my good men, every one.
> For Foreman, he can dance alone.
> Foreman, he can dance alone. . .'

'No, Missis, not him.'

'Ah, here he is, sweetheart. You just take a look in his trousers. Go on, don't be shy. Go on, take a peek.'

'No, Missis...'

'Where's the harm?'

All February Mum was like a zombie from Outer Space. She didn't seem to notice me and Foreman rabbiting about in the house at all. In the morning she went down the Co-op and then she come back home at tea-time knackered and quiet and sat in front of the telly till it was time for bed.

Dix come in some nights with her kids and they all sits down by the telly and just watches and watches. It don't matter what. They watches whatever. One night I gets up out of bed and I goes down to the front room and watches them. I get the flipper switch and fiddles around all over the shop. I give them a bit of Channel Four film in Frog where you has to read the words and they don't seem to mind that and then we goes over to *Newsnight* with a couple of geysers droning on about the economy and they don't turn a hair. I messes round till one. The silly buggers was lapping it all up. I finishes with this programme with some arty doctor chap blathering on about the meaning of life to a load of short-haired hippies and it was so boring I wanted to shiv the lot. But did my zombies bat an eyelid?

When I turns the set off they all got up, still being the Living Bloody Dead and Dix and her brood goes back home and Mum goes upstairs.

I says to Foreman about it when I went back. But he grabs me and starts to do it again and I forgets about them being crazy because you can't think about nothing else when Foreman's doing it.

He goes out every now and again does Foreman to get rat-arsed and he don't let me tag along. So I goes over to Langley when he does and I tarts about down round the town centre. He don't care. He knows I'll bring him some cans back anyway.

I got a bank account now.

End of March Mum got pinched. She'd been thieving from the till and the fuzz arrive and haul her off down the nick for a couple of days. My Uncle Mick come over from Fosshampton and bailed her out. He said he thought she'd get off with a fine because she ain't got no record and what the hell was the matter with her? I says I reckons she's sick but she won't see a doctor. He wanted to know who Foreman was and when I says he's my bloke he cut up nasty. Starts bad-mouthing him. I give Mick a well-lethal shiv and he shut his mouth and pissed off sharpish. Good riddance to bad rubbish I told Foreman but he just grunted and rolled over.

I near on gived up school. Who needs it? Sometimes I goes in for Community Studies now and again so's I can sound off and listen to them all agreeing with me like a load of sheep. It's a bit of a giggle and I just does it for fun, see? I might go in for politics perhaps. I'd be good at that.

When April come I got this bad turn. It wouldn't have happened if Foreman had stayed home like he was supposed to. But no, the bastard's got a big thirst and he's off down town. So I done my eyes over and nips across to Langley on the train. I done a few tricks and I thought I'd swank around the Town Hall bars and pick up some more trade but halfway along up the High I gets ill. Real ill. And while I'm trying to spew up and wondering what the hell it was I ate I hears this ripping sound and me best bloody dress starts splitting away at the seams. I got the sodding biggest bun in the oven you ever see. All at once. One minute a size twelve – the next I'm practically ten months gone! With my dress hanging around like I been in a hurricane. And Christ, did it sting! I starts bawling out and screaming and it being Saturday I gets a decent crowd. Some old classy bint comes out from one of the posh side streets and starts bossing my audience about. They get me an ambulance and about time too I says when I gets in because I'm wet all down my legs. Waters broken says one of the ambulance creeps and so I gets rushed into St Cath's with all the deedoos going.

Didn't take long to push the nipper out but it really bloody hurt. I ain't going through that, never again. I looks down at my belly after and I got these bastard scars just above my hips. Stretch marks says the nurse. And my breasts are all hard and big and they're leaking for God's sake! They wants me to breast feed but I ain't having none of that. Sodding disgusting. The kid'll make do with powdered milk, I tells the sister and I gives her the mean eye. Stopped her mid-lecture, that did.

Mum come in to see me the next day and she just sits there beside the bed staring at the kiddie as though it was something amazing. When the bell goes, end of visiting, she gets up and stomps off without a word to me like 'How are you?' or 'What can I get you?' Charming.

Next day I gets up and nicks some clothes out of a side ward while the woman's in the bog and I gets dressed and takes the babe and discharges myself. I'm going straight off to give the old girl a piece of my mind. What did she think she was doing playing a trick on me like that, hey?

'Ah, you had the kiddie, did you, Nipper? Let's have a look at her.'

'Yeah, no thanks to you. I thought you was going to take care of me?'

'Well, I did, didn't I? Best to have the baby in a nice clean hospital with lots of doctors and nurses to keep an eye on you.'

'I thought you was going to do it for me?'

'What, you mean you thought it'd be nice having the kiddie out here by my insanitary little stream? I ain't no midwife, sweetie, I never said I was. Or did you think I was going to have it for you? I ain't no bloody conjuror neither.'

'Ain't you?'

'Not so's you'd notice. A harmless eccentric, that's me.'

'Where's Foreman then? I stopped off home and he's gone.'

'Ah, yes. Well, Foreman got tired.'

'What you mean, Foreman got tired?'

'They all have to have their sleep, dear. You're a demanding girl, see? You exhaust them after a while.'

'But what am I going to do now? What about me?'

'Oh, I got a treat lined up for you, sweetheart, but you has to wait.'

'What treat? Why do I have to wait for it?'

'You heard me talk about Littleman, ain't you?'

'Yeah. But Littleman's invisible, you says.'

'True. But on a certain night in the year he ain't. He's good solid flesh just the same as the rest of us.'

'So what?'

'He wants you. He wants you bad. He wants you so bad that he thinks he might spend the whole of his one night with you.'

'Listen, Missis, why the shit should I get worked up about that?'

'Language. Because, Nipper, Littleman's better than Ringman and Longman and Foreman all rolled into one. He's the best there is. The tops. And the things he can teach you. The power he can give you. Makes me feel faint just to think about it.'

'What sort of power?'

'Ooh, real power. The power to get what you want just like that. You can have money, clothes, servants, fast cars, villas in the South of France, men, anything you bleeding like.'

'But I got that now.'

'No, love, what you got now's just a shadow of what you could have if you let Littleman spend the night with you.'

'If it's so good why don't you go with him instead of me?'

'It's you he wants, sweetie. He only wants you, see? And as for me I get my thrills by seeing you enjoy your self. I like your appetite, Gemma. It feeds me.'

'What d'you mean?'

'Forget it. Just you nip up to Yalderton Ridge the last day of the month and I promise, you'll have the night of your life.'

'I don't know. I'll think about it.'

'Don't think about it, girl, do it. I ever let you down before?'

'No. Well, I dunno. I might. OK? I might. 'Bye. See you.'

'Aren't you forgetting something?'

'What?'

'Your baby, Nipper. Your little baby what you're going to give me to look after like you said you would.'

'What you want her for, Missis?'

'I got a kind heart, see? I reckons you might neglect the little one once you got your hands on Littleman. Give us the baby, sweetheart, and I'll see she wants for nothing a mother can give her.'

'I don't know...'

'Come off it, Nipper. You truly want a baby hanging round your neck once you're gallivanting round the world with your men friends?'

'Suppose not. All right. But I'll check up on her, see?'

'Good girl. You'd be unnatural if you didn't want to see her now and then. You just come and ask and I'll show her to you. OK?'

'Yeah, suppose so.'

'And don't forget. Be up the Ridge on the thirtieth. You won't regret it.'

'Might.'

It was hard waiting. Even though it was only a couple of weeks I was close to busting. Most nights I went down town trolling but it was stupid. After Foreman it didn't seem as if any guy I could find to screw knew how to do it. I started to dream about bloody Littleman and woke up howling. Mum took no notice. Once I'd got rid of the brat she'd lost interest. She was on the Social now because the Co-op wouldn't take her back. Hardly surprising, silly bitch! Fancy thinking she could get away with lifting money out the till! Still, she was quiet enough and give me no cheek when I got iffy which I do regular when I has to go without it.

Christ, them days went slow. Sometimes I'd plan out what I was going to do once I'd got this extra zip the old girl had said I'd get. I'd buy myself a Rolls or better still, a Chevvy, and I'd get a hunk to be my chauffeur and I'd go on the biggest spending spree anybody ever went on. Other times I'd think up faces for Littleman – Nick Nolte or Kevin Costner – and then

I'd think about what the rest of him'd look like and groan. Yeah, it was a shitty time for me. Had to go round with crossed legs most days.

When the day come I was in the bath all afternoon. I shaved my pits, my legs, near on everywhere. I done myself up real careful and got my black dress out so's to look dead seductive. Not what you might call suitable for messing around in the woods up on the Ridge but the weather was fine and I'd got a spare pair of stockings ready.

In the bus going up there I was so fidgety I had to keep on changing seats. The bus creep tells me to sit down but I don't shiv him because we can do without a sodding crash. Jesus, I was impatient. I kept thinking when I was the boss round here I'd get the buses to stop only two or three times. This bloody bus stopped all over the shop. It even bloody stopped when there wasn't anybody wanting to get on. So I started to think about how I'd zap creeps when I come into my power. How I could even zap the old girl. Teach her a few lessons. A little respect. And then I goes back to thinking about Littleman. My hands is sweating and that's a sure sign I'm ready for it. Christ, was I ready!

It was near dark when I gets off but I knows my way up the Ridge backwards since last summer and I belted up and tore through the wood heading for Ringman's stone. There weren't no sign of Littleman so I sat down to catch my breath. After a while I hears the old girl singing bloody Top of the Pops. I can do without this, I thinks, but I knows better than to interrupt. Somewhere away in the woods she's droning on as usual:

> *'Dance, Littleman, dance,*
> *Dance, my good men, every one,*
> *For Littleman, he can't dance alone,*
> *Littleman, he can't dance alone.'*

Oh, so Littleman can't dance alone, hey? He needs a girl to make him dance. I'm bloody trembling now at the thought.

It were getting real dark but I knew Ringman when he steps out from behind his stone and I knew Longman and Foreman who come with him. I know them by their smells, specially Foreman. They comes up and touches me sort of gentle and exciting and in a little I begins to pant. They carries me into the wood and we comes to a clearing place and they puts me down very careful, still stroking away. Then I sees the old girl sitting on a log, smiling at me like I was her true nipper and she lifts her hand and points over to a dark corner and crouching there is Littleman. I wants him straight away. He's big and blond and he looks at me like he ain't ate for a year. Well, he can eat me all right.

'Gemma,' says the Missis, 'let me introduce you to your dad.'

I begins to laugh and then I sees she ain't joking. For a minute I wonder whether I should run off but my legs is all weak. I licks my lips and goes hot.

I says, 'What the hell? I'll try anything once.'

I takes off my clothes and lays down inviting in the middle of the clearing.

Headline story, Langley Evening Argus, 15 May 1992:

MURDER VICTIM USED IN SATANIC RITES?

The body of a young girl, found yesterday in woodland below Yalderton Ridge, was today identified as that of fifteen-year-old Gemma Hearnesley of 14, Coebrook Grove, Grigbourne. Her badly mutilated and partially eaten remains were discovered by a farmer's dog in a remote spot below the Ridge.

Chief Inspector David Marsh of the County Constabulary, who is in charge of the case, stated categorically today that the police are treating Gemma's death as murder. Police from all over the county were out in force this afternoon combing the area for clues to Gemma's assailant.

Chief Inspector Marsh went on to say that although the body was naked and had remained concealed for about a fortnight, forensic reports showed that there was no sign of a sexual assault made on the victim. However there were certain indications at the scene of the crime which suggested that she might have been subjected to some form of black magic ritual, though the evidence as yet is far from conclusive. Her other injuries have been ascribed to scavenging animals.

Two men, Neil Hogarth (31) and Dougal Smith (23) were arrested in the early hours of the morning after tip-offs from local people. Both men are members of a group of New Age Travellers encamped on common land near Yalderton Heath and have been described as Satanists. Later they were released after questioning.

Mrs Lynda Hearnesley, the mother of the victim, was unavailable for comment. However, all day, letters of support and comfort have been arriving at her Grigbourne home from relatives and friends. This afternoon some of Gemma's classmates delivered flowers and messages of sympathy to her door, shocked and stunned by the news of her death. Mrs Hearnesley's neighbour, Mrs Dixey Foster, said that Gemma's mother was too distressed to comment. She added, 'Gemma was a lovely girl, popular with us all. Nothing was ever too much for her. When her mother was ill earlier on this year Gemma nursed her devotedly through it. We are all horrified to hear of her death and the sooner the police catch the madman who did this the better.'

Another neighbour expressed his opinion that the reintroduction of capital punishment would act as a deterrent for this type of crime.

Moira Flaherty

JULIET McCARTHY

BIRTHDAYS WERE never celebrated in my family. There were only the two of us, my mother and I, and she looked upon the traditional milestones which other people celebrated in their lives with scepticism.

'Ah, sure they're only a year closer to the grave. What's there to be so happy about?'

But I remember the summer I turned fifteen with special clarity. It was the summer I met Moira Flaherty, a young woman from Tullamore in Tipperary. She was a girl really, hardly much older than I and she was on her honeymoon.

I always loved the name Moira. I wished my parents had given me an Irish name instead of Teresa. Moira sounded wild and provocative, a little like the girl that lurked beneath my colourless exterior. I was named after the Little Flower, Saint Teresa, who got to be a saint by being obedient and kind and doing ordinary chores without complaint. I was afraid that by being christened Teresa I was in some way predestined to be humble and self-effacing, qualities I noticed were not particularly admired, not even by the nuns at school who favoured the girls who were saucy and bright.

In my adolescent ardour I preferred saints like Joan of Arc who led armies and died at the stake or the beautiful virgin martyrs who were blinded or beheaded for their faith. I would die for my religion but even then I did not know whether or not I would have the courage to live day in and day out like the patient Saint Teresa.

Of course, I've since learned that it's often easier to die for one's beliefs than to have to live up to them and that perhaps Saint Teresa was more heroic than all the virgin martyrs put together. But that was before I met Moira Flaherty, Mrs Flaherty. I never exactly met her. We were never formally introduced and she only stayed at the hotel for three days, but I have never forgotten her.

My mother and I were on holiday in Dublin, an unprecedented thing really, for a family of our means from the country, but Mother read a great deal and had aspirations for her only child. She was a widow, a housekeeper for an English doctor and his family, and despite the fact that she despised them and ridiculed their airs, she often imitated them and had definitely acquired their taste for the finer things in life.

In addition to seeing the tourist attractions in Dublin, we spent hours on Grafton Street browsing in expensive department stores and admiring the fine linen and crystal.

The hotel where we were staying was not unlike a dozen others in the neighbourhood. It had once been a private home. It stood in a row of identical Georgian houses overlooking a park. Neither time nor diminished circumstances had altered the elegance of the simple brick facade with its delicate wrought-iron railings and graceful fanlight that beckoned over the front door. It was owned by an enterprising Dubliner named Julia Dowd. Guests could get room and board for a reasonable fare if they did not mind doing without a private bath or toilet. In those days one did not run into many foreigners staying in the small, private establishments. The Americans preferred hotels like the Shelborne and the Gresham, close to the shops and the theatre. Mrs Dowd's guests were mostly Irish or English or an occasional German who complained about the lack of heat and the general inattention to housekeeping.

I thought the Vicenza, as it was grandiloquently named, was lovely. I never tired of admiring the imitation Turkey carpets or the sombre collection of portraits that adorned the parlour walls. I especially looked forward to meals, when all the guests crowded into the dining room to sit at their appointed tables and be served by three sullen-looking girls who also did the washing up, as well as making the beds and doing the linens. Conversation was at a minimum. The people were no less formal or friendly because they were few in numbers or shared the same bathtub.

The maids were pleasant to me, I suppose because they seldom saw anyone very young. Mrs Dowd catered to the middle-aged. She did not want any high spirits to disturb her guests or ruin her reputation.

It was the maids who had alerted me to Moira Flaherty's impending arrival and provided me with the titillating information that she was on her honeymoon. They were much more knowledgeable about such things than I but the four of us were beside ourselves with excitement over the prospect of having a new bride under the same roof. Would she be pretty? Shy? Nervous? What of the groom? I spent the entire day wondering about them and anticipating their arrival.

My mother and I were in the parlour when the taxi finally deposited the celebrated couple on the doorstep. Lucy opened the door for them and saw to their baggage while Mrs Dowd steered them into the parlour for a glass of sherry to revive their spirits after the long train ride.

I could hardly take my eyes off the new Mrs Flaherty. Her navy-blue suit was inexpensive and ill-fitting and she tottered clumsily on brand-new, white heels. But to me, unsophisticated and impressionable, she looked radiant. Her skin was fair, not sallow like mine. No one would have asked her if she felt unwell. In fact, we both had blue eyes and red hair, only the colour of her eyes was like the sky on a brilliant June day and mine looked like its reflection in a cloudy pool. Her hair was long and curly, not limp, well-behaved curls, but a lively, confused mass of ringlets that seemed to have a life of their own and refused to be tamed by the silver barrettes that held them off her face. She looked like a schoolgirl sitting there with her knees together and her hands folded in her lap, not like a bride. The only concession to the occasion was a spray of white roses pinned to the lapel of her suit.

I tried to catch her eye, to smile at her. I wanted to let her know that she was among friends but she didn't look at anyone in the room. She kept her eyes fastened on a portrait of a woman that hung over the mantel. Years of having pride of place above the grate had left a grey film of soot and grime over the painting so that the colour and details were no longer distinct, although one could still perceive the haughty expression on the woman's face. She looked as if she could not abide hanging on the wall in the cluttered parlour. A sneer of distaste grazed her thin, pale lips.

Mrs Dowd hovered solicitously over the newlyweds. She spoke in a low, ingratiating manner, exchanging trivial confidences with Mr Flaherty about a mutual acquaintance in Kilkenny, the gentleman who had recommended Mrs Dowd's establishment to the groom. They both ignored Moira.

What, I thought, had that beautiful girl seen in Mr Flaherty? He was at least twice her age, a respectable farmer no doubt, from the looks of him, but dour. When he wasn't talking his mouth turned down at the corners and there was a perpetual frown on his forehead. His hair was thinning and even though he had tried to comb it artfully to disguise the fact, one could see his scalp, pink and tender as a baby's where it was protected from the sun under his hat. His face and hands were deeply lined.

I loathed him. I was physically revolted by his appearance which I examined with the cruel, critical eye of a child, noting the fierce eyebrows and coarse, grey hairs curling out of his ears. The handsome young man I had envisioned sweeping his bride up the staircase had turned out to be old and ugly. I did not have the heart to finish my hot chocolate.

Reluctantly Mrs Dowd arose and suggested the couple retire. As if on cue Mr Flaherty stood up and beckoned his wife. She thanked Mrs Dowd for the sherry which she had barely touched and followed him out into the hall. He mounted the steps slowly and solemnly as if he did not want to appear too eager to be closeted away with his bride, for despite his nonchalance, he could not have been indifferent to the bemused and curious onlookers who watched them ascend the stairs.

I wondered if anyone had remembered to put a few shillings in the meter to take the chill off the room, but then Moira Flaherty was undoubtedly used to undressing in bleak rooms and sliding between sheets that stung with the cold. Perhaps Lucy had drawn a bath for her so she could undress in private away from the scrutiny of that dreadful man. I hoped so. I couldn't bear the thought of him watching her while she went through the ritual of undressing, unfastening her skirt and letting it slide down over her hips, peeling off her stockings and stuffing them into the toes of her shoes, unbuttoning her blouse and exposing her breasts in the flimsy little bra.

The parlour, which was always decidedly chilly, suddenly felt warm and oppressive and I started to perspire. The woollen vest my mother made me wear to protect my chest from the dampness started to itch under my jumper and I could feel my cheeks burning.

Mother and I were about to retire when Mrs Dowd returned. 'I gave them my best suite,' she said. 'I picked some flowers from the garden and put them in a vase on the nightstand. Made it a little special.' She leaned over in what she thought must have been out of my earshot and said: 'It's not often I have honeymooners staying here.' She rolled her eyes as if to emphasize the excitement and delicacy of the situation. Mother nodded.

'Most young people want someplace a little fancier or else they can't afford to go away at all. But Mr Flaherty is the sensible kind.' She smiled. 'He's very comfortable. Owns a dairy in Tullamore. If you ask me that girl has done very well for herself, a young snip of a thing from the looks of her.'

My mother did not look up but I could tell from the tone of her voice that she was annoyed with Mrs Dowd.

'He looked a bit old for her,' she said. I couldn't believe it. My mother, who disdained idle gossip, discussing two strangers with that nosy old busy-body. My mouth must have opened in disbelief for she shot me a withering glance.

'Why, he's a widower,' Mrs Dowd said by way of explanation. 'His wife died last year of a tumour. He's three children older than the bride.' That seemed to tickle her. 'Didn't waste time finding another, did he? If he's not careful he'll have a whole new litter. Now just tell me why a fine man like Mr Flaherty would want a silly shopgirl for a wife,' she said indignantly, but she didn't sound very convincing. She sounded as if she knew the answer.

Mother must have cast one of her deadly glances in the direction of Mrs Dowd for she looked taken aback and apologized for forgetting there was a child present.

'Well, and I'm sure they'll be quite happy all the same,' she said sweetly. She patted my cheek. 'Wasn't Mrs Flaherty lovely now? What a complexion. Only Ireland has girls that look like that.'

Why, oh, why, wasn't I one of those raving Irish beauties, I thought sadly. I wouldn't waste myself on a balding middle-aged farmer.

Mother gathered up her things. 'Come along, Teresa,' she said. 'It's getting late and we have a big day ahead of us.' We went up the stairs, down the narrow hall, past the room where Moira Flaherty was confined with her bridegroom. There was a sliver of light shining under the door.

In the morning at breakfast the maids were unusually cheerful. They kept nudging one another and blushing and when they disappeared behind the swinging door into the pantry one could hear them giggling and whispering. The other guests did not seem to notice, but I knew the object of their mirth was the empty table in the corner reserved for Mr and Mrs Flaherty.

Breakfast was served from seven-thirty until nine. Promptly at nine the breakfast dishes were cleared away and the table set for tea. Lucy was preparing to dismantle the table when the couple walked into the dining-room. They made their way between the tables and sat down facing one another. I was relieved to have an unobstructed view of husband and wife.

Mr Flaherty was wearing his Sunday suit and white starched shirt with a stiff, detachable collar that pressed on the folds of his neck. It looked like he was being garrotted, the knot from his tie squeezing the air out of his pipes and turning the fleshy furrows of skin purple. He had cut himself while shaving and there was a gathering clot of blood on his chin which he kept blotting with his handkerchief. His expression was unchanged from the previous evening, the deep line between his brows, the mouth that turned down at the corners. He propped *The Times* on the table in front of him while his bride poured the tea.

I had expected, what? To see some sort of transformation, at least in the girl. But there she sat in the same navy suit with the identical, enigmatic expression on her face. What secrets did she know? How had she changed? How could she face a room full of strangers with such indifference?

When we returned from Mass Lucy took me aside in the upstairs hall and good-naturedly confirmed my worst suspicions.

'How do you know?' I asked incredulously. She laughed.

'The sheets. You can always tell by the sheets.' I was confused, but I did not doubt that Lucy knew what she was talking about. She seemed to be an authority on those unfathomable rites.

Mr and Mrs Flaherty appeared regularly at all the meals. They never conversed. He sat staring at his plate or the newspaper and she picked at her food or, when he signalled, poured the tea. She was careful to fill the cup exactly half full with hot milk and add two heaping teaspoons of sugar.

I saw her one morning when she was coming from the bath. She had a raincoat on over her nightgown. She seemed startled to meet me in the hall and brushed by without a word. I watched her open the door and go into her room, hoping to catch a glimpse of, I know not what, but I was disappointed. The only thing I saw before she closed the door was the vase full of wilted flowers on the nightstand.

The last time I saw Moira Flaherty was the day she was leaving to go home. I found her on the landing, leaning on the window-sill gazing out over the rooftops. It was a warm day, the window was open and she had discarded her jacket. When she saw me she turned and smiled.

'It's a grand day, isn't it?'

'Oh, yes,' I said, startled by her attention.

'You're not from around here, are you?' she asked. I shook my head. 'I could never live in the city,' she said, which surprised me because I thought all young people longed for the excitement and gaiety of Dublin. My friends and I talked constantly of the time when we would move to the city and put our country ways behind us. I leaned on the window-sill and tried to imitate the wistful, faraway look in her eyes. We were the same height.

'I'm going home today,' she said. She had kicked off her shoes and was standing barefoot on the faded carpet. Her feet were surprisingly small and dainty and her toenails were painted bright red. I wondered if the first Mrs Flaherty, the one who had died of a tumour, ever painted her toenails red. I doubted it; she probably would have disapproved of nail polish.

'And have you enjoyed your stay in Dublin?' I asked boldly. Her face became fixed. The dreamy look left her eyes. I had broken the spell.

'The food does not suit Mr Flaherty,' she said solemnly. She leaned down, retrieved her shoes and retreated up the stairs.

When I went into our room my mother was lying on the bed with the curtains drawn and a wet cloth on her forehead. She was suffering from a migraine.

I sat in a rocking chair in the corner and watched the almost imperceptible rise and fall of her bosom. She was not very old at the time, in her early forties, but her hair was almost white. Her mouth hung open in the abandonment of sleep and she was snoring. She always slept with her mouth open but when I accused her of snoring she denied it – presumably on the grounds that ladies did not make undignified noises or, worse yet, acknowledge them. I continued my critical scrutiny with a growing unease. Mother looked old and very fragile lying there and I was suddenly frightened. It occurred to me, for perhaps the first time, how hard she worked to keep us intact, to afford the school I attended and provide the little extras she considered essential for a young lady. Hard physical labour, scrubbing floors, washing, work that was rarely appreciated and more often criticized. I never heard her complain about the work although she bitterly resented the doctor and his wife for their arrogance.

She went to Mass every morning and we said the rosary every night before we went to bed, but her religion was not an escape, it was a bulwark, private, unsentimental.

I thought how little I really knew about my mother, about her girlhood, her marriage. She seldom spoke of anything personal. When I asked about my father she said he was a decent man, which wasn't very enlightening. My only recollection of him came from his photograph on the mantel which was taken while he was still in school. He was slender and delicate looking. People often remarked on our resemblance but of course, he was such a remote figure in our lives it was difficult for me to imagine any connection with that serious young man.

Mother met him several years after he had been immortalized in that photo. He was a bookkeeper for some company in Cork and her aunt introduced them. She told me once he was very fastidious, but I didn't understand what she meant by that. My friends' fathers were often boisterous or rude. Even the priests I knew liked their drink and tobacco. Fastidious?

At any rate, he died unexpectedly of a haemorrhage in his brain. One minute he was talking to the man next to him and next he was slumped over his desk. It was a blessing he went so quickly, my mother always said. The doctors told her he would have been paralysed and dumb and I think she was relieved that she had been spared looking after him.

'A blessing,' she'd say. It was the only time I ever heard her refer to my father with any tenderness. It was as if she regarded his death as a personal favour.

My mother sat up in bed and squinted over at me. Her face looked pinched and white.

'How do you feel?' I asked.

'Oh.' She shrugged and sank back on the pillows. 'Good for nothing.' She tried to smile. 'I've spoiled our day. It never fails.'

'They went home today,' I interrupted.

'Home? Who?' She didn't sound very interested.

'The Flahertys.'

'Ah, yes.'

The room was almost completely dark. The sun had gone down and the city was bathed in that long, pale twilight of summer. Slivers of grey light were barely visible where the shade did not quite meet the casement.

'Why did she marry him?' I asked, more to myself because it was not in my mother's nature to discuss other people's affairs. 'He's so old.'

I heard her sigh and I could tell that my question had provoked her. I thought if she hadn't had a headache I would be in for a lecture on not judging other people or gossiping like the contemptible Mrs Dowd, but she surprised me by saying: 'I'm sure she had her reasons. I just hope for her sake she doesn't regret it. And for his sake too, poor devil. He had no right to marry that child.'

I was startled, as much by the passion with which she spoke as by what she said. She was obviously agitated. She sat up in bed and was massaging her temples.

'Pride,' she said aloud. And then under her breath, 'And lust.'

Pride? Lust? What did my mother know about such things? I could not believe anyone with her thin shoulders and primly pursed lips could know anything about lust. She always wore the brown scapular pinned to her nightgown and kept the rosary beads under her pillow.

'It's a disgrace,' she said bitterly. And she stood up and began to pace back and forth in front of the window.

'I don't understand,' I ventured. 'It isn't as if she had to marry him.' I hesitated. I knew sometimes couples did have to get married because the girl was in the family way. It was always common knowledge in town, which bride walked up the aisle sweet and unsullied and which ones were in trouble. But somehow I did not think Mr Flaherty had compromised his pretty wife and anyway, I had it on Lucy's authority that Moira had sacrificed her virginity three nights ago and left some mystifying sign on those sheets. But I could never tell my mother I was privy to such squalid information. She would never have forgiven me. So I blurted out: 'Well, no one can force someone to marry against her will.'

'Oh, Teresa,' she said. I did not recall her ever address ing me so tenderly. 'People do foolish, reckless things out of fear, pity, loneliness.' Her voice trailed. She raised the shade and stared out over the rooftops, the dark, uneven shapes barely discernible in the waning light. She had that same look in her eyes that I had seen in Moira Flaherty's eyes that afternoon, as if she were puzzled, trying to understand some great mystery that kept eluding her.

Finally she said: 'That old fool downstairs thinks she married him for his money. Well –' she shrugged as if defeated – 'perhaps, she did. They said that about me when I married your father. If he had any I never saw it. We lived in a flat he shared with his sister. She treated me like an intruder. She raised him, you know.' I didn't. Him. He had a name, Michael, but I'd never heard her refer to him by it.

'She doted on him. Cooked all his meals, washed and ironed his shirts, pressed his trousers. My handiwork never suited her.'

I didn't want to hear any more. I wished we had never come to Dublin, never set eyes on Moira Flaherty. I knew my mother would never have revealed these secrets to me if we were at home. She leaned her head against the transom and closed her eyes.

'I don't know why I married him. I had nowhere to go when my aunt died and I was afraid to live alone.' She started to laugh. 'I was lonely. I wanted...' She turned and looked at me as if waiting for an explanation.

'Your father was kind to me,' she said.

Did she marry him because he was kind? She never mentioned love but then I could not imagine my mother young and impulsive, her flesh pricked with desires which for me were still unfocused and confused.

The shade, caught in a sudden draught, tapped against the window-pane like someone knocking softly and insistently to be let in.

'Last night I dreamed about him.' She sounded surprised and annoyed that after so many years he would have the nerve to intrude into her dreams. 'We were in the parlour downstairs. You were there.' She smiled at the absurdity of that and then went on. 'Mrs Dowd was playing the piano. She was very jolly. He was sitting next to me. He wanted to hold my hand. He didn't say anything, he wasn't even looking at me. He was watching Mrs Dowd and smiling, but all the while he kept moving his hand closer to mine. His hands were covered with brown freckles. I didn't know what to do. I didn't want him to touch me.'

She pulled her wrap around her and refastened the sash as if the familiar ritual might exorcize the ghost of my father from her memory.

'Is that all?' I asked.

'I think so.' She hesitated. 'I don't remember.' She went across the room and switched on the lamp beside the bed.

The light, which added little cheer to the dreary room, seemed to bring her back to her senses. She smiled bravely while she rummaged through her handbag for her tablets.

'They're too strong,' she said. 'I woke up and I didn't even know where I was. And all those dreams,' she added. 'Such nonsense. I never dream.'

She shook two pills out of the bottle into her hand, regarding them as if they were responsible for her aberrant behaviour. But they were the only thing that gave her any relief and I knew she was weighing the alternative of spending the night vomiting in the draughty toilet down the hall or having her sleep haunted by memories.

'Well, I'll just take them tonight,' she said finally. 'If I don't get rid of this headache I'll be in no condition to travel tomorrow.'

If my mother had any more dreams she didn't tell me about them.

In the morning we dressed, packed our suitcase and went down to breakfast. It was raining. The empty table that the Flahertys had occupied was framed by the window overlooking the garden. We ate in silence, absorbed by the storm that raged outside while we sat safe and dry, nibbling our toast. The excitement that the Flahertys' presence had generated in the quiet little hotel had vanished. Lucy lurked in the corner with her tray under her arm, scowling at the guests for eating so slowly. She drummed her fingers impatiently in time to the pattern of rain beating on the flagstones.

'We must be on our way, Teresa,' Mother said as if my lingering had caused us to be late. 'I'll settle with Mrs Dowd. Go along and get the suitcase and go to the toilet,' she added. Lucy smirked and the man at the table next to us glanced with distaste in our direction.

At the top of the stairs the door to the Flahertys' room stood open. It had been dusted and swept, the linens changed. As it was the dearest room in the hotel it was seldom occupied but Mrs Dowd kept the door open so that all the guests could at least glimpse the modest luxuries she provided as they traipsed down the hall to their meaner rooms in the back of the house.

I hesitated in front of the door, torn by a desire to explore the deserted room and my mother's injunction to hurry.

The bed stood against the far wall. It was old fashioned with an imposing mahogany headboard. A peach-coloured satin bedspread, frayed along the hem, was aligned carefully on the bed and a row of small, crocheted lace pillows were placed in precision against the headboard. I ran my hand over the material and marvelled at the smoothness and sheen of the satin, but the rest of the room was disappointing. There was a large wardrobe opposite the bed, a chair and a wash basin in the corner, the greedy electric meter that measured out the heat, and a dressing-table in front of the windows.

I tried to picture Moira Flaherty sitting in front of the mirror combing her hair but I couldn't conjure up the image. It was as if she had vanished and left me with a vague feeling of sadness and loss which I did not understand.

I turned to go when a streamer of silver ribbon lying in the bottom of the wastebin caught my eye. It was a wedding corsage. I stared at it lying abandoned among the rubbish. The petals of the roses were brown and curled around the edges, the spray of fern brittle and dry. Wedding flowers should be pressed between the pages of a heavy book, a token of cherished memories.

I looked up, half expecting to see Moira Flaherty standing beside me struggling to unfasten the corsage, but it was my own reflection I saw in the mirror. I had changed, not to outward appearances of course. I was still a thin, ungainly fifteen-year-old girl. But now I was privy to a terrible knowledge. I felt infinitely sad, wise beyond my years, and afraid.

There was still so much I had to learn. But I was sure I would not be waylaid by foolish dreams. They lay abandoned with the wedding flowers in that dreary hotel in Dublin. And if sometimes I was wont to forget the lesson I learned that summer, I recalled the sad and haunting look in Moira Flaherty's eyes.

Magdalen

ALISON ARMSTRONG

IF THE PRISONER has a name she has forgotten it. She is a machine, needing oil. Brodie's piston comes and goes and she feels he is trying to rub her out altogether.

Brodie is so-called because he never takes his clothes off, and when he leans over her, his jacket falls open to reveal the label: 'Brodie & Sons: Tailors of Distinction.' Brodie is over fifty, with pale eyes and a bald head like a long thin egg. His cat's arse mouth tightens when he nears his climax, and he comes like the dregs of talcum powder being squeezed from an exhausted tin. Pfft. His suit is black and ancient – perhaps even older than he. It smells of another person's salty rheum and their last medication on earth. It also smells of eau-de-Cologne, because with there being no running water in the Tower, Brodie insists she saturates herself with eau-de-Cologne before and afterwards. She has to douche with it as well and the stuff stings her unlubricated cunt. It's a kind of burning-out of Brodie, so in a way, the pain is welcome.

Brodie's Tower is square and squat, and it stands on the top of a small tree-covered hill. The prisoner can see above the trees as she lives on the top floor, in a room once occupied by Mary, Queen of Scots. There are no four-poster beds now, though, but there is a sash window – Victorian, and rotting. There is a chaise longue with a split skin; a table, a chair, a bottle of eau-de-Cologne, a can for the necessary, a mirror and a wind-up gramophone. There is also a pile of rugs and blankets, and a print tacked over a damp patch on the plaster. Although there are damp patches everywhere there is only one print. One day the prisoner peels it off the wall for a closer look. It shows a woman in a medieval dress, that falls about her toes like overlong curtains. The dress is low-necked and the woman's breasts look as small and hard as sour apples. The dress is red, and a dragon with a big mouth yawns behind the woman. Brodie says it's ready to swallow her up, but she doesn't seem bothered and she leads the dragon on a long golden chain. She is poker-faced; perhaps because the artist wasn't skilful with faces, but her name or title- 'Magdalen: A

Whore(?)' written on the back of the print – suggests an open expression wouldn't suit her.

One more point about Magdalen. She has long bracken-coloured hair, falling loose to below her knees. The prisoner has hair the same colour that falls to her thighs. It is growing fast but Brodie won't let her cut it, even though it gets tangled when she thrashes around in her weird dreams. After every pfft he measures her hair with a metal tape he carries around in his pocket, and every time he finds it has grown about three inches.

Apart from her room, the Tower is derelict. Beneath her feet there are floors of dereliction, ending with the cellar, or dungeon. A rotten door that's been wedged half open for years, lures tramps and children into the dark unpaved region below. One evening Brodie catches a tramp there, who is doing something wrong, something unspeakable. Brodie holds his rifle fastidiously at the man's head and pokes him out of the cellar, but he (Brodie) can't stop the foul thing happening...

Brodie is angry when he relates this. Beneath his anger, the prisoner senses his alarm. When Brodie measures her hair, the steel tape becomes a gun against the skull.

Now, she thinks the floor she stands on might collapse and she will fall down and down again into the cellar. The square, squat Tower swallows people, like Magdalen's dragon. The soft earth in the cellar is probably digested people and if her floor gives way she will have a gentle landing. But she doesn't want to land where some smelly old tramp has been.

Perhaps he wasn't very old.

The sunlight, a chute full of mites, falls into the room through the rotting window. It touches the print of Magdalen and seems to make her po-face wink.

Brodie does not wear a watch, so the prisoner has no idea of time. Out of the window, she can see a village which has moving cars, and satellite dishes fixed to the houses, but it's like a village inside a glass dome. One shake and silver snow will fall.

Brodie plays Wagner on the gramophone. He also plays Highland dances and (for light relief) Gilbert and Sullivan. He has read that music is the food of love, and love is what he wants. He doesn't like the sex, because it is dirty. He prays for the strength to desist, but Magdalen gets between him and God.

Some days the prisoner isn't a machine needing oil; she is a foot inside a rubbing shoe. Sometimes Brodie has to stop and get off, in order to wind up the gramophone or change the needle. When the music starts again, the crackles of the old 78s express her own dry skin.

But her dreams have long, soothing fingers. Not only do they rumple her hair, they disturb the bedding and taunt her with sensations. She starts to believe that Magdalen is responsible: Magdalen and that great yawning dragon at her back.

Oh.

Brodie tells her that Magdalen covers a patch of damp. That is her only function, and she does the job very well. Brodie plays Tristan very loudly, and sings along to the tenor part. Afterwards, he measures the prisoner's hair, and is cheered to find that it now comes down to her knees. Hair growth, he once read in a reputable magazine, is a fine gauge of amatory fulfilment.

What if I fall pregnant, thinks the prisoner when Brodie has gone. She grimaces as the eau-de-Cologne bites once again. She is being cured, like leather, or ham. Magdalen grimaces back, sick of being a cover for a patch of damp.

That night, Magdalen sends the prisoner a special dream. The dream's eyes are green, like a witch's, and each iris holds a million fragments of a soul she can't fathom. All she can see are the eyes, but with her hands and her skin she feels the dream's long back, the slight rise of its buttocks, the taut, wiry muscles of its shoulders and arms. She feels it waiting, in a gentle inquisitive way like a poor boy wanting to enter a church. But she can't let it in.

The dream cries, silently. Its tears overflow, fall and wet her skin.

... She wakes – thinking, it's not Magdalen's fault things didn't work out. The chaise longue she uses as a bed, now has a sweetish, dirty smell, like honey going bad.

Brodie brings her two presents. The first is a tortoiseshell dressing-table set, once owned by Queen Victoria. The prisoner checks the brush for royal scurf before tugging it through her own hair.

The other present is a pair of amber earrings, each drop containing a tiny prehistoric fly. Brodie tells her these came from Atlantis, under the sea. He also tells her she is beautiful.

Then he plays *The Mikado* on the gramophone, and afterwards, the tape shows her hair has grown three whole inches. Brodie is pleased, but doesn't show it. The shape of his head gives her an idea of him: he is an eggshell trying to be a whole egg.

Poor Brodie.

But when she walks, she thinks splinters are rubbing together.

Brodie brings her regular meals, packed neatly into sandwich boxes. For washing, she has to stick with the eau-de-cologne until he brings her new dresses. Then he supplies four large Thermos flasks full of hot water, a bar of ladies' scented soap and a giant fluffy towel.

There are three dresses; one blue silk, one in green velvet and one in ivory satin. They are in the same style as Magdalen's dress, and when the prisoner tries them on, her breasts are pushed high and hard. Brodie laces her up the back, so tightly she can hardly breathe. Her skirts stretch drumskin tight across her hips, then fall wide and loose and crumple at her feet. She can barely move, but she feels beautiful. Her hair is wet from being washed and falls to below mid-calf. It is now as long as Magdalen's.

Brodie leaves her in the blue dress, but unlaces it so she can take it off to sleep. He takes the other two away, for if they stayed in the room, the damp would spoil them. When Brodie has gone, the prisoner lets her hair drape out of the window, to dry in the breeze and the last, intense rays of the evening sun. The breeze ruffles her hair gently, and lulls her almost to sleep. She wants Magdalen to send the dream again, and she wonders if the dream has anything to do with the man in the cellar. Brodie said he would shoot that man if he found him on his property again.

There is no electricity, and Brodie does not allow candles. When the sun is down, darkness is near absolute on a moonless night, and the shapes of things make stolid, sentry-like ghosts. The prisoner sits on the chaise longue and shivers because it is cold. She wonders if the dream will be scared off by her new finery, but she knows he is somewhere in the room.

The nerves in her spine scream as he draws close behind her. She doesn't turn round. His mouth is wet on her neck, and his teeth are sharp. His beard growth rasps slightly and though his hair mingles with her own, she feels its otherness. She wonders if the right thing is happening to her, but Magdalen doesn't care about the right thing. She sends girls and women hot, dirty dreams and watches, grinning and chuckling, until dawn.

He sits behind the prisoner, rocking her back and forth and tunnelling into her bunched-up skirts. He is clothed tonight, and patches of her skin encounter rough material. His smell is all the love juice since Adam and Eve, which has never been washed away, and he is nameless – driftwood, cast up by a dark sea. His arms link across her waist and pull her tighter and tighter until their bones touch through the yards of crumpled silk.

What if he is ugly, she thinks.

But she knows his green eyes are beautiful.

When he comes, it is nothing like Brodie's miserly pfft.

When the prisoner wakes, the room is filled with a grey dusty light. She ought to have taken off her dress before she slept, because now it is stained and crumpled, and it smells bad. She puts eau-de-Cologne on the stain, which leaves a worse mark, but she can say she had an accident with the bottle. She also finds two sore bites on her right shoulder, which (she decides), Brodie did when he forgot himself.

She hangs the dress out of the window, to try to get rid of the creases.

She has to greet Brodie wrapped in a blanket, and he is not at all pleased. Yet when she says 'you forgot yourself', his cat's arse stretches in a tight smile, and, accompanied by the wail of the bagpipes, he tries to forget himself again.

Brodie brings her a rope of pearls, once gambled and lost by a mistress of King Charles II. Each pearl is the full moon, and they look cool and magical against her blue dress. But this dress is taken away, to be replaced by the green velvet. For this dress, Brodie brings her kohl and green eye cosmetic and heavy gold bracelets from Imperial Russia, set with topaz and malachite. She wonders if the treasure would turn to dust if the Tower fell down. She wonders, too, what Brodie will do when her hair stops growing.

Then Brodie grows suspicious of the lovebites and she tells him about the other man. She adds, tearfully, that she was forced. So Brodie gets anxious and spends long hours on watch with his gun, and packets of sandwiches. He combs the basement, but prefers to sit on the roof – from where he can see his enemy approach. In his black suit, he resembles a crow. She hears him scuffling from time to time as he changes direction, and she also hears the odd slate crash to the ground below. Silly old sod.

As an extra precaution, he changes all the locks on her door. When he visits he keeps putting the wrong key in the wrong lock, and she has to listen to him fumbling and tutting for an eternity. Magdalen thinks this a huge joke, and the short black dash of her lips occasionally trembles.

The prisoner hopes and fears that *something* will happen, soon.

Brodie removes the prisoner's green dress and brings her the ivory satin. This colour suits the amber earrings and her bracken-coloured hair, but does not suit her jail-pallor. Brodie brings a gift of heavy gold chains – a type (he says) once popular in Germany. He insists that she wears them, but they rasp her as the piston comes and goes; and when he measures her hair, he finds it has not grown a fraction. In fact, it has not grown since she got those bites.

'You're not very good, that's why,' she tells him.

The cat's arse tightens so much, it swallows itself. He looks as though he has been warmed up from the dead; yet even so, he is calculating.

'You hurt,' she adds, bravely. 'You hurt every single time.'

Her head is a chamber of echoes; a shell brought inland and cut off from the real sound of the sea. When Brodie strikes, he will crash her echoing limbo – and there will be retaliation because she has blown a man apart.

'Is that so?' he asks quietly.

'Yes.'

The prisoner waits to be struck, but it does not happen. Brodie leaves the room, postponing it. She hears the door clang and several locks slide shut. Not long afterwards, she hears his feet disturbing roofslates; perhaps the same slates that kept the rain off Mary, Queen of Scots.

Then she hears a shot.

Then she hears the tiles clatter off the roof, taking with them an object that falls like a bag of wet cement.

The prisoner rises from the chaise longue and shuffles to the window. She walks sideways so her labia don't rub together. By the time she reaches her window, the dust has settled and she can see the tiles partly covering a heap of old clothes. Poor bastard...

Soon Brodie will come back down. He will place his rifle carefully against the wall and say that right has triumphed. Being victorious, he might not punish her for what she said.

A trick of the light makes Magdalen grin, knowingly. But what can she know? She is cardboard, covering a patch of damp.

A late tile falls off the roof – knocked by Brodie's clumsy feet. Brodie wears stout black shoes which he keeps in excellent repair; the man he's just shot went barefoot. His toes were as sensitive as fingers, but they were grimy and were covered in old cuts and bruises. He was after revenge, and Brodie's sandwiches; and he almost got there. But at a calculated moment, Brodie turned and shot.

The story *has* to finish that way, because if Brodie falls, so must his Tower. She can picture the other man clearly now, and he was dirty and ugly, with long matted hair and the beginnings of a straggly beard. If she'd seen him at night, she would not have touched him.

She feels hot; old leather turning back to skin. It is time to do something. It is time to brush her hair...

Queen Victoria's hairbrush hits a knot. The prisoner closes her eyes and tugs and tugs, and on the dark screen of her lids she sees two exploding wheels of pain. These are yellowish green, and when she stops brushing they stabilize. In the centre of each a black hole emerges, which pulses gently as the surrounding colour dilates. Each wheel, each eye, is a sorrowful, microscopic world that she is too big and clumsy to join.

The prisoner opens her eyes. A cape of hair is no protection, when scrutiny comes from within. The man's green eyes were beautiful, but they were misplaced, like emeralds hiding in filth. He was not very old.

There is a metallic crash, sounding as though Brodie has dropped his rifle while descending from the roof. Brodie hates carelessness, so this must be irksome, and he will arrive in a bad temper. The prisoner thinks she hears a curse but it is hard to tell because the echo is distorted by the Tower. It makes the stonework tremble, but nothing falls.

It was (she thinks) a bad curse, quite ungodly.

She used to wake, sometimes, with that rotting honey smell on her fingers

– but that was before she came to the Tower. Now, the smell competes with the odour of damp, and she is sickened by them both. She leans back on the chaise longue, covered, as far as possible, by her bracken-coloured hair. In preparation for Brodie, her body takes on a doll-like rigidity. Every time she thinks, this is the peak of pain, but there is always a little more.

> Humpty Dumpty sat on wall,
> Humpty Dumpty had a great fall,
> All the King's horses and all the King's men
> Ate scrambled egg for a week.

(He doesn't mean to laugh; he is content staring at the prisoner, who is like a princess to him. But recent events have stressed him, and the recollection of that long thin egg rolling off the roof, is too much to contain.)

She turns sharply, and his instincts make him cower. He is squatting, legs crossed, on the table behind her. Next to him lie Brodie's gun and Brodie's keys. He is bigger, more angular, than in her dreams, and she thinks (stupidly) that his bones are too big for his skin. He is crouched like a broken chair, with soiled and tattered upholstery.

He recovers, and rakes his hair off his face. Then he grins at her. The grin belongs to an urchin. The eyes, with their harrowing lustrous beauty, do not.

She regrets, silently, that she has nothing to offer him, not even a biscuit. It's Brodie's fault, not hers. He kept her short, so she would maintain her figure. The man – who is very young, not much more than a boy – wears a black jacket over his shoulders, like a cape. One pocket bulges with a paper bag that held sandwiches. He pulls out the paper bag, splits it open and picks up the crumbs with his tongue. He does this very seriously, and not a crumb is wasted. His tongue is deep pink against his scruffy black beard, and it has a soft, rounded tip. As he works he looks up through his hair and watches her, almost without blinking, until she wants to freeze, or become *real* china.

He crumples the paper bag and stuffs it back in the pocket. Then he reaches into his shirt pocket and with care, takes out a half-smoked cigarette. He lights it and smokes with his body hunched around it, protectively. His hands are stained and bony but the fingers are graceful; the nails are bitten down to the quick. A pilferer's hands, she surmises. Unlike Brodie, he used the door keys silently, if he used them at all.

'How did you get in?' she asks.

He shrugs, and she does not ask again. Those hands contaminated her – yet he was gentle, and the thought of him could moisten her now if only she were not so tinder dry. She burns like a bush fire. It is Brodie's fault, like the absence of tea and biscuits.

The man uses the tabletop to stub out the cigarette. He doesn't know any better, and looks anxious when she frowns. The Tower ought to shudder dangerously, but it does nothing, perhaps because the table is unpolished, lumber room stuff. She smiles in forgiveness and complicity, and he grins back. He appears to take her smile as an invitation, because he slides off the table. Standing, he loses some of his angularity, unless it is hidden by his shirt and trousers which belonged, several wearers back, to a fatter person. An old sweater is tied around his middle, and this almost hides the knife dangling on his hip, sheathed. He steps towards her, and excitement threads a string through her belly and starts pulling her where she might not want to go. He stands behind her and, leaning over slightly, trails a fingertip down the centre of her face. When he reaches her mouth, she nibbles gently and glances upward. What she sees is a black jacket lining and a flash of the label: 'Brodie & Sons: Tailors of Distinction'.

The prisoner knows that, if she wanted, she could bite the finger to the bone.

A is for Axe

MIKE McCORMACK

A IS for Axe

Six pounds of forged iron hafted to a length of hickory with steel wedges driven in the end. During the autopsy the coroner dug from my father's skull a small triangular chip which was entered as prosecuting evidence by the state. It was passed among the jurors in a sealed plastic bag like the relic of a venerated saint.

More than any detail of my crime it is this axe which has elevated me to a kind of cult heroism in this green and pleasant land of ours. I am not alone in sensing a general awe that at last small-town Ireland has thrown up an axe murderer of its very own. It bespeaks a kind of burgeoning cosmopolitanism. At last our isolated province has birthed a genuine late twentieth-century hero, a B-movie schlock horror character who is now the darling of downmarket newsprint.

As I was led to trial several of my peers had gathered on the steps of the court house. Long-haired goateed wasters to a man, they sported T-shirts emblazoned with my portrait and short lines of script: *Gerard Quirke for President*, they read or, *Gerard Quirke – A Cut Above the Rest*. My favourite: *Gerard Quirke – A Chip Off the Old Block*.

B is for Birthday

I have picked through the co-ordinates of my birth and I find nothing in them which points to the present calamity. I was born on the twentieth of October 1973 under the sign of Libra, the scales. It was the year when the sixth Fianna Fáil administration governed the land, added two pence to the price of a loaf and three on the pint. In human terms it was a year of no real distinction; if there was no special degree of bloodshed in the world of international affairs neither was there any universal meeting of minds, no new dawn bloomed on the horizon.

I have these details from a computer printout which I got from James, a present on my eighteenth birthday. He bought it in one of those New Age shops specializing in tarot readings and incense that are now all the rage in the bohemian quarters of cities.

I was named after St Gerard Majella whom my mother successfully petitioned during her troubled and only pregnancy.

C is for Chance

Chance is at the root of all. 3, 12, 20, 10, 27, 8. My date of birth, my father's date and my mother's also. These are the numbers my father chose on the solitary occasion he entered for that seven-million-pound jackpot, the biggest in the five-year history of our National Lottery. And for the first and only time in his life the God of providence smiled upon him.

D is for Defence

I had no defence. To the dismay of my lawyer, a young gun hoping to make a reputation, I took full responsibility and pleaded guilty. I was determined not to waste anyone's time. I told him that I would have nothing to do with claims of diminished responsibility, self-defence or extreme provocation. Neither would I have anything to do with psychiatric evaluation. I declared that my mind was a disease-free zone and that I was the sanest man on the entire planet. As a result the trial was a foreshortened affair. After the evidence was presented and the judge had summed up, the jury needed only two hours to reach a unanimous verdict. I was complemented for not wasting the court's time.

E is for Election

As a child nothing marked me out from the ordinary except for the fact that I had been hit by lightning. I had been left in the yard one summer's day, sleeping in my high-springed pram when the sky darkened quickly to rain and then thunder. All of a sudden a fork of lightning rent the sky and demolished my carriage. When my parents rushed into the yard they found me lying on the ground between the twin halves of my carriage, charred and blackened like a spoiled fruit. When they picked me up they found that the side of my head had been scorched by such a perfect burn that, were it not for the ear it had carried with it, you could have admired the neatness and tidiness of it. While my mother carried me indoors my father stayed in the downpour, shaking his fist and bawling at the heavens, cursing God and his attendant angels.

In the coverage of my trial much has been made of this incident and the fact of my missing ear. Several column inches have been filled by pop psychologists who have repeatedly drawn parallels between the lightning strike and the axe. All have sought to deliver themselves of fanciful apocalyptic axioms. It surprises me that at no time was a theologian asked to proffer his opinion. I feel sure he would have found in the incident some evidence of a hand reaching out of the sky, a kind of infernal election.

F is for Future

My life sentence stretches ahead of me, each day an identical fragment of clockwork routine piled one upon the other into middle age. I do not care to think about it. Seven months ago, however, after my father came into his fortune, I dreamed of a real future. Hour after hour I spent in my room working out the scope and extent of it, embellishing it with detail. Eventually I polished it to a gleaming prospect of travel in foreign climes, sexual adventure and idle indulgence. I mapped it out as a Dionysian odyssey, a continual annihilation of the present moment with no care for the morrow. It would take me in glorious circumlocution of the earth all the way to my grave, ending in a fabulous blow-out where I would announce my departure to the assembled adoring masses, an elegant wasted rake. I was careful enough to leave blank spaces in the fantasy, filling them out during moments of conscience with vague designs of good works and philanthropy. I confess that these were difficult assignments, my mind more often than not drew blanks. My belief is that I had not the heart for these imaginative forays. My cold and cruel adolescent mind was seized mainly by the sensual possibilities and I hungered cravenly for them.

G is for God

My father stayed in the downpour to decry the heavens and my mother pointed out in later years that it was at this moment God set his face against us and withdrew all favour. Whatever about God, it was at this moment that my father turned his back on all religious observance, an apostasy of no small bravery in our devout village and probably the only trait in his personality I took after when I entered my own godless teens. A steady line of self-appointed evangelists beat a path to our door to try and rescue him out of the cocoon of hunkered bitterness into which he had retired. But my father's mind was set. The God of mercy and forgiveness was nothing to him any more and the community of believers were only so many fools. He could be violently eloquent on the subject. In black anger he would wrest me from the cradle and brandish me in their faces.

'There is no God of mercy and forgiveness,' he would roar. 'There is only the God of plague and affliction and justice, and we are all well and truly fucked because of it. This child is the proof of that. More than any of you I believe in Him. I only have to look at this child to know. The only difference is I have no faith in Him.'

These rages would reduce my mother to a sobbing shambles. She would recover, however, and then redouble her observance on his behalf, attending the sacraments twice daily to atone for his pride. Icons flourished in our house and the shelves and sideboards seemed to sprout effigies overnight. My father ground his teeth and reined in his temper.

H is for History

I have admitted my interest in killers at the pre-trial hearings. However, even now, I maintain that it is nothing more than the average male teen infatuation with all things bloody and destructive. Like most young men of my generation I can rhyme off a list of twentieth-century killers quicker than I can the names of the twelve apostles. At school I listened critically to the tales of the great ideological killers. I became convinced that the century was nothing more than a massive fiction, an elaborate snuff movie hugely budgeted and badly edited, ending with an interminable list of credits. I came to believe that beneath this vast panorama of warring nations and heaving atrocities the true identity and history of my time was being written by solitary minds untouched by ideology or political gain, solitary night stalkers prowling alleyways and quiet suburban homes, carrying their knives and axes and guns and garrottes. And I believed also it was only in this underworld that concepts of guilt and evil and justice had any meaning, this world where they were not ridiculed and overwhelmed by sheer weight of numbers. Bundy, Dahmer, Hindley, Chikatilo, Nilsen, the list goes on, an infernal pantheon within which I will now discreetly take my place.

I is for Indolence

After my leaving cert, I signed on as a government artist – I drew the dole. It was an issue of some scandal in the village, after all my father was the possessor of probably the biggest private fortune in the county.

One evening after signing on I sat in a local pub putting a sizeable hole in my first payment – I was quietly discovering the joys of solitary drinking. On an overhead TV I listened to the news and heard that the national unemployment figures had topped three hundred thousand for the first time. The figure was greeted with equal measures of awe and disgust.

'Christ, it's a shame, all those young people coming out of school and college and no jobs for them. The country is going to hell.'

'In a hand cart,' another added.

A third was not so sure. 'I don't know,' he said, a large straight-talking man. 'Half of those fuckers on the dole have no intention of working, they'd run a mile from it. And it's not as if there isn't plenty of it to do either, look at the state of the roads, or the graveyards for that matter. A crowd of bloody spongers the whole lot of them, if the truth be told.'

It was a brave thesis, particularly so in a townland surrounded by subsistence farms, the owners of which topped up their incomes with government handouts.

But he was right, at least in my case he was. I went home that night and for the first time in my life I knew what I was. I was a sponger, a slacker, a parasite, a leech on the nation's resources. Like most of my generation I had neither the will nor imagination to get up and do something useful with my life. And what was worse I took to my role joyfully, safe in the knowledge that I could fob off any queries by pointing to the statistics or by saying that I was indulging in a period of stocktaking and evaluation before I launched myself on the world with a definite plan. I could loftily declare that I was on sabbatical from life. Only in solitary moments of truth and pitiless insight would I speak the truth to myself: I had no worthwhile ideas and no courage, I was good for nothing.

J is for James

The only shaft of light in my childhood years was the presence of my friend James. Throughout my trial he was the one constant, sitting in the public gallery with his hair pulled back in a tight braid, chewing his bottom lip. I could feel his eyes upon me, placed like branding irons in the centre of my chest. Now he comes to me every week, bringing me my record collection piece by piece and my books, Hesse, Nietzsche and Dostoevsky, a young man's reading, or so I'm told.

James was more than my friend, he was my champion. I would be at the centre of one of those taunting circles, my tormentors wheeling about me, dealing out cuffs to the side of my head and insults. 'Ear we go, ear we go, ear we go,' they would chant. My defence then was to disappear down inside myself, down into that part within me which was clear and painless, a place lit by fantasy, ideas, books and music. Almost inevitably James would round the corner. I would see in his eyes the dark fire that was already igniting his soul.

'Leave him alone, you pack of cunts,' he'd yell. 'Leave him alone.'

Then he would wade into the centre of the circle, shouldering me aside, his Docs and fists flying, working his surprise to the limit by scoring busted noses and bruised balls. Sooner or later however he would find himself at the bottom of a pile of heaving bodies, curling into a tight foetal to ward off the kicks and blows that rained down on him. Just as suddenly my tormentors would scatter, yelling and whooping, leaving James bloodied and bruised on the ground like carrion. In those moments I used to think that James was the victim not of his love for me but of his own rampant imagination. Now I can see him rising from the dust, his face bloodied and running like a clown's make-up and I curse myself for my cynicism.

K is for Kill

The axe swung through the air and cleft my father's skull in two and he lay dead upon the floor.

L is for Lug

When I reached my teens I grew my hair to my shoulders. By then, however, it was already too late to prevent me from being teased mercilessly and earning a succession of nicknames. My peers were never short of cruel puns and covert abuse whenever I was near. 'Ear, ear,' they would yell whenever I opened my mouth to speak or, 'Ear we go, ear we go, ear we go,' whenever we gathered to watch football matches. From national school my name was Lug and in secondary school the more technically minded tried to amend it to Mono. But Lug was the name that stuck and I hated them for it, hated them for their stupid wit and their lack of mercy. But I did not hate them as much as I hated my father on the day he discovered it. He returned from answering the phone in the hallway. It was one of my 'friends'.

'Lug,' he said gleefully. 'Christ, they have you well named there and no doubt about it. We used to have an ass with that name once, Lugs. Mind you, he was twice the creature you are. He could work and he had a full set of ears.'

I burst out crying and ran to my room. I stayed there the rest of the afternoon, weeping and grinding my teeth. I eventually dried my eyes and took a look at myself in the mirror and I resolved then that no one would ever make me cry again.

M is for Music

Because of my impaired hearing my love of music has caused much wonderment. Again this has proved a fertile snuffling ground for those commentators desperate to unearth truffles of reason in this tale of blood and woe.

I am a metal head, a self-confessed lover of bludgeoning rhythms in major chords and rhyming couplets dealing in death and mayhem. My record collection, now numbering in hundreds, reads like a medieval codex of arcana; Ministry, Obituary, Bathroy, Leather Angel, Black Sabbath and so on. My greatest solace now is that I can listen to these records in the privacy of my cell without maddening anyone. If there was anything certain to unleash my father's temper it was the sound of these records throbbing through the house. He would come hammering at my bedroom door.

'Turn that fucking shite off,' he'd roar. 'Christ, you would think a man of your age should have grown out of that sort of thing long ago.'

But I never did grow out of it and I don't foresee a day when I will. The horror of this music is rooted within me as deep as my very soul and I would no more think of defending it than my father would his own lachrymose renditions of 'Moonlight on the Silvery Rio Grande'.

N is for Never

As in never again. At the bottom of our souls all young men are sick. We do not grow sick or become sick nor is it some easy matter of hormonal determinism. This sickness is our very nature. Having suffered from the disease myself I know what I am talking about. It manifests itself generally as a disorder of the head, a slant of the imagination that preoccupies us with mayhem and blood, slashing and hacking, disease, waste and carnage. There is not a young man of my age who, in the privacy of his own heart, has not thought of killing someone. Many times James and I would sit fantasizing about a kill of our own, our very own corpse. We weighed up the options like assassins and narrowed it down to a single clean strike in an airport terminal bathroom where there is an abundance of unwary victims and suspects. We were armchair psychos, already tasting the blood. Most young men grow out of this sort of thing, taking to heart second-hand lessons in mercy and compassion, turning in wonderment and revulsion from their former selves. Some never learn and continue to stalk the earth with weapons, amassing victims in the darkness. But the truly wretched ones turn away also, not out of principle or humanity but from the antidote at the heart of the disease itself, the terrible soul-harrowing and puke-inducing disgust.

O is for Obituary

QUIRKE (MARY ELIZABETH) died suddenly at her residence, Carron, Co. Mayo, 2.I May 1993, in her fifty-ninth year. Deeply regretted by her sorrowing husband, Thomas, her son, Gerard, and a large circle of relatives and friends. Removal to the Church of The Immaculate Conception, Carron this (Wednesday) evening at 7 o'clock. Requiem Mass tomorrow (Thursday) at 12 noon. Funeral afterwards to Cross Cemetery. No flowers. House private.

> *Your story on earth will never be told*
> *The harp and the shamrock*
> *Green white and gold.*

P is for Patrimony

Four months ago James and I stood in a green field behind our county hospital, two unpaid extras witnessing a dedication. There was a small platform bedecked with ribbons, a few local politicians, the diocesan bishop and my father. The field was populated by a motley collection of patricians, merchants and outpatients, a few nurses hung at the fringes. Incredulity hung in the air like a fine mist. We were here to witness the sod-turning on the foundation of The Thomas Quirke Institute for Alcoholic Research, a laboratory annexed to our county hospital and funded in equal measure by European grant aid and the single biggest bequest to the health services in the history of the state, my father's entire Lottery win. I listened as the politicians spoke on the straitened circumstances of the health services and on the pressing need for an institution of this sort in a province ravaged by alcoholism. My father was commended as a man of vision and philanthropy. I saw the bishop sprinkle holy water on the green earth and invoke the saints to guide the work of the institute. Then my father stepped forward to turn the first sod, his public awkwardness belying his easy skill with the spade. The audience whispered and shook their heads and as the earth split and turned I saw my fortune vanish before my eyes. In honour of the occasion James and I left the field for the pub across the road and got sinfully and disastrously drunk.

Q is for Quietus

We sat in the kitchen drinking the last of the whiskey. It was two in the morning and darkness hummed beyond the windows. James was slumped at the table, his head resting in his extended arm, clutching a glass. His speech came thick and slow.

'Every penny,' he was saying, 'every fucking penny gone up in smoke and pissed against the wall. I wouldn't have believed it myself if I hadn't seen it with my own two eyes. And everyone of them bursting their holes laughing at him behind his back. The Thomas Quirke Institute for Alcoholic Research, no less. Sheer bloody madness.'

'Give it a rest, James. I'm fed up hearing it.'

It had been a long day and I badly needed sleep. A monstrous headache had begun to hammer behind my eyes.

'Are you not mad, Ger. Christ, I'd be mad. A whole fortune squandered in one act of vanity. You're his son, for Christ's sake, it wasn't just his to throw away. You're his son and you could have been set up for life.'

'I know, James. It's all over now, though, and there's nothing anyone can do about it. It's all over.'

'I'd kill him,' he said suddenly, rising up and swinging the bottle wildly. 'Stone dead I'd kill him. He hadn't the right, he hadn't the fucking right.'

My father entered at that moment, his face flushed with drink, the knot of his tie well over his collarbone.

'Hadn't the right to do what, James, hadn't the right to do what? Go on, you young shit, spell it out.'

He was standing with his legs apart inside the door, the cage of his chest rising and falling. He looked like a man who was going to reach for a gun.

'I was just saying it was a real pity that all that money couldn't be put to better use where right people might benefit from it.'

'Is that so? And I suppose if it was your money you'd have known what to do with it.'

James' head was lolling heavily, a wide smirk crawling to his ears.

'I'd have given it to the poor of the parish,' he said, guffawing loudly and gulping from his glass. 'Every last penny. And I'd have put a new roof on the church,' he finished, now giggling helplessly.

'And I suppose you wouldn't have left yourself short either, James. You being one of these poor that prey so heavily on your mind.'

He was leaning with both hands on the table now, towering over James. He wasn't totally drunk, just in that dangerous condition where he could argue forever or lose his temper suddenly.

'Do you know what it is, Mr Quirke, something I saw today? Everyone of those people were there patting you on the back with one hand and smirking behind the other. Telling you what a great man you were and then going away bursting their holes laughing at you. I saw it with my own two eyes.'

James had lost the run of himself now, he didn't care what he said. I stood between them.

'Cut it out both of you. James, it's time you left, I need to get to bed.' I began hauling him to his feet.

'He'll leave when I'm finished with him,' my father hissed, squeezing out the words between his clenched teeth. 'When I'm finished and only then. What about you, James, were you laughing?'

'I didn't know whether to laugh or to cry, Mr Quirke. I was in two minds.' He was swaying drunkenly now, bracing himself between the chair and the table. 'I didn't know whether to laugh or to cry. I was standing there thinking that some people have more money than sense.'

My father lunged at him, his outstretched hands reaching for his throat. James keeled backwards, spilling the chair and my father landed across him, bellowing in rage and surprise. They grappled wildly for an instant. I threw aside the chair and James' boot flicked up as he rolled over, catching me under the chin and knocking me sideways into the table, grabbing the tablecloth and bringing the bottle and glass shattering to the floor. We scuttled to the end of the room and my father came off the floor clutching the neck of the bottle at arm's length.

'I'll cut the fucking head clean off you,' he roared.

He moved towards James slowly, as if walking over broken ground. It was at this instant the axe rose into the air, just off my left shoulder and passed in a slow arc over my head. And it was at this instant also that there was a sound of breaking glass and the light went out. The fluorescent bulb showered down around our shoulders as the axe clipped it and there was a sudden pass of cold air in the darkness, a grim sound of something splitting with a soft crunch. I rushed to the wall and turned on the bulb.

'Oh Jesus, oh fucking Christ.'

My father lay face down on the floor, his head split open and the axe standing upright in it as if marking the spot. He was dead beyond any salvation. James was doing some frantic crazy dance about his head and there was a smell of shit in the room.

'Oh Jesus, what are we going to do, what are we going to do?'

I was stone-cold sober then, hiccuping with fright but perfectly in control. I started dragging James towards the door, hauling him by the collar.

'Go home now, James, there's nothing you can do. Go home.'

I pushed him out into the darkness and slammed the door. My breathing came in jagged bursts and I needed to sit down. I righted the chair and sat at my father's head, a four-hour vigil into the dawn with no thought in my head save that now, for the first time in my life, I had nothing.

When the grey sun rose I stepped into the hall and rang the cops.

R is for Responsibility

Not for the first time James was picking himself up off the tarmac, wiping the blood from his face. I was after telling him rather imperiously that his imagination was running away with him. He was having none of it.

'Those fuckers walk all over you,' he sobbed. 'When are you going to stick up for yourself ?' He was near crying.

'I can take care of them in my own time,' I said cryptically.

'Well, it's about time you started. Look at the size of you, you're well able for them, what the hell are you afraid of ? And your father too – Christ, you put up with so much shit. You have to be every bit as cruel as they are. You have to meet every blow with a kick and every insult with a curse. You shouldn't take this any more, it's not right.'

'I never asked for your help,' I said coldly.

'Well, this is the last time,' he yelled. 'From now on you can be your own martyr or your own coward. I want nothing more to do with it.'

'No,' I said, 'you'll always be there. You can't help it, you have the imagination for it.'

I walked away, leaving him sobbing on the ground.

S is for Summary

Even now, in the fifth month of my sentence, I still receive weekly visits from my lawyer. There are loose ends still in need of tying up, details to be put to rest. He informs me that public interest in my case has not waned, apparently its notoriety is being seen as indicative of some sort of widespread malaise in the minds of our young people, a kind of national tumour in need of lancing. He tells me that there is much probing of the national psyche in the media.

More recently he has presented me with a sheaf of proposals from publishers and film producers, all of them looking for the complete story, the first-person account. I have refused all of them, returned the documents through the wire mesh. I have no interest in the superfluities that necessarily accrue within the scope of the extended narrative. I have chosen this alphabet for its finitude and narrow compass. It places strictures on my story which confine me to the essential substratum of events and feelings. Within its confines there is no danger of me wandering off like a maddened thing into sloughs of self-pity and righteousness.

T is for Truth

Under oath and on the Bible I swore to tell the truth. I confined myself
to the facts, which may or may not be the same thing. I believe now that
this preoccupation with the facts is exactly the problem with all kinds of
testimony. A clear retelling of the facts, no matter how accurately they
record actual events, is a lamentable falling short of the truth. I know now
that the true identity of things lie beyond the parameter of the facts. They
lie in the treacherous and delusive ground of the fiction writer and the
fabulist, those seekers after truth who speak it for no one but themselves
with no motive of defence or self-justification. This is the terrain in which
someone other than myself will one day stake his ground.

During the days of testimony I saw James leaning forward in his seat,
chewing on his bottom lip which had blossomed out in cold sores under
the stress. His eyes bored at me from the other end of the courtroom as I
confined myself to the facts.

U is for Unravel

The thin bonds of our family unit sundered completely after the death
of my mother. On some unspoken agreement my father and I commenced
separate lives within the narrow scope of our house and small farm. I rose
each day at midmorning when I was sure he was about his business in the
fields. I ate alone in the kitchen, staring in mild surprise at the creeping
ruin which had taken possession of the house. Now that neither of us
seldom bothered to light any fires, paint had begun to peel from several
damp patches on the walls. A light fur like a shroud clung to the effigies
and icons all about and the windows scaled over.

Yet neither of us would lift a hand to do anything. We were now
caught in a game of nerves, each staring the other down, waiting for him
to crack. But neither of us did, we were too far gone in stubbornness and
pride. The dishes piled up in the sink and cartons and bottles collected
everywhere. The house now reeked of decay.

I came down from my room one evening and he was at the table,
drinking from a bottle by its neck. I stopped dead inside the door and
continued to stare at him. We spoke at the same time.

'This place has gone to hell.'

And still neither of us made a move.

V is for Visit

Now that I have all my records and the last of my books I have begun
to sense a distance opening up between myself and James. It gets worse
with every visit, a widening fissure into which our words tumble without
reaching each other. Most of the last few visits have been spent sitting in
silence, staring onto the blank tabletop. We have made sudden despairing
raids on old memories, seeking frenziedly among old battles and fantasies

for warm common ground. But it is hopeless, it is as if we were retelling the plot of some book only one of us has read, and not a very good book at that. I am surprised by the different ways we have come to remember things. I tell him of one of his heroic interventions on my behalf and he grimaces and speaks dismissively of a rush of blood to the head. He tells me a bitter incident of crushed youth and violent temper and I wonder who he is talking about. We are different men now and we hold different memories.

This week he had a real surprise. He sat across from me with his eyes lowered on his hands, the curious air of a lover about to confess some long and on-going infidelity about him.

'This is the last time I'll be here, Gerard,' he mumbled. 'I'm going away – America.' He had developed a twitch along his jawbone since his last visit and I noticed that his nails bled.

'When did you decide?'

'A few months back, seeing you in here and all that. Everything's changed, it's all different now. I've got the medical and a job set up in New York. It's all set up,' he repeated. He continued to stare at his hands.

I was obscurely glad that it was going to end like this. James' days as my protector were at an end and my incarceration was his loss also. I knew our friendship had exhausted itself – consummated might be a better word – and I knew that I was looking at a young man whose mission in life had been completed.

'I hope it goes well for you over there. Make big money and meet lots of women. American women go mad for paddies, I'm told. It's the dirt under the fingernails. Tell them you live in a thatched cottage, I hear it never fails.'

He smiled quietly. 'I don't know what I'm going to do. Probably work for a while and save a bit of money. I'd like to go to college.'

'That's good. It's good to have a plan, if only to have something to diverge from.' I rose from my chair and held out my hand. 'Best of luck, James. I hope it goes well for you.'

'So do I. And thanks, Gerard. You were the only real friend I ever had.'

'It goes both ways.'

'Goodbye.'

'Goodbye.'

I watched him leave and I tried to remember a time when I had ever seen him walking away before. I couldn't.

W is for Wisdom

My father made it clear to me that life wasn't easy. It was his favourite theme, particularly in those drink-sodden days after my mother died. He would fall upon me roaring, snatching the headphones from my ears.

'I suppose you think that it will be easy from now on, ya useless cunt,' he'd roar. 'I suppose you think that it's all there now under your feet and all you have to do is bend down and pick it up. Well, let me tell you here and now that it won't be like that, it won't be like that at all. No son of mine is going to be mollycoddled and pampered and I'll tell you why. Because you'll work for it, like I did when I was your age and every other man of my generation. Because, and make no mistake about it, you young cur, it's work and nothing else that makes a man of you, a real man, not like those fucking long-haired gits I see you hanging around town with.'

He was well into his stride now, pacing the floor and breathing heavily.

'Started work after national school we did, every man jack of us, footing turf at two shillings a floor, nearly a hundred square yards. And damn the bit of harm it did us. It made men out of us, real men who knew the value of money. Now all this country has is young fuckers like you spending all day on your frigging arses, eating and drinking the quarter session with no thought of tomorrow. I'm sick of the fucking sight of you.'

He would grab a hank of my hair then, and lift my face up, his whiskey breath burning my skin.

'But if your mother was alive there'd be a different tune out of you, I'll bet. She'd have put skates under you and not have you sitting here all day like a friggin' imbecile.'

This was the inevitable point of breakdown, the moment at which all his vehemence would drain away, rendering him mawkish and pathetic. He would collapse by the stove, weeping and snuffling into his hands.

'Oh Mary, Mary my love.'

I did not know which was the most terrifying, the honest and direct terror from which there was no escape, or this genuine grief which was his alone.

X is for Xenophobe

We watched the interview on television the following evening. A study in western gothic, it showed the three of us standing in the doorway, my mother staring into her hands, plainly abashed by the attention, my father square-jawed and sullen, glowering darkly at the camera. At their backs I rose up between them, a half-wit's leer covering my face. The bright young interviewer, all smiles and bonhomie, waved a microphone in my father's face.

'Mr Quirke, you are the latest Lotto millionaire, the biggest in its history. It must have come as a complete shock to you.'

Father avoided the bait skilfully. 'No,' he said drily, barely hiding his contempt. 'When you have lived as long as I have it takes more than a few pounds to surprise you. I just checked my numbers on the Nine O'Clock News and when I found out that I had won I went and had a few pints in my local like I always do.'

'You didn't throw a party or buy a drink for the pub?'

'I bought my round as I always do. I've always had money to buy my own drink, anyone will tell you that.'

'Now that you have all this money, surely it will bring some changes to your lives, a new car or a holiday perhaps?'

'The car we have is perfectly good,' he answered bluntly. 'It gets us from A to B and back again. If we wanted to live somewhere else we wouldn't be living here. There'll be no changes.'

The interviewer hurriedly thrust the microphone to my face.

'Gerard, you are the only child of this new millionaire. No doubt you have high hopes of getting your hands on a sizeable share of it,' she said hopefully.

'My father has a sound head on his shoulders; he'll not do anything foolish with it,' I said simply, barely able to keep from laughing.

The interview ended in freeze-frame, catching my father with his jaw struck forward in absurd defiance and the half-wit's leer spreading back to my ears. In the news coverage of my trial it was this image which defined the tone of all articles. The national press barely managed to suppress a tone of there-but-for-the-grace-of-God righteousness. Their articles were consummate exercises in mock anguish and between-the-lines sneering at their dim western cousins. Some day soon I expect to read accounts of sheep shagging and incest purely for tone.

Y is for Yes

Yes, I have my remorse. All that night I sat over my father's corpse and watched the blood drain from his skull over the floor. I was experiencing an object lesson in how death diminishes and destroys not just life, but memories also. All that night I had trouble with my recollection. I could not square this overweight, middle-aged corpse with the towering ogre who had terrorized and destroyed my teenage years. That was a creature from a different era, a prehistory of myth and violent legend. It had nothing to do with this small West of Ireland farmer, this lord of forty acres with his fondness for whiskey and cowboy songs.

There was a clear and horrible disparity in that room, a terrible and universal lack of proportion.

Z is for Zenith

On the first morning of my detention a small deputation of prisoners greeted me in the exercise yard. I was amazed to see that they bore several gifts for me – a ten spot of hash, a quart of whiskey and a list of warders who could be bought off for privileges. I stood bemusedly trying to conceal these gifts in my baggy overalls, watching the bearers retreat diffidently across the yard. Evidently my reputation had preceded me, elevating me on arrival into that elite category of prisoner who were not to be fucked with. I had a secret laugh about that. This of course is on account of the axe. There is no doubt but that the nature of my crime has made it a transgression of a different order, even in here, where there are men doing time for crimes that are barely speakable. Knives or guns are understandable, they are the instruments of run-of-the-mill savageries. But an axe is something else again. It is the stuff of myth, the instrument of the truly sick of soul.

From the beginning I have received fan mail, curious and vaguely imploring missives from faceless well-wishers. Dear Gerard Quirke, Not a day passes when I do not think of you alone in the isolation of your cell. You are in my thoughts every day and I pray for the deliverance of your wounded soul.

Today I received my first proposal of marriage.

I have begun to think again of my future and I have made some tentative plans. Yesterday I signed for an Open University degree in English Literature and History; it will take me four years. Now my days are full, neatly ordered within the precise routine of the penal system, meals and exercise alternating between longer periods of study and my record collection. At night I lie in this bed, plugged into my stereo and smoking the good quality dope that is so plentiful here. The lights go down and peace and quiet reigns all about. I spend the hours before sleep remembering back to the final day of my trial and I acknowledge now without irony the wisdom of that judge when he handed me this life sentence.

The Welfare of the Patient

ANNA McGRAIL

SHE LEANS against the wall, in the only space of shade in the bright afternoon, and smokes a cigarette while she watches ambulances arrive, families leave. She didn't want to come to the hospital, didn't want to come near him at all, but she had promised. She could turn back now, walk away down the hill, but she is far too aware of convention to ignore it and thinks of the stain her absence would leave upon her reputation. She grinds the cigarette out under the heel of her sandal and brushes her fringe out of her eyes with the back of her hand. She is ready.

The main doors open as you reach out to touch them, inviting. It is cooler inside than out. The light from the ice-cube shaped fluorescent tubes is a mixed blue and pink, brighter, more searching than daylight.

The nurse leads her without a moment's hesitation, once she learns who this is, down the linoleum-tiled corridor and into the right room. It must be the right room because it has his name on the door, official lettering in a small wooden slot, but she does not recognize him, not at all. Not at all, she who knew him better than anyone. She walks in and smells turpentine disinfecting the air.

'I wondered when you'd get here,' he says.

'I didn't bring any flowers,' she says. 'I see you have some anyway.' There are old roses in a glass vase on the window sill.

'What would I want flowers for?' he says. 'You might have brought grapes, though. Isn't that what visitors are supposed to bring patients?'

'Only if they end up eating all the grapes themselves,' she says. 'I don't like grapes.' She places her shopping bag in the corner of the room, takes a can of lemonade from the top and opens it. Very carefully and deliberately she throws the metal tab into the wastepaper basket. She sits down on the moulded plastic chair that is the only concession to visitors, kicks off her sandals and presses the soles of her feet, one by one, against the cold iron frame of the bed.

'You may sit,' he says.

'Thank you.'

'They took nail clippings yesterday,' he tells her. 'What do you suppose they do with them? They've already had blood, urine and my spleen. There'll be nothing left of me.' He lifts his arms, thin as hazel wands, and the tube in the vein in his right wrist moves with him. She is startled. She had not expected him to be able to move by now. He smiles coyly as she stares, on display, the tendons in his limbs visible, strung tight as piano wires.

'Look at this,' he says. He moves his fingers against the light and casts shadows against the white wall, fuzzy at the edges, black in the centre. 'Look. Amazing figures formed by the hand.'

'A rabbit,' she says dutifully. 'A bird, no, an eagle. A Siberian crane. A lesser spotted hedgehog.' At last there is a shape she cannot guess and she grows impatient, shaking her head from side to side.

'It is an angel,' he says, laughing, bending his fingers once again. 'See, here are her wings.'

'What a talent,' she says, pretending to see now, to admire.

'My own invention,' he replies, pleased. 'Sorely missed at parties, I bet.'

'Every night,' she says. 'I don't suppose they allow you to smoke in here.'

'What do you think? You should stop. You'll live longer. Although you'll live longer, anyway, won't you?'

She drinks from the can, the carbonation burning her tongue. Already the lemonade is getting warm, the promising condensation on the cold metal surface disappearing. She tries not to look at the blood, seeping from beneath the bandages. He picks at scabs, idly, short fingernails unhinging the ridged surface. She tries not to look at the marks on his arms. In his wrists, a network of blue veins is clear, as if his skin were becoming steadily more transparent. It is as if he has begun to live in distant oceans, in sunless depths, metamorphosing into a deep-sea creature, the luminous sort, with internal organs visible beneath the skin. The thin arteries beat in the unsteady rhythm of his heart, a display of the mechanics of life that some might consider to be in poor taste.

'It's your turn now,' he tells her. 'Entertain me. Isn't that what you've come for? Do a couple of card tricks or something. Take my mind off things.'

She smiles. 'How are they treating you?' She knows he needs to talk and she can afford to be courteous. She has the time.

'As well as can be expected when they don't know how to treat you. Perhaps they'll name a complication after me. Fame and fortune await. This isn't like Kansas any more, Dorothy.' He laughs. 'Tomorrow I could come down with a whole new range of impressive side-effects. Lycanthropy, for example.'

'I think the full moon is past. I'll consider myself safe.'

'As well you might, Mrs Talbot. They say the innocent need have no fear.' He grins at her, the striations on his skull becoming darker, and bares his fangs, triumphant as a wolf at the head of his pack. She stays still and waits, watching him stretch taut then subside, aching. Sweat glitters down the side of his face and wets his tongue.

'How are you sleeping?'

He replies that he never shuts his eyes, he cannot, must not. Sleep always takes him to the places at the back of the eyes and he doesn't want to visit those strange countries again. 'There are terrible strange animals here at the end of the world,' he says. 'Nameless and nerveless.' He picks at a piece of loose cotton on the quilt, tracing the remains of a pattern. His hands pluck the covers closer to him with crab-like movements, crustaceans on a journey of their own. He shivers, as if he were cold.

'Lying here under your sheets all the time. Your imagination must be morbid.'

'A car accident,' he says. For a moment, she can see this. Sweat matting his hair, staining his skin, the cold wind on his face, his sore bones scraping along the roadway. There is blood on the tarmac, oily and viscous. 'That's the sort of death I'd like,' he says. 'That's the one for me. Definite. Quick. No hope. Not this.'

'None of us can choose,' she reminds him. She says it quickly and moves on, before he can think through the implications, but she is too late.

'I did choose,' he says. 'I knew the risks. So did you. And I can choose now. Anytime. I could leave here for a start.'

'But where would you go?'

'And who would have me?'

'Who will have any of us, once we've come as far as this?'

'As far as we can go,' he says.

'Not quite,' she says. 'It isn't over yet.'

She considers a ceremony in a grassy field, his family and friends gathered at last, now there is nothing more to be afraid of. The sun is shining on the fresh soil. The trees stretch endlessly like banners on the green slopes. Beyond that is the desert. The sky turns to white where it touches the white of the land, far at the horizon, beyond colour.

'No,' he says. 'Not yet.'

The shells of conversation are lower and louder. 'Try to think of it as a gift,' she says. 'Most of us ignore the inevitable, bowling along until the bus hits us. Try to think of it as a chance.' Her voice is as gentle as she can possibly make it.

'A chance to do what?' He is angry. 'No matter what I do now, it isn't going to make any difference. I've had all my chances, hundreds of them. Where did they get me? Here.'

Exhausted, he leans forward to throw up in a tin basin. Heat presses. She asks him if he wants a drink of water and reaches for the paper cup. There are two clear bottles on the bedside table. He tells her no. One is gin, the other formaldehyde. They smile, confidentially, friends again.

Sudden quantities of very strong sunlight pour in through the window, illuminating their collusion, making everything incandescent, reflecting off the dust into multiple rainbows. 'Look at that,' she says, dreamily. 'Dust is the most beautiful thing I know.'

'Such words belong to the patient,' says the patient. 'I should be thinking about dust. And I have been. I've thought everything about dust that there possibly is to think. And my conclusion is that one day not only will I be dust, but this room, this building, this country. Dust. Dust. It's not a new conclusion, I realize, but you can't expect original thinking at my time of life.' He reminds her that a day will come when the entire universe has worn itself out, when there is no further energy available for use, when all is at maximum dissipation and disorder. 'This is known as the heat death of the universe,' he says smugly. He draws her attention to the floor, where there are several cereal flakes, three safety pins and some petals from the fading flowers. 'Things are falling apart already.'

She says she doesn't believe it, although she is accustomed to things dissolving and dying. 'Like those flowers,' she says. 'It's the price of being alive. No one is immune.' The sky outside the window bleaches in the heat, loses all colour and silvers like a mirror, reflecting back the earth. She smiles to think of everything becoming warmer and warmer in the heat death of the universe, all bonds fracturing, all obligations meaningless, until even the separate molecules are broken.

'Visitors are supposed to make small talk,' he complains. 'I'm not here to give lectures. Talk to me about inconsequential trivia. Take my mind off things. Tell me something I don't already know.'

'I may not see you next week,' she says, sitting up straight and pressing her spine against the back of the chair.

'I already knew that,' he says. 'Or, at least, I already guessed it.' He twists his fingers. They are slightly sticky. She cannot tell whether this is from fear or simple sweat.

'Is there anything you still want taking care of ?' she asks, brisk now, polite, concerned. 'Letters written? Library books to be taken back?'

'There's lots of things to do,' he says, 'but I can't see me fitting them all in now. Fulfilling my potential as a violinist, for example, I never got round to that. Then there was being called to the Bar. An exhibition of my oil paintings at the Royal Academy – whatever happened to that idea? Do you know, I once even considered having children.'

She looks at him. 'You'd have made a good father, on the whole,' she says.

'It leaves someone to mourn for you,' he says, 'if nothing else. In my next life I'll start as I mean to go on. Make lists. Never procrastinate. Seize the day. I'll tell you something else I've been thinking about: there isn't enough time left to make amends. Not to everybody. Not to everybody who deserves it.'

'There are still things you can do,' she says, 'that will make a difference. To you. To us. You can die a hero and not a victim, for a start.'

'Want me to go out and kill a monster?' he says. 'You have strange ideas about what a man can do on his deathbed.'

'You don't have to lift a finger,' she says. 'Listen to me. You can be a hero by admitting you're afraid. That's all it takes.'

'I'm not afraid,' he says. 'What do I have to be afraid of now? The worst is over.'

She leans forward, takes his hand. His skin rests lightly against hers, clammy, insistent, and she tightens her grip. 'Think about it.'

He looks at her and looks away. 'I can't think,' he says. 'It's another deficiency I've acquired.'

She sees the shadows beneath his eyes, violet lines. The heat has made him quiet. She releases his hand. 'Aren't you tired?' she says. 'You must be tired by now. I am.'

'You'll be lying here one day,' he says. 'This place or somewhere like it. You don't know what tiredness is.' His breathing is harsh.

'I know what pain is,' she says. 'It will soon be over.'

'Cassandra.' His voice is so small she hardly hears. 'What do you think will happen? Does anything happen next?' She lets the small voice talk into the silence. 'I've always believed there wasn't anything else. I've lived like there wasn't anything else. No God, no devils, no angels. I don't want to go into the afterlife and come face to face with something I've never believed in. What sort of Judgement will there be? If there is no judgement, there will be nothing. Just darkness. Just emptiness. You could tell me, you know. Please, Cassandra, tell me what you think will happen.'

'You know I can't tell you. No one can.'

'I could take out an insurance policy, I suppose. Do you think I've got time for a deathbed conversion? Perhaps you should call the priest. I've got things to tell him, confessions to make.'

'You wouldn't talk to him. I know that much. No more than you would the last time I got him here. I'd be better off arranging the violin lessons, instead.'

'I am so frightened,' he says. 'I never wanted to die alone.'

'I promised you,' she says. 'You won't.'

He wants to hold her hand again. She puts the lemonade on the bedside cabinet. The lines on his palms are ragged and pale, they used to be etched more deeply. He smiles and shrugs his shoulders. His hair is the colour of warm caramel. His eyes are surprisingly blue, as blue as seas should be. 'I shouldn't rely on you like this,' he says.

'Some of us always depend on the kindness of strangers.'

'No,' he says, sharply. 'You are no Blanche to be driven mad by what you see.'

'No,' she says. 'Not that. I could be Florence Nightingale. You could have an injection. A sedative.' She puts her arms around him.

'How about choirs of angels to sing me to my rest?'

'I might manage angels dancing on the head of a pin, given sufficient notice.'

'In formation?'

'If that is what your heart desires, Cinderella.'

'Tell them to start with the paso doble.'

Clouds are beginning to appear, fist-sized on the sky, and it is getting dark outside, now that the sun is hidden.

She sees he might cry. 'Hush, baby,' she says, as softly as she can. 'Hush. Sleep.' She can hardly see his face.

She kisses his forehead, which is white now. His hand against hers, incessant in its movement, seems to weigh nothing at all. There is nothing holding him to the bed. He says goodbye. 'It is,' he tells her, 'a far far better thing I do.'

'Damn right,' she says.

'Tell them,' he says, 'curfew shall not ring tonight.' He closes his eyes.

'My hero,' she says, and smiles and cradles his head. She is patient. She waits. Even as she watches, he stops breathing. The tumult in his hands stills. The shadows remain in the corners of the room, solid bars of darkness. Now all she can hear is the fizz of bubbles from the lemonade, the liquid flattening. She can still taste the sugar on her tongue, leaving a film on her teeth of incipient decay.

She lets go of his hand and lays it on top of the sheet. It is caught in an arch, the last movement in a dance of extremities and terminations. She presses it flat and pushes the fingers together. Her task completed, she gathers up her belongings, puts the can in the yellow container marked 'Clinical Waste', removes his name card from the door and steps out into the air. She is efficient, as well as neat. The city smells of turpentine.

A cold wind starts to blow as she walks down the hill to the train station. Far at the horizon, the sky is grey where it touches the grey of the land. It begins to rain, slow drops the size of coins intermittent against the paving stones. Now she is Azrael, the Angel of Death, who never cries, although she often feels lonely. She walks with all the time in the world through the late afternoon.

Football in Busanze Camp

DICK BAYNE

MOTHER AND FATHER are dead. I don't mind.

Swedi and Juma, my brothers, are dead too, and that's a pity because we used to play some good games. My sister Joanna looks after me now. I like her; except when she cries, because it makes me feel uncomfortable.

She told me they played football with Swedi's head. I was hiding in the maize, but she saw. The soldiers cut it off with their pangas and started kicking it. They made Father join in. He had to take a penalty, and when he missed they shot him. Joanna didn't know what a penalty was, but when she described it I told her.

I like football. At home there was a pitch with real goals. I used to watch when the big boys played, and made a ball out of woven grass to kick with my friends. So I was glad when I arrived here in Busanze with Joanna, because I saw a crowd kicking a ball. Now we play football every day.

At first there was only a grass ball, but then the Whitemen gave us a real one. Not the Whitemen who brought the plastic sheeting we use to make our shelters, and not the ones who showed us how to dig holes for when we squat. The ones who came and pushed pins into our arms.

I was hiding, but Joanna found me and made me join the line. She said she would give me an extra biscuit. The Whitemen bring the biscuits too. When they had put a pin into everybody they gave us the football.

My friend Nason looks after it. He's older than me and quite big, but lets everybody join in.

When we're not playing football there are the two hills for running down, and on the really steep parts you can slide if you have a piece of sheeting to sit on. There are the rows of shelters which are perfect for dodging through when someone is chasing you. The sheeting is blue, so if you go to the top of the hill you see all these humps in lines, like giant blue piles of cow-dung.

In the valley there's the stream where Joanna makes me have a bath. We splash and shout and throw water. At home splashing wasn't allowed because Mother had to fetch it all from a pump.

Joanna's more fun than Mother. She lets me go out and play almost all day. When I start to feel hungry I come back to the shelter and have some food. I have biscuits in the morning when I wake up, more if I want during the day, and we have rice or beans in the evening. There's plenty of food because the Whitemen bring it.

Our shelter is small – as it's just us two, Joanna says – with only half a blue sheet. We get wet when it rains, but so does everybody else. The squat-hole is just down the hill, so there's a bit of a smell. Home used to smell too.

I don't think about home very much. Once, when Joanna was crying, she asked me if I remember what it was like. I said no.

But I do remember sometimes. When I wake up in the morning and it's still too early to go and play. It makes me uncomfortable, like when Joanna cries, and I take my grass football and kick it up and down until Nason comes out too.

After a while we take his piece of sheeting and go to the slide. Lots of our friends are there: so many you have to push to get to the best place at the top. I take turns with Nason, and then we both try to sit on the sheeting together. I fall off and cut my elbow, so we go to the stream to wash away the blood. It's funny watching the red drops fall into the water. They make tiny stringy clouds in the pools, but where the current flows fast they just disappear.

While we are by the stream the Whitemen come in their big white car. They have a special hut, covered with enough sheeting for ten shelters, where they look at you if you don't feel well. We watch them until they leave again. The smaller children run after them shouting 'Greetings', and the Whitemen laugh and try to repeat it; but if you look carefully when they get into the car and leave the children behind, they have stopped smiling.

After the big car has disappeared in the dust, Nason goes to fetch the football and we try to play a game like they used to on the pitch at home. There are too many of us, and everybody chases the ball, so it's not really much like a proper match, but we do have goals and two teams and I like it.

The sun is quite low when I start to feel hungry, and go back to the shelter. Joanna is cooking the rice.

After eating I lie down and go to sleep. When I wake the moon is very bright and I look outside. There is a soldier with a gun on his shoulder and a panga in his hand. The blade shines big and white in the moonlight.

He is standing by Nason's shelter and looks as if he is waiting. I slide forward a little, till my head is outside, so I can see better. The soldier looks over his shoulder, away from me, and raises the panga.

There is a loud noise, like when Nason pretends the cooking pot is a drum and Joanna tears strips of cloth to put 'down there' when she bleeds, but both mixed together. I know it is the sound a gun makes because I heard it before, when I was in the maize and they shot Father and Mother.

The soldier hits Nason's shelter with the panga and starts shouting. Suddenly the noise is coming from all around and I know there are other soldiers with more guns firing. Lines of what look like shooting stars, only redder, go sweeping across the sky. After a loud pop, a bright white light appears above the hills and hangs there, making the night day.

Joanna tries to drag me back inside, but I wriggle away. I am watching the soldier. He hits the shelter again and it begins to fall down. Nason's father comes out. He is bigger than the soldier, but doesn't even look before running away down the hill. The rest of the family come out and run too; it looks as if the soldier is laughing.

Nason is still inside. The soldier drops the panga and takes the gun off his shoulder. He points it into what is left of the shelter and I see him make a little jump backwards. The noise the gun makes is just part of all the other noise.

Nason crawls out of the wreckage and tries to stand up. It takes him a long time because one leg isn't working, and he is trying to keep the football under his right arm. In the end he drops the ball and it bounces away. Then he is standing opposite the soldier and I can see he isn't really a soldier at all. They're the same height, but Nason looks stronger.

They look at each other for a moment, and then the boy-soldier laughs again. He pushes Nason with the gun and watches him fall slowly backwards as his leg folds up. Then he turns and begins to walk away.

I hear Nason shout through the noise. The word is 'Baby'. The boy-soldier turns again and the gun comes up. He points it at Nason for a long time, then swings to find another target.

The first shot misses, kicking up a spurt of sand. He does something to the side of the gun and then his whole body shakes to the drumming-ripping sound. The football disappears in a cloud of dust then skips high into the air.

The boy-soldier watches the ball fly and then fall, not bouncing but flattening to the ground like a ripe-rotten mango dropping from the tree. I want to kill him.

Barcelona

JONATHAN CARR

IT'S NOW six minutes since the pilot informed us – with, in the circumstances, what seems to be unjustifiable calm, that both of the engines have failed and we are sinking towards the earth at an alarming rate. In fragments, he tells us the present score, which is that flaps have been flexed to stall our descent, flammable kerosene has been dumped, the airport knows there is something up and radio contact is being maintained. There's nothing to worry about. I'm listening to the announcement and I'm not sure what I think or feel.

He came on the cabin speaker system and told us and the immediate passenger response was disbelief. He said that about a half hour ago one of the two turbines had spluttered and died, but that the other had been fine. We could fly normally with one engine. During this half hour, while cabin staff sold duty free and collected empty plastic glasses, he had tried to restore the engine to its previous form, but it was having none of it, and sat limply on the wing, nothing but an unwanted extra in the drag coefficient to which we are all now unpleasantly awake. When the other engine followed suit, he decided to share the news. Thanks, Mr Pilot.

It would have been nice to have longer to panic, was my first thought. Perhaps just for once the standard paternalism from officialdom could have been dropped and we could have decided, as adults, how to handle our disaster. But I wonder – does it really make any difference?

In the first minute following the announcement, the passengers sat in a bewildered lull. There is surprisingly little to do when you've been told of your imminent death. Conversations and tears followed, flowed, in the second minute, and the cabin crew swept along the aisles comforting people. In the third minute, some of the cabin crew broke down too, and the economy class cabin was seized then of the scale of its misfortune. People stood up and paced about. A queue for the toilet developed. Sick bags were used.

By the fourth minute, a delirium had settled among a group near the exit, that gazed out hopelessly at the static turbine, at the shuddering wing. Beneath us is one of the most beautiful views I've ever beheld from a plane, London at night, but today, I can't really focus on it. I'm beside my father on the window seat of a Boeing 737 from Barcelona to Heathrow, and he's in the aisle and looking around and I have no idea what he's thinking. My father and I look alike, and in old pictures he is the image of me at twenty-three, which is what I am now, and has retained some of his looks. At the check-in the woman at the desk grinned at us as she passed the boarding cards through a machine.

'How nice!' she cooed. 'A father and son on holiday together.'

My father grunted and I tautened my lips into a sort of smile to cover the fact that the whole trip has been a mistake and we currently loathe each other more than ever.

Dad is not a very wealthy man, but he cut a couple of deals late on in life that netted him nearly a million and so travel is one of his main pursuits. After I'd packed in my job and had some free time he invited me out to Spain to hang out and maybe catch up on some things we've missed and no doubt tell me what a mess I'm making of my life.

If I think about it I am back there listening to him. His voice quivers as he grandly issues the invitation. I know that the subtext is that I can barely afford cabs, let alone plane fare, and that he's doing me a favour. When he asks me, I'm kind of not with it and I'm not sure.

'Um, I don't know, dad,' I tell him, my hostility building. Why the fuck should I do this for him? He's humiliated me enough. I have never been to Barcelona, and I think of the city becoming inextricably linked in my mind with my dad and somewhere I then, because of him, don't want to go back to, like Tokyo, where he ridiculed me in a restaurant, age thirteen, for asking him to send my food back because it was cold (it was sushi), or like Dallas, where I supposedly ruined his chances of a deal with some fat oil people by meeting up with them late for dinner, and in jeans, and talking too loosely about my dad's business at home in London.

'I'll, em, call you back, dad,' I say on this occasion, and as he replaces the handset I can hear my mother saying, in a loud whisper the new phone captures fully, 'He doesn't want to go, Michael.' And then there's a click and I feel ridiculously predictable and despise both my parents for knowing how I'm feeling.

So then I flick through Spartacus and Barcelona looks pretty good and I call back, with forced jolliness, and tell him I'd love to go.

*

In the fifth minute, the cabin crew are offering people drinks and handing out doubles of things until there is nothing left and in the nonsmoking section people are breaking open packs of duty free cigarettes and chain-smoking them. The pilot comes on to say we might not make the runway but there are other places to land, maybe Gatwick, which is closer, and he's checking out his options, but it may be that we'll have to risk a landing in a field somewhere near the M25 and I'm not really listening and I'm thinking about my drugs in the hold and wishing I could take something but then I realize that nothing I have would probably kick in before we crash so it would be a futile exercise. Then I'm wondering whether they do a post mortem on the bodies they find in a plane crash and thinking about my mother's embarrassment when she is told by someone that her son's blood was rich in amphetamines and marijuana, but in the end this thought is quite funny and reminds me of when she used to tell me about putting on underwear you wouldn't be embarrassed to be found wearing in a car accident.

Then I'm thinking about us travelling economy and my family's frequent accusation that my dad would never pay for first class seats because it's a rip off, and I'm wondering if the irony is amusing to the people up front in Club Europe, because although they paid three times as much as we did, death will sweep through their section of the plane first.

I smile to myself about this for a moment and I remember that Richard Branson once said that if the seats in an aeroplane were arranged to face the rear of the craft the statistical chance of survival in a crash is masses higher, and then I'm sad to think that even though all of the airlines know this, none of them have tried it because they're worried that nobody will then fly with them. And I have a vague recollection of a product my father once sold that was basically unsafe and I remember him justifying this to himself and saying that safety doesn't sell anything and as I look at him now I want to ask him about this and find out if he thinks it's kind of ironic.

Even though dad will not fly first class, the family all have these Executive Club lounge cards so we can have free drinks and newspapers pre-flight, and I can see that my dad thinks it's pretty cool to stride past the peasants in the common areas up to the lounges, although these lounges are consistently full of drunks and plebs too. We were in the lounge today and I had three large gin and tonics, quickly, and my dad watched me and sipped orange juice because since he became richer he's stopped doing unhealthy things and clearly intends to live longer. 'Afraid of flying, are you now?' he asks me, his copy of The Financial Times being folded and replaced on the rack beside him.

I glare at him and light a cigarette, and his mouth tightens further. 'Not... afraid... of flying,' I reply calmly. 'I just need a drink.'

My dad checks his watch and though it is past noon in Spain, London is an hour behind and my dad obviously thinks this is a bit early for a drink. 'It's a bit early,' he comments, evenly.

'It must be opening time somewhere,' I tell him, looking up at the departure screen which lists a whole lot of flights I'd rather get on, in particular one to Rio de Janeiro which will be hot and full of horny boys and most importantly is six thousand miles away from my father.

'In fact,' I add tersely, 'it's opening time in bloody London.'

My dad shakes his head slightly, as though I am impossibly wayward and he cannot believe it was from his loins I sprang in 1972. But then his face softens and he smiles a little, which is a bad sign as it generally precedes some little recherché snippet of wisdom.

'I suppose when I was your age I was smoking and drinking all the time,' he tells me. 'But it was different then, smoking hadn't been linked to cancer. You could drink and drive... people never talked about cirrhosis.' He tails off, and I laugh out loud at the idea that a responsible person needs a law to explain to them the dangers of drinking and driving, at the idea that knowing about the risks of smoking drives people from it, rather than intensifying its appeal. My dad probably wants to ask me what's funny but doesn't, maybe afraid of what I'll say, and now picks up *The Economist* and studies that. But then he mutters, 'You'll be sorry when your body packs up when you're forty-five. Your forties are much closer than you think.'

And I'm thinking about the drugs I take and if they quicken the ageing process and I realize with a shock that in my suitcase is some grass and some whizz someone in a gay bar in Barcelona gave me, and which I hid in the pocket of the case because I knew my dad wouldn't look there and I have almost forgotten about it. I can picture the scene at Heathrow clearly, with the normally calm and obedient patrol dogs dragging the guys along on taut leads, foaming at the mouth, dashing round, and the guilt on the faces in the customs queue draining away, replaced with disdain as the dogs land on my case, flattening it, barking madly. Also, I know from my friend who was searched that customs people have lots of extra powers to detain you that aren't available to the police, and I think about this and it frightens me a little.

'I think... I want to stay in Barcelona a bit longer,' I say to my dad, as I think of ways to get my case off the flight.

'Eh?' He puts down the magazine and frowns at me. 'What do you mean?'

'I want to have a couple more days,' I say.

'But I've not got that type of ticket,' he says. 'You'd have to pay for another ticket.' My dad thinks I am being ridiculous and that this is to do with spending the flight with him. I stare at him and my fantasy of the dogs at Heathrow expands to accommodate the shocked and unbelieving face of my father and I can't be bothered to argue and in some ways think it might be worth it just to see his face.

But as we sit together now, six minutes after the announcement, I'm wishing like hell that I'd got off the fucking plane and stood my ground because now I'll never get to see my dad's face at the imaginary drug bust and the whole plan is ruined. My dad is turning the safety card he's plucked from the seat pocket and is looking it over thoughtfully, but it now seems absurd, a story about a perfect crash landing, as smooth as an ordinary one, with women's high heels off and everyone bent forwards, then everyone sliding down inflatables in an orderly, dignified line to the hard, real tarmac.

'We're going to be okay,' my dad for some reason decides to tell me and I stare at him and after a long time I say, 'Why are you... telling me this?' He doesn't reply, just keeps on staring at the safety card, holding onto it, and the stewardess leans in to us and querulously asks us if we want something to drink.

I am looking at the stewardess and she looks artificial and exhausted, and young, maybe not more than twenty, and she tries to smile at me but she is too upset to reassure anyone, and I realize that she is the person who went through the safety announcement just after take off. I wonder what she has been taught about how to behave in a crash situation but I find I have no idea what the training might be.

'I'll have a Jack Daniels,' my dad tells her and she passes him two little airline bottles and looks at me, waiting for my order.

'Um... gin and tonic, please,' I say, and I get the bottles and she forgets to give me tonic and as she walks off to another row of seats I'm looking at her and wondering why she's forgotten and I shout her over and my dad spins round and looks at me and says, 'Christ.' Then he falls silent, slowly snaps open one of the bottles and drinks all of it in one go. Moments later the stewardess is streaming along the aisle saying the bar service has been 'suspended'.

I get my tonic and mix the drink and watch it slowly go flat, not touching it, and outside the ground looks closer but then I'm not sure and there are so many lights I wonder how the fuck we can land in between them and I wonder for a while whether the pilot is allowed to put the plane down where he wants to, even if it's in a residential area and people will be killed when we hit the ground. I develop an urge to go up front and watch the crash from the cockpit and sit behind the pilot as the nose of the aeroplane dips towards a field and finally splinters and the glass in the windows shatters, but then I decide that it wouldn't be like that, that what's more likely is that the cockpit is just instantly crushed and there is no time even for glass to respond by breaking, and I turn this thought over and eventually it makes me smile.

'I was once in a plane crash, you know,' my dad tells me. 'Well... not a crash, as such, but a fucked-up landing.'

I listen to my dad say 'fucked' and I realize I have never heard him say it before and he seems a bit more human for a second, but then the content of what he's said takes shape in my head and it's just incredibly irritating, because my dad has always done everything before and you can never have an experience he hasn't had. I remembered the restaurant choices I advanced in Barcelona when he consulted me about where we would eat and how each time he'd been there or knew somewhere better until in the end I just lost it with him and said, 'What the fuck did you ask me for, then?'

So now I think about ignoring him but he clearly wants to talk, so, still staring at my gin and tonic I tiredly say, 'Oh yeah? When was this?'

'When you were about four, in Rio de Janeiro.'

'You've never mentioned it before,' I remark, suspicious, wondering if he's making it up. Not that this would surprise me, since he must find his way to be equal to or better than any situation, even if it is his own death.

My dad shrugs. 'Never thought about it. I was going to Argentina, and we had a stop in Rio, and everything was fine until we landed, when the plane suddenly veered off to the left and I was sitting in the upstairs cabin in the jumbo and it was obvious that the brakes had failed or something, and we were heading for the terminal building.' He pauses, and I am looking at him in a new light – a crash survivor, and I think that actually, this is not a bad story, although I am annoyed by the casualness with which he's absorbed the experience, and long for him to admit he was – even momentarily – not absolutely confident that he'd get through it.

'And then the plane eventually stopped and by this time all these red lights had come on, and the emergency exits were opening and there was this announcement in French, because it was an Air France flight, and everyone had to get up out of the crash position and get down the chutes and run, so we did that and ran from the plane. When I looked back, one of the engines was on fire and the plane had buckled so that its, like, back was broken, but there were no injuries and it was all okay.'

I take all of this in and stare at him, and the stewardess comes back and sweeps away the drinks, looking nervous as hell, and around us people are agitated as they feel the plane judder and lurch towards the ground, with a steepness I haven't experienced before though I have flown a hundred times.

*

I try to think about dying and what that means, but my mind is turning over and going back to the first night we had in Barcelona at a restaurant my father had chosen and I am miserable at the table because near us is a group of four gay men and my dad has been watching them looking at me and admiring me and we both know we have no words for this and that we'll ignore it, and as I light my fifth cigarette since we sat down and look again at the menu, which makes no sense to me, one of the guys says something to another and they all look over at us and laugh. It's like, the most embarrassing thing.

'You're smoking an awful lot,' my dad observes. I stamp the cigarette, just lit, out into the ashtray and fold my arms and try to steal an unsuspicious look at the only one of the gay guys who is attractive but I can't quite pull it off and so I just lift my beer to my mouth and almost drain the bottle. My dad smiles blandly at me and hoists up his menu.

'So, what would you like?' I stare at him and back at the menu.

'It's all in Spanish,' I halfheartedly complain. 'I don't know what stuff is.'

Now that I have cued him in, given him a role, my dad flexes his Spanish, which he is depressingly good at, like he's good at everything, and he begins to translate the menu.

I decide to get drunk and once we finish the meal my dad suggests we go to a bar, and so we trawl the streets and somehow wind up in an area that's gay and I'm hoping that my dad doesn't realize but suddenly, excruciatingly, he says, 'This looks like your kind of neck of the woods,' and I nearly die and just keep walking.

Eventually we get back to the hotel, and the bar is full of locals and my dad decides we're going to have sangria and we sit on bar stools by two women in their mid-thirties who are alone, and tourists. My dad leans towards me.

'What do you think?' he says, teasing me but not funny.

'About what?' I ask.

'About...' he looks over at the two women, and one of them, who is taller and quite attractive, smiles back. I can't believe that, seeing as I have come out to him recently, he would say this to me, even as a joke.

'Dad,' I say, and my face is a humourless mask, and I realize that I cannot talk to my father, that I can't bear his company.

'So, ladies,' my dad asks one of the women, 'what are you drinking?'

I shudder and turn away, and although I know that my dad is just fooling, I imagine him on other business trips, away from home, and wonder if he's had affairs, if he's been unfaithful.

'Oh,' one of the women is saying, pleased, 'white wine.'

'White wine,' my dad nods, and he motions to the barman to refresh their drinks. He turns to me and I sense that I am about to be introduced and I try to assemble some sort of smile as my dad says, 'I'm Mike and this is my son, Mark.' My dad gestures to me apologetically and adds, 'He's, um, a bit shy.'

One of the women nods and smiles and says, 'I'm Alma, and this is my friend Michelle.'

'Hi,' says Michelle, displaying crooked teeth, and I notice that her face looks stretched over her cheekbones and I think for a second that I can see little scars, maybe from a facelift, but as I'm revising my estimate of her age upwards she turns away and it's too dark, really, to see.

My dad is smiling at the women and we watch as they are served with wine.

'We're from Birmingham,' says Alma, playfully, and I place the accent and groan quietly and my dad nudges me as though I am some troublesome child. The three of them are staring at me and then Alma turns to Michelle and smiles. 'A father and a son on holiday together,' she says. 'Isn't that nice?'

'Yeah,' Michelle agrees, looking us over, 'that's very nice.'

I have had enough and I lose my smile and announce that I'm tired and I want to go to bed. My dad glares at me and I glare back and stand up, and it seems that in this look he gives me now is summed up all the disappointment I have caused him, and I realize that no matter who I become or what I do I can never please him, and it will never be enough. He turns to the women and says, apologetically, 'Well, have a good night. It's been nice...'

'You stay, dad,' I say, almost aggressively, but my dad doesn't seem like he wants to.

'What's up with him, Mike?' Alma asks and I'm already turning away and leaving the bar but I am close enough to hear my dad chuckle softly and say, 'Oh, problems at work and... stuff. He's, em, going through a few changes.'

I am walking quickly towards the lifts and my dad is two steps behind me and I just want to get away from him and sleep.

We are all waiting for the pilot to come back on and tell us what is happening, but he doesn't, not yet, and I'm starting to panic and wish I'd drunk the gin and tonic and I stare at my dad with about a million things to say, saying none of them. And now I'm thinking of the last conversation I had with my mother, which was a not untypical one.

I am sitting in the living room of our house and I'm watching MTV and there are all these great new videos on and I'm, like, engrossed, and my mother comes in and starts asking me what I want to eat for dinner.

'Well... I'm not bothered,' I tell her, still staring at the screen, but she just stands there and she's tediously going through the options and it seems like we've had this conversation a million times and it seems like it's the only conversation we've ever had.

'Mum... just... whatever, okay?' I say, but still she persists and will it be steak or maybe a takeaway and eventually she gets so irritating I have to huffily put a tape in the video and record what I'm missing on MTV and turn to her and listen.

'Mum, steak is fine. Whatever you want is fine,' I tell her, and she gives me the saddest look and looks at the TV set and then retreats from the room. And it doesn't seem like a very good last conversation to have had with your mum, to me.

The pilot comes on and tells us we are to make an emergency landing at Gatwick and this will happen in about three minutes, although from the window I estimate that had we been flying normally the height we have left to lose would take twenty minutes of flying time, and I can feel the plane dip and head down with shocking purpose. And the stewardess comes on and in a voice with at least a shred of confidence, says, 'Seats upright. Place your forehead on the back of the seat in front of you. There will be several bumps. Leave all your hand baggage and move as quickly as you can to the exits and slide down the escape-chutes. When you are on the ground – run.'

So I'm starting to really worry and I hunker down as she's instructed and from this new vantage point I can see that my father is, like, trying not to cry and then I can feel the pressure of tears and I try to ignore them and then I say, 'Dad,' but not loud and he turns to me and smiles, and then grins.

'We'll get through it, son. Don't worry.'

And I want him to give me a hug, like he hasn't in years, and I say, 'Dad,' and I'm choking and the plane seems to be sliding somehow to the left.

'I love you,' my dad tells me and I frown and say, 'I love you too.'

He says, 'I'm sorry we couldn't... get it together this weekend. I'm sorry for... things. But you're my son and I love you.'

I listen to this and I think red lights have come on in the cabin and there's this terrible silence as we wait for the impact and the plane makes hardly any noise, which is just, like, so fucking eerie, and I wonder where the ground is and if we'll make the runway.

'Dad,' I say again, and I'm not sure what else I can say but I feel kind of close to him and it feels, actually, okay.

The 737 smacks the ground and I can feel the fuselage shudder and rock and my ears press and my head feels like it must be through the seat in front and I'm barely aware of it but my teeth are locked together and my eyes are closed and I'm waiting for something, like a searing heat or sudden pain but instead there's just this tug of Gs at my body and while my head is shooting forward my legs think they're being pulled through the floor and I can see my sunglasses jump from the rack and shoot forward beneath the seats in front of me.

The plane is shooting down the runway for what seems like forever and there seems like there's this hesitant application of brakes and then more and I'm shunted into the wall and then the plane begins to vibrate spitefully and then actually jump and even leave the ground and now I'm thinking, oh fuck, it's not going to stop and I think of the story Jimmy, my boyfriend, told me, of how his convertible left the road and went into this spin but that in the end it stopped and he was, like, fine, and I hope that we'll be lucky too.

Now there's this crunching sound and the plane feels like it's turning and the tail is developing all this weight and suddenly, there's a jolt that I think almost breaks my neck and the plane stops.

For long seconds nobody can believe that the plane has come to a halt but the air stewards are rushing down the aisles and as I sit up there is this noise which I realize is seatbelts clicking and the exits are open and I notice that the oxygen masks have come down and all the overhead lockers have flown open and there are jackets and bags in the aisles. A queue forms along the aisle and people are quiet but press nervously towards the exit as we wait for the stewardess to tell us the chutes have inflated, and women are pulling off their shoes. People are saying, 'Please, please,' and the stewardess is telling people to sit and jump and the plane clears at surprising speed, although it's full. My dad catches my eye and kind of smiles and when it's our turn we slide down the chute and run from the plane which I now see has scooted off the runway and is about fifty yards from the terminal building. People are crying, but there is exultation and the grass is strewn with people lying down and the stewardesses are trying to comfort people, and the plane looks fine from where I'm looking, not buckled or broken, not in flames, and in my ear I can hear my father talking to me, looking ragged but fine.

'Well, I told you we'd be all right,' he says. 'This was all right.'

I smile at him, and right there on the grass, in total shock, I step towards him, and give him a hug, which he returns powerfully, and it's all over.

Strange Weather

MARIA CARUSO

THIS IS the first thing I noticed: a change in the sound of the wind at night as it blew the leaves of the cherry tree outside my bedroom window.

The tree's branches had always brushed against the glass, a sleepy, sweeping sound, sometimes stirring me out of sleep. It was a sound I thought of as lonely but never frightening.

But one night the wind became husky and rough, as if something wild were beating the tree, something out of balance, hissing among the branches. It was the kind of wind, though more extreme, that is the precursor to a thunderstorm in Michigan. But no thunderstorm arrived, no rain at all. I sat up in bed, watching the cherry leaves quiver, and wondered what was coming.

The next day it started – an awful stillness, and heat. The sun came closer, hovering. I could not stop going out to look at it, thinking it was too strange to last – that soon the sky would darken and a breeze stir itself and rain hush down. I could not keep cool in that weather. My face and shoulders took on a permanent red flush and in the mirror my eyes looked bright blue in contrast, the colour of something a girl would buy in a dime store.

At my high school the boys stopped waiting until they were out of sight of the schoolyard before bursting into dusty, vicious fights. And when I walked by the neighboring farms I saw the farmers spit and raise their fists like cartoon characters, angry at the sky. Everyone I knew began to look vaguely the same when the weather set; thirsty, blinking and surprised.

I was not so poetic a young woman that I thought myself responsible for the drought, or perhaps it's truer to say if I had those thoughts they were quickly followed by the knowledge that I was clearly not that powerful. I was fifteen years old and I knew my boundaries even as I pretended greater authority than I possessed. I was half one thing and half another that summer. I knew how to take a stitch in human skin but I believed if my bedroom door was not left open exactly three inches I would die before morning.

Like a portrait of a passionate woman, painted with her back to a little window through which the viewer can see a bolt of lightning striking the ground, the drought was my backdrop. The irritating heat matched my disposition, magnified it – I felt surrounded by anger and dread. You can ask anyone who has ever been in a drought if it isn't true – there is no better word to describe it than sullen. The rain refuses to fall. And under this refusal, this sullenness, is its reason.

Alone on the farm with Steven, day after day, I scarcely had to scheme to get him to do what I wanted. He felt so sorry for me. We lived on junk food and saw every movie playing at the Lido. We rode in his rusty pick-up truck, rattling as far as Saugatuck to watch the sailboats drag themselves through the waves, or to Port Huron for the horse auctions – prize geldings drooping, their flanks shiny with brushed sweat. Anything I wanted to do.

On days when he could not leave the farm but had to stay and work with our hired man on something that went wrong, again and again that summer, with the irrigation system, I paced the house. My body was the only thing in motion, and that made me feel both powerful and exhausted. The curtains hung at the windows as if they were carved from stone. The front porch was scattered with insect shells, crisp as if they had been baked. I stepped on them to hear their sharp crack. Steven saw me as he passed by.

'Go inside Cassie,' he said, 'you'll just make yourself hotter out here.'

I ignored him, rocking on the porch swing for two minutes and then walking out to check the mailbox for the second time that day, though I knew no one who would think of writing to me. I went back into the house. In the kitchen I opened every drawer, fingering the contents. My mother's sewing scissors, in the shape of a heron with rounded legs; a box of rusted screws of my father's, a rose corsage, dried to the color of rotting crab apples. I was not looking for anything but I was angry I could not find it, and I slammed the drawers shut, one after the next. After I slammed the last one I put my hands to my head, pulling at the roots of my hair. I looked up to see Steven, leaning against the doorframe and watching me.

'You're just like your mother was,' he said.

I barely knew him.

We were still in the stages with each other where he would ask me what kind of music I liked and did I want jam or maple syrup on my pancakes. I saw him hiding, and her as well, their pleasure in each other, maybe because they thought it might embarrass me. But I saw everything. Their horrible, immense happiness when they saw each other after she came home from the store or in from the garden, the way they went up to bed together. I could feel their footsteps on the stairs, trying not to race.

I had not even known him long enough to have the necessary argument with him where I was supposed to scream that he was not my father and he was supposed to say of course he wasn't, he would never try to take my father's place. We had not settled into even that much peace.

My father had been dead a long time. He remained for me mainly in photographs and certain objects; coveralls hanging on nails inside the barn, a hunting hat with fur earflaps on the shelf in the coat closet. I did not expect anything from my father, anymore. That he appeared, smiling, in a picture with me on his shoulders seemed sufficient, seemed father enough. It was my mother from whom I expected everything. It was my mother who cheated me.

After her funeral Steven and I drove to a spot by the river. At first we didn't get out the car. The river, through the trees, was just a thin slip of movement. My face was swollen and sore. Steven reached over and held me, for the first time ever besides quick hugs. He held me as if we were no longer strangers.

'It will be all right,' he kept saying. My breasts were tight against his chest and I was unable to think, unable to imagine what he meant.

When I asked him what would be all right he said everything. He did not look into my eyes but he said everything.

Then he got out of the car and walked towards the river. I followed him, ducking behind trees so he wouldn't see me. He kept looking back in the direction of the car, again and again, and I believed I was watching a man who wished to lose something.

Ever since I was old enough to balance in it I loved to sit out in our tyre swing and watch the cars shoot by, the people inside turning their heads to look at our farm. 'That's the LaFave farm,' I imagined them saying to their children – and I thought somehow the name was written on the land itself. We lived west of the highway, and as evening came I saw them squint through their rolled-up windows to see the hay barn and the silo and the house, the rows of corn streaking by like the long striped skirt of a running girl.

In town everyone called it LaFave's farm, and they meant by this not that it was the farm belonging to my family but the farm belonging to my father. His death did little if anything to dissuade a sense of his ownership, and I occasionally heard someone in the grocery store ask my mother how the LaFave farm was doing, as if she were part of the hired help. The land too seemed to know it was his – when he was alive plants sprouted and thrived under his authority. He would not have let it be otherwise. And I was like the plants, knowing always what he expected of me. I would not have dared to make a mistake, and my childhood fantasies were rife with instances of disappointing him. I used to have a recurring dream in which the three of us woke one morning to find the fields of winter wheat stretching to the horizon around us gnawed to stubble, an act which I knew I had done during the night, crawling between the rows, moving my sharp teeth to one plant after the next, watching the sky for signs of morning, hurrying, hurrying.

Steven was at best described as a reluctant farmer. Neighbours came to give him advice and I watched from my bedroom window while he toed the dirt with an unlaced boot, looking out at the dry corn rows and letting their talk blow over him. For a while they came often, shaking their heads and pointing at sections of the crop as if they were unruly children. But I knew he never meant to be a farmer; he married my mother for her lively grace, and ten years younger than she was, he took on the land at her insistence. It was not his to begin with, and I think he remembered how it belonged to the man who loved her first.

When the neighbouring farmers stopped coming by altogether Steven began to solicit my opinion on every aspect of his farming, telling me always exactly what he planned to do, naming for me the pieces of equipment he would use as if afraid of making a mistake.

Finally he worked only a tenth of our land, in narrow strips surrounding the house. He let the hired man go. If I sat very low to the ground in the front yard I could pretend everything was as it always had been.

It became very quiet, in the middle of the drought. I was afraid I would dream of rain. It was the worst thing I could imagine – dreaming of the sounds of water and then waking to the unchanged heat, waiting for it to hit me full force – this was my real life.

The dryness began to seep into our bodies. Steven's face reddened from the sun except for the tiny white lines around his eyes where he constantly squinted when he was outside. My hands were so dry I could barely stand to turn the pages of a book. I tried to help him some days, but the heat was overwhelming. Mostly I just stayed in the house, watching the fan in the kitchen turn.

One day I summoned the energy to make oatmeal cookies. I supposed it was so hot whatever the oven might add to it wouldn't matter. When I heard Steven's footsteps on the porch I ran to meet him with a plate of the cookies and he smiled when he saw me.

'These are for you,' I said.

He pulled off his shirt and used it to wipe the sweat from his face and arms. 'Did you bake them on the kitchen floor?' he asked.

'The floor was too hot, I put them into the oven to shade them.' I felt shy, and afraid I might have left something out of them, the sugar or something important, but he ate a couple at one crack and reached for more.

'Is there anything to drink?' he said.

I went into the kitchen and when I came back out I saw he had moved onto the porch swing and was forcing it slowly back, holding it there with the tips of his boots. When I handed him the Coke he said, 'Cassie, we need to talk about what we're going to do.'

I sat down on the floor of the porch with my knees pulled up, watching him. He took a long swallow from the bottle, his throat working. A fly buzzed near him and I leaned forward to brush it away. He drank down the bottle and wiped his mouth with the back of his hand.

'I think we should sell the farm,' he said. He looked out at the scorched land, sienna and gold; beautiful, but not the colours it should be. The cottonwoods that lined the highway were parched. In the distance the corn moved from a rare breeze. Neither the sound nor the breeze reached the house so it looked like the plants moved from agony, or restlessness. Earlier in the day I stripped some leaves from a corn stalk and examined them. Steven watched me for a moment and then asked if I knew what I was doing, if I was looking for something. But I was just looking at the colours of the thing, creamy white where it should have been green, streaked through with red like all its blood was coming to the surface, like some transparency was beginning.

I tried to look out where Steven was looking, not just the same direction but the exact rock or post or piece of horizon. My hands began to shake.

I though about once when I was stung by a bee. It was at Easter, and my father hid my Easter eggs under the chickens in the coop. I had always been afraid of going there, the chickens were so nervous and confused, and once a big hen flew right into my face and knocked me over, leaving long scratch marks on my neck. My father said he was hiding the eggs there so I would get over my fear – that if I wanted the eggs enough I would.

There were always a lot of bees around the chicken coop – I think because there was an old honeysuckle vine back there. I had been stung on the bottom of my foot more than once from stepping on one. So while my father watched me I went out to the coop, walking carefully through the grass in my white Easter dress. I pushed open the door with one hand, then the other. The bitter yellow-jacket sting to the palm of my hand took my breath away. But I knew my father was watching so I kept walking. Inside the coop it was as dark as night. The hens shuffled softly in their places and the air was thick with dust. My hand hurt so much I was surprised it did not glow in the dark. I could not believe so much pain could be invisible. I reached under a hen: nothing. Another: again, nothing. Under the third hen I felt an egg – but the trick was to emerge with an Easter egg, not just the ordinary sort. I held the egg in front of me, trying to see it. It was warm in my palm and I let the bee sting rest against it. I emerged from the dark of the coop, almost not daring to look at it. My father came towards me and I saw the egg was the blue-green of the sea, the colour of the thinnest part of a wave, before it breaks. Someone had written my name on it, in pink, with hearts above and below. I handed the egg to my father and he told me I was a good girl. When I showed him the bee sting he took my hand and kissed it. When I could I pulled away from him and went to where my mother was sitting on the far side of the house in a straight-backed chair. I laid my head in her lap and she stroked my hair.

'We could go down south,' said Steven, 'where my family is. Georgia.'

'Oh, Georgia,' I said. Georgia meant as little to me as a foreign country. I felt as if I had been invited to a circus or some other exotic, mountebank-driven event.

'It's nice. It's got good weather,' Steven said. He looked at the sky.

'I think we'll just stay here.' I said, politely but with some finality, as if I were settling something and there were no further need to talk about it.

'It's good you're telling me how you feel,' he said, and it sounded like the first part of something else he was going to say but he didn't say anything more.

He fried pork chops for supper. While he fixed them he told me about his sister Clary, who owned a gas station and lived with a woman named Janet. He said Clary was the sweetest thing on God's green earth, and then he amended himself by saying he didn't believe in God. He looked at me sideways to see how I was taking the news, and I told him when I was little I thought God lived in the birdfeeder in the backyard because there was a little cross on top of it. Then he started to sing *Amazing Grace* very, very off key. He plowed through the song as if it were a sun-baked piece of earth, and he the tip of a rusty old blade. Then the pork chops were done, not tender and melting like she used to make them but rubbery and black at the edges. He put them on blue plates, with store-bought bread and sliced tomatoes, still warm from the garden. He peppered everything on the plates, including the bread. He smiled and we began to eat and while we did I told him about when I made my first communion how I expected to die of happiness like Saint Agnes did and I was terrified to go up there. I tried to make it as funny as I could, waving my knife around to emphasize, and he laughed in all the right spots. Good pork chops, I said.

I never did learn to like going in the chicken coop, but I did it every day, late in the morning. I gathered the eggs from the limp chickens, trapped beneath their thick feathers. Every egg a plain colour – brownish, white or cream.

I dusted my mother's bone china and her bookcases full of Russian and English novels and cleaned the bevelled glass of the front windows but only from the inside. I spent my afternoons weaving long scenarios for myself about how I would get the farm back if Steven sold it.

A man stopped by one afternoon, walking slowly up the drive with his hat in his hand. He called out to me when he saw me watching him from the porch. He asked if Mr LaFave was looking for anyone to help out. His dark hair fell over one eye, drawing my gaze to the other and I said, without meaning to, that no one could help him now. Made braver by my uncharacteristic flippancy, and braver still by my loneliness, I coaxed him to drink some lemonade on the porch with me. He said he wouldn't mind and I listened to the creak of the swing while he waited for me to make it, hurrying to mix the sugar in, stinging a cut on my hand with the lemon juice.

I brought it to him, embarrassed before he even tasted it, and it was, as I knew it would be, too sour when I drank it there with him – though I tasted it twice when I mixed it in the kitchen and it had been all right then. He stayed on the porch swing and I sat on the steps, looking up at him. I ran my fingers through my hair, feeling his eyes on me.

'You're Cassandra, right?' he said.

'How do you know me?'

'My family used to live around here, a long time ago. I just remember you, for some reason. I remember the house.'

'This house isn't so special.'

'No. But you live here – that makes it different. I remember your mom, too. Black hair. How's she doing?'

'Fine,' I said, 'she's not here now.'

'You used to wear your hair in pigtails, down low under your ears. My little sisters always wanted their mama to fix their hair the same way.'

I blushed and drank my lemonade. I held still when he came and sat next to me on the steps, keeping my eyes down. Everything was motionless and hot. He touched my hair. He told me I was so pretty. He asked me what it was like, to be alone in the house. I felt myself leaning towards him, listening to his voice, which was burred and low.

'What's a little thing like you doing here by yourself?' he said.

'Everyone has gone,' I said.

'You sure?'

'Well, I have a cat,' I said – thinking it might make him laugh.

'That all?' he asked, not laughing, his voice serious and close to my ear.

'That's all,' I whispered.

He put his hand into the top of my dress, touching my chest like that was all he wanted and then he slid his hand lower. I felt I was giving something to him; that he would think I was sweet if I let him. I wished I had just had a bath. I wished my skin smelled of orange talcum and verbena. But he put his face against me as if I were the nicest thing he'd ever smelled. It felt better than anything. Like he was stirring up the cool inside of me. He put his mouth to my nipples, outside my dress, wetting the fabric. I wanted something I could not put a name to. Can I kiss your mouth? he said. Kiss me, I said.

He was kissing me, his mouth slippery and hot, his tongue reaching into me when Steven came around the corner of the house.

'Cassie,' was all he said, and he said it like one word could be a question.

The man stood up, looking at the ground, wiping his mouth with the back of his hand and I was embarrassed for Steven to see the man wiping me off of his mouth.

'You better go,' said Steven.

'All right,' said the man.

I covered the front of my dress with one arm, holding my shoulder.

The man jumped the railing on the porch, stumbled slightly, and walked down the drive toward the road. He did not look back. When he was gone Steven turned and went into the house and I followed him. He sat down in the front room and worked the laces on his boots loose.

'He's a farmer,' I said.

Steven didn't say anything and I said, 'He'd know how to farm this land.'

Steven kicked his boot away and said, 'Then maybe he can have it when we're gone.'

'I'm not leaving. You go if you want to.'

'You haven't got a choice, Cassie, what are you going to do? Stay here by yourself?'

'I am here by myself,' I said. I think I expected him to get angry.

He rubbed his forehead with his hand. 'Don't you think I know that? Of course you are. But I can't do it. This place was your mom's – everything here was hers.'

'Don't you want to be reminded of her?' I said.

When he answered me he spoke so slowly I leaned toward him, waiting for his words.

'Not just now, I don't. Can you understand? Please try.'

'I don't even know who you are. I wish my mother never married you.'

After I spoke we looked away from each other, but it was a small room – there wasn't too much to look at. We both looked towards the window and as we did the draperies lifted, the air so hot it wasn't like a breeze at all, just a shifting.

When he got up and went into the kitchen I thought it through. If only my mother had never married him. I'd have the farm to myself. Everything would grow for me, like it had for my father. I could do whatever I wanted, all the time. My mother would come back, somehow, to keep me company. I followed Steven into the kitchen and told him I would not leave. I said it like I meant it. My father always said to me: say it like you mean it, Cassandra, or no one will believe you. My father said so many things to me like he meant them. Like there was no room for my dissension. I will not leave, I said. Well that's just great, said Steven.

'I am not a drinking man,' said Steven.

He was not talking to me. I was up in my room, my ear to the heating vent on the floor next to my bed. I could hear the voices downstairs clearly. He was talking to a woman. She giggled.

'You're drunk,' she said to him.

'May well be,' said Steven, 'but I am not a drinking man.'

'Maybe that's why you're drunk,' the woman said, and giggled again.

He must have gone to the window then, and pulled back the curtain, because he said, 'Everything you see before you is mine. As far as the horizon are my own lands.'

He sounded like a king in a cartoon but the woman said, 'gosh,' in a hushed tone. They were quiet for a minute and then I heard the woman say, 'Why don't you take this thing off?'

I shut the vent, as softly as I could, and got into bed. My mother made my quilt, white with every shade of blue in scattered squares.

I must have fallen asleep then because I woke to Steven talking to me. I am sorry about everything, he said. I didn't open my eyes. I shifted as if I were still asleep, turning away from him. He put his hand on the quilt, touching my shoulder through its layers.

'I'm sorry about everything,' he said again, more softly, 'I have tried to do this, but I don't know how to be anything to you.'

A couple of days after that Steven woke me very early in the morning. It was still dark. I sweated under a thin sheet, angry with him for bringing me into the heat when I had been ignorant of it only a moment before. I wanted to pull the sheet down to my waist to let the warmth escape from under it but I couldn't with him standing there.

'There are some things I need to do, Cassie,' he said. He spoke slowly, clearly, as if my ears might still be asleep. The keys to the truck shook in his hand.

'Can I come with you?'

He did not answer right away. He put his hand through his hair.

'No,' he said.

I did not argue with him. When he left the room I couldn't fall back asleep. My legs were wet where they had lain against each other and my hair clung to my face. I listened to the sounds of him leaving the house, getting in the truck, starting the motor. I went to my window because I wanted to see him drive away, the tail lights of the pick-up glowing and then fluttering and then disappearing.

I went downstairs and began to clean the house. I pulled out the ammonia, the brushes, the bottles of cleanser. I learned from my mother it is possible to calm yourself by scrubbing. When my parents fought they often drove off, to have their fight away from me in the car. They always came home to a shining house and when I was a little older my mother would joke with me they fought so they could come home to a clean house. The night I got the call from Steven at the hospital, telling me my mother had collapsed in a restaurant, I turned the house inside out to clean it. Lemon ammonia, the grit of cleanser, the sound of a mop wrung out in the sink, these things stave off fear. Of course, they are not the final arbiters, they stave off nothing forever.

He had not taken the clothes from his closet. I checked and for a moment felt better, until I saw my mother's dresses hanging there too.

I plotted, during the afternoon, of how exactly to get him in as much trouble as possible. I took a long cold bath and put on a blue cotton dress he once said looked pretty on me. I imagined the voices of the neighbours, shocked and concerned at what had happened to me. Abandoned. I made dinner, thinking that might bring him. I sat in the kitchen while I ate it and tried to think of nothing, watching a sweat rise on my clean arms, feeling my dark hair collecting the heat and holding it at the crown of my head.

I went outside and could feel myself pale under the strong light. Everything was bright, bright. Steven kept the birdbath filled and birds sat in the water, occasionally ducking their heads under and lifting their wings in quick succession. I walked to the stone bath, the water like a bowl of light. The birds quietly flew off and I dipped my hand in, the water soft around my fingertips. A car drove by, coming slowly out of the distance like a thing that would never arrive, finally passing with the squeak and crunch of gravel, rising dust that hung in the light like a veil after it passed. Its passengers did not look up at the farm, at me. I thought he was not coming. He was the same age I am now. If I were him, would I have come?

I imagine his day's driving took him out of that strange weather altogether; that he gained, at his furthest point away from me, a day of ordinary summer, with a breeze, maybe with clouds. He never said to me directly, then or later, that he tried to leave. And sometimes I thought I was wrong for believing it.

When his truck pulled into the drive, in the late evening, I felt a surge inside me. I thought for certain I had hoped too hard for his return – I wanted it too much and therefore he would not come. That he came knocked down a piece of the philosophy I lived by, all my childhood. He sat in the truck and I clattered across the porch and down the steps and across the yard to him. I put out my hand and reached through the window of the truck to touch his shoulder. But he was dreamy, far away.

I would like to ask him, still, to show me how far he got. I would like to ask him to take me to the spot where he turned around to come back. I would like to stand there, for a moment, to see what he was looking at when he decided to retrace his path, back to the farm. I imagine a road cool and lush, shaded with pine trees.

The branches of the cherry tree brushed against my window, a soft, yearning sound. The rain was like everything I'd lost, falling from the sky. It melted against my windows and sluiced down in waves, over and over. I had awakened from a dream that my mother had uprooted everything in the vegetable garden, that she wanted me to help her. I watched the rain for a few moments and then I pulled a nightgown over my head and went to wake Steven.

When I stood at the threshold of his room I hesitated. His room was a solitary, separate place, ghostly blue. I could hear him breathing, steadily, low. He was lying on his stomach and I touched his skin with my fingertips.

'It's raining,' I said.

He turned toward me, lifting himself on an elbow, and then looked out the window. The rain pinged off the eaves.

'It is,' he said.

I said his name, thinking he wasn't understanding.

'O.K.,' he said. 'It's raining. It's raining. What do you want me to do? It's over with. The corn couldn't suck up water from a flood.'

'Please.'

'Please what? It's too late, Cassie.' He sat all the way up.

'It's only too late because you want it to be,' I said.

'I didn't ask for any of this. Listen to me. It wasn't supposed to happen this way. And I can't fix it. I only get to decide what happens some of the time. A very small percentage of the time.'

I turned away from him and started to cry. He got out of bed and stood next to me. He touched my back. I could feel his fingers shaking through the cotton of my nightgown.

I said, 'And me, I wasn't supposed to happen like this either, was I?'

'You? Don't ever say that,' he said and his hands circled my arms.

'Everything about you happens just how it should,' he said.

'My mother isn't coming back,' I said.

'She'll always be with you, Cassie. She'll always be with me.'

'Oh big deal. Big deal,' I said. He held me then, and I cried a long time.

It was not until the summer before I was to finish my last year at college that Steven and I returned to Michigan, to see the farm and what became of it.

We parked out on the road at evening, shy of steering up the tree-lined drive. From a distance the farm looked perfect. We walked up underneath the trees, and as we drew close I began to see the great disrepair, paint peeling off in sheets, cracked windows, a missing front step. The porch swing was suspended from only one end, with a length of knotted rope.

I did not look at Steven. A woman came out onto the porch and shielded her eyes with one hand, squinting out at us. As Steven went towards her I turned away, heading towards a birch copse between the yard and the fields. I hid myself in the trees and looked out at the farm, breathing deeply. For a moment I let myself imagine nothing had ever happened to me – that I still lived here – days passing, waking at night to the low sounds of my parent's voices.

My eyes settled on Steven and the woman in the doorway. They laughed about something, and Steven waved in my direction, though I don't think he could see exactly where I was. I came out from my hiding place, walking through the yard slowly, trying to look as if I were not particularly interested in anything. I traced the circling of ivy on the old stone bird bath. There were leaves under the water and I fished them out. Everything was not as I had left it. The hay barn looked smaller, and the distance between it and the house not as far as it used to be.

Steven introduced me to the woman and I smiled.

'She says it's been raining like crazy this summer,' Steven said.

'So how long did you live here?' the woman asked him.

'Well, really,' Steven said, 'I only lived here for a while.'

'But I thought you said...'

'It belonged to my wife,' Steven started to say. 'It was her first husband's...'

'No, it was Steven's farm,' I said. 'It was ours.'

I turned and walked to the tyre swing, threaded my body through it so that I was facing the road. Steven was still talking with the woman and I could hear snatches of their conversation. Beautiful, I heard Steven say, beautiful, beautiful. I spun on the tyre swing and saw the decaying buildings, rusty old cars on cinderblocks where the kitchen garden used to be, but also the trees, in rich full leaf, the crops thick and sturdy like specimen examples in encyclopedia pictures.

After a few more minutes Steven came down the steps of the porch and we walked back to the truck together. Before getting in I turned to raise my hand to the woman on the porch, but she had already gone. We drove away, and he reached over and touched my hand. The cottonwoods swayed above us, the leaves making their sweet rush of summery noise.

Officer Shenstone's Nigger

R. D. GALBRAITH

SHENSTONE MUST have seen that nigger from the bar. That was where he always stood at that time of the day on that day of the week. After the whole thing was over I had a word with Israel to see if I could squeeze anything out of him – you know, to see if Shenny was acting strange that day, if there was something out of the ordinary. Of course, the man was born useless and he couldn't tell me nothing worth listening to. Anyway, Shenny went in to do his duty by way of asking Israel (he's no Sheeny by the way, his mother just liked the sound of the word and didn't know any better), if there was anything he should know about.

'Nope,' was what Israel said. 'Ain't no trouble here Shenny.' Israel could get a little familiar sometimes, but Shenstone knew an idiot when he saw one and never let it bother him.

Let it also be said (although I hasten to say I had a high regard for the man), that the brevity of Israel's reply never stopped our good Officer Shenstone from accepting the free beer which, if he waited long enough (and he usually did), was always offered.

I'd often watched him there. He had some style, no end of little ways about him, but always the same. There was a reliable feel to the man. I can see him as if he was standing there now, drinking his beer and drawing the first finger of his hand across his mouth to draw a little mustache of foam off. He was a quiet man, would never speak if it wasn't necessary. He'd just stand there and think his thoughts and watch himself in the mirror. His father (it was even before my time), had been a schoolteacher, and some folks seemed to think he'd come down in the world. Another thing; he'd never married, or not by that stage anyhow. That was a puzzle to some people, for Shenstone was a fine looking man.

And so on that day he must have looked to his left, creasing up his eyes at the hot brightness of the early afternoon beyond the bar-room window and seen that damn nigger just sitting on the sidewalk, up to no good.

'Israel,' said Officer Shenstone. 'You seen that boy before?'

'Nope,' said Israel, twisting a linen cloth into the bottom of a glass.

Then came one of those occasions, all entirely accidental so far as anybody has ever been able to work out, on which Israel said something meaningful: 'He don't belong here.'

With two inches of beer left Shenstone scowled out at the nigger, willing him to stand up and walk away. It had been weeks since his job had actually forced him to do something and this wasn't the right day to end the run of good luck. This period of peace had been earned by him sending the last nigger out of town with a lump on the back of his head the size of a Grade A goose egg. Even so, as Shenny well knew, such stories faded quickly from niggerdom's collective memory and frequent refreshers were by far the easiest way of keeping the town decent.

With nothing but a couple of slips of foam left in the bottom of his glass, Officer Shenstone stuck his thumb in his belt and walked out of the bar. He crossed the street and planted his shiny boots right under that nigger's nose, but he wouldn't move a muscle. We all thought there was going to be trouble right away. Shenny was a man with a reputation after all. All he could see of that nigger was the back of his woolly head staring down at the dirt, so dusty it was like an old man's, and his shoulders, powerful already although he was hardly more than a boy. No shoes and a pair of dungarees with more holes than threads in them. Shenny gave him a good kick on the shin and told him:

'I'm talking to you, boy.'

The boy looked up, creasing his face up in the glare and seeing Shenstone's great black form, standing there like he was God Almighty himself. Alec and I had just come out of Miller's (we'd been fixing the fan there), so we stopped under the shade of the awning to watch the proceedings. Still the nigger said nothing and I thought; boy, you're going to get it carrying on like that. You're going to get it good and hard. I could see Shenny's fingers itching around the handle of his billy. I could almost feel that bump rising on the back of my own head.

Shenny knew we were watching by then. He turned a bit and glared at us like we were going to be next. His shirt was sticking to him and his face was red as a bitch baboon's ass.

'Where you from, boy?'

The nigger just put his head down again and stared at the street. I thought he was going to get it there and then, but at the last moment he had the sense to point up the street and say: 'That way.'

'Well thank you, sir. That's an answer to my question that is. You'll tell me where you're from if you know what's good for you, boy.'

The nigger pointed up the street again, like this was his own town:

'That way, about twenty miles. More maybe, I dunno. From Stenton.' He settled his head down again between his knees.

Shenstone looked about himself: 'Is there another nigger here, boy, or are you talking to me?'

'Stenton, sir,' said the nigger.

"Swat I thought you said. Now tell me boy, what's stopping you from going back there?'

Again he was asking for it. He said nothing, just put his head down and clasped his hands around the back of his neck. Alec was laughing and called out to Shenstone:

'Do your duty, Shenny!' but he just ignored him.

The nigger wouldn't say a word. A full half minute passed without a sound. It was like a photograph; the nigger crouching on the sidewalk, his bare feet on the burning street, Shenstone standing there with his hands on his belt, pouring with sweat, waiting for an answer, Alec and me leaning in the shade outside Miller's waiting for the action. Then there was this noise like nothing I'd ever heard before, like halfway between some hound howling and some sort of siren. The sound began to break up into huge gasping sobs, and then we realised. He was crying. Weeping like a child, curling himself up like he was trying to disappear, his whole body jerking. We could hear Shenny starting to curse and blaspheme and look up and down the street like he wanted to be sure there was no one there. Apart from us four, it seemed that the whole world had died of the heat, and we could hear every word that was said.

'Listen boy, I'm not going to have some nigger bum salting the streets of this town d'you hear?' We could see that he was trying to be quiet, but it was no use. He wailed like an animal with its leg in a gin. All Shenny had to do was book him for vagrancy and run him out of town with a lump on his head, same as the last one. God knows what he was thinking of, but whatever it was, that was when the whole business started. I still can't understand it; it was all so unnecessary.

He said to the nigger: 'Can you work, boy?'

I guess we were all about as surprised as each other. It certainly shut the boy up. It took him a good while (and he wasn't the only one), to realise that Shenstone was actually offering him something. He wiped his face with his forearms and stood up, tall enough to look Shenstone in the eye.

'Yessir,' he said, loud and clear. 'I can work. I'm willing, sir.'

'Well,' said Shenstone, 'you can't go near decent folks smelling like that. Follow me.' The nigger trooped after him like he was his foreman, round towards the railway depot.

That was the last I saw of him till the whole business was over. The rest I pieced together from talking to folks in the town. Shenstone took him to the back of the depot where there was an old standpipe and no ladies. He told the nigger to strip off and wash himself with the water from the standpipe. He did as he was told, meek as a lamb, while Jack and a couple of the other railway boys looked on from the staff rooms over the way. Shenstone disappeared and came back a few minutes later with a loaf and a couple of red apples he'd presumably bought in Miller's. He found his nigger standing there, naked, drying himself in the sun, told him sharpish to get his clothes on, gave him the bread and apples and left again, telling him that if he moved from that spot he'd give him ten days in the cells and a lesson he'd never forget.

In the half hour he was gone he crossed the town, went up the hill and called at the Athlone house. By that time it was already getting a bit seedy, but I remember it in its heyday. It was the widow Athlone's father who first made the money and had the house built before the first war as a retreat from the city. The place was run almost like a colony. All sorts of finery would come down from the north to spend the vacations (they were the sort of people who had vacations), with the Athlone's and for a month the place was like a Broadway show. Then some more money would have to be made and the house would be shut up for most of the rest of the year.

The present Mrs Athlone and her husband began to make more frequent use of the house and when he died she sold up in New York and came down here to settle. A strange decision in a way, and she's always been some way apart from the rest of the town. Of course that never stopped her from ruling the place; chairwoman of the Woman's Voluntary Committee, coordinator of this appeal or that, first port of call for the nearest Democrat. Never had much to do with the woman myself, all I know is that a few years back she was unwell and little of her has been seen since then. The house was let slip and the servants became a little free with what was left of the Athlone fortune.

Only the doctor was seeing her regular then, and after the dust had settled I got the story from him. It seems that Shenstone never intended to see Mrs. Athlone herself. She still kept a gardener then and he was the man he was after. He went to the outhouses to find him but before too long was accosted by one of the house staff and told that 'Mrs. Athlone would see him now.' I laughed when I heard that. That was the widow Athlone alright, that was her through and through. So what could he do?

He was shown into the ballroom which I guess hasn't been danced on in a generation. Apparently it was all but empty; just one small corner by the window at the side which was furnished like an old-fashioned parlour. From there Mrs. Athlone could look down the driveway and watch the comings and goings, including Shenstone's coming. It seems they got off on the wrong foot from the very start. Shenstone explained (or made up as the case may be), the idea that he had heard of some work that needed doing about the place and that he had a young man who needed a few dollars worth to pay his way back home.

'I can't imagine why you have heard that, Mr Shenstone. I gave no such instructions.'

Shenstone explained that he'd heard it from the gardener.

'And did you think that I employ a gardener to make decisions for me?' Shenstone said he was sure she didn't, he must have been mistaken, excused himself and was on his way out when Mrs. Athlone decided she was interested after all. She had little enough human contact then and I reckon she wasn't about to let go of it whether she liked the sound of it or not.

'What sort of young man,' she asked.

'Just a young man down on his luck,' said Shenstone. 'A young man who needs to make an honest dollar or two to pay his way back home.'

'A young man you would prefer to get out of town, Mr Shenstone?'

'I think that's what we'd all prefer, mam. I just thought there might be another way of doing it. If there's any work to be done I thought it might be convenient. I understood you had, well, social interests.'

This irritated her no end; 'presumption' she called it, 'height of presumption.'

'A young man, you say.'

'That's right, mam. A young, man.' That was the only way Shenstone described him. The doctor said she seemed obsessed by this, went on and on about it like he'd lied to her. They were a sly pair, I'll say that. Then Mrs Athlone started to worry about the money.

'I am expected to facilitate this young man's departure?'

'It's normal to pay a man for his work, mam, but I wouldn't want to impose. If you can oblige with some work then I'll put something aside and you can decide later what it's worth.'

She just turned round and returned to her gazing out the window, dismissing Shenstone with the opinion that if he thought it was wise he could tell his young man to come and talk to her gardener. And that's how they parted, I suppose with some sort of an understanding but exactly what wasn't easy to say.

Shenstone walked back to the centre of town, leaving a five dollar bill on the salver in the hall as he left. When he got back behind the railway depot he found his nigger there squatting in a patch of shade, apples and bread gone, sleeping like a dog. The boys in the staff room were a few hands further on, but otherwise hadn't moved from the table by the window. He gave him a vicious kick, waking him with a jolt.

'You don't smell much better, do you boy?' The nigger stood up smartly and looked Shenstone in the eye.

'I've got a chance for you if you're willing to take it.'

'Yes, sir.'

'Let's make sure we understand one another first. This town isn't a charity. You get a few dollars-worth of work and you use it to get out of here, to go back where you came from or wherever you like. No one here will care. Got it?'

'Yes sir,' said the nigger, 'I understand.'

'Follow me,' said Shenstone and off they trooped up to the Athlone house.

When they got there the gardener had been spoken to by Mrs. Athlone and everything seemed straightforward. One of the sheds by the side of the house had a heap of raw wood in it from trees in the grounds that had been blown down in the big storm the year before. The gardener handed over an axe you could have shaved with, told the nigger to heave that wood out, put it on the block and get choppping. I never heard any complaints from the gardener. It was a day to sweat your life out just standing still, but he never stopped. After a while he just rolled his dungarees down to his waist and kept on going till sundown. Doctor told me that Mrs. Athlone never took her eyes off him. She must have sat by that window a third of the day, her face white as death, just watching that axe rising and falling like it was part of some machine. Before the end he must have disappeared behind the pile of chopped wood with Mrs. Athlone just sitting in the gloom listening. I was up there myself some weeks later or I wouldn't have believed it. The gardener swore that no one had touched the pile since that night. There was one last thing that capped the whole business. By the time it was full night they had to tell him to stop, but they wouldn't give him his money. They told him to come back the next day to finish the job and then he'd get his bill. I don't take sides in these matters, you know that. All the same, it was a mean way to save five dollars.

By the time Shenstone next saw him there was a small crowd there already. It was the sort of news that travels fast. Like the rest I'd heard it on the rumour mill and got there a little before him; I'd been doing a bit of work on that side of the town. They'd done it from the old walnut tree. There was Officer Shenstone's nigger (as he was soon to be known), hanging there from the one big bough that stretches over the water. His head was all cricked to one side, the rough rope cutting into his neck. They'd stripped him naked, cut off his manhood. There were already flies clustering around the wound and on the surface of the river the ripples of a big catfish moving below, stirring up the dirt, smelling his blood. The Sheriff and some of his men were there, standing around. There was even a couple of Feds taking notes and photographs before getting into their fancy car and driving off to make their report.

Shenstone arrived a couple of minutes after I did. I suppose he must have known what to expect; I got the impression he'd had the chance to prepare himself. He had that stiff way of walking like he was about to bang someone on the head as soon as they stepped out of line. He planted his boots in the mud right by the edge, stuck his thumbs in his belt and stared at the nigger without saying a word. The body began to sway a little as a breeze picked up, the rope creaking on the bough. There was a fair amount of business behind him; the Sheriff and his men talking and the growing number of onlookers asking each other to explain the obvious. The Sheriff's men began to go around asking and I told them what Alec and I had seen the day before, which at that time was all I knew. They didn't seem interested, for the very good reason, I suppose, that they already knew about it. Everyone knew about it, but we all wanted to pretend otherwise and Shenstone's frozen, silent back was making it more difficult by the minute. Before long an itchy silence settled over us and people began to move away. Others who hadn't seen the show yet, looked from a distance but didn't come right down to the bank. One of the Sheriff's men crawled along the walnut bough and cut the rope, another waded in to grab the end and pull the body in, yanking it onto the mud like he was pulling a boat up a beach. He let it drop just a few feet from where Shenny was standing. He turned with nothing in his face, just nothing and walked out of there without a sound, without a look in the eye for any of us.

Now I don't know if this is true, but it don't take much to believe it. The word was that a few days later Shenny received an envelope from the Athlone house. From Mrs. Athlone, I suppose, though there was no name, no letter, just a five dollar bill.

Well, it was never the same for Shenstone after that. Within a few weeks most us weren't ever to see him again. I caught sight of him once, years later, in the city. He was still in uniform, still looking a fine man, but he wouldn't look at me. A lot of people could never quite forgive him for what he did. It came as a terrible shock to some to realise that a man in whom they had put their trust could be so... how to put it?

So unsound.

Expect Jail

NICK KELLY

EVERY WEEKDAY for the past three months my wife and I have been riding the Piccadilly Line, the section from Acton Town to Cockfosters.

These journeys have been the most exciting events of our thirty-one year marriage, more delicious than our honeymoon, more fulfilling than the day I became a partner with my firm (Whelkstall & Amersham, 1 Lincoln's Inn Fields, London EC1R 3AU, Telex: Bluechip, London), more thrilling than even the births of our two now full-grown sons, Edmund and Alexander.

Alicia, my life's companion, knows me better than I know myself. I think she had been planning for my retirement for months, years maybe, although she never so much as mentioned it to me.

For myself, to be honest, I had given it very little thought; like most professional men, I suppose I had just assumed that it would be all late lie-ins, rounds of golf, a glass of good wine with every lunch, at least two with every dinner, plenty of reading, long leisurely conversations with other similarly carefree friends and perhaps a new hobby, such as water-colour painting or researching my family tree.

How surprising then, eleven days after my grand retirement dinner at the Savoy, to find myself in tears in my favourite armchair in my study, not knowing what to do with myself and the fearfully empty hours that stretched before me.

But, apparently, not a surprise to dear Alicia at all.

'There, there, my old bulldog,' she crooned to me, dabbing at my wet face with her no-nonsense matron's handkerchief. I had not even realised that she was in the house. She must have sensed that that day would be the day of my disintegration, and postponed her appointments (she is the chairwoman of the Committee of Friends of the Victoria & Albert Museum) to be ready to appear by my side.

She did not wait for me to offer an explanation. I suppose she knew that I would not have one.

Moving slightly away from my chair, she lowered her head, just letting me catch the mischievous glint in her dark eyes: 'I think it's time we did a little work on our Naughties, my darling' – she smiled at my obvious shock – 'now that we've got all this time on our hands.'

'But what can you mean...?' I breathed.

She stooped slightly forward, and with her slim gloved hands – she was, I now noticed, dressed for going out – she lifted the hem of her neat skirt to her waist: she wore no underthings!

My vision clouded and starred as if I had bumped my head. The sudden understanding of what she was suggesting, the sudden realisation that she was perfectly and happily serious, made my stomach acid with lust.

'The Naughties' was our phrase for our one recurrent shared sexual fantasy, a fantasy that had had its first, tremulous airing some six years into our marriage (Alicia was, of course, the first to take the plunge by relating some of her imaginings one night to her weary and ever-so-slightly-bored husband in order to make him sit up and take his nose out of his bedtime book).

We would be on a train, or some other form of public transport together. We would be sitting next to one another, but we would pretend that we were strangers and would not talk to each other, or take any discernible notice of one another's actions. I would be reading a paper, so that my face would be hidden to most of the other travellers. Alicia would catch the eye of some fellow passenger sitting opposite. He would be a handsome man, not young, by appearance a successful doctor or lawyer. She would smile at him. My newspaper would be completely blocking my view of her, but I would be able to peep surreptitiously around the other edge and see his reaction to my wife. Alicia would then, very discreetly, make some rearranging movement with her skirt, allowing this handsome man to see that she was wearing no underwear. I would only know the precise moment of her revelation to him by the change in his expression. He would show a flicker of amazement, but then regain his controlled, professional composure. She would repeat the movement some minutes later, and then once or twice more if necessary, to make him understand that it was no accident. Eventually he would drop something (a coin, a book) onto the carriage floor, and using the retrieval of this as an excuse to stand up he would reseat himself beside my wife, so that she would have one of us on either side. They would then start to talk. Although they would speak quietly, Alicia would make sure that her words would be just audible to me, anonymous behind my paper, though his might not. She would then begin to say outrageous things to him, sexual things, carnal invitations and suggestions. Although his verbal responses would be muted, by peering around the edge of my paper across the carriage I would be able to see his physical reactions to her reflected in the carriage window in front of which he had been sitting until just a few minutes before.

That was it; The Naughties never went any further, nor needed to. Just the relating of the scene was enough to make us as erotically-charged as schoolyard virgins. And I suppose, in truth, I had never given it serious consideration outside of our own, lights-out love-making. It was always a private thing, a joke with just enough truth to be really amusing. There was, to misappropriate a phrase much in vogue with the younger partners at Whelkstall, a glass ceiling: a barrier beyond which The Naughties could never even contemplate going.

But now, as Alicia stood beaming before me, I realised that the glass ceiling had evaporated. There was no reason why we should not do it. We would do it. Why shouldn't we?

My bold, brave, darling Alicia!

There have been more than twenty by now. We chose the Piccadilly Line over the other local option, the Central, principally because of its extremities: our plan would work better when, city striving towards country, the gaps between stops became longer, and we felt that we were more likely to find suitable candidates (late-middle years, professional, of good stock and breeding) travelling to Cockfosters and Southgate than to Hainault or Ongar.

They have been tremendously varied.

The first, perhaps because Alicia was new to the practice and unsure of herself, was the youngest: he cannot have been much more than forty.

He was a big, burly man, with a face that looked ready to fly into a rage at the slightest provocation. He had little guile, and his jaw dropped comically open when he first became aware of my wife's selective undress. He coughed very loudly and looked immediately away, reddening furiously. For the next minute or two he was beside himself, mortified, staring down at the carriage floor, fiddling with his big, ugly watch, waiting for my wife or one of the other passengers to laugh at him or demand an angry explanation for his unforgivable behaviour, as if he had himself removed Alicia's knickers. When he finally realised that nobody else in the carriage had noticed anything untoward, he allowed himself another furtive glance. This time, finding that my wife, so far from objecting to his interest in her, was unmistakably pleased, he allowed his eyes to linger, and, as I could clearly see, his body began to react, causing him to shift awkwardly in his seat and dig his hands deep into the pockets of his expensive (but not perfectly cut) grey pinstripe. When (as we had discussed beforehand) she looked directly into his eyes, smiled, and discreetly patted the vacant seat to her left with her gloved hand, he hesitated only for a moment (one last check to make sure his intolerable behaviour had really gone unnoticed) before clumsily crossing to sit beside her. She used the same kinds of words as she had always used to me for The Naughties. I could not hear how he replied, but his posture – viewed in the window opposite – was not masterful; he craned his head so that his ears were almost at my wife's lips, as if to ensure that she did not feel the need to raise her voice. Later on Alicia told me that he had not responded to her with any erotic talk of his own. All he had been able to bring himself to do was mutter 'yes...I know...yes...,'and make one final, adolescent suggestion of a rendezvous later in the week in a hotel. This (as we had arranged) was politely turned down. At Southgate (the last stop but two) Alicia said a friendly 'goodbye, so nice to have met you' and, to the man's utter horror, we both stood up simultaneously, linked arms and left the train. We found a nice, ordinary café near the station where she gave me a complete run-down on The Shy Quantity Surveyor.

Number Two, much older and more suave, was The Aftershave Greek. He barely raised an eyebrow at the initial approach, as if middle-aged women flashed him on trains every day. He did talk back, but, perhaps predictably, it was in the hackneyed imagery of English soft-pornography, all barrow-boy clichés. When we left him at Arnos Grove, he hardly reacted at all, turning his attention back to his briefcase, as if he had had better things to be doing all along and had only talked to her out of courtesy.

After him came The Nearly-Millionaire, The Cummerbund Man, Doctor Smarmy, The Councillor, Little Lawman, Big Lawman. These nick-names owed more to guess-work than hard information: rarely did one of our subjects reveal much about himself outside of his fantasies.

The encounters, of their nature, were very brief. I think the longest – Little Lawman, Knightsbridge to Turnpike Lane – was only about twenty minutes. It is to my wife's great credit that she managed to glean such a rich yield of erotic information and experience in such short lengths of time. But, then again, Alicia has never been a dawdler, nor an utterer of platitudes. I truly think she has a talent, an ability to cut through to the fundamentals at astonishing speed. I had noticed small hints of this capacity before, but these last three months have been a revelation.

Some were terrified throughout their little adventure and barely spoke at all. Some were predictable in their smuttiness, like The Aftershave Greek. Some had fantasies which seemed so mundane that it was difficult to be sure whether they were completely sexually pedestrian or, on the contrary, so acutely sexually aware as to be able to find pleasures where less sensitive fantasists could see nothing of interest at all. And some were born erotic tale-tellers, relaxed, powerfully descriptive, sparing with profanity so as to preserve its full exquisitely shocking effect for when the moment was just right, full of surprising and exciting counter-suggestions, giving far more than they received from Alicia.

It may seem surprising that we have never been confronted by the same subject twice. But, in fact, the more advanced in years one becomes, the more one is a creature of routine, and by varying the time of day travelled and the carriage entered – and, of course, by keeping our eyes open – we have not had any embarrassing second meetings. (Once we did see The

Cummerbund Man entering a door at the far end of our carriage, but we managed to escape before the doors shut, and I'm sure he noticed nothing).

On all but two occasions, Alicia politely terminated the encounter and we left her admirer at Southgate, Arnos Grove or an earlier station if necessary. On the days when we got a 'catch', we never travelled as far as Cockfosters. It would obviously have been unwise to disembark at the same station as the gentleman concerned, and my wife seemed instinctively able to tell how soon his destination was approaching and take appropriate action. Quite how she managed this, I am not sure. Possibly some urgency began to creep into his mumbled carnality, or he tried to shift the conversation from fantasy-relating to actually making erotic proposals (always gracefully ignored or declined). At any rate, Alicia almost invariably took the person by surprise with her farewell and we would step out of the carriage just as the automatic doors began to slide shut. We would then spend a wonderful three-quarters of an hour huddled close at a corner table in some cosy hostelry like student lovers, discussing that day's gentleman, his attributes and his shortcomings, and speculate from what we already knew of him as to what else might lie unrevealed.

Our journeys back to Acton Town – we decided from the start to confine Alicia's attention-seeking activities to the outbound trips – were full of giddy, hard-to-conceal excitement. For no sooner were we back in the sanctuary of our large bedroom than we would tear at each other's clothes and gurgle and gasp with lust, laughing and moaning as we consumed each other. I used to imagine our intimate life as about average, good enough but necessarily dulled by familiarity and the passage of years. Now, I occasionally feel that we must really have been rather a staid couple as regards these things. I find myself wondering whether any of our close married friends have been enjoying the kind of relations Alicia and I have just discovered ourselves capable of throughout their own long marriages. For she has been set ablaze by the intimate attentions of these total strangers she has encountered, as I have by the knowledge that their attentions will be unrequited and that, whatever their qualities and charms, at the end of our tube trip, it will not be they that beds my irresistible wife, but I. Together we revel in the treasure-trove of intimate data that she has gleaned from the gentlemen she has spoken to on our expeditions, their stories, their bragging, their own fantasies and insecurities. We have amassed an unrivalled database of erotic detail, which we can access at any time. We – at our age, can you credit it? – have become experts in the clandestine craft of sex.

As I say, on only two occasions has an encounter not resolved itself in the ordinary way, by Alicia suddenly abandoning her suitor, taking him by surprise as she and I made our clean getaway.

The first was six or seven weeks ago. The rather intense little man we later christened The Repentant Perv, who had initially leapt at the bait of Alicia's bare thighs, and who had regaled her with some of the most forthright stuff that she had yet heard, seemed all of a sudden to be smitten by belated guilt, and, breaking off in mid-mutter with a stricken 'Excuse me, please,' he jumped up from the seat and rushed off the train at Turnpike Lane in a state of extreme agitation.

The second was today.

He got on at Green Park, a busy station. It was just after ten o'clock, but in Zone One the rush hour is never really over, it just eases slightly. I noticed him straight away.

He wore a long blue overcoat, buttoned up, a mustard-coloured scarf, and black leather gloves. His black shoes gleamed. His hair was thinning and completely white. His air was relaxed. He was clearly a successful and distinguished person, possibly a barrister or a senior clergyman. He could even have passed for a member of parliament, the kind who has inherited a safe rural Tory seat from his father and effortlessly retained it over five consecutive general elections.

He was an extremely handsome man, but his presence was of a kind that even had he been grotesque one would still have paid him attention.

The seat immediately opposite Alicia was already occupied by a young mother who struggled to control the fidgety three-year-old on her knee. There were two other seats free further along the carriage. But he was content to stand, it seemed, his gloved hand enfolding the ball-ended safety grip that hung from the ceiling, his body swaying easily with the train in a manner that belied his obvious years.

Alicia had noticed him too. I did not have to see her face to understand this. I simply felt, through some surprising intuition, her gaze lock on to him.

At Leicester Square, the struggling mother and her son left the train.

There were many people crowding in through the doors, and it seemed likely that the seat would be immediately re-occupied by a lank-haired girl in a floral dress and clumping army boots, but – with startling grace – the man released his grip on the hanging handle, glided along the aisle and sat down in the place exactly opposite Alicia, just before the obviously amazed girl could reach it.

What a move!

I had never in the course of our recent adventures been so tempted to say something to Alicia, to make some kind of contact with her, just to express my excitement, just to share it with her. But naturally I did nothing of the kind, knowing that on no account must I jeopardise the encounter that seemed certain to take place.

I knew that this fellow was something special.

I fixed my eyes on his face, holding my *Telegraph* up in front of me but in such a way as to allow me a narrow unobstructed view around the right-hand edge (Alicia, as usual, was sitting to my left). I knew that by the time the train had reached Covent Garden, my wife would have made her first move.

Extraordinarily, I saw no start of surprise or shock, not even the merest flicker to signify that my wife had uncrossed her legs. He sat, perfectly comfortably, his hands clasped lightly together as if in an attitude of prayer. Yet I had distinctly heard the swish of skirt against stocking-top.

And it was not because he had been looking elsewhere and had not seen. In fact, he was looking directly at her. I could not at first decipher his expression. His brown eyes held her steadily. He did not change his body position in any way, neither craning eagerly forward nor folding shyly inward, the two most usual responses to Alicia's revelations. And, unless I was deluded, his mouth was actually twitching as if he was suppressing an attack of the giggles.

He sat like that, twinkling at her, for several minutes. I dared not look at her, of course, but she must surely have been as surprised as I by the lack of any of the standard reactions.

Notwithstanding this, she must have finally decided that it was time to make her standard hand-patting-the-seat offer, for he stood up in a leisurely fashion, and moved across to her side.

'Well, thank you, that would be very nice indeed.'

He spoke quite normally, and made no effort to lower his voice. He was, to my surprise (but, then, everything about this man surprised me), an Irishman. You could not, however, have confused his tones with those of Ian Paisley or Bob Geldof: his accent suggested culture, learning, wisdom, affluence. I suppose the nearest likeness I can find for him among my admittedly limited set of images of the Celts would be that of Oscar Wilde.

He lowered himself into the seat and, as I could now see reflected in the window above the place he had just vacated, he was no less relaxed than before, his hands once more held loosely together. He seemed to have no self-consciousness whatsoever.

I heard Alicia make her standard opening remark, using the phrase which she invariably used when her prey had taken the bait and was sitting beside her. Her voice seemed a little uncertain, and she spoke more quietly than usual. She asked her admirer to tell her exactly what he had seen that had made him want to come over to sit with her.

'Oh, I could just tell that you wanted a bit of an old chat.'

His voice seemed to boom around the carriage, though none of the other passengers appeared to hear. I just wasn't used to hearing Alicia's gentlemen speak out loud. (Previously, strain though I might, I had never picked up much more than muffled sibilance or grunts).

Alicia herself was clearly taken aback. She paused for some seconds.

When she asked her follow-up question – but had he liked what he had seen when she had uncrossed her legs? – her voice was even lower than before, like a mother whispering to a roaring child in the vain hope that he will reduce his volume to match hers.

'Well, you're certainly a very attractive woman,' he replied, with a laugh in his voice, 'but, to be honest, I'm not much of a ladies' man, and I expect that someone with a little more experience in the field would be a better judge when it comes to that kind of thing.'

He had not taken the hint; in fact, I think his voice was a little louder still.

My wife, for the first time in three months, was seriously rattled. I did not have to look at her to know that. Our genteel Mr Wilde seemed to have no concept of what was required of him, and little tact or discretion. People around us would surely overhear him. Perhaps, despite initial appearances, he was a drunkard or mentally unbalanced. Perhaps he would begin shouting at the top of his voice, telling the entire train that this seemingly respectable lady here beside him was a sexual deviant. Perhaps he'd leap gracefully up and pull upon the emergency lever.

The train was beginning to slow down as it approached Russell Square. I sensed that Alicia was waiting for the precise moment to stand up, grab me by the arm and rush me out of the carriage just before the doors shut. This mission would have to be aborted.

But just then, Mr Wilde spoke again, and this time his voice was much lower, barely audible to me.

'But I would enjoy talking to you. I'd enjoy that very much, my dear lady.'

I looked across at his reflection. His head was now much closer to hers. His posture was just as relaxed, but somehow, magically, whereas before he had sat like a stranger sits beside another stranger, now he complemented Alicia as if they were a long-married couple. No casual witness would have doubted the propriety of his connection to her.

The train pulled up, the doors slid open. But the tug on my sleeve from Alicia that I was expecting never came.

As the doors shut again, and the train began to pick up speed, I realised that my wife had decided, in an instant, to prolong this disturbing encounter. More than that, something in Wilde's voice and manner had suddenly struck home, had turned Alicia's fear into trust.

And, as the journey continued, and as he spoke to her, Alicia seemed actually to forget where she was. She ceased to be aware of the other passengers or of the ebb and flow of the passing tube stations. She also forgot about her husband, sitting mutely to her right.

Always, during our little adventures, I had been aware that, although I played the part of a total stranger, a passive, covert witness to her behaviour, everything she said or did was for my benefit, for the benefit of us both. This secret understanding was what made her escapades so thrilling.

But, as I quickly became aware, this encounter between Wilde and her had somehow been transformed into a truly private contact, no longer one engineered by Alicia to be shared between us later. Wilde had taken her somewhere else, had spirited her away from me.

He spoke and she listened. His voice was not loud now, but somehow every word he spoke reached me, every pause, every gentle stress.

'Life takes us on strange journeys, does it not, my dear?' he began.

'I was born just sixty years ago, on a small farm in the west of Ireland. I was the second of eight children, six boys and two girls. It was a lovely part of the world. The land was not great land, but it produced a higher yield than any other farmland in that area, which was a tribute to my father, and to his father before him, and to the hard work that they put in. It fed us all, anyway, and clothed us and sent us to school.

'My older brother was very bright. He was just fifteen months my senior, but the gulf between us was much greater than fifteen months. He had an ability to retain information and to process it the like of which I have never known before or since. We were in the same class in school. When the teacher would start showing us something new in chemistry or mathematics, Fingall would always be the first to pick it up. He truly had a raging thirst for knowledge and learning.

'While the rest of us happily helped out at harvest-time, destroying as many haystacks with our playacting as we ever built, freckling our noses and reddening our bare backs in the hot sun, skinning our knees as we tripped and chased each other home at dusk along the stony narrow boreens which ran between the rock-walled fields, Fingall would be sitting palely indoors, straining his eyes at some book he would have had specially ordered from the mobile library that passed once a fortnight.

'When he was sixteen, and I had just turned fifteen, we sat the National Intermediate Certificate Examination. For the young people in our locality this would generally be our final contact with education, and most of us were not sorry to see the last of the damp pebble-dashed schoolhouse. Once the Inter was over, we would be grown-ups, workers, part of the real world.

'Fingall got nine 'A's. He got three prizes, for achieving the highest marks in the whole of Ireland in mathematics and biology, and the third highest in chemistry. Each prize – a medal – came with a letter of congratulation signed by the Minister for Education.

'A news photographer came out from Galway City, and another all the way down from Dublin, to take pictures which later appeared, with laudatory captions, in the papers concerned. For the Galway paper my parents were asked to pose with their genius son, and so they did. My parents had only ever had one photograph taken of themselves before, on their wedding day, and in the cutting – I still have it somewhere – they are like rabbits caught in headlamps. In between their two awkward, nervous faces, Fingall looks almost casual, as if he had not a bother on him, as if he was bored.

'It was not boredom on Fingall's face, however. It was resignation.

'The morning of the arrival of the Minister's letters, Fingall had requested a private chat with my father. Once in the back room, he told my father that he wanted to stay in school, to study for the National Leaving Certificate, to seek a scholarship to go to university in Dublin and to take a degree in the Sciences. He wanted to become a forensic analyst, to join the police force.

'My father, not knowing what to say in response to this flabbergasting proposal from his normally silent eldest son, sent one of my younger brothers to ask Father Lannigan to call down to the house. Father Lannigan ran the school, and had taught us Irish and Latin. He and Fingall had never got on. Fingall's brains and his unanswerable questions and his logical argumentation outraged Lannigan. He was a jealous and ignorant man, a man threatened by progress and science and all forms of intellectualism. I think he thought Fingall was a heretic, perhaps even the Devil himself.

'When my father told Lannigan about Fingall's plans, the priest instructed him that on no account should he let my brother have his way. What about the fine farm that my father and his father before him had built up with their honest toil? This country was founded on tradition, Lannigan said, a Christian tradition and a rural tradition. Patriots had died to ensure that this land belonged to a good Irish family. The Convention that land should pass from eldest son to eldest son was sacrosanct. Without Convention, without the strength of knowing where we all stood, Ireland would quickly go to rack and ruin. It was my father's duty as a Christian and an Irishman to banish these dangerous notions from his son's head, by force if necessary.

'Force was not necessary. I suppose that nowadays a youngster might consider running away from home or a father might decide to go against the wishes and advice of his priest, but that was not the Convention in those days and in that place.

'Fingall stayed on the farm, and, after my father died, he dutifully took up his inheritance. He never read another book from the day of Lannigan's visit. He spent his life working the land, a job which he hated and for which he had no calling.

'I would gladly have stayed there and helped him, for I loved working out in the open air and could not imagine another, indoors life. But that would have run against Convention too; a farm was not built up over generations only to run the risk of being split up again among squabbling siblings. Daughters were expected to marry into other nearby farms, and younger sons to leave the area entirely, to look for work in the villages, the towns, the cities, and very often overseas.

'I came over here when I was eighteen, though it broke my heart to leave.

'Things went well for me, I was very lucky. I stumbled, somehow, into some kind of an education, I worked out how things were done over here, and I did all right.

'In forty years I only went back there twice, for two funerals: my father first, and then, barely five months later, my mother. Fingall received us all, all his younger brothers and sisters, grown now and awkward sitting in the little parlour in smart clothes bought in Galway, Coventry and Chicago. He wore my father's threadbare second suit. It was all he had to wear. He didn't argue with us or discuss things with us, or with any of the other mourners, and I knew that he never did with anyone any more. He only made small talk.

'I was back there again last week. For Fingall's own funeral. He never married. He hadn't been well for months. I bought a suit for him last Christmas, I had it made in Savile Row. Although I made light of the gift in the card I sent with it, he was not fooled, I'm sure. We both knew that I had bought him a suit so that he would at least have something decent to wear in his coffin. It was a little too big for him, in the end.

'After the funeral, and the dinner and drinks with my greying brothers and sisters and all my multi-national nieces and nephews, I was told by the solicitor Kilbride that Fingall had left me the farm.

'In the will he said that I was to have it, I 'who should have had it all along'.

'So here I am, six months from retirement, with the farm I would have happily lived on all my life.

'But I'm too old to work it, of course. And I never married either, nor had any children. If only I could have lived Fingall's life; if only he could have lived mine.

'I tell you, dear lady, Convention made a mockery of us.'

He paused for a little time. I realised that, while he had been telling Alicia (and, incidentally, myself) this story, I had become completely oblivious of my surroundings. I had fallen under his spell, just as Alicia had. I had been unaware of the train's stops and starts, or of the other passengers' movements. I began to focus my eyes again. My arms were stiff from holding the paper up, still open on the Obituaries page. When I lowered it to look around I saw that we were alone in the carriage, the three of us. And I realised from the landscape passing outside the windows that we were now travelling overground and were already past Bounds Green, past Arnos Grove, past both Southgate and Oakwood. The next stop was the last, Cockfosters.

I felt suddenly afraid, and for the first time in the entire encounter (in fact, for the first time, really, in all of our adventures of the past three months put together) I half-turned in my seat, and faced towards my wife. What should we do now, when the train stopped, how should we deal with this unexpected development? I realised that she had not spoken since the story began. I needed her to make a decision, to be her resourceful, intuitive self, to get us out of this pickle.

But Alicia was unavailable to me. She, too, was turned in her seat. Her back was to me, she only had eyes for Wilde.

He spoke again, but with a slightly different tone. He was not telling a story now.

'Of course,' he said softly, 'if I could find a beautiful woman somewhere who could put up with me and my foibles, and who wouldn't mind living out her days with me, just the two of us together, in a little cottage in the loveliest corner of the universe...'

I heard a strange sound: Alicia sighing, just once, but not in a way I'd ever heard before.

'... Well, then, perhaps I could have my last laugh at Convention's expense.'

I really thought, at that moment, that I had lost her to him.

I realised that I was the stranger, not he. The rules under which Alicia and I had boarded this tube train, under which we had lived our whole married lives together seemed suddenly to have been rescinded. I had never imagined that our special bond together could be broken, was vulnerable to attack. All my life, since the day we left the church together, I had felt that she and I shared a small bunker for two, from which we could laugh at the world and at each other, impregnable and safe. But Wilde had seen something in her, a yearning or a need, which I, her husband of thirty-one years, had not spotted. It would not have been a spectacular thing to witness, perhaps, but the combination of her concentration, her back turned to me, and that small, alien sigh, was as profound and shocking to me as if she'd turned around from the kitchen sink and plunged a knife into my stomach. I have never felt so lonely.

The brakes squealed as we slowed down into the terminus. Wilde spoke again.

'Why don't we go and have a cup of tea together...'

Alicia moved to stand up, her face turned towards his and away from mine. So this was how it would be, I thought. She would leave me for him.

'... Just the three of us?'

As we walked along the road to our regular Cockfosters teahouse, he explained that he was a policeman. His name was not Wilde, of course, it was Duignan, Chief-Inspector Michael Duignan. There had been several unusual complaints from passengers, in consequence of which a plain clothes policewoman had been assigned to travel on Piccadilly Line trains looking for a suspect answering Alicia's description. She had spotted Alicia, and, from several seats away, had witnessed the Repentant Perv incident. Waiting to see which station Alicia would alight at, this WPC had been rewarded with the sight of my wife and I linking arms and departing together.

'To be honest, in a situation like this, in the old days, I would simply have done nothing,' he told us, his eyes crinkling kindly at us across the formica-top table, 'what harm have you caused anybody?'

He took a sip of his tea. He was as relaxed as ever, no different to before.

'But, there's been a lot of pressure on us lately, what with all this talk of family values' – the expression was clearly distasteful to him – 'from various idiotic hypocrites in high places, and it was decided that you should be arrested and charged.'

He looked at Alicia, whose face was still drained of colour, as I suppose mine must have been.

'But I'm not very impressed by these people and their zeal for Convention, so I persuaded my superior to let me approach you to give you just a warning.'

He was smiling at us as he spoke, now, and it was the smile of an ally, a confidant.

'I'm really of too senior a rank to be dealing with this kind of matter myself, but, because they know I'm retiring shortly after a long and distinguished service in the force, they humour me a little. They find my interest in you two quaint.

'You see, I really did want to meet you. I wanted to tell you that if you can't bring yourselves to restrict your adventures to more discreet locations you are liable to be arrested and prosecuted, which I know you would both find embarrassing. It's my duty to tell you that, and now I have.

'But I also wanted to meet you so that I could tell you' – and his lips were once again twitching as they had when he had first sat down opposite Alicia – 'how much I admire your guts, the pair of you. I envy you your closeness. Well done.'

He then shook our hands in turn, bid us a warm farewell and left the café.

We travelled back to Acton in silence. We would be all right, despite everything. We would be fine.

I unfolded my *Telegraph*, and for the first time that day, I made an effort to read.

'Expect jail, judges warn porn peddlers,' ran the headline. From tomorrow I shall be taking a different newspaper.

Ground No More

HWEE HWEE TAN

'WAH-LEOW,' Loong swore. 'The ground no more man.'

Gone was the white flash of concrete in the sun. Instead, a hole exposed the grey jagged underbelly of the pavement.

'*Ai-ya* I tell you if we were in Singapore this kind of thing won't happen.' My father shook his head. 'All these Dutch pavements, so lousy.'

Spontaneously collapsing pavements were one of the many things we got used to after KLM posted my father to their head office in Den Haag. As a huge chunk of Dutch soil is reclaimed land, the earth beneath our feet used to be formless sea, and thus liable to crumble at unexpected moments.

'This cat was just walking along you know,' my brother Loong said, 'Then the pavement suddenly pah-boam! The cat fell in – splat! Like pancake. Good show, man.'

'Cat?' I ran outside. I lifted the cat from the hole. My fingers felt the throb of its heart beneath the brown fur.

'The cat not dead,' I said. 'Just unconscious.'

'I take care of the cat,' Loong said.

'Yah, like you take care of my Snoopy – with a knife. I take the cat to the vet.'

'Pa, tell her give me the cat,' Loong said to my father. 'I need the cat for my A-level biology experiment.'

'Give cat to Loong,' my father said. 'It's only a stray.'

I pressed the cat against my chest. Its warm breath brushed my face.

My brother grinned. Then he told my father the magic words that would persuade any Singaporean parent to let their child get away with murder – 'If you give me the cat for experiment, it'll help my biology marks a lot.'

Singaporeans are obsessed with grades. Take that fifteen year old, leukaemia-stricken boy who was given a full page spread in our national newspaper, the *Straits Times*. In other countries, if you're a kid dying of a terminal disease, you do interesting things e.g. try to break a world record by collecting the most get-well cards, or meet Michael Jackson.

Does the Singaporean boy take this golden opportunity to do any of the above, before he snuffs it?

No.

Instead, he studies his butt off for his O-levels. He achieves six A1s, but doesn't live to see it.

What's the use of ten O-levels once you're six feet under?

My parents don't understand, for they believed that there was a positive correlation between moral fibre and good grades.

So although my brother was a cancerous polyp on the anus of humanity, when my parents looked at him – he was mainly glasses and freckles – they saw a cross between Einstein and Francis of Assisi.

So my father pried open my arms, took the cat, and gave it to my brother.

My brother was my parents' Loong – their dragon. He was the strong, smart and charismatic child who would fly to the top.

They named me *Piao Piao* – 'Pretty Pretty'.

The less said about that the better.

My parents let their dragon get away with anything. When I was four, Loong's favourite game was to turn off the light when I was in the bathroom.

'Toilet monster going to eat you girl,' Loong said. 'His claws going to burst out of toilet bowl, grab your buttock and drag you down to hell.'

I jumped off the toilet seat. My panties dangling at my feet. Loong pointed at my vagina and laughed.

Things changed when I was seven, after I attended the Methodist Girls' Primary School in Singapore. Every assembly, the chaplain would deliver a short sermon. One day he spoke about the armour of God – the shield of faith that blocked the flaming darts of the Devil, and the sword of the Spirit – the Word of God, sharper than any two-edged sword.

So the next time I went to the bathroom, I took a Bible with me. When Loong switched off the light, I sat down on the floor and pressed the Bible close to my chest.

Loong switched on the light. His dark brown rubber flip-flops slapped against the wet floor, leaving a trail of black footprints on the white tiles.

He grabbed my Bible and hit me across the face with it. It jerked my head around hard.

My face felt hot and large.

I clasped my hands, waiting for the next blow.

'Not bad, not bad. Good stuff,' Loong stuck up his thumb in approval. 'Love suffers long. Gooooood Christian.'

He giggled. His hand swept and knocked my head to the other side. 'You sit here. We going to have big fun later on.' Loong left the bathroom.

My face felt thick, hot and awkward. I went to the sink and bathed my face in cold water.

The flush had gone from my left cheek but it looked a little swollen.

I sat back down on the floor. My skirt soaked up the water from the cold tiles. I shivered.

I pinched my nose to block the smell of urine. We were poor in those days, and to save money, my parents commanded us to flush the toilet only after every third use.

Loong came back with my Snoopy and a knife.

As I said, back then in Singapore, we were poor. We didn't have a proper lamp in the bathroom like we do now. All we had was an orange lightbulb that hung from a cord. The bulb swayed while the knife sliced through the air.

I brought Snoopy's shreds to my father. 'I want you to kill Loong.'

My father laughed. 'Don't be stupid. Snoopy so old, falling apart anyway. Tomorrow I bring you to Toys 'R' Us, buy you new Snoopy, okay?'

A month before the pavement collapsed, my father announced that the Lim family was also moving from Singapore to Den Haag.

Charlie was Mr Lim's son. He wanted to join the FBI or the CIA when he grew up, thus he chose an appropriately American name for himself.

I never knew anyone who wanted to be American so badly.

Charlie was a total Walter Mitty type. When we shared a room with Charlie during our vacation at Pasir Ris, Charlie woke up at four a.m. shouting, 'Battlestations! Buck Rogers reporting – Wilma, get those starboard lasers ready!'

One afternoon, when he was eleven, Charlie spent two hours tailing three cyclists.

'Wah, just like in 'Hardy Boys',' Charlie said. 'You know those people who hire bicycles from East Coast Park? They not supposed to take bike out of the park you know.' (We lived in an apartment that was across the park) 'I saw three boys riding bicycles on our estate. Their bicycles got East Coast Park logo. So I follow them.'

'So what? You make citizen's arrest?' Loong said.

'No. I saw them ride into the underpass to the park. Which mean they hire bike from the park. My suspicion correct! No need to follow them anymore.'

My brother laughed.

Charlie smiled. 'I was good huh? They never knew I was behind them.'

Now to understand the full impact of what my brother said, you have to realize that back in the Seventies in Singapore, profanity was not widespread. Back in those days, you didn't say 'shit' or 'damn' until you were sixteen.

So Charlie is swelling with pride, and Loong keeps laughing. Then he says, 'You know what? You're one pathetic motherfucker.'

However, Loong was the Head Prefect, and received at least four book prizes annually, so his words only made Charlie want to gain Loong's approval even more.

When we went to the Lim's house-warming party to welcome them to Den Haag, Charlie was constantly at Loong's side, making sure his glass was filled with Pepsi.

'Charlie, you going study at the British School or not?' Loong asked.

Loong put his hand over his glass as Charlie tried to fill it with Pepsi. 'You got vodka?'

Charlie shook his head.

'In Holland men don't drink sissy thing like Pepsi. I bet you never drink vodka before.'

Charlie went red. 'Of course I have.'

'I bet you're still a virgin.'

Thus began my brother's campaign to make Charlie a *gei ang-mo* – a fake Caucasian.

Europe, Loong told Charlie, was a place where academic excellence and ethics had gone out of style, where it was good to be bad, and you cultivated decadence until it blossomed into sophistication.

So like Loong, Charlie got his ears pierced. Like Loong, he wore torn Levi jackets, peered through his Ray-Bans, and slouched around with a Marlboro in his mouth.

At night, they went to Loong's lab in the garden shed, where they tried to grow marijuana. They smoked pot, popped E, and got stoned on electric jelly and hash cakes. They were bad. They became European. Gone were the Singaporean, bespectacled, calculator-punching, aspiring engineer types. They were lean, mean, Continental machines.

Two days after Loong took the cat from the pavement, Charlie ran out of the garden shed, leaving a trail of vomit in his wake.

My brother laughed. 'Charlie's frightened about my biology experiment in the shed.'

'What happened?' I asked.

'Nothing. I just skinned the cat, took the flesh off, reconstructed the bone structure. Great experiment. I'll get an A, sure thing.'

'Make sure that you burn the carcass,' my father said. 'If not neighbour come here and complain about the smell.'

A week later, Loong performed another experiment in the shed, mixing Fanta orange with methylated spirits. He told Charlie that the drink was a cheap and legal way of getting high.

My father looked out of the window at the flashing lights on the police car. 'I tell you if we were in Singapore this kind of thing won't happen.'

Loong told the police he was sorry. He was a victim of his environment, he said. He had been nipped from the shelter of Eastern values in Singapore, and thrown into a decadent Western society, where if you got good grades, you were labelled a dork, nerd or swot. You had to prove that you were tough through drink and drugs.

The red light from the police car flashed outside my bedroom window.

Two months ago, orange hazard lights flashing outside my window kept me awake all night, for immediately after we reported the broken pavement, fixit men rumbled up with their cement truck, blocked off the hole with red-and-white striped tape, and surrounded the gap with the orange hazard lights. They fixed the hole with the quick efficiency of the experienced, like men used to patching up spontaneously disintegrating pavements. When dawn broke, the hole was filled.

After Charlie died, Loong threw himself into studying for his A-levels, and my parents never mentioned the incident again. My brother had patched up his 'accident' as quickly as the fixit men.

In the morning after the men had repaired the hole, my father walked onto the pavement, and stood there for ten minutes. I waited at the doorstep. 'Everything okay,' he said. He stamped his foot on the ground.

I knew better. After the ground collapsed, stepping out of the house became a great leap of faith. But after a while I pretended that the ground was a firm foundation, a solid rock. Similarly, my parents pretended that Loong was fine, that his good education gave him a concrete moral base.

Even if you can't trust the ground beneath your feet, you have to pretend that you can. You can't think of how you could suddenly be walking on air. If you did, you would never step out of the house. Staying in the house wouldn't help either, 'cos God knows, the house may collapse on you. You can't live life with that kind of fear.

Believing in Loong's explanation was like filling the broken ground with sticks, straws and stones. I told my parents about the true Rock, the cornerstone that was rejected. They wouldn't listen to me. Education was my parents' foundation. They knew no other ground to walk on.

It was the anniversary of Charlie's death last week. Loong had moved to England to read biology at Cambridge.

Everyone still believes that the boy who got all As for his chemistry, physics and biology exams, wasn't smart enough to think that orange juice and methylated spirits would get someone high.

Loong was smart enough. Smart enough to persuade Charlie to drink the lethal concoction. 'Drink it,' Loong must have told Charlie, 'Everybody's doing it.' I could imagine Loong standing over Charlie's corpse, laughing, like he did always. 'So stupid,' he probably said. 'Trying to get high. You're one pathetic fucker.'

On my way to school, I bought five different publications.

During lunch, I walked to a coffee-shop near our school. I cut the first letter – a 'M' from *Haagsche Courant*, the second letter, a 'U' from *GQ*, the third, sixth and eighth letter 'R' from *Der Spiegel*, the fourth letter 'D' from *Rolling Stone* and the fifth and seventh letter 'E' from *OK!*. I pasted the 4x2 letters on a postcard.

I sucked my cigarette. It finished burning, and I put it out amid the shells of the pistachio.

I tore the postcard and threw the shreds into the ashtray. I sent Loong lilies instead. The card attached said, 'Charlie's still dead. As always, I think of you.'

Loong sent me a card with Snoopy thanking me for the flowers.

Outside, the white pavement shone like burning magnesium in the summer light. I squinted at the ground, searching for cracks, but I found none. The light bounced off the ground that burnt as white, as solid, as concrete as it did the day before it collapsed.

The Window-cleaners of Bjec

PHIL WHITAKER

WE ENTER Bjec just before noon, another of the dozen or so towns we have to pass through on our way towards Srenica and the latest flare in the fighting. Koblinski's at the wheel, smoking a Winston. Martin Pusey's snoring in the back. Strange road signs, stunted trees, squat buildings, drift past my gaze.

Two days ago, when we first arrived, these things captivated my attention. But the novelty's worn off and I'm thinking of Sue again, back in Hornsey – tormenting myself with thoughts of who she might be seeing now I've gone.

'Straight over?'

Kob's voice hauls me back. He changes down as we reach a junction, beyond which our tarmacked road funnels into a narrow cobbled lane, old houses on either side. I clutch at the map open on my lap, planting a finger at random.

'Um...' I search rapidly, finding the area of grey shading labelled Bjec. The road seems to pass through the centre of town. 'Straight on, yes.'

The Mitsubishi starts to judder as the wheels hit the cobbles.

'You missing her?' Kob asks.

I look across at his profile. Stubble forms a hazy rim around the otherwise solid jaw. His arms are stretched straight, hands gripping the top of the wheel, eyes fixed on the way ahead. The Winston pokes up between his fingers, its trail of smoke eddying with the vibration of the Jeep.

'A little.'

I told Kob about Sue during the long flight east, Martin sitting in the row behind, headphones in his ears. Any topic of conversation seemed fair game in building bridges between us, new colleagues heading into the unknown.

I made her out to be something she hadn't been for a long time, not since she landed her staff job at the Beeb and I went freelance, following her to London like a pining dog. It seemed a convenient fiction at the time.

The Mitsubishi hits a pot-hole and I watch a pellet of ash, shaken free by the jolt, glance off his fingers and land on his trousers.

'Gonna find it tough out here, missing someone,' he says.

The ash rolls, disappearing on the other side of his leg.

'I'm sure I'll cope.'

I hope my tone will convey shutters coming down. I want to be left to brood in peace; wish I'd never mentioned Sue. Far from attracting his sympathy, my story of the lover left behind provoked the observation that he had never seen any use for a woman back home. He told me he preferred to find one when and where he felt the need.

Behind me, I hear Martin yawn and stir. Kob remains silent, apparently concentrating. The houses either side of us close in. Paint flakes; walls lean; wooden window bays jut out. The lane seems too narrow and I fear for our wing mirrors. Kob takes a hand from the wheel, drawing on his cigarette.

'So. Did she mind you coming out?'

A reluctant smile twitches my lips, in part at his persistence but also in recognition of his perceptiveness. Kob is wasted as a cameraman, I decide, should be a reporter. When I told her, what I wanted more than anything was for her to mind. Instead, enthusiasm. In her eyes, unmistakable relief at being able to cast me adrift. I reach across to Kob's top pocket and fish for a cigarette from the soft pack.

'No,' I tell him, 'she didn't mind. She was pleased for me. What hack wouldn't be?'

Kob glances down at my hand, extracting the Winston. He grunts and passes across his lighter. Ahead of us, the lane is blocked by a group of pedestrians, walking towards the town centre. Heads turn to check out the vehicle behind. Kob brakes, slowing to a walking pace, fingers tapping the wheel. The Bjecs are animated, their steps jaunty. As I light the Winston, Martin asks where we are.

My reply is rendered in exhaled smoke: 'Bjec, birthplace of the President.' My head reels with the first rush of nicotine.

The lane gives on to a sizeable cobbled square, its surface undulating. Kob stops as the jeep noses into the open. There's a central fountain. Drab shops and offices, products of the concrete revolution, line the market place. Not for the first time, I'm struck by the irony that before his rise through the Party hierarchy, the President trained in architecture. In a couple of places older facades have survived, relics of the era before annexation. Their great stone blocks and high windows hint at the values of other architects long dead.

More Bjecs, following us up the lane, squeeze past our stationary jeep. From other gaps between shops, citizens spill into the square. They head for the one striking building, towering above its fellows at the far side. Twelve or so brown brick storeys are piled skywards.

Each successive level is somewhat narrower, though the differences lessen the higher the tower rises – no mere pyramid this. The effect is of graceful sides sweeping upwards like gigantic staircases. It's quite unlike anything I've seen so far in this tiny state. A mass of people are ranged round the building's foot.

'Any ideas?' Kob asks, rasping the handbrake ratchet.

I shrug, puzzled, at the same time grateful for the distraction, veering the conversation away from the personal.

Martin rests his forearms on the backs of our seats. 'Some kind of rally, maybe?'

'Guess so,' I reply. 'Stick it over there.'

Kob revs the engine and nudges the 4x4 though the milling Bjecs, pulling over by the glamourless display windows fronting a branch of the state department store. Martin and I disembark, but Kob stretches across the front seats, peering out through my open door.

'Want me to hang on here, while you check it out?'

I hold his gaze for a second, trying to gauge his concern. Kob has come back from numerous theatres where journalists, failing to pay heed to caution, have themselves created the news. But we've heard of no unrest this far north, deep in a part of the country still loyal to the President. I look around. No-one seems to be displaying more than a passing interest in us, as they head over to swell the crowd on the far side of the square.

'No, Kob, lock it and leave it. And we might as well take the kit. We may have something.'

Kob comes round and opens the rear door. He and Martin pull out their cases. By now, the square is half-full and the numbers still entering from the lanes have slowed to a trickle. I put the crowd at a couple of thousand.

'Jackets, or no jackets?'

Kob holds up a flak jacket, as if for my inspection. There's a suspicion of an amused tugging at the corners of his mouth.

'I really don't think so. Do you?'

'You're the boss,' he says, slinging the jacket back.

'Yeah. I guess so.' I watch him shoulder his camera case, slamming the jeep door.

The crowd is close-pressed and noisy. I pause at the back, taking stock.

'Where's best?'

'The front, I reckon,' Kob passes me. 'Stay close.'

'Try losing me!' Martin shouts after him, sloping his directional microphone like a rifle against his collar bone. I hesitate, nonplussed, then tuck in behind them as we start a halting, weaving progress towards the middle of the throng, and the brick tower beyond.

Kob cuts our path, alternately excusing himself in dialect and shouting

'Comin' through' in best New York. His camera case is cradled in his arms. Voices speak a language I hardly know; rising, falling. There's a smell of alcohol. Shouts, laughs, dart at my ear. People jostle; nearly everyone sports Presidential-red ribbon in one form or other. Tobacco, straw; perfume, stale sweat.

My gaze alights on an old man, squatting on a wooden stool amongst the standing crowd, arms resting on knees, chewing reflectively. A small boy jinks into my path. I stumble against something hard. A woman staggers, a cage hanging from her arm. Flapping; wings beat wire; downy feathers launch like shuttlecocks. I mumble apologies in English. The woman tries to calm her hen, gives up, shouts at me. I gesture towards my disappearing companions. A teenage girl gives me a rueful smile as I pass.

Martin's furry microphone bobs above the heads a way off in front. I catch him as he shies from a small monkey, screeching at him from its vantage point on a man's shoulder.

'Well, waddaya know, 'Kob shouts back at us as he breaches the front of the crowd.

Elbowing through behind Martin I see a broad crescent has been roped off around the base of the tower. The six-foot something Koblinski is already straddling the waist-high barrier. As his trailing leg clears the rope, his torso dips to one side, and I catch sight of the unmistakable huddle of another film crew.

Martin hesitates as he reaches the cordon. 'Go on,' I answer his look.

He flicks the rope up with his mike and ducks under. I follow suit, catching some bemused looks from the Bjecs at the front of the crowd as I straighten up again. Kob has reached the other crew, flashing what I take to be his press card. As Martin and I stride over to join them, he's handing out introductory Winstons.

The other crew is local. The middle aged sound engineer sports a drooping moustache. Martin drifts over to join him. Kob seems to be managing a conversation with his counterpart, a tall youth whose bulky camera is mounted on a tripod. The third member of the group is a petite woman, around thirty, dressed in matching skirt and jacket. Her hair is dark and drawn smartly back. Slav cheekbones, Western shoulder-pads. She makes eye contact as I arrive and returns my smile. We shake hands.

'Geoff Barker, ICN.'

I struggle to assemble a name from the phonetics of her reply. I think it might be something like Katya Tayarby.

I hold up a finger: 'Katya, excuse me.'

She smiles again, nodding, and I turn to Kob, to find him sitting on his heels, rummaging in his case. The local cameraman's attention has passed to his cupped American cigarette.

'Kob,' – he looks up – 'any idea what's going on?'

He hauls the camera free of its casing. 'You're the reporter, Geoff. You tell me.'

With that he stands, holding his Panasonic out for the Bjec cameraman to inspect. There was quite a bust up over the question of interpreters when we first arrived. I didn't think we'd need one till we got nearer to Srenica. Kob – despite his basic grasp of the language – was all for engaging one for the whole trip, but then he doesn't have to manage the budget.

I flirt with the idea of a tactical apology, but decide he's unlikely to call off his sulk here and now in any case. I try Katya again. She tells me 'yes' and nods vigorously when I intone 'English?'

She calls me 'Yef', after several rehearsals, something I find endearing. I point out the motif embroidered on her jacket's left breast and ask, 'What is 'TRB'?'

There's a sticky moment till she gets the gist, 'Ah! Tayarby is television of the North!'

I give an exaggerated look of comprehension. 'Right! We...' I gesture at Martin and Kob, 'are ICN.'

This reiteration gets nothing more than a slowly fading smile and a look cast at the cobbles underfoot. I've run out of small talk so I point at the crowd, sweeping my hand in an arc. 'What's happening here? What is going on today?'

'Ah yes, today, it is wash the window.' She smiles with great charm. 'The window.'

She points and looks up at the towering building behind her. I follow her gaze. There's a whole lot of windows all of which look remarkably similar. 'Any one in particular?'

Her crinkled nose tells me the limits of her English. I try a different tack. 'What exactly is "wash the window"?'

'Wash the window? Yes, it is, um, to clean the glass?' she waits for my nod, 'in the tower of the President.' Again she flourishes a smile and points.

The tower of the President... The phrase sets off some gopher deep inside my mind, burrowing amongst the research I did for the trip. I turn once more to Katya. 'So this is the tower the President designed himself?' (I get the nose crinkle again.) 'Your President... made this tower?'

'Yes, yes! This is right!'

She seems genuinely excited that I know this fact. I'm rather taken with the way she clasps her hands beneath her chin and draws a sibilant breath, as though I've tickled something erogenous. I sense a story. Perhaps the President is going to appear. What else would bring all these people here, to the tower he bequeathed to the town of his youth?

Someone tugs my sleeve. Martin's come over. 'Have you seen that?'

'What, Martin?'

'That.' He turns me round. Tucked at the far edge of the crowd, alongside offices festooned with the state bank's logo, is the only other vehicle in the square. It's seen better days, but it's unmistakeably an ambulance.

At that moment a hesitant cheer runs through the crowd, followed by applause. The TRB cameraman abruptly loses interest in Kob's slim Panasonic and, ramming the Winston between his lips, swings his own camera round for some crowd shots. The engineer picks up his mike and starts fiddling with his control belt.

'Please,' Katya's hand is on my arm, a light touch which for a second commands my whole attention.

She steers me, Martin following, to the far side of her crew, beckoning to Kob en route. Suddenly the cheer becomes a roar and the glass doors at the front of the building open outwards. A group of perhaps two dozen uniformed figures emerge, pausing for a moment before trotting, as a phalanx, down the steps at the building's entrance. Each has a submachine gun slung over his shoulder.

TRB are busy. Katya is back with them, holding a ridiculously large microphone with a square 'TRB' box round the handle. It looks like a White House prop. The camera is on her. She's talking excitedly. Her expression causes me a pang of regret – the look is too familiar: barely suppressed triumph, the kick that comes from reporting significant events.

How many evenings did I sit alone in the Hornsey flat, watching Sue on the news – the Houses of Parliament in the background, microphone in her hand? That same animation on her, a look I only ever saw as she stared out at me from the TV screen. A look which was invariably replaced by one of weariness by the time she returned home – alcohol on her breath from her after-work drinks – too tired to do anything other than go to bed, to sleep.

Finishing her piece, Katya takes a measured step to one side, allowing the camera an uninterrupted view of the group of figures now at the bottom of the steps. I recognise the black uniforms of the state police who, I only now appreciate, have been singularly absent from such a large gathering.

I study a few humourless faces. A man in a suit, wearing what looks like a mayoral neck-chain, steps forwards. He raises a megaphone to his lips and starts barking at the crowd. A ripple of 'shhh's washes back over the massed onlookers.

At the end of his short speech, the Mayor waves. his loudspeaker above his head, and the crowd start a collective whooping and yelling. I look at Kob. He shrugs. Katya is chattering into her mike again, her voice almost lost in the din.

'Will you look at that!' Kob bellows in my ear.

I look over to see the ranks of police parting. In their midst stand three men, each clad in a bright blue jump suit. The bottoms of their trouser legs disappear into heavy, laced boots. Their backs are burdened with large steel cylinders, like scuba-diving tanks. Tubes loop from the bottoms of these, trailing round and tucking into belts beset with metal implements and coils of rope.

Kob takes a cigarette from the packet in his shirt pocket and waves it butt first, leaning in towards my ear again. 'The fucking Ghostbusters!'

The Ghostbusters (I take his point) stand quite still whilst the raucous crowd gradually settles. The one nearest to us is a youth, no more than twenty. His brown hair is gathered back in a pony tail, revealing a forehead livid with acne. The middle man is stocky, martial; hair shorn almost to the scalp and a spider's web tattoo strung across his cheek. The third figure ill-befits his paramilitary garb. His belly overhangs his belt, his jump suit stretched tight by the flesh beneath. I'm fascinated by his thick framed glasses. They're made of the same black plastic as the National Health specs I had to endure as a child. In studying the fat man's face, I notice wet tracks shining on his cheeks. The pride which I thought I detected in the Ghostbusters' static posture suddenly looks more like fear. I look back to Kob, who's lighting his Winston.

'Worth shooting?' he asks.

I nod and he moves over to join Martin. 'Come on, Marty.' They start connecting leads.

Katya has finished her piece and the TRB camera is being relocated further from the tower. They're having trouble getting the tripod to stand squarely on the irregular surface. As I start towards them I become aware of a slithering singing noise, like a distant underground train. I can't pinpoint its direction, but those at the front of the crowd are looking up. I turn in time to see three ropes unfurling in free-fall down the front of the building. There's a triplet of emphatic thwacks as the rope-ends hit the ground. After their precipitate entrance, the ropes sway coyly.

With one shouted command from the Mayor, the nearest two Ghostbusters – Pony Tail and Crew Cut – turn and walk slowly up the steps, each to their own rope. The Fat Man hesitates. A policeman prods him in the side with his machine gun stock. Head dropping, he turns and joins his fellows, taking up position at the unclaimed rope. The crowd remains quietly attentive; occasional laughter pealing out. I hear the screech of the monkey.

'How much more of this we gonna film?'

Kob talks without taking his eye from the viewfinder, head craned back, camera tilted way up. His tone is exasperated, but he's already turned down my offer to fetch his tripod from the jeep.

'Quiet, Kob!' Martin says sharply, adjusting a level, other hand pressing a headphone against his ear.

'Knock it off, Marty,' Kob mutters. 'You can't need more background.'

I leave Kob's original question unanswered, turning my attention back to the three blue figures, spraying water from their portable tanks at the windows lining the fourth storey. It's taken them half an hour at least to get this far. The whole thing is something of an anticlimax after those expectant first few minutes. But the set-up is intriguing: the weight of the water-tanks, the difficulty of the climb.

I have a sense of having happened upon some local tradition – Bjec's version of Siena's palio maybe, or Pamplona's bull-running – bizarre though the 'sport' of window-cleaning seems.

Katya has been running an almost continuous commentary ever since the men started climbing and I've yet to get more out of her. I'm tantalised by the idea of filing a report to contrast with the images of destruction that have been beaming out from the rebellious south; some quirkly glimpse of the humanity of this hitherto unheard-of people. I intend interviewing Katya as a passable English-speaker – afterwards. I have a notion of the flattery she will feel, when I ask her to be filmed for a Western news programme.

In the eighteen months after I followed Sue to London, I watched her become more and more involved with her new colleagues. I listened jealously as male names recurred in her conversation: producers fixing her up with exclusives, fellow political correspondents giving her tips. They're only trying to help, Geoff. I think it's very sweet of them, actually. I told her they were only interested in giving her a leg up so they could sneak a look under her skirt. Don't be so paranoid, she told me. But on the few occasions I was invited out with them all, I saw the looks, hungry to devour her.

They ignored me, a two-bit hack doing occasional freelance stuff for in dependent production outfits. I sat, watching her laughing as they mocked the quirks of various politicians, recycling gossip from the Westminster tea-rooms. I had nothing to say – an awkward hanger-on from her previous life as a provincial reporter.

Then the ICN job came up. I jumped at it – hoping a return to mainstream journalism would even up the imbalance between us. But there'd been too much sniping, too many hasty words. When I told her I was leaving, to go on this assignment, I hoped for some reaction, some inkling that I was still important to her. She said I could leave my stuff at the flat and we'd sort it out when I got back.

I cast a further glance at Katya. Her eyes flick momentarily in my direction. Perhaps my coming here will give me the opportunity of evening up a different sort of imbalance.

'These guys're nothing more than glorified window-cleaners.' Kob's disdainful words break into my thoughts.

'There has to be some reason why this lot've turned up,' I point out, looking at the massed spectators.

The crowd have remained attentive. Each time the window-cleaners finish a level, there's an appreciative round of applause. As they launch off that ledge, rope-climbing to the next storey, an excited chant starts up: 'Higher! Higher! Higher!' – Kob deigned to translate this. The crowd have even taken to giving the Fat Man, who tends to bring up the rear, an ironic sort of cheer as he finally hauls his broad beam on to each successive ledge.

'They seem to find it very entertaining,' Martin chips in.

Kob gives Martin a sarcastic 'shhh' then says, 'Must be one hell of a boring town.'

'It could be something political,' I speculate. 'Maybe they get banged up or something, if they don't turn out to watch the President's tower get its wash.'

'Mmm,' Kob muses, redundant eye screwed shut. 'Or maybe there's just nothing better on TV.'

I laugh at this, and look again at Katya and the TRB crew, still huddled round their camera.

Suddenly Kob winces, left hand gripping the back of his neck: 'Jesus!' He slides the Panasonic off his shoulder and lowers it to the ground. His head sags forward and he rolls it from side to side, massaging vigorously. I resist the temptation to point out that he'd get a flatter angle filming from behind the crowd.

Applause again. The crew-cut window-cleaner holsters his hose, his section done. He shuffles back along the ledge and grabs his rope. 'Higher! Higher! Higher!' the chant starts. There's no audible diminution in the crowd's enthusiasm. Crew Cut gives a little jump and starts to hand-over-hand, boots scuffing the brick for purchase.

'Aah, fuck this,' Kob mutters, rubbing his neck.

Pony Tail and Fat Man have finished their cleaning and are also at their ropes. 'Higher! Higher! Higher!' Crew Cut is up at the fifth storey now, way above us. Pony Tail and Fat Man are inching up to join him. I find the inexorable rise mesmerising. Kob is tugging the cable from his Panasonic. There's the ironic cheer as Fat Man heaves himself on to the next ledge. Pony Tail is lagging behind. 'Higher! Higher! Higher!'

'Hang on, Kob,' I shout.

The chanting is louder.

Words coming faster.

A sudden, passionate roar. Two thousand voices raised in excitement.

I look up.

A blue figure, hurtling, arms backstroking in unreal time.

'Fuck...' Kob, in the corner of my eye.

The figure hits the cobbles. I duck out of instinct. There's clapping, cheering, whistling. I don't know if I hear the impact or imagine it.

'Fuck...' Kob, fumbling with his lead.

I straighten. People are jumping, arms held aloft. Grins are wide with absolute glee. It's a cup-final goal, an extra-time winner. A hat in the air falls somewhere unseen.

'Fuck...' Kob, hoisting his camera.

A boy of about twelve, at the front of the crowd, is shrieking. A man, maybe his father, flicks chunks of red gore off his shirt with a hankie. In front of them, Pony Tail. The back of his head is flat. A sunburst of blood on the stones. The water tank has thrust his back into an arch.

Kob has his camera trained on Pony Tail. Martin has dropped to one knee, mike held out like a pistol. At the far side of the ellipse of clear ground, a man with a peaked cap ducks under the rope barrier. He carries a white case with a red cross. He stops his trot some yards from the body, turns and walks back to his ambulance.

From out of the crowd, the monkey emerges, scooting past him, a red flower in one hand. Reaching Pony Tail, the monkey screeches, lips baring teeth, and throws the single stem. The flower rolls across Pony Tail's chest and falls off the other side.

'Unbefuckinglievable.'

We're crouched in the back of the Mitsubishi, parked outside a bar on the outskirts of Bjec, engine idling to keep the battery charged. The three of us are peering at the tiny screen on the computerised editing suite. Kob winds the digitalised footage back a short way, then re-runs it.

At that height, with Kob's back-breaking angle, Crew-Cut and Fat Man's torsos appear to be missing. All we can see are the tips of their water tanks peeking out above blue backsides, and their legs scrabbling as they struggle to pull themselves on to the ledge. I've no idea which storey they were at. Nor how tired their arms must have been. Suddenly Crew-Cut leans back, peels away; rapidly enlarging then flashing out of frame.

'That's where we should cut it,' I say. Kob rocks the fine-position toggle back and forth, and Crew-Cut bounces in and out of the screen like a crazed trampolinist. A press of a button electronically tags the film, at the point where Crew-Cut vanishes.

We fast-forward through the next sequence, where Kob tried vainly to track the falling window-cleaner. The rushing brick and windows form a stroboscopic blur.

'Jesus,' Kob says. He hits pause and sits, neck bent forward, fingers pressing on closed eyelids. Martin and I wait silently. After a while, Kob runs the film again, tagging it once he catches up with the twisted body on the square. Crew-Cut has somehow contrived to land both face and arse down.

'Not too long on that,' I say.

Another tag and Kob starts to fast-forward. 'D'you want the monkey again?'

'No. Once'll do.' I'm aware of my heart: I don't think its rate has dropped to normal all afternoon.

'Okay. Fat Man, Fat Man, Fat Man.' Kob scans through minutes of film, flashing by in quadruple time. We watch the Chaplinesque climbing and cleaning of the one remaining window-cleaner.

'There!'

Kob slows to real-time and edits-in the segment with Fat Man's legs flailing, for what seems like an eternity, before he too plunges to his death.

'How long're we aiming for?' Martin asks.

'Three minutes max, including the interview,' I say.

Kob calls up the time elapsed. 'We'll have to axe some of Fat Man.'

'Okay, it's too long anyway. Just keep the bit where he goes. I'll do a voice-over to link it.'

'Sure thing,' Kob rejigs the Fat Man footage. He then runs the tape on, editing-in the interview with Katya. We listen carefully as she explains that the window-cleaners were convicted terrorists.

'Read: freedom fighters,' Kob remarks.

Any of them, Katya continues, that had managed to clean all their windows, would have been freed – one man was, the previous month.

I'm disturbed, watching her on the screen, by the fervour in her voice and eyes. Kob, nearly a foot taller, has filmed her from above. The angle broadens her already wide shoulder pads. My drawn face appears on the screen, tinny voice coming out of the speaker.

I ask why the window-cleaning has to be so dangerous – 'Viewers in the West will wonder why there aren't gantries, um, equipment, to allow safe access to the outside of the building?"

Katya shrugs. At the time, just for a moment, I thought she hadn't understood – her nose crinkled. Seeing it again, I recognise disdain.

After a pause she says: 'The President did not made his tower like that.'

'Shit architect,' Kob says, tagging the tape a final time.

We have trouble getting a satellite link. At least that's what I tell Kob and Martin, deliberately fudging the dialling several times. I send them to the bar, saying I'll join them once I've got through. They head off, leaving me behind in the jeep.

Alone, I hook up with a CommSat and transmit to London. After it's relayed, I run the original footage through a couple of times. Even this soon afterwards, the shock I felt has largely gone, replaced by moody detachment.

Watching the window-cleaners falling, I wonder what they died for. I know about their particular struggle. But I also know that even if it succeeds, history says another will follow in its wake, and another after that. Disaffection with political leaders is perennial. I can't shake the image of Fat Man, with his clumsy glasses, cheeks wet, staring out at the crowd. I wish Kob had captured that; the picture in my mind encapsulates the futility I feel.

I raid Kob's cigarette stash and open a fresh pack. I'm on my third, sitting between the Mitsubishi's open rear doors, when he comes out of the bar. I watch him walk towards me.

'Okay?' he asks, joining me at the tail of the jeep, fingers of one hand gripping the necks of two bottles of beer.

I nod. 'Should be a CommSat overhead in a bit.'

He sits beside me, handing over a beer and lighting up a cigarette. He takes a drag, looks at me carefully and says, 'Things'll get better. At least down south they're actually fighting, not getting fucked like a bunch of Christians.'

I take a swig from the bottle. 'For what though?'

He gives a sardonic laugh. 'Freedom? Democracy? Fuck knows. It's important to them though.'

'If they saw democracy in action they wouldn't be so keen.'

Kob taps his Winston, ash falling to the dusty ground. 'Sure, but at least we get to chuck our lot out without getting killed in the process.'

I nod and we sit in silence. My thoughts turn to Sue. Things seem in proportion suddenly; our feuding – of over-riding importance at the time – now appears a petty irrelevance. All the old clichés go round my head: I don't know how to convey it, explain that we shouldn't have let our problems snuff out the good things between us. I want to say to her: so we split, we move on, maybe we find other partners. Things'll seem good for a while, but difficulties will arise again. They always do. At some point we'll have to stick with someone, work it out, not throw everything away. Why not now?

For a moment I wish she had been here too, shared the same experience. But I have the gloomy realisation that it's too late. We've been fighting too long and I can see her, relishing the freedom and the lack of aggravation which my departure will have brought.

Kob stubs his half-smoked Winston out on the bumper. 'Well...'

I look towards the bar. 'Go on,' I tell him. 'There's no knowing what Martin'll get up to if he's left alone too long.'

Kob chuckles, standing.

'Thanks for the beer,' I say.

He gives me a casual salute and walks off.

I promised myself I wouldn't call her, clinging to the faint hope that my absence would make her rethink. There was also the idea that I'd be punishing her somehow. Now all I want to do is speak to her. I clamber back in the jeep, returning to the transmitter. Eventually I get a call through. It's late and she's in bed, but she comes to quickly at the sound of my voice.

'Geoff, I saw it. It made the Ten O'Clock, first after the break. How horrid. You okay?'

Her words are delayed by a split second as they bounce from earth to satellite to earth again. I tell her I'm fine. While I speak, I check my watch: they must have turned the footage round fast to get it on the evening bulletin. I sketch in some details for her about my companions, recounting Kob's panic when he realised he'd stopped filming at just the wrong moment. As I talk, my mind races, sparked into life by the sound of her voice. I want to be back in the Hornsey flat.

'How're things with you?' I ask. I'm irritated by the flatness of my own voice; resolve to brighten it. 'How's London?'

'Oh – so so...' I hear her sigh.

'Sue, I've been – '

At the moment I speak, her next words reach me through the time delay.

'I'm – I miss you, Barker.'

Instantly, the distance between us closes, the past months as irrelevant as the miles from London to this tiny town a quarter the way round the globe.

Kob looks up as I join him at their table. Martin is over by the counter, trying to order more beer from the aproned landlord. The bar has a floor littered with butts and trash but at least it's quiet.

'She alright?' Kob asks.

I nod at him and half smile. Wasted as a cameraman.

We stay in the bar till darkness falls; spend the night in threadbare rooms upstairs. The next day, hungover, we continue our journey south towards Srenica, and the latest flare in the fighting.

Algebra

JOSEPHINE CORCORAN

SOMETIMES I THINK about the old days. We led a simple life. Anna cooked thick vegetable soup while I chopped wood on the tree stump outside our kitchen window. After the logs toppled onto the path, I stood straight, the axe heavy in my swinging hand, tasting vinegary sweat on my upper lip, watching my breath sail through the frosted air. The smell of collapsing parsnips, carrots, black pepper and cream turned my head to the watery window, to see Anna sipping from a steaming wooden spoon and my daughter frowning, carefully turning the pages of a book.

My daughter ran through our house on tip-toe, her blonde curls flopping. Anna stitched creamy lace to the edges of her dresses and bought pieces of velvet ribbon to wrap in her silky hair.

Dr Winston told me my wife had made an angel. He wore a brown, knobbly tweed jacket. I could smell the rain that had drenched it on cold, howling nights as he ran from his steamy car to houses full of hope and fear, excitement and dread. I could smell the rain that had seeped inside the bubbles of wool as he pressed his icy stethoscope on wheezing, rattling chests.

He gripped me by the shoulders and offered me a sooty smelling cigar and told me my wife had produced an angel.

'Nothing to worry about. Nothing to concern yourself with. Just a little bobble of flesh. Nothing untoward. A little angel. We'll wrap it in a tiny bandage and it will crumble away. Congratulations.'

My wife never mentioned it. She has always been a calm, unexcitable woman, as steady as a sturdy rocking chair. Sometimes I felt a quickening of my heartbeat, a rush of blood, a sound in my ears like a shell from the shore. She'd wrap me in her sturdiness at times like that, hold me, rock me, and her body would soak up my heartbeat.

We brought our daughter home from the hospital and called her Angel.

The nurses said her curls were like a halo. It was unusual, they said, for a baby to have so much hair, and to have eyes so bright, brimming with light. Our home was a converted barn, the heavy stone walls were washed with white paint, the ceilings were high. We stayed in one room most of the time, warm and safe together. We built up a wall of logs and loaded them carefully onto the wood-burner. Angel slept in her cot in the corner while Anna stitched warm fleecy linings into my shirts and mended the worn away patches of my corduroy trousers. The logs cracked and spat, crumbling red and black. I read books that Anna had found for me in the library. Her sister drove her there once a week, while I worked as a lumberjack, deep in the forests, dwarfed by the giant trees that gave us our income. I stood still within the forest sometimes, hearing my own blood flowing through my bones, hearing the bones of the trees bending, bowing, breaking, and a picture of Anna and Angel in the library shimmered in the freezing forest air.

Angel's baby breath, the spit and snap of the red hot logs, Anna's thread breaking, the crackle of the pages of my library books; these are the sounds that creep into my dreams.

There was no crumbling away. I realised what it was when I changed her one evening. Anna usually tended to her but she was ill in bed with a bad cold. It was a shocking winter, Dr Winston said.

'Complete rest, whisky, hot water and fresh lemon juice, and you take care of the little one.'

He had never thought to mention it again. I unwrapped the bandage and saw it and knew. But it was a desperately tiny thing, as tender as a string of fat on a piece of ham. I'm a practical man. I work with my hands. In those days I slept peacefully at night, untroubled by complicated concerns. I took this piece of surplus fat and tucked it tightly away, hidden, out of sight. It fitted perfectly and seemed to cause no trouble.

Anna's colour returned. The wall of logs diminished and the forest air became tinged with sprightly birdsong and sprinkled with lime coloured leaves. I tugged my thick woollen jersey over my head and smelt my sweat evaporating into the forest. Anna opened all the windows and swept woodshavings from the path.

Years passed. Sapling trees swelled with juice and seeds and thrust their bulging roots deep into the rich, red soil. I watched them devouring the earth, sucking in its energy to power their own rapid growth. It seemed that they climbed higher and straighter by the minute. I heard their blood pounding.

Angel liked the home she'd been born into. Anna taught her how to

sew. She was very careful and patient for a child, her stitches were neat
and intricate. At school she won the Needlework Prize and they mounted
samples of her work in a glass case. Anna asked me to teach Angel about
wood. She said she wanted her to try things that hadn't been available for
her. Times were changing, she said, and, after all, some of the boys in her
class were keen on cookery and handicrafts. But I couldn't interest Angel
in woodwork. She laughed at her own weak arms that could hardly lift a
chisel or a plane. She loved cooking and sewing and reading her books.
The friends that she invited home for tea were all quietly spoken and
polite. They sat together at our kitchen table drawing pictures and singing
songs. They helped Anna make thick, raisin cookies or picked flowers
from the edge of the forest, and pressed them carefully in pastel coloured
books. They showed no interest in scaling the swaying trees outside our
house, or wading through the gushing brook that ran around it.

Another winter fluttered down like a black magician's cloak,
swamping us in shadowy half-light. Angel was in her final year at the
small, local school. Next year she would move to the Senior School,
on the other side of the forest, a long bus ride away. We knew that she
was troubled by the thought of change. She made me a beautiful blue
shirt for my birthday, with my initials embroidered on the breast
pocket, and burst into uncontrollable tears because the cuffs were a
fraction too tight. Anna said her moods were fragile, she needed all
our patience and reassurance.

   We decided to go up to the mountains over Christmas, rent a log cabin
and watch families of roving grisly bears from our frosted-up window. We
were going to tell Angel that night, after supper, as we were sitting around
the wood-burner. We wanted to give her something to look forward to, to
imagine and plan for, to picture in her head on long winter nights.

   We needed to stack up logs for the cold weather ahead. I swung my axe
and let out a cry as I brought it down to split a grizzled tree trunk, the
gleaming blade biting into the crusty, exploding bark. I paused, panting
and sweating, my hands on my hips, watching my wife sprinkle salt
crystals into a pan of bubbling soup, and saw my daughter's blonde head,
bent over a lap of needlework. She looked up then and her eyes were
spilling with worry. Uncertainty shivered across her face, then she saw me
looking, smiled and bent her head down again, to her sewing.

It was Angel's last day at school before the Christmas holidays. We were
going to set off to the mountains that afternoon. Angel kissed us goodbye
in the morning and set off with her hockey stick and a tin full of mince
pies. On their last day, the schoolchildren played hockey and sang Carols,
before closing with a Christmas party at lunch time.

   Anna tidied up the house before we left and we loaded suitcases, boxes of food, blankets, books and wrapped presents onto our truck. We were going away for one week, and we joked that we would only use a fraction of what we'd packed, but the cabin was miles and miles from anywhere and we wanted to be comfortable and safe. We closed all the windows tightly and locked all the doors. Anna sat close to me in the truck as we drove to pick up Angel.

Fragile flakes of snow fluttered across the windscreen and Anna placed her warm hand over mine on the gear lever.

Angel was standing alone, a little way along from her school, on the edge of the pavement, almost in the road, shivering and holding her school jersey up around her throat. We wondered why she wasn't wearing her winter coat. A large group of children and parents stood huddled together nearby, looking at our truck as we pulled up. Anna took her hand away from mine. Angel tried to smile when she saw us but her face jumped and trembled uncontrollably. We opened the car door and she climbed up over her mother and sat beside me, shaking with cold. She pressed her hands between her knees and then I saw the bruises, the cuts and the smears of dark, muddy blood on her legs. I knew that smell; dark, intimate, Anna's unspoken smell, and the tears, the moods, all made sudden sense. I put the truck into gear and set off for the mountains. As we pulled away a shower of stones rained across from the group of parents and children and thudded angrily against the side of the truck.

'Keep driving,' Angel said. 'Drive fast,' and I remembered Dr Winston's scratchy wool jacket, the roughness of it as he'd grasped my arm, the smell of so many nights of rain, his sooty cigar fingers fumbling with the tiny bandage.

Angel's time had come when she was out on the blustery hockey field. She'd felt a falling away inside her and Mrs Bonner had seen the trickle of blood. She'd taken her quickly to the sick bay and given her two fluffy sanitary towels. She hadn't meant to look, she'd turned away while Angel fixed herself up, but she was taking such a ridiculous amount of time and had gone so suspiciously quiet that Mrs Bonner knew she must have got herself into a terrible mess. She'd swung around to help saying in a no-nonsense, experienced voice, 'You'll soon get accustomed to these, Angel, we all do,' and then she saw it hanging there, meaty, hairy, swinging. No longer a tiny bubble of surplus fat, easy to tuck away, it had fallen out of Angel in a cascade of gloomy blood.

She never talked to us about the rugged cuts and deep violet bruises. We could only imagine the boots smelling of dog shit pressed against the back of her blonde head, the rough hands that pinned her down, the curious fingers, as white and hot as candles, pushed furiously inside her.

We stayed inside the log cabin all week. Winter spread its sinister cloak around us. Anna cropped Angel's hair with her dressmaking scissors and wound pieces of cloth cut from dresses tightly around her disrupted chest. She cut down some of my shirts and overalls and we stayed quietly together, listening to the bears sniffing outside our bolted door.

After Christmas we drove the truck to a small town on the other side of the mountain and I found work in a paper mill, lifting and packing. The mill owner employs Anna as a housekeeper and we live in a cottage in his grounds. We send Angel to the Senior School here, but we call her Andrew now. The mill owner's wife says she wishes her boys were less rowdy and how lucky we are. I work hard, the wages are good, and we no longer struggle for money. There's no need anymore for Anna to patch up my worn out clothes.

In my lunch break I eat my sandwiches by the gushing river that turns the wheels of the mill. I listen to the cogs clicking, the water splashing, and I think about Angel sitting in the classroom of her new school. I can see her sitting quietly and still at her desk, not catching anybody's eye, not moving or speaking, just sitting still and concentrating on the blackboard. I can hear the scratch of the chalk as the teacher scribbles on it. I can hear the children whispering to each other when his back is turned. I can hear them giggling and their desk lids banging. I can see Angel's blonde head bent over her algebra, looking at the x's and the y's, and the x's times y's, and I can see her frowning, trying to make sense of it all.

Last Days at the Asylum

JULIA DARLING

I AM discussing the similarity between intersecting train tracks and knitting with Rose in the common room. I'm smoking a nice fat rollie and I've got ten left in the tin. It's a shiny, yellow kind of day, and the teaspoons in our saucers reflect our moon faces. Marcus is over there, still in his pyjamas. He's eating a banana. Days like this, when the trees stand still on the lawn outside, despite a frisson of wind, and the long corridors purr, I'm quite happy at Saint Gerts, just off the A231 near Wolverhampton.

It is at the summit of this realisation that a bearded man comes in with a herd of nurses, all nodding and pointing, and the breeze changes direction and becomes an ill wind, clouding the spoons and rustling the thin white curtains.

He tells us that his name is Doctor Cluster, and he's come from somewhere else with a technique that he learnt in America. We look at him with our mouths open. He won't let us go with his eyes. He picks up my ashtray and gives it to the nurse, who holds it as if it's religious.

Doctor Cluster believes in something. He thinks this something will cure us all. It starts straight away, the procedure. It's to do with washing methodically and hygienically, and putting your shoes under the bed, facing East. He gives us a bit of paper with the rules on. He says they are boundaries, 'Like the hard shoulders of motorways, or railway sidings?' I ask through my open mouth.

'Yes, David,' he says, like he's just learnt my name.

He wears cheese-coloured trousers, and a loose silky shirt. His voice has a honeyed twang, as if it's been sunbathing. His beard is a hessian shadow on his chin.

I look at the bit of paper. The first instruction is NO SMOKING IN THE COMMON ROOM OR ON THE BEDS. After that it is so dense with words that I drop it into my pocket, and let it rumble away to itself.

We watch Doctor Cluster moving around the hospital as if he is a dog and we are cats with our hair standing on end. From the moment we meet him he never stops suggesting difficult things, like making us go for bus rides, or telling us to telephone directory enquiries. He stands behind us on such occasions, making notes about the way we hold the receiver, or the voice we use to speak to other members of the public. Often his instructions are complicated tricks, with snags. For instance he gives us money for the phone, but the coins don't fit, so we have to go and change them in the office. Stupid tricks.

2. ALWAYS BE POLITE TO HOSPITAL STAFF

Then he tells me that I'm going to live at Gateway Mansions, instead of Saint Gerts, and that he will take me to see it himself, along with Marcus and Rose. Getting there is a palaver. We each have to buy our own tickets on the train. I get a tight feeling when I hear the hoots. People stare at us. I feel inappropriately dressed. I stare at the no smoking signs.

Gateway Mansions is an inarticulate, high building on the edge of the city. I am to share with Rose, who never stops knitting, and Marcus, who is fat and rumpled. Apparently it is going to be our home. Doctor Cluster guides us through the intercom system, and into the lift. We all stand together trying not to hum, as we are pulled up through the building to our so-called flat. He shows us the keys and how to turn them in the locks, and we each practise. He is very patient. It's a bit like learning to drive, and I tell him so, but Doctor Cluster doesn't like that kind of comment. He wants us to say, 'Yes, I understand,' or 'That's nice,' or 'Thank you Doctor Cluster.'

When we get inside I notice that the windows are locked and that the rooms smell of chemicals from the bowls of artificial pot pourri that are on each windowsill. Rose politely comments on how well the corners were hoovered.

We sit in a row on the sofa, looking at the television that is switched off.

Marcus says, 'Think I'll just go for a walk if you don't mind,' but Doctor Cluster just smiles and says, 'Not now Marcus.'

I put my picture of Elvis up. Doctor Cluster told us to bring a special thing, so I did. It's the one of him dripping with sweat in his white cat suit with the mother of pearl accessories, and it reminds me of my father, who is also dead. Marcus has brought his medical dictionary. Rose has her collection of T. S. Eliot. We are all on our best behaviour. Notches in Doctor Cluster's stick.

After we have familiarised ourselves, Doctor Cluster says we should have five minutes silence in order to feel the vibrations of Gateway Mansions. I'm not sure this is a good idea, but I keep quiet, and sit with my eyes tightly closed. My mouth moves, but I don't let any words out. There is so little nicotine in the atmosphere that I nearly suffocate. Rose stops knitting and Marcus doesn't shuffle his feet at all. In that silence I hear a train hooting in the kitchen, but luckily when I open my eyes and look there is only blue formica.

I am glad that I am going to be moving in with Marcus and Rose. We have all been at Saint Gerts for over ten years. We all like a game of Beat Your Neighbour Out Of Doors, and Yatzee. We are three of a kind. We have a joke sometimes. I have a go at Marcus about his stomach that brims over his belt, and Rose calls me The Professor and pokes me in the ribs. We are friends. But we'd never been friends outside Saint Gerts. We'd never done all our washing in the same machine, for instance, with all our socks weaving together in the soap. And we'd always had a bell to ring if we dreamt something unkind, or fell out with each other. We are all different versions of mad. I am scared-mad. I wrote books once, but all the characters came alive and hated me. They said I had hurt their feelings. I am very afraid of hurting people's feelings. It feels to me like a wound. Marcus is voices-mad. He gets instructions from radios and televisions, telling him to do drastic things, like take his trousers off and run around parks. Rose is icy-mad. She will sink into a depression that surrounds her like feathers, so that you can't get near her. You know when it's about to happen because she stops knitting, and her hands drop down to her lap and whatever she is thinking slowly comes unravelled. It's upsetting. But Doctor Cluster said that none of these madnesses would happen. He said that if we followed the procedures then everything would run smoothly, even making toast and having visitors. I suppose that we wanted to believe him. I liked the idea of myself lying on a sofa eating rice crispies from my own bowl while Marcus did the ironing in the formica kitchen. Oh yes. I was keen, and said so, and Doctor Cluster said, 'Good, David, I'm very pleased to hear that,' and put his hand on the shoulder of my pullover, sending ritualistic messages through my bloodstream.

'I think we should celebrate!' he says, so loud that the cups tinkle in the cupboards.

3. THINK POSITIVE

Back at Saint Gerts we sit on our beds and wait for Doctor Cluster to ring a bell or make an announcement. Then some young grumpy nurses bring in trestle tables and one of them says 'Give us a hand David,' and I do, even though I hurt my finger on a hinge. 'What does he think this is?' snarls a Scottish nurse. 'The last supper?'

That made me get the giggles, which get worse when the chefs come.

'Hello!' booms Marcus as half a dozen spotty young men in chef's hats appear carrying silver dishes on their heads. Rose says 'Excuse me? Don't you want the palace?'

One of them goes red and mutters that they are from a cookery college in Wolverhampton.

'Are they going to cook us?' whispers Rose, luckily, as I stop giggling then. The young men in chef's hats are putting menus on the tables. I edge up to one of them and stare. The first course is chilled salmon.

'Do I have to pay?' I ask, as Doctor Cluster appears with a bunch of balloons.

'No David. There's a budget.' He says. Sounds like a kind of biscuit.

I scamper outside to the soft lawn where the poplar trees are. There is something consistent about this row of trees. They are like wise doctors, standing together, talking. I don't want to tell Doctor Cluster how frightened I am. I am afraid of hurting his feelings. So I imagine trains instead. I like trains and stations, and the way that the rail tracks go straight and are fixed to the ground. I had a train set when I was young. It was a complicated circle with tunnels and bridges. For hours I would sit with the trains going round and round. If a train derailed I would cry for hours.

Rose yells out of the window, 'He says we've got to get dressed!', and I stub out my fag, even though I straight away wanted another one, and wander back to the ward. The place has got even stranger. There are balloons hung from the windows, and streamers falling from the lamps. All around me patients are struggling to do up shoes and fasten hooks. Doctor Cluster gives each of us a new set of clothes. I have a Marks and Spencer polo neck and some grey trousers. I look like a schoolboy who is about to be bullied.

Everyone in the ward is talking at once. We all know that big changes are coming at us like a train approaching a broken bridge.

The adolescent chefs are laying out white plates and polished glasses. One of the patients thinks it's his birthday and an argument breaks out. The nurses haul him out protesting so he will never get to taste the chilled salmon. He goes back to pre-rehab. He makes us feel superior.

We all sit around solemnly in our places. Doctor Cluster blesses us. I hear one of the nurses muttering, 'This is bloody crackers!'

'We are celebrating your return to society!' bellows Doctor Cluster, raising his sharp fork.

The salmon tastes very clean. We have a toast to our new lives; to Gateway Mansions, and front door keys.

Doctor Cluster is enjoying himself a lot. His cheeks are flushed and he has congratulations written all over him. He gets out a video camera and films us as we eat our strawberry mousse. Perhaps I am enjoying myself. I'm not sure.

'Who is he?' I whisper to Rose who is holding her spoon as if it's a knitting needle.

'Yes,' says Rose, unhelpfully.

I think Marcus must have heard an instruction coming from the leftover fish head that still lay on the table, because he springs up then and runs towards the camera as if he might grab it from Doctor Cluster. For a moment the ritual goes awry, like eggs falling off a shelf, or a train derailing at high speed. I shut my eyes. Feelings will soon be hurt, I thought. But it's alright. Marcus remembers to pretend. He slows down. When I open my eyes he's filming us drinking coffee from blue cups. Doctor Cluster holds him with his eyes. I'm thinking, I really did want to go to Gateway Mansions. At least, my eyes and my fingers do, but not my mouth. My mouth wants to hurt Doctor Cluster's feelings. My mouth is unable to be grateful. I seem to be swearing. There are words stuck on the ceiling like when you throw spaghetti and it sticks.

'Stop that David,' says Doctor Cluster. 'You're talking nonsense!'

'I'm old enough to be your father!' I trumpet.

'He's the only one making any sense at all,' mutters the cynical nurse, handing me back my ashtray and I light three cigarettes in quick succession. Then I hear myself shouting 'Who do you think you are? Jesus?' and suddenly we are all looking at Doctor Cluster, and I know I have hurt his feelings as bad as I possibly could have done. The nurses stare at him as if for the first time, and then Marcus starts to laugh, and Rose joins in, and soon we are all guffawing, running up and down the long ward, stabbing the balloons with our knives, filling the room with bangs. The boy chefs are hiding under the beds and Doctor Cluster has lost control of the steering wheel and he's thinking, 'I hope the authorities don't hear about this.'

After we have all been sedated, he walks around the ward undoing the balloon strings and straightening the curtains, while I lie on the bed, watching. He has lost something. Whatever it was he had has drained away, leaving an empty little man that you wouldn't notice on a station platform. It was the last supper. Doctor Cluster sits in an office now. I think he's writing a book. I wonder if I'm in it?

Got a postcard today from Marcus and Rose. It starts Dear David. It's a picture of a goldfish in a bowl. They are sharing Gateway Mansions with an ex-anorexic from Ward Eight. They have both written on it. Rose's writing is like stalks, and Marcus writes in round irregular hoops. I stick it up above my bed. Rose says that someone is always hoovering in another flat. Marcus misses the poplars. Elvis Presley is still covered in sweat. They send their love to Doctor Cluster, but I won't give it to him. I'm keeping it for myself. I light a rollie. Soon it will be teatime.

Losing Track

TOBIAS HILL

PAST THE last billboard is where the desert starts. Off the blacktop, on to the dirt. The sidewalks just tail away. No one comes out here.

'No one hears the trees.'

'What?'

I don't say anything.

'There are no trees, Calvin. Keep walking.'

'Okay.'

I look up to read the board as we go under. Harry Connick Jnr is playing the Excalibur. I hear a dog bark, way back. There's so little noise out here. No one hears the trees fall. I keep walking. I'm trying to write in my head.

'Good boy. Just walk. You make me happy when you walk. I'm happy, you're happy. Happy campers.'

I'm trying to remember the skyline behind me. It has no buildings or mountains or trees. Just neon. I miss it. I'm measuring off the yards away from it. I don't know when to stop. Walk (scrub grass, packed earth). Listen (chuff and trudge of dirt). Feel. I can smell ginger.

One time, I was getting dinner in Circle-K, it was after the midnight shift and nothing left except BeenFeest burgers and a Yahoo. Socrates the shop-boy, he's telling some guy they got no cappuccino Haägen-Dazs. One minute they're arguing and the next he was shot.

I read in a book that a bullet travels faster than sound; you don't hear it till it hits. First the feeling, a kick in the guts, then the sound. Like a joke. Bugs Bunny with his face all burned black, and then a little flag coming out of the gun, BANG! Socrates laying on the freezer-cabinets, saying I'm sorry, I'm sorry in his Latino voice. Blood icing up pink on the cold glass.

I want to hear it first, is what I want to say. If I get shot ever. People get shot all the time in Vegas.

*

'Okay Calvin, you got the job. Congratulations. I tell you what they tell me. Which is: you dress nice, you never screw the customers, and you never, ever screw the company. Oh, and take the wristwatch off. You don't want to wear that in the Palace.'

That's Sebastian. He's management. There's marlins stitched into his silk necktie. Knuckles raw. When he talks his hands curl up and the knuckles go white. He likes the way I deal.

'Now here's a tip from your new boss just for free, son.'

His breath smells of hot-dogs. Meaty sour-sweet. We're in the Eiffel Lounge, seventeenth floor. Croupier interviews. Croupier means dealer. This is back in April.

'People lose two things in Vegas, three if you count cherries, but mostly our customers have only two things left to lose and they're both the same thing. Take their time, you take their money. Take their money, you take their time.'

He leans across the table. 'But you take care of your time, Calvin, and you shit green presidents. Like me. Let them lose track, yes? And never lose track yourself. This is the Palace. There's always money to be made. You like money, right?'

The Palace of Versailles. I like it here. I work on Plaza Five. There are no clocks, but I got used to that. I got used to the noise too, the slots and crowds and big-win bells. There are clock-radios in the four-poster bedrooms, alongside the check-out times, and from the stained-glass arcade on first floor you can see the giant digital over the Midnight Hour wedding chapel on Las Vegas Boulevard. That's all.

There's this poem called 'The Lotos-Eaters' by an English Poet Laureate, where people eat fruit and the world goes plain out of their minds. That's what the Palace is. Lotos fruits, all different kinds. Lemons, cherries, plums and bars. It's from the Greek. When I get off work I always read a poem. It's a sign of worth. Then I sleep. I got a place with a view near the Golden Nugget. Mostly I just work, though.

I got a black Casio I keep zippered in my waistcoat pocket. Fifty metres water-resist. I won it on the Trawler-Crawlers in basement three. To check the time whenever I go to the men's room. I keep track.

I do cards, triple-shifts. My eyes are twenty-twenty for long periods. I got potential.

Sebastian is from Culiacan, that's Mexico. He doesn't talk about that much. Him being a foreigner, he doesn't talk about that. One time he told me. We were drinking. He probably forgot now. Back then he used to take me out drinking uptown. He drank silver tequila chasers. He said, Money in the desert. This is where we live, Calvin. Only we don't get it. The money. We get green baize and burger bars. If I could turn it all back. Make it liquid. Liquid money. You like money, Calvin? Sure you do.

Once I'm walking home, late night. The stoplights outside my place, someone's stolen the colour filters off of them. It goes green, white, white. It makes me think of Sebastian. Making it liquid. I stay away from him.

Then it's four months later and there's this woman.

Midnight Hour is two elevators away and she isn't wearing a wrist-watch. I've been checking on her between deals. I'm on blackjack, table E14, E is the row, fourteen's the aisle. Today I was on baccarat shift but I changed with Sevvy, I always do because Sev says baccarat muff has got class. That's what he says.

I checked the time too. On the Casio, just now in the locker room. This woman, she's been losing a lot of time but not much money. That's smart. No big wins, just give and take. I guess I didn't start counting until she took off her hat and I saw her hair. For definite, she's been playing that same slot for seven hours and just gone ten minutes.

The hat's a Panama. Not real Panama. The kind of thing they give away with Chicken à la Colon at the Dunes. Her raincoat's army-surplus. That's how I know she's from out of town. Wearing a raincoat.

She comes out from the elevators and stops when the noise hits her. Wheels and dice and the three thousand slot-machines. She looks at it like she was only going to the mall and took a wrong turn someplace. Wrinkles her nose at the smell. The tang of static and electric motors, like pennies and oysters. A carnival ground with no sky is what she sees. The inside of Las Vegas. In the first alley of slots she stops again.

She touches one of the machines. A Desert Bandit, hubcap chrome painted with red and green diamonds. An accumulator, that's when the money goes up and up the longer it waits. Tokens come crashing down somewhere, over on the Cashcades. Her hands snap shut.

Two young girls trail away from the third slot on the left. She walks up to it and takes off her hat. She runs her fingers across the arm and doesn't jump at the little tug of static. Just smiles. I smile too.

I lived in trailer-parks with my Ma when I was young, and that's why I have good vision. Looking at the world through moving windows. It was practice. I see everything mostly. Gas station faces, WELCOME TO, rain coming beyond porch windows. Faces turning a winning card, private Fourth-of-July's, lips moving when they need to pray.

This is all wrong. This isn't what I want to say. I'm walking up a desert ridge away trom Las Vegas. The man behind me shouts *Keep going Calvin, good boy*. This is the place where no one hears. There's not enough time. What I want to say is

Before the hair, I see the way she stands. Ankles touching, like a woman waiting on a cold street. Lipstick too. Gloss. She looks like the street-people, one of the young ones who hang out down by the dog station.

The Greyhounds I mean. The ones who call up for pizza and steal it from right out of the trashcans when nobody collects it.

That's what she looks like. Hungry. She looks up at the chrome ball of a security camera and smiles. Then she takes off her hat and I see her hair.

It's ginger. Not ginger like the word. Ginger like ginger: the lion-fur of the root when you cut against its grain. I can't take my eyes off of her. Sometimes I feel this way with women I can never meet. At a window. In a photo. On a subway train. She's very beautiful.

I'm not a dozen feet from her. Her coat-pockets are full of silver dollars, she's running one hand through them while she plays. So I guess she didn't walk in by accident after all. She plays well, too. I keep watching while the blackjack players burn and bust. I can tell the time just from their drinks. GTs and Marys in the afternoon, rocks and straights as evening comes in. After an hour she changes arms, starts pulling with her left. Milking the slot while she flexes blood back into her right hand.

Then Hutch the floorman is behind me with his hand on my shoulder. Just too tight.

'Everything alright here, Mister Halliday?'

That's me. Calvin Halliday. 'Yes, sir!'

I don't say nothing else and Hutch's hand loosens up, so nothing else was the right thing to say. Hutch is like Sebastian's Rottweiler. They drink uptown a lot, I guess. Hutch is built like a wall but if his head wasn't tucked into the neck of his tuxedo, he'd lose it and not even worry. Like them lizards with their tails.

'Make sure you give our customers your undivided service and attention. Make their stay a happy one.'

'Yes, sir.' I don't talk too much as a rule anyway. I don't do patter like some dealers. I ridge the cards, cut them, deal. There's only two players but I couldn't tell you their faces. I win a hand. Take bets. Look up.

Hutch is with her. Not standing too close, not close enough to scare her. Touching her when he can. Her arm to guide her to the slot, her hand to the lever. The light shines off his dress shirt and his teeth and for a moment it looks like they're dancing.

Then she moves back from him, stands with her arms wrapped across her belly while he grins. He spins the slots for her. He gives her his personal demonstration. Now he's telling her his joke about jerking off the slots.

She waits for him to go. Just standing, head down. She looks tired, her arms must be hurting by now. She just lets them hang.

He goes. She never smiled, not even when Hutch was telling his jerk joke. I watch her for hours as the Palace fills and empties. Lipstick and light all the colours of carnival-glass. I see her mouth move when she prays and loses, hear the bells when she wins a hundred.

Once she looks over at the mirrored glass that's Management.

Sebastian is there, leaning against the glass. Watching her with his arms folded sharp against his tux. She looks away then. There's some kind of feeling in her face. Just a twist of muscles, it could mean anything strong. I see that. I keep track. My eyes are good.

A truck goes crashing past on the 115. It's a long way back now. It just makes the desert seem quieter. A place emptied out of life. I can hear the man breathing as he climbs. Soon it'll be time to stop walking.

Not yet. Not yet. Wait.

She's very beautiful.

One time I saw Madonna in the Flamingo café and this woman, she's beautiful like Madonna. The way people watch her. They want to be with her, a part of her. Like the waitress at that café will tell her grandchildren how she met Madonna, and when she gets Alzheimer's, she'll tell them nothing else all day, how Madonna took extra sugar and cream and how she licked her spoon. A part of her.

I wish I could be with her. Someone this beautiful, the world must be different for her. I try and imagine it. Maybe she gets used to it. She looks cold.

Seven hours, ten minutes. There's shadows under her eyes the colour of new bruises. When she pulls the bandit's arm she grins. It's not a smile. It's her teeth coming together with pain.

A working day she's been here. All that time on the same slot. Never coming over to the five-dollar tables, not even trying a different bandit. She's fed a lot of silver into that one machine, and milked some of it back out. Third Desert Bandit on the left. Maybe she saw it in a dream.

The eye-shadows make her look like that boy in the Charlie Chaplin movie. *The Kid.* She's so young. I want to know where she ought to be, a whole working day and all that cash gone by.

I have to keep track of the table. There are cards in my hand and I don't know what they are. This is what I'm good at, but I'm not doing it good. I don't like that.

There's an old guy in blue jeans with four cards, he's got numbers written all over the backs of his hands. Another man standing behind, drinking Long Islands, sometimes sitting to play and sometimes not. A couple with East Coast haircuts, Jesus, I'm not even watching them. The wife clicks another red disk down and drinks her sweet martini. Lipstick on her teeth and glass.

Couples you got to watch because they slip up together for a kiss and then maybe slip cards. I lose the hand too. The East Coast lady kisses her man on his bald spot. The Marlboro Man swears, crosses out the numbers on his knuckles with a ten-dollar Palace fountain pen.

I keep watching her, though. The woman. She could be gone each time, and that's why I have to keep looking; I might never see her again. She doesn't take her eyes off the machine. Chews the insides of her mouth. I do that, when I'm thinking. I want to know what she's thinking. One time when I look up I can see Sebastian in the floor-to-ceiling cut mirrors. He could be watching me, or just looking through me. It's hard to tell from his eyes. He looks bored.

I deal. Cut. Play the cards. Head down. There's a rhythm to it. If I get the rhythm right, I can keep track without ever looking at the Casio.

'Any more bets?'

I try not to watch her. I try hard to keep my eyes on the baize. Red chips stacked up in their black rings. Small-time gambling, five dollars a hand. The systems man works with one-dollar silver discs, clicking them together in his hands. All nerves and addiction. The green table is everything.

I stop hearing the noise of the gambling halls. For a while I stop thinking of the beautiful girl who dreams of one slot machine. There's just me and the players now. I go for unsafe hands; five card tricks or splitting fives. If I win I don't smile. My face don't show nothing at all. I bust a six-card hand and deal again. The haze of smoke hurts my eyes and I blink. Once, twice.

'Deuce and nine is eleven showing, ladies and gentlemen. House shows one queen and holds. Standard bet is five, House wins draws. Does anyone wish to raise the bet?'

'Can I play?'

She's standing right next to me. I never heard her come up. I can smell something on her, perfume or her hair. Her voice is hard and nervous, teenaged. Nevada accent, and mostly Nevada means Vegas. I keep getting her wrong.

Her nails are bitten short. No paint, no gloss. They don't match her lipstick. She's wearing no socks. Just sneakers. The rubber peeling off of them. She's talking again. I have to talk back.

'You're welcome to play ma'am, soon as the next game starts.'

'Oh, sure. I'm sorry.'

She watches while the House wins and the man with systems on his hands gets up and swears and walks away. She smiles at the East Coasters as she takes the empty seat. The husband won't look at her. He sort of nods at the space around her. I can understand that.

'Just a couple of hands. Then I have to take five.'

'Yes ma'am. Good luck.'

I'm not supposed to say that. I say it quiet, so maybe she won't hear with the casino background noise. But she smiles at me. There's gaps between her teeth. I'm surprised because it doesn't make her less beautiful. Only less perfect.

'Thanks. But this is no big deal. Just a chaser.'

She sits back. She talks fast, her voice going up a little at the end of every sentence. It's her accent. It makes everything a question I want to answer. I deal the cards. Ace showing, eight down.

'To go with the slots.' I don't plan to say that. It just comes out. I look up.

She's not smiling. Her pupils have gone small in their green irises. When she smiles again the pupils stay small.

'Excuse me?'

'A chaser, you said. To go with the slots.'

She starts to look behind her at the Desert Bandits, then stops. 'You were watching me?'

The way she says it, it's something bad. Like she was naked. I try to smile but it's hard, I want her to stay, I know it shows now. 'It's my job.'

'To watch me playing slots?'

'Well, just to watch all the players. Ma'am.'

'Hey. Speaking of jobs.' It's the East Coast wife, tapping a red disk on the baize.

I start to apologise again. Then Sev is behind me, down from the baccarat gallery, whispering garlic breath in my ear. It's the end of my shift and I didn't even know.

'Chow time, Cal.' He clucks his tongue against his teeth like the ranchers out in Clark County. Lowers his voice. 'Hutch says go get changed, you look like a 'coon in heat, you're disturbing the customers.'

I follow his eyes and she's watching me. I want to say something. Just so she remembers me. But there's no time. I pick up the cards. When I talk I'm looking at her.

'Excuse me, ladies and gentlemen, I hope you've enjoyed your time with me, and I'll be handing you over now to another of our highly trained croupiers, Sevvy. I hope you have a good evening.'

And then I just stand there, looking at her. I can't stop myself. Hutch the floorman comes up, he's saying something, laughing, pulling me out of the way. I want to tell him he's hurting me, but it sounds so weak. I don't want to sound weak with her there. I catch my footing and don't fall.

When I look up she's still sitting there, watching me. She shakes her head. Then she puts down her cards and goes. She just goes. She doesn't look back.

'That's it, Calvin. You can stop now. Turn around so I can see you.'

I lost my breath a little, coming up the ridge. The desert is out ahead of me, I know that. But in the dark there's nothing. Only wind coming with the smell of rock dust and cactus pears. I could be on the edge of the Grand Canyon, it's that dark.

'Turn around, Calvin.'

I could do that. Look back at Las Vegas. The Strip laid out in neon from the Tropicana on in. I'd like that. But I want to be sure. If I hear it first, or if I feel it. If I look, I'll never be sure.

I keep walking.

I lied. That bit about what I do, work and sleep. I write too. That's what I do, like what I want to do is what I mean. Like this, writing in my head. It's instead of talking.

I do poetry. You can probably tell from my style. I'm not so good, I don't really know why. My Ma taught me. We used to do poems when she was driving.

> *When the moonlight's deep,*
> *banked up against walls,*
> *you can skate on it*
> *or pack moonballs.*

That's what I wrote last night. Lying on the worn-down bed in my rented room, thinking of her. I've never seen snow, only sand which might be the same sometimes. On TV I have. Seen snow.

I lie in my room, thinking of her. I've never seen someone so beautiful. Not up close. She's like snow. I think of her hands, running through pockets of silver. That's how I'd touch her. If I could ever.

I think of it all night, half-dreaming. Sebastian in the mirrors, the third slot on the left, silver dollars streaming out like liquid. Making it liquid. I think of the way he watched her. Bored. Intent. There's light on the ceiling coming in off the Golden Nugget and game arcades. Red and gold. Like her hair when she walks under the striplights and chrome.

Then it's today. I'm still waiting to sleep. I can tell when it starts to get light without moving. The neon fades against the ceiling, thinned with sun. I go down to the public phone outside and ring Lakeisha at the Palace to change my hours.

It should be Sebastian I call. I don't want to talk to him now. I get Lakeisha to put me on blackjack again. Table E14. She doesn't ask why. One time she called Sebastian a pimped-up bumfuck hick. Only once, though. She told me since then she's never been alone with him, not anywhere. She makes sure. I like her.

I eat a hamburger breakfast and walk to the Palace. The stoplights are mended now, but it's early, there isn't much traffic. The lights click through patterns by themselves. Red-amber, green, amber. I try and think what I'm going to do. I can't think. Like I'm hiding it from myself.

I knew she'd still be there. I'm not talking smart. I think slow, I need time. But I thought all last night and I see mostly everything. At the Palace I check the jackpot updates outside Plaza five. The Desert Bandits are up to three million three hundred twenty seven thousand dollars seventy-seven cents. The Cashcades and the Louis XV are higher, nearer four.

Lakeisha lets me check her file copy and it says the same. But there's a note on the Bandits, faded-out with photocopying: URGENT AUG. SEE % SLOT REF. 212. Percentages are odds. Lakeisha doesn't have odds records. That's different from jackpots, only top management sees those. Sebastian could get them, I guess. If he wanted them bad.

There are no windows in the gambling hall, no line of sight out to the sun. You can tell it's daytime, though. There's a different crowd, not so many couples. This time of day lots of the tourists are out in the Mojave, looking at orange poppies or Joshua Trees. What's left are the addicts, the systems-people, the last-chance players.

There's less laughter, more time. My table goes quiet around late-afternoon and I look up. She's been there the whole time. Third slot on the left. Not losing too much. Moving only a little as she plays. Saving herself.

One thing about millionaires and poor folks; they think about the same thing, money, all the time. One way or the other, money is what makes them what they are and they have a hunger for it. Once you got it, that hunger, you never get rid of it.

That's what she's like. It's in the way she treats her silver dollars. Loading them slowly, not wanting to let them go, warming them with her hands, talking. She'll never have enough of it. She loves it, like Sebastian. *You like money, Calvin? Sure you do.* It's in the way her eyes sparkle when she's watching the machine. Wet.

I put the cards down and look up. I know what I'm going to do. The cameras will see me, because they see everything. I could lose my job just for leaving the table.

It doesn't matter now. I walk up to her. She has her back turned, so she doesn't see me till I'm right there. I didn't plan what to say and I don't want to say the wrong thing, but there's no time. She turns and I start to talk before she recognises me.

'I know what you're doing. With the slot and Sebastian.'

A cheer goes up from the crap table crowd. I have to shout a little. 'I don't mind. All I want you to do is talk to me. And let me talk to you. And then I won't tell no one.'

'Just talk?'

She doesn't even stop to think. Maybe she was expecting me after yesterday, I can't tell. Her eyes are punched-out blue with exhaustion. 'Where? Somewhere private?'

She's laughing at me a little. I nod and she looks away.

'I'll have to ask Sebastian. No. You'll have to ask Sebastian for me. Somewhere where the cameras won't see you. Tell him we'll be an hour. Go.'

I walk away between the knuckle-crack of roulette tables. I try not to think about what I'm doing. My chest hurts, it's the excitement.

Sebastian's office is behind the security room, but I don't need to go back there. There's just him and Hutch on cameras for Plaza five. They've been watching everything I done.

He looks up at me, Sebastian. Just looking without expression, then back at the screen. 'You're off your table. I should fire you.'

I go over. On the close-circuit is the woman. She's waiting by the Desert Bandit. Not looking up. I guess she knows we're watching anyway. She doesn't look beautiful like this. It's gone like figures in landscapes from a car; a woman sleeping, a face. The car moves on and the angle is gone, there's just mesas and dunes. I can't get it back.

It's not important. What matters is I'm not here to watch people play. I'm part of this now. I don't understand it all yet but I'm trying to learn. It feels good. Sebastian sighs and stands back. He looks at me like he's expecting me to say something. So I do.

'You're keeping track, right?'

'Right, Calvin.'

'Right. I saw that. But there's always money to be made. You said that too.'

'Yeah.' He sounds real tired.

'Are you making money now?'

Hutch swears and looks away. 'Calvin. Please,' Sebastian says. His hands are fists, blood draining back from the joints and bones. 'She could win any second. Any second now. Just say how much you want.'

I look back at the screen. 'What's her name?'

They wait. It's quiet in here, soundproofed. I talk into the quiet. 'I want to be with her. Just for an hour. Just talking. She says it's okay and to tell you, she'll be an hour. That's all I want. You can have the money.'

Hutch starts laughing. He does it real quiet, but when I look at him later there's tears running down his face and it's hard to tell if he's laughing or crying. Sebastian just goes on looking at me a long time. He lights a cigarette, even though smoking's not allowed inside the security rooms. All the time he looks at me until he lets out the first mouthful of smoke.

'So go.' He shrugs. 'What are you waiting for?'

'What's her name?'

He grins. His teeth are like hers. 'Whatever you want, Calvin. Right now you call her what you like.'

'Goodbye Calvin.' He says that as I'm going. A cheer goes up as I step outside. Someone winning big over on the crap tables. I walk between the watchers and players, the floormen and waitresses. I can feel the cameras following me. A pressure on the back of my neck. I don't look up at them.

She sees me coming across the hall and leaves ahead of me. In the elevator we don't say nothing, it's just the two of us. The TV screens playing *Happy Days* with the sound down. Muzak Sinatra. Not looking at each other at all.

We get out at the Atrium and walk outside and it's already dark, the moon round like an oven-dial, hot against our faces as we walk. She's fast, I have to run a little to keep up. She's taller than me, I didn't see that before. I guess I don't see everything. I try and concentrate on her face.

She talks without slowing down. A little breathless. 'Stop watching me. Stop it. What do you think I am, MTV?'

'I'm sorry.'

She sits down on a concrete bench. I didn't know she'd do that, I have to go back to her. She pulls out a packet of cigarettes and lights up. I sit down. There's nothing else to do.

She's blowing smoke, shaking her head. 'I don't believe it.' Then she looks at me, not talking, just shaking her head like yesterday. I try and think of something to say.

'Don't believe what?'

Her eyes keep moving, like she's trying to see inside my head. She's frowning. Not angry now. She looks amazed. 'You know they'll kill you. They can't just shut that slot down. Someone could be hitting that jackpot right now. If that happens, they'll kill you. They'll just walk you out into the desert and shoot you.'

'I only want to talk.'

She leans forward with her elbows on her knees and puts her head down. 'What do you want to talk about.' Grinds the heel of a hand into her tired eyes.

It's not going right. I stand up. This wasn't how it was supposed to happen. 'I want to go somewhere else. I mean us. I want us to go somewhere. If you want to. Are you hungry? We could have dinner together.'

She stands up and smiles. A kind of grin which don't have much to do with feeling. It's just the bone showing through. 'It's your time. What's your name?'

'Calvin. Halliday.'

She doesn't give me her name. We shake hands. Cars go by on the Strip. Faces looking and looking away. 'Actually I'm not hungry, Calvin. Can we just get a drink somewhere?'

'Oh sure.' I look around for somewhere. But you can drink anywhere in Vegas, any time. 'How about Union Plaza? Is that okay?'

She takes my arm. I feel it like static. 'That's fine, Calvin. We can walk.'

And we do. Down towards Fremont together, the sound of a siren somewhere behind us and the warmth of her, the warmth of her arm, closer than I ever imagined it could be. After a little while her breathing changes, slows. I feel her relax against me.

'What are you doing here, Calvin?'

I shrug. 'I just ended up here.' We walk through automatic doors. The elevator closes around us. I want to tell her. To explain. 'I'm just road trash. You know, Vegas has been a place for road trash and white trash ever since the Mormons bought it off the Paiute for eighteen bucks.' We find a table. She orders drinks. Turns back to me and nods and smiles.

'I like it here, is why. It always feels – if it ever got out of season, the Strip would be the biggest ghost town on earth. But it never is.'

'Never is what?'

'Out of season. I like it that way.' There's a tall glass of alcohol the colour of apricots. I pick it up and drink. It burns. 'The neon meadows. Like coming on water in the desert. That's why I'm here.'

She's nodding, looking past me. I don't turn round to see if there's a clock there. I don't want to see that. 'How about you?'

Her eyes focus in. 'You know what I'm doing here.'

'I mean why?'

She doesn't answer. Just frowns at me for a while, then looks down. 'You're a very strange person, Calvin.' She sits forward. 'I'm here for the money. That's what I want. That's all I want. I don't care if I die with no friends, no fuck, no family. As long as I'm rich. Do you understand that?'

'Sure.'

She smiles. A real smile, the first time. 'No you don't. What do you love, Calvin?'

I could say her. I don't say that. 'Poetry. Really. It's what I try and do. It's hard.'

'Tell me some poetry.'

'I can't.' It's true. I can't even look at her now. Her voice is different. Quiet. 'I'm no good at it.'

'So tell me what you want to write about.' She sits back and drinks. Her glass is almost empty. I take a breath and talk without looking at her.

'Well. The rain, maybe. Mostly it never rains but sometimes it does. Saved-up and coming down hard. Like an accumulator. Raining millions. Have you seen that?'

She nods, *sure*.

'So when that happens I go walking by myself, the Strip and Downtown. The boulevards and backstreets are full of reflections. Neon and laser-spots and glitterballs and spangleboards.

'I walk nearly all night, some years. There's the smell of food from air vents and the light all around, it keeps me warm. Up to the Trop, down around Glitter Gulch. It's like walking in the sky. Then next morning it's gone. Dried away into the desert. So fast. It's frightening. That thirst.'

I stop talking. She hasn't looked back at the clock. Her eyes are trying to find a way round mine again. My hands are sweating. I wrap them round the cold of my glass.

'I want another drink. You want another?' I nod and she orders. I close my eyes while she's looking away. In the dark I lose my balance. I haven't slept for a while now. We wait for the drinks to come.

'You know, when I said what are you doing here, I meant here. With me. I meant why did you do this.'

'Would you have come with me if I hadn't?'

'No, but–'

'I've never talked to someone like you. Nothing ever happens to me. I'm the dealer, it's not supposed to. But I just wanted to talk to you. You're so beautiful.'

'Thank you.'

'It's my pleasure.'

She doesn't touch me. She just smiles, her face softening into it. She looks beautiful again. Maybe it's enough. Then Hutch is there, I see him coming across the room, multiplied in the smoked-glass mirrors.

'Calvin.' The dress-shirt has come out. He still looks like he's been crying. He has one hand in his jacket pocket, the fingers curled tight. 'I've been looking for you everywhere.'

She doesn't look at me any more. She stands up, her eyes going wild. 'It happened didn't it? Hutch? It's gone, isn't it? Oh shit.'

'Get up, Calvin.'

They look down at me. Together they're similar people, I can see it. It's a trait, like green eyes or a love of meat. 'Calvin the poet. Calvin who thinks he's God's gift to fucking oxygen. Get up.' Quiet voice. It could be her speaking. I can't tell. I stand up and she looks away.

'I feel like you're polluting the air in here. I'm going to have to ask you to leave the building with me. You're fired, by the way. Now let's go.'

I want to tell him they could try again. Or that I'll keep quiet, I can. I could do that.

Instead I think of her, her hair. I wish I could have touched it. At the street I look back for her, but she's gone. I start to write it down, in my head.

The Strip is long and quiet, Hutch ten steps behind. I listen to his steps as we walk. We come to where the city stops and the desert begins and he tells me to keep going.

No trees, no one to hear them fall. Once I look round quickly and he's standing under the last billboard, hands in his pockets. Shadows from the sodium lights fall down over his eyes. Then he starts up again and we go on. A long-haul truck passes on the empty road. Then the road is gone. I'm on the ridge. There's nothing but the smell of dust and stone.

'That's it, Calvin. You can stop now. Turn around.'

I keep walking. I just want to hear it first. Before the pain. I want that fact. Behind me the man with the gun is shouting my name. In my pocket the Casio alarm goes off, and as I pull it out I hear the sound of the jackpot and I smell the colour of her hair.

Gathering

CARRIE WORRALL

THREE FIGURES climbed steadily up the rough slope behind the barn, leaving dark trails in the dew-grey grass. Reaching the dry stone wall that divided the field from the moor, they turned along it a short way, then stopped to climb the intake gate. One of them waited to help another over the gate while the third, already some way ahead, continued up the moor edge. The morning was quiet and damp; shades of grey and green faded into a dull purple of heather towards the sky.

At the roadside below, a man leaned against the wall and watched the walkers. He could not make out who they were. They were not carrying rucksacks, but they weren't locals either – two men and a girl from the way they walked. Level with his knee, the black and white head of a border collie was cocked on one side. Ears alert and neck tense, the dog watched the strangers; when one of the three dislodged a stone, it rattled down into a dry gully and the dog's swift panting ceased for a second. A whine and an enquiring eye at his master, who made no movement, and the young dog lost interest in the three figures, almost invisible now against the dark heather. Nose down, he sniffed for rabbits along the wall-back. The man watched the walkers for a moment longer, until first one and then the other two stood up against the light sky. He watched them as their silhouettes shortened out of sight and vanished. Then he bent down to attend to the mole traps he was here for.

In the still morning on the moor top, now out of sight of the dale floor, the three figures walked on. The day would be fair when the mist blew off; already there was a warmth in the air. Cobwebs like white cotton draped the tufts of heather, and snail trails glistened on the stones and yellow earth. It was almost completely silent, except for the faint stirring of life in the valley below: a dog barking here and there. A tractor started up with an insect buzzing, though they wouldn't be turning the hay yet, with this heavy dew. Horizons were becoming clearer as the bright mist sank into hollows and clung in wisps to the earth, dissolving in the sun.

The leading figure stopped to let the others catch up. He stooped to re-tie the lace of his walking boot. The leather was soaked dark with moisture off the long grass in the field, and now dust and heather buds decorated the toe of the boot, clinging to the damp. As he straightened up, a couple of sheep clattered out of the gully and across the track, pushing through the heather away from him. The ewe was shedding her fleece, leaving her back white and gleaming beside the dirty grey rug that draggled at her sides. Her rud-mark was hardly visible now; another day or two and she would be quite anonymous. Her hefty lamb was unmarked. A wily mother, she must have escaped notice on the moor or in the forest back at lambing time. Just as the two younger walkers reached their waiting guide, the silence was pierced by the single pure note of a plover. They listened. It came again, a soft close whistle, fading at both ends, as if it were a perpetual note just coming into focus for a moment.

'It's going to be hot,' said the girl, out of breath and sweating already from the climb.

'As well we set off in good time, then, isn't it?' The sharp tone of the leader's reply reminded her of her complaints earlier in the morning. She had hated the early call, the cold water. She had complained about the stiffness from unluxurious sleeping, about the toilet facilities, which were non-existent. She was not used to roughness, in people or in her surroundings, and felt her obvious superiority to this man undermined by his scorn for her refinement. Not that it was refinement that made her cringe at using the back of a wall as a toilet, burying her own faeces like an animal. No, that was just civilisation; what makes us better than animals. Without it... sheep. Her train of thought petered out as she concentrated on not tripping over the heather or putting her foot in a rabbit hole, of which there seemed to be a remarkable number, treacherously deep, hidden and angled to break a leg.

'Watch out for the shell-holes!'

Shell-holes? She could not for the life of her imagine why anyone would bomb this desolate lump in the earth, but refused to admit to ignorance, keeping silent.

'It was a firing range. Used it for target practice. There's a burnt out old tank up here somewhere and a pillbox. Watch your feet, you could break a leg. You probably thought they were rabbit holes.'

She fumed silently. Of course he knew everything better than she did. Of course she was stupid and ignorant. She was the one at Cambridge, though – what was he? Just some nutcase her brother had picked up at some local history lecture. They shared a cosy little obsession with ancient history. Oh yes, he'd made a real study of that, hadn't he? With dates and tribal histories, and ritual reconstructions. Big deal. Her brother was just as bad; delighted by the whole stupid adventure. He probably enjoyed crapping in fields.

'Is it far?' her brother asked. Now if she had voiced the question, there would have been some cutting, sarcastic comment. But to her brother...

'No, we'll be at the tumulus by lunchtime. Then we can decide what to do.' This was said with a frustrated glance over his shoulder at the girl lagging behind.

'And then what?' she snapped.

The older man didn't even hesitate in his step as she stood still, braced for a fight. He just laughed his infuriating, sarcastic laugh and walked on. A look of sympathy from her brother didn't help, and she watched the two men walking away from her towards a faint bump on the horizon. The mist had finally cleared and the moor-edge was melting and re-forming in a flickering heat haze. Not for the first time, the girl wished she had stayed at home.

'Funny lot, those walkers we had in last night,' said the landlord to his only customer, who leaned conversationally over the bar. The front room of the pub was cool and dark despite the summer. Stone paved floor, wooden settles and iron tables kept it cool. Around the plain woodchip walls, photographs of darts and cricket triumphs; the famous names of county cricket; a nineteenth century map of the dale. The electronic calculator on the wall by the dartboard looked slightly out of place. The firegrate was full of cigarette ends and crisp packets it was too hot to burn.

'I saw them off up the intake this morning, early.' The farmer drank deeply. 'By, that's good!'

'They asked if they could stay in the barn. The lass looked like she was after bed and breakfast, but the lads were set on sleeping rough. I don't mind so long as they don't burn it down. Just the one night they said.'

'Where were they from? I've not seen a car parked anywhere.'

'Two of them looked like brother and sister, from down south somewhere I'd say. A bit well-spoken. T'other fellar's accent was more like Leeds or over that side. I thought maybe he was a teacher or something, but he said not. Come to think on it, he didn't ever say what he did. The young ones are at college.'

'Maybe they've parked somewhere up Kirkdale, for a walk back to the car today. They've got a good day for it, anyway – it's another hot one.' As if to prove his point, the farmer drained the last of his pint. 'I'd better get back for dinner. You hay-timing this aft?'

'Aye – got to make the most of this weather,' nodded the landlord.

Outside, under the van, the black and white collie lay panting, half watching the chickens scrabbling about at the top of the yard, too hot to bother. His master's step and the tinkle of the pub doorbell brought his head up, and he left the shade, waiting to be let into the back of the van. The farmer stood blinking with his hand shading his eyes, as he looked up to the hilltop, squinting as he caught a flash of white disappearing behind a wall.

'Have you still got a ewe out on the moor, Doug?' he called to the landlord who was bringing out a crate of empties.

'Yep – saw her yesterday. I must've missed her with my lot. She's been knocking about since it got dry, comes down here for water. Too hot to chase after her now, she'll likely come in for clipping with Bar's ewes.'

'We're gathering up at Clifftop tonight. I'll keep an eye out for her.'

The farmer let his dog into the back of the van and went round to the driver's door. Opening it, he felt the heat, and let it stand open for a couple of minutes before getting in. The smell of hot plastic and petrol mixed with the scents of dog and sheep – he wound down the windows in both doors before starting up and pulling out of the yard. His hay was in, his few sheep clipped the day before, and he looked forward to a kip in his cool front room before the gather that evening.

In the dry heat on the moor top, the girl was lagging further and further behind the two men. Her brother had turned round a couple of times, but it was not as if his sister was getting out of sight, and the track was clear enough. The yellow-grey earth was cracked and bright, dotted with white stones. The path was only occasionally overgrown or distracted by well-trodden sheep tracks. The young man was feeling fairly irritated by the presence of his sister. She had insisted on coming along, and had done nothing but complain. She had moaned about leaving the car such a long way from the pub, even though their guide had explained why: it would shorten the walk today. It also felt right somehow – arriving on foot, leaving on foot. The whole point was to try and re-create that historic day, centuries ago, when so many people had walked miles to hear the tribal chiefs and take part in the sacrifice. What did she know about sacrifice?

It seemed obvious to him that they should spend the night before in as primitive a place as possible, yet she had wanted to stay at the pub. He had relished the cold water, she had barely dabbled her fingers in it. There was something necessary and spartan about everything their guide had suggested. This morning he felt vigorous and young; life was flowing through him with the growing heat of the day, and it was good to be here, with this man who had suddenly become so important in his life. He felt connected, somehow, to all the infinite threads of being that link us now to the darkest ages of our history. He wanted to walk and walk, to stretch his body.

He glanced back over his shoulder. His sister was plodding slowly along, head down, suffering from the weight she'd put on in the last year, and from the gin last night. There again, she had ruined the pure excitement of the evening by getting drunk and flirting with his friend. It had made his blood boil and the fact that she hadn't got anywhere didn't help. Every time she was treated to a sarcastic comment or rebuff, he felt guilty for being pleased. No wonder she was in such a foul mood this morning. He wished they had never told her about the trip, or let her come. She had seemed interested, but in what? Typical bloody woman – things are okay in theory, but when it comes to reality... He half-ran a few steps to catch up with the other man.

'You shouldn't have told her about this trip,' said the older man, without a sideways glance. 'She's just going to slow us down. We'll make the burial chamber, but we'll not get to the site of the gathering before six, and even though it's light until late, we won't be back at the car before dark.'

'What should we do?'

'Well,' the older man looked at the student walking beside him. They were almost the same height and despite fifteen years or so between them, they walked with the same easy stride. This boy was his; he could read admiration and enthusiasm in the young eyes that scanned his face. 'Let's wait and see when we get there.'

Their goal was clearly visible now, below the splintering horizon, a stone ring marked by a leaning wooden post. On top of the post, a rusty metal star showed that this was one of the many tumuli, burial grounds, scattered across these moors. Graves of ancient tribes hiding high from the invader... In illustrated school history books, those times are always dismal and raining, or pictured in a lifting mist like this morning. Somehow, the bright hot day evaporated the mystery, and the young man felt disappointed. Perhaps it would be better close up. Perhaps the disappointment was connected to the hunger that had been creeping up on him for the last half hour. Perhaps they could eat soon.

Warmed by the day, the purple heather gave off a glorious smell of dust and honey; the purple was rich and deep. The smooth curves of the hillsides were clothed in a royal robe, an altar cloth embroidered here and there with vivid emerald green bracken patches and grey-white rocks to fool the shepherd. Underfoot, the ground was light and porous, dried sheep droppings paled into dust, and the dark patches of moss were black and crumbly. It hadn't rained for ages.

A world and a short walk away, men sweated under the shade of a corrugated iron roof. The heat stifled conversation, but the mood was cheerful. Outside in a close pen, sheep were packed, heads up, panting. A young girl balanced on the bottom rail, leaning over the hot animals and watching for any to drop to its knees and go under. Every two or three minutes, another would be fetched to the clipping shed, a three-stride drag across the yard. The pen was three-parts empty, but the sheep crushed tightly together at the far end, the cracking of their teeth and horns sounded like breaking ribs.

Above the panting and shuffling of the animals and the drone of the clipping machines, a van radio crackled the cricket commentary through an open door. Dogs lolled in the shade, too idle to snap at the heels of the up-ended sheep. The hot weather made the grease lift away from the skin, made the sheep easy to shear. Below each tangled grey mat, the creamy-yellow clean wool gave way in swathes, leaving the sheep dazzling white and baffled. Blinking and shaking their ears, they skittered out into the field, a bright new red mark across their rump. Behind the clippers, a man and a woman were wrapping fleeces, trimming the dirt and rolling them tightly inside out into neat creamy bundles. The smell of hot wool was itchy and their hands soft and red with wool-grease.

One of the clippers straightened up and cast his eye over the remaining sheep in the pen. Easing his shoulders back and stretching his legs, he said:

'We'll finish these by dinner time.'

'Aye, and the Aussies'll have finished us by then, an' all.'

A low laugh ran round.

'Could do with getting back in good time this aft – we're gathering up at Clifftop tonight. Hope this weather holds out another day or two.'

'I think our lads over in Headingley could do wi' a shower right now.'

'They *are* a bloody shower, way they're batting!'

'Weatherman said it was going to break soon. Glad I led my hay in yesterday.'

Up at the top of the yard the kitchen door opened to the yowling of cats and a woman shouted, 'Anyone ready for dinner?'

'Give's half an hour and we'll be finished.'

'Right. You'll all stay and eat though? It's all done.'

The door closed and the cats went back to the cool of the coal shed. Hurried at the thought of dinner, the men were quiet and concentrated, one ear on the cricket until that too stopped for lunch.

'T'only thing can save us now is rain,' said someone gravely.

'No chance. Not in daylight, any road.'

When the two men reached the tumulus, they stood still and looked at it. The girl's brother was hungry, but felt that any comment to that effect would be inappropriate. He glanced at his companion's face, and was surprised by the aggression he read there. The man was standing, his features tight with concentration, arms at his sides, fists clenched. His eyes were squinting against the glare of the sun, but he was obviously staring at the mound, overgrown with short-cropped rough grass. Dry droppings and wisps of wool caught on the heather showed that the hump was used as a windbreak and shelter for the moorland sheep. The older man began to walk around the burial mound, very slowly, scrutinising it closely without getting any closer to it.

Feeling self-conscious, the boy followed him, half expecting a burst of mockery at any moment, half afraid of this new mood. Until now, their guide had been matter-of-fact, practical; explaining, on the drive up, the history of the place and his own archaeological interest. The whole adventure seemed fun and interesting; a good way to spend a couple of days in the long vacation. Then, it began with the barn, a new aspect had opened up; an almost mystical sense of excitement and mystery. The two men had sat up talking into the night, while his sister slept, talking as equals about history and humanity and life.

Now, something indefinable crept into the mood once more. That such things had happened here, in this very place, so many hundreds of years ago to the day; that they should revisit the sacred places, where decisions were made and lives offered up in a vain attempt to invoke the protection of long-dead gods. A tense expectation charged the air, changing everything. Even the heavy heat of the day now seemed fitting.

This was reality: sunlight glancing off sharp stones, dancing on the bleary horizon. His romantic vision of mist and grey rain was history's shroud, the obscurity of the past. Under the pounding sun, breathing the heather-loaded air, time had no meaning. Then and now were one. The sun had been, was now, ever would be; deadly life-giver, warming and fermenting or drying the skeletons of the earth to dust. Hanging in the hot, still air.

The boy felt dazed by this circling in the heat. Sweat was trickling between his shoulder blades, sticking his shirt to his back. He became aware of a distant rumbling, a far-off roar which grew swiftly to a deafening crash. He threw himself to the ground instinctively as the jets crashed across the sun, bright and dark and shattering the air. The aircraft swung easily around the curve of the moor and swooped down into the dale. The grace of the movement seemed disconnected from the destructive roar they left echoing and threatening the hillsides. The sheer speed and force of them left him shaking. He heard himself being laughed at, and reached up for the hand held out to pull him back to his feet.

The man's grip was strong, and he held on after the young man had stood up, laughing: 'It was only an aeroplane! They still practise up here in fair weather. You should have seen your face!' Letting go finally of the boy's hot hand, the man slung the canvas bag he'd been carrying off his shoulder. 'Shall we eat?'

'Maybe we should wait for my sister.' Normality rocked back into place.

'How hungry are you?' The other man grinned conspiratorially as he began to unpack the canvas bag he'd been carrying over one shoulder. 'She'll be a while, yet. We'll save her some. Maybe it would be better if we went on from here by ourselves. She can rest here for an hour or so and then head back the way we came – it's an easy track – we'll pick her up from the pub tonight.'

Biting into a cheese sandwich, her brother could only nod.

*

When she had watched the terrifying jets out of sight, the girl looked back at the two men. They were unpacking the bag on a patch of green in front of the hillock. She wasn't hungry; she felt nauseous with the heat, and she cursed her unfitness again. And her stupidity in drinking so much the night before: her whole dehydrated body craved water. She wasn't hungry, but they might have waited for her all the same. She quickened her step, frowning at the unbearable sun.

The two men were kneeling on the grass, facing each other, unpacking the bag one item at a time, as if in some ritual. From where she was, they seemed to be moving unbearably slowly. Each thing was drawn carefully from the bag and examined before being passed to her brother, who set it down on the earth with the same slow attention. For some reason, this methodical slowness irritated her, as if it were a deliberate taunt, and she hurried to break it with her own gasps and complaints. She was walking much faster now, and breathing heavily. The sun pressed down, hammering a headache into the back of her eyes; the blood thumped in her head and she screwed her eyes up. Just to get to that heap of stones, to flop down on the springy turf and have a long drink… She was close enough to the men now to see their lips move and they even seemed to be speaking in slow motion. She broke into a stumbling run.

All she could hear was the pounding of her head as the shimmering horizon seemed to grow steadily darker. The edges of her vision closed in, framing the bright green grass and the kneeling figures. She saw her brother eating, saw the other man's hand touch his face gently, saw her brother turn, painfully slowly, to look at her. His expression changed so gradually that she could see every muscle move. His look of horror grew as he looked at her running, as if the flesh were crawling around his features. Slowly his mouth widened and dropped into a shout which she did not hear above her own heartbeat. The pressing sun won and she tripped, blacking out the rushing earth as she fell.

'We must get her out of the sun,' he said.

I must get out of the sun, she thought.

'Ready? Lift!' Strong arms, hard hands, it felt as if they were all over her body – she couldn't twist or struggle. Then a sudden relief of shade. She opened her eyes cautiously. She was propped against a heap of stones, in the tiny patch of shade offered by the tumulus.

'Are you okay, Sis?' He always asked the most stupid questions. She nodded, the movement making her head throb. Then that other voice, darker and soothing: 'I don't think you should go any further. Why don't you rest here for an hour or two? We'll leave you the bag. When you feel up to it, walk back the way we came. You know the track.'

Suddenly relieved at the thought of being quiet and alone, she smiled at their guide. His face was full of concern, the first warmth he had shown towards her since they set out. 'That's the first good idea you've had all day,' she said. 'I'll have a rest here and then head back.'

'We'll go and get the car, drive round to the pub and pick you up. If you want to just stay here, we'll come and fetch you later, but it would be better if you got back to the pub.'

It was the kind of voice you couldn't disagree with; firm, calm, perfectly reasonable.

Her brother handed her a water bottle and put the bag down beside her. 'There's a couple of sandwiches and an apple in there – you should eat something.'

The two men hovered around her while she drank.

'Go on, then,' she said, eager to be rid of them.

'Are you sure you're okay?' Her brother, still anxious, wanted absolution from the guilt he felt for getting her into this mess.

'Yes, just go, will you? I'll be fine. See you back at the pub.'

They left her gratefully.

'We might as well take a look at the meeting site, on the way back to the car,' said the man. 'She just needs to rest.' He cuffed the back of the boy's neck lightly, dropping his hand to rest against the small of his back for a moment. 'Cheer up – she'll be fine.' And despite himself, the young man's steps were light on the turf as they struck out across the moor. He felt as if he had left the very last of his cares behind him. Now the rest of this glorious day was all his own.

The van followed the Land Rover up the battered road onto the moor top. In the back of the Land Rover, a black and white collie snapped at his neighbour; tense, expectant dogs bristled with rivalry and energy now that the heat had gone out of the air. The Land Rover turned north at the shooting road, the van south. The heat had gone, but the air was still thick, especially up on the moor with the early evening scent of heather like liquid in the throat. Men and dogs were dropped off around the moor, sometimes within sight of each other, always within earshot of a whistle.

When the woman driving the van had dropped the last man, she switched off the engine a while and got out to look at the evening. There was not the slightest breath of wind, and a haze lay over the moor, distorting shape and distance. She stooped to pick a branch of heather and leaning in through the open window of the passenger door, tucked it behind the mirror. Pity it wasn't white, for luck. It was still quite light, and should be for some time, these long summer evenings. The sky was no longer clear, though, but a muddy yellow. The clouds had built up quickly at the end of the afternoon, and a black smudge approaching from the east heralded a storm. She hoped it would hold off till the men got back; it would do the earth good if it rained, but wet sheep tomorrow would stop them clipping, and there were folks who hadn't got their hay in yet. She turned to get back into the van, and was startled by the cry of a curlew, long and dying in the evening air. It came again and was answered, and looking up, she saw the birds, wheeling and plummeting. Someone is defending his territory, she thought.

The drive home along the rutted track was slow, and just as she reached the field gate, she had to brake sharply to avoid a ewe that leapt out of the dry ditch, right in front of the van. The creature hesitated mid-track, confused by the vehicle, then careered off downhill into the bracken which hid the field wall. She had lost a lot of her wool already, and was unidentifiable from this distance. Close up, her earmarkings and horn-burn would show whose she was. There shouldn't be a man this close to home yet, nor a dog, but the sheep was obviously running from something on the moor. She thought again of the warring curlews, and then drove home. Her husband and their neighbours would be hungry and ready for a drink by the time they'd walked the moor tonight.

There was a slow, rhythmical drumming; a deep pounding of ancient drums. Against a shadowy backcloth, a purple altar, curved like the hip and thigh of a reclining woman. Figures circled the altar, formless shadows. They moved slowly and silently. The girl became aware that the altar was her own body, clothed in the moor, fused into the earth like a deep stone. The silent figures turned around and around, moving so slowly. Their faces were covered, arms hidden beneath dark cloaks. She smiled as she recognised her brother, though she couldn't see his face. She thought quite distinctly: 'and now the next thing must happen.' As she lay on her side, she felt heavy objects being placed on her hip and waist. As if from above, she saw they were a loaf of black bread and a broad-bladed silver knife, with a pale handle gleaming like moonstone.

One of the figures approached her, drawing back his hood to the quickening rhythm of drums. She smiled to recognise the man who had brought her here, and he smiled back, taking hold of the silver knife to cut the bread. She thought clearly: 'don't cut me' and lifted the loaf from her hip, placing it instead on her neck. The man pressed down very slowly into the loaf, and she could see the knife cleaving the heavy black bread easily, coming closer to her neck. The dull pressure of the blade increased until she knew it was about to cut her throat. She tried to cry out, but her mouth was full of heather, sticky with honey, and her body was immovable stone. There was a clap of thunder, the earth split in a blinding gash of light, and the girl opened her eyes, choking and panting.

The sheep gathering was well under way when the storm broke. The first rattles of thunder up and down the dale had given warning, and the men sighed or swore as they continued their slow walk. Each dog ran a sweeping arc, rooting individual sheep out of dry gullies and bracken patches as tall as a man. The hot heavy sheep trotted or galloped, tangled grey fleeces swinging from side to side under their bellies. The black and white collie was too keen after a day of inactivity, and snatched at the shaggy mats of wool, trailing grey wisps from the corner of his mouth.

'Lay off, Tip! Pack it in! Go steady on there.' Rising, falling, querying whistles sounded around the moor, like some strange bird chorus. Curses and shouts followed dogs that missed sheep or got too close. 'Don't rush them or we'll have 'em to carry home.'

'Get by, Tip! Get back there!'

The evening was foreshortened by the storm clouds darkening out the sunset. Even though they had started early, the men knew it would probably be dark and wet by the time they got back. Thoughts of supper and a quiet fire were distracting, and Tip's master sent him back twice after a rock that stood like a pale sheep in the half light.

Around the moor, the dog-run net closed in, easing the sheep in and down to the intake above the farm. A wide rippling funnel of wall led to the field gate which the three walkers had climbed that morning and which now stood open. A fleeting breeze passed, carrying more bleating of sheep and cheerful shouts. The animals were now moving in knots of five or ten, coinciding in a thickening grey mass. A tiny late lamb, bright in the dusk, was too slow to keep up and had to be carried. As the men now walked closer together on the rumbling moor top, the tired dogs had less to do. The warning shouts eased off, and Tip trotted wearily at his master's heels. The flock was finally together, and as the sheep moved down into the funnel they packed closer into a sluggish grey sea. It started to rain in huge heavy drops. The problem now was bracken; a forest which covered the sheep and disguised the outline of the field wall. Too easy to leave an escape route back onto the moor. Dogs were brought back into action, darting into the bracken jungle, only to reappear ten yards further along, bouncing up to get a better view. A cunning old ewe lay low in the bracken-covered ditch, close to the wall, working her way slowly uphill, back towards open country. Her lamb followed closely.

The girl felt sick, and her head was splitting. The memory of the dream seemed more real than this waking. She had been lying close to the entrance to the tumulus, her head on the canvas bag. Looking around, she was surprised to see how low the sun was, filtering between massive clouds. Her neck and shoulders ached from sleeping on hard ground, and she struggled to sit up. The light was yellow and dusty, slanting in shafts like a hazy lantern into the valley. She started to push herself up, and her hand touched something smooth, sharp and ridged, tucked under an overhang of heather. She picked it up. It was the complete skull of a sheep, jeering white and empty-socketed. A couple of long yellow teeth still clung to the upper jaw and the laughing mask was framed by two curling sharp horns. Disgusted, she threw it away from her, and it fell with a dry rattle into the narrow entrance to the burial mound. The hole was half veiled by thin heather and a few white wisps of sheep wool. She was suddenly awake, and knew she had to get moving if she was to get back to the pub before dark. The thunder rolled again and she felt the moor cower beneath her, closing its stones around her. The darkness would come soon, with half-remembered stories of ghosts and gatherings and sacrifices, and the sweated memory of a dream.

She tried to stand up, but a jabbing pain in her ankle brought her to her knees. Her head was spinning with the thunder roaring around her, and as the first heavy wet drops fell on the back of her neck she was violently sick.

That and the cold water helped. Lying on her back, face into the rain, she opened her mouth to catch water. She was quickly drenched. The storm was now in full voice. She shuddered and crawled back to the only shelter there was. Squatting close to the opening, her back to a stone, she tried not to think about what lay in the darkness behind her. She watched the storm as it trawled the dale, pummelling the moor top. The grey clouds were never still, their changing patterns and forms becoming less distinct as the last of the daylight faded. Sheltered beneath the low hump of the tomb, the girl waited for the storm to pass. Then, night or not, she would try to get back.

The cold from the rock seeped through her damp shirt and the fine spray of water splashing off stone clung to spiders' webs in tiny droplets like a delicate dew. The thunder rolled on, echoing round the flanks of the hills. She hoped her brother and his bloody guru were soaked, too.

Two men stood at the centre of a flattened earth platform – at one corner a tree grew twisted by moor top winds. This was the highest place for miles. A burnt circle in the earth, spent matches and discarded ring pulls showed this had served as a campsite recently – but now there were just these two.

'We'd better get back,' said the younger man, quietly.

'Afraid of being struck by lightning?' The familiar tone of mockery was back again, but it no longer had the same effect.

'Not really.'

They had arrived at the gathering place with the first rumble of thunder, and had watched the storm swirling around before it finally broke. From here, a view of dales and forests fell away on three sides while the moor stretched northwards to the horizon. Exhilaration, joy, freedom – the mood of excitement and release the boy had felt since parting from his sister had grown steadily as they had walked, hot and silent. And now this magnificent thunderous welcome from his ancient gods! He had jumped up onto the flat platform with a whoop of pure joy. Stretching his arms out wide, he had spun around and around, whirling his cotton T-shirt round his head like a flag, drinking in the space and emptiness of the place. Suddenly aware that the other man was watching him, he stopped. They looked at each other, and the boy could not read the expression in the other's face. He held his gaze as the other man stepped up to him, suddenly close.

'Good, isn't it?'

'Yes,' said the boy, 'Thank you.'

Their hug was briefer, and more awkward than the man had expected. The boy inhaled the smell of sweat and rain, and thought of men embracing before they went to fight. Armies destined to be slaughtered had gathered here. Holding onto this man, he suddenly felt as if he were saying goodbye to something. Taken aback by the thought, he let go and stepped back.

'Come on,' he said. 'We're going to get soaked. My sister will be frantic.'

'She can take care of herself.' The man stepped forward again, tried to repeat the embrace. But the boy turned his face away, twisting a shoulder into the man's chest.

'Don't,' he said.

'It's alright, you know. This is a place of mystery. Anything can happen here, and when you leave the place, it may be as if nothing has happened.'

The boy pulled away again, and looked at the man. Their eyes were level. 'Don't spoil it,' the boy said. 'Please. I want to head back now. I'm sorry... It's been a brilliant day.'

'For Christ's sake,' snapped the man, and the sudden coarseness of his language shocked the boy more than anything. 'You'd think I was going to rape you or something. It was just a bloody hug.'

'Damn and blast you dog! Tip, where are you? Come here to me!'

Dripping under the rain, the men were herding the sheep through the gate into the field. The wet grey animals streamed through like a flash flood of the storm, scattering and spreading out over the field. Heads down, ignoring the storm, they were discovering the coarse green grass of the intake after several lean weeks on the dry moor. Ewes were too absorbed in eating to answer lambs separated from them on the way in, now bleating damply in the gloom. Dogs were finding out the last stragglers from the bracken, which was already wet enough to soak a man ploughing through it, dragging a stubborn sheep by the horn.

Just on the edge of sight, fatally visible by the white bald patch along her spine, a ewe was escaping steadily away, taking her lamb back to the moor. She placed her feet neatly and quickly in her familiar gully, where a trickle of yellow water was already running off the hard-baked highland. Her lamb, nervous at leaving the others, jumped from one side to the other, skittering and skidding. He kicked down a stone, and the collie looked up. Only the white half of his face could be seen, and the glint in his black eye. He was sodden and panting, but instinct sent him back up the track after the ewe, now invisible.

There followed a curious battle in the storm. The dog soon got round in front of the sheep, and dropped like a stone to the ground. She, hesitating and also weary, stood still. The sheepdog crept forward, head low, haunches flowing smoothly, his movements almost imperceptible. He snapped his lolling tongue back into his mouth and seemed to be holding his breath, eyes fixed on the sheep. She, stamping nervously, turned her head and nosed her lamb, tucking him in beside her. Then she looked back at the dog, nodding and shaking her head. Instead of turning, she stepped forward, shaking her horns at him, head down. And another step. The young dog seemed astonished. He lifted his belly off the ground and moved in a weaving curve in front of her, willing her to turn back. The ewe was no longer taking any notice of him. High-kneed and head set, she trotted in a straight line, occasionally stamping or ducking her head in the dog's direction. Tip swung out, round and ahead of her again, and again dropped low, trying to unnerve her by sheer willpower. The rain beat down on both animals, and the odd whiteness of the dog's half mask and the sheep's spine stood out in the wet dark.

The man, coming over the moor edge, shouted after his dog again, and whistled. Ears up, Tip's attention slipped from his quarry and she broke past him, head down and galloping, her matted wet blanket of fleece flaying from side to side, spraying water. She did not stop, and the man soon lost her against the dark heather. The dog, torn between his master's repeated whistles and the escaping ewe, looked after her, straining and whining. The man walked right up to him and took hold of his collar. The wet leather was slimy, and bending down to pat the dog's steaming sides, the man felt his hot breath and smelt the sweaty excitement in him. His hind leg was trembling, jumpy.

'Bloody keen, aren't you? Well, we're so wet anyway... might as well bring her in tonight. Go on then, get by!'

He released the dog and, watching him disappear up the track, trudged on after him, enjoying the vertical rain and glad his hay was not still out in the field.

The girl must have dozed off, for when she opened her eyes the light had gone completely from the sky. It was still raining, but the storm had moved on, thundering threats across from the next valley. She felt numb, her foot was throbbing, her whole body ached with cramp and her mouth felt dry and swollen. She opened her mouth wide to breathe and was aware, suddenly, of another presence. She could hear a heavy, panting breath behind her shoulder, from inside the tomb. She could almost feel the hot breath, a strong smell of animal fear. She was frozen, the muscles in the back of her neck tense, a numbness crawling down her spine. A reasonable voice somewhere inside her head told her not to be so stupid, as wide-eyed, she turned slowly to look behind her. She saw nothing but blackness, and the tension drained away in a surge of relief. With a last laughing flash of lightning, the storm lit up the mouth of the grave for a split second, and she saw the grinning skull, lifted from the ground and fleshed; horns shining wet and hollow sockets filled with eerie green fire. She did not see the lamb tucked away behind its mother, deeper still inside the chamber. She screamed, and her mind flew out of her throat, carrying her voice above the rumbling thunder.

'I'll be off then,' the farmer stood in the doorway of the pub. The rain had eased off to a soft dripping from eaves and gutters. The night was cool and calm. In the back room of the pub, her gaze fixed on the floor, the girl was sipping hot tea. She had changed out of her wet clothes into a borrowed sweater and jeans, but she was still shivering.

'Aye,' said the woman. 'She'll be right in the morning. Needs to sleep it off. Her ankle's twisted, must've gone down a shell hole.'

'Easily done.'

'Fancy those lads leaving her like that!'

'Maybe she left them, tried to get back on her own,' he suggested, uncomfortable. 'She says they'll be coming here to pick her up.'

The woman smiled. 'She hasn't said much else, yet. Too much sun, I should think.'

'I'll drop by tomorrow, but let me know what happens, won't you? Shook me up wi' that scream, she did; must've been Tip that scared her.' He smiled ruefully. 'And to cap it we lost that old ewe we were after!'

The woman laughed too, imagining the tale as it would be retold over and over again in the pub, about the time he went up on the moor after an old ewe and came back with a young gimmer instead. She called softly as he got into the van: 'And watch what you pick up on the way home!'

His answer was drowned by the van engine.

Leaning on the doorpost, letting the cool, moist air float into the warm kitchen, the woman watched his headlights bump out of the yard and into the road. She heard the van, every gear change, speeding back down the dale. The air was still, refreshing after the day's heat. It had been a funny day. She couldn't really say she was sorry there would be no clipping up at Clifftop first thing tomorrow; a nuisance but a bit of a relief, too. Inside, there was a cheer from the bar as someone scored high on the dartboard. If they were parked up in Kirkdale, those lads would be turning up soon, and then she'd give them a piece of her mind. Nudging a hopeful cat back out into the yard, she shut the door.

The blurred moon rose, lighting up the clouds around it with a yellow glow. The heather began to breathe again into the night air, and the wood smell of peat mingled with the stink of sheep as the ewe rested with her lamb in the dark shelter.

Do You Like Oranges?

KEVIN DOYLE

IT IS difficult for me to accept that Ricardo is dead. Physically, of course, he is. I buried him myself just one month ago in a plot near Rye on Port Philip Bay. His casket was small and light to carry. His funeral was large and reasonably well attended. It marked me even, the occasion – and I felt his passing – this ending of my closest friend. I shovelled the clay with others, and I saw it break and spread on wood. Myself, I threw pages of a diary into his burial earth. A couple of days later I even returned to sit quietly with him, and his grave was as permanent as any. Yet I feel him alive. He is here with me today as I stand on this finger of land, thousands of miles from Australia and from the place where we met. I am looking up hill at a small white-washed bungalow, at Coughlan's house, and I am thinking what a long journey home this has been. But I am back.

Strangely, until Ricardo's death, this journey back here was never going to be made by me – I had decided that and I had turned my back on the past and the idea of retribution. I can claim no insight on this, I was simply afraid and I didn't know if I was ready; I didn't know if I would ever be ready. Australia is a place where you can forget and maybe that in my innocence is why I went there. It was certainly far enough away. But I still remember the fear – and the sense of being hunted with no place to run – that drove me from this country. That I can never forget.

Death has brought me back and death is probably what I will leave behind. You see – and I had actually forgotten this – but I have always been the person that listens to the graveside orations, the person in the crowd that sullenly and resolutely decides to act on what is being said. Ricardo's funeral was no different in that respect – how could it be? A different continent maybe, a different lineage of rebellion maybe, but the same in every other way.

Ricardo took cyanide. A spoonful. When he died he was alone in a small apartment in Fitzroy in North Melbourne. He planned everything meticulously and he left a note, an explanation of sorts: *Forgive me*, it said, *I am ashamed of what I am doing and I am sorry*. The note was signed, Ricardo Mann and it was dated wrongly June 7, 1979, instead of the actual date of his death, July 7, 1990.

What really took me back here to Ireland? Ricardo's death and a broken bond? Some sense of retribution? Some cataclysmic end that I could bring upon myself and my nemesis here? I have looked up no one since my return, not one single person in this place and country that I once called home. Not even my ageing father whom I have not seen in all these years.

I realise that I have no interest. It's as if there is only one thing on my mind. Just this one idea: to see Coughlan and consider. I could do it, I have thought that already. I have had him in my sights. Yesterday, as he walked alone along the lane by his home, I drove right by him. I could have killed him there and then. And it would have been very easy. But I have a presence of mind now – I drove on quietly.

Ricardo's sister, Consuela, is also dead. Killed by a bomb explosion in 1986 in Viña del Mar, Chile. An assassination attempt on a General Tomás Klesse. Her remains were never returned.

Ricardo's father, Javier? Missing too, presumed dead. A trade unionist until late '73 in Valdivia, Chile. Last seen in early January 1974, days before his forty-fifth birthday. He was facially disfigured and he appeared unable to co-ordinate his movements.

Ricardo now, dead too. Suicide. July, 1990. *Torture sequelae* unresolved. Survived by his mother, Maria (Valdivia, Chile). Rest in peace.

Almost ten years ago, on a warm, May afternoon in the town that I come from: that is where all this began for me. The year is 1981 and it is the height of the hunger-strikes. I am walking alone, along a terraced street not far from my home. It is late afternoon, nearer to five o'clock than four, and I am thinking about moving out of home, of getting away from my father. But he'll take it badly. Why? he'll ask. What is wrong with here? You don't have a job yet, he'll say, and you don't have any money. Stay a while longer, he'll plead, until you have work at least. This is what I'm thinking when a voice says, 'Hey!'

I look. A car pulls along the kerb, goes ahead of me a bit. A heavy-engined car, purring warmly. Black. Well built.

'Is your name Michael McCarty?'

At a bar in Union Hall on my second day back in Ireland I put a book on the counter and I say to the barman, 'The man who was just in here drinking his pint, do you know him?'

The barman nods.

'He left this book behind,' I say, pushing it towards him. The book is a hardcover. It has gold inset lettering: *Property of the Special Air Services (Rhodesia)*. The barman doesn't look. He picks up the book and puts it behind the Murphy's tap. 'I'll give it to him,' he says.

I take my drink. 'Take a look inside,' I say, 'at the photographs.'

The barman is surprised. 'Why?'

'Just do. Open it,' I say, coaxing him

He does. His face is expressionless. He stares. When he looks back up at me, he says, 'Are you sure Mr Coughlan left this book?'

I point to where Coughlan was sitting. 'That's where I found it,' I say, lying.

I walk over to the car. The man who called out to me is in his late forties, I guess. He has a well-receded hairline with tight ginger curls on the sides and on the back. His locks are silver-white. He hands me an open black wallet: *Detective-Sergeant J.P. Coughlan*, it says. There is a picture of a much younger man and a badge: *An Garda Síochána: Special Detective Unit*. Underneath the badge is a harp crest.

I see another man beside him, in the driver's seat, much younger, in his thirties maybe. He smiles. Coughlan speaks.

'Would you mind if I asked you some questions, Mr McCarty?'

The back door of the car on my side opens. A man gets out, more middle-aged. He is wearing a grey-black suit and a shirt and tie. He has wavy, black hair. He's stocky but short.

'About what?' I ask.

'That depends,' Coughlan replies.

Melbourne, 1982. Five months after my arrival in Australia. The Yarra River. Two canoes glide along the water coming down stream. At first I can barely see the figures. As they come closer, they wave. I don't wave back. The canoes go under the bridge.

A minute goes by, maybe more. I prepare to jump. One of the canoes backs out from under the bridge against the current. It deftly turns to hold at right angles to the flow. The nose of the second canoe also re-appears. Again I see them wave.

'Are you okay?' I hear. The voices are distant. My pants are wet. At the MCG grounds, a football match is in progress. There's a score and a roar. Everything seems distant. Again the shout comes. A woman's voice. 'Are you okay?' Suddenly I get off the bridge wall. For a moment I stand on the side of the busy roadway, then I begin walking towards town, up Footscray Road.

Coughlan gets out of the car. The door swings shut behind him. He's reasonably tall, about my height, five-eleven maybe six foot. He's casually dressed, in a bomber jacket with cords. It looks wrong, not quite the thing for a man of his age. The two men close around me. Across the road a woman stops to look. She moves on again.

Coughlan points at the badge on my lapel. It's green in colour. The writing, in black, says, *H-Block: H for Hunger and H for Hell.* He fingers it. I step back.

'Been busy?' he asks.

'Not really,' I say.

The shorter man lifts my knapsack from my shoulder. I hold onto it with one hand. He yanks it from me, roughly. Coughlan smiles. 'What were you doing at the Exchange?' he says.

'Giving out leaflets,' I reply. I look at the stocky man. He has my knapsack open. He removes a bunch of leaflets. He hands some to Coughlan. Coughlan sifts them. He stops at the leaflet about the hunger-striker, Bobby Sands. He holds the leaflet out for me to see. 'A bit late in the day for Sands isn't it?' He smirks; Sands had died two days earlier. I don't say anything.

'And you're on your way home now, is it?' the other man asks. He feels the side pockets on the knapsack and reaches inside; he doesn't take his eyes off me.

'What's it to you?' I say.

'Answer the fuckin' question,' Coughlan says.

I nod. The car engine revs.

Coughlan holds up another leaflet. It says, *Political Status Now!* 'Give out many?' he asks.

'A few hundred,' I say.

The stocky man hands me back my bag. He indicates towards the car door. 'Get in,' he says. I back away more but Coughlan grabs me by the arm. 'In,' he says. The other man grips me as well. I'm pulled towards the car. Coughlan shoves my arm backwards and up. The sullen man whispers: 'Your bones are bending son.'

I get into the car.

One day Ricardo and I are alone at the Centre. I'm helping him with a mail-shot. He's inserting the letters into the envelopes, I'm doing the address labels and stamps. After a while he asks me when I plan to go home. To Ireland you mean, I ask. Of course, he says, to Ireland, where else? I'm not going back, I say.

I am put into a large room on the third floor of the Garda station. My clothes are taken, everything except my underpants. I am told to wait. The room is empty apart from a small formica table and a chair in the centre. There is a long wooden stool like a church pew, against one wall. At the far end, diagonal with the door, there is a fireplace that has been closed off.

I wait for a very long time or so it seems. Maybe it is an hour or two or three. I begin to feel cold.

When Coughlan returns he is alone. He has a briefcase and the leaflets that were in my bag. He tells me to get off his chair and stand. He points to a place in front of the formica table. 'Stand there,' he orders.

His appearance has changed. His hair has been re-combed, and there is a smell of aftershave. He is now wearing regulation police pants and an ordinary blue shirt. The shirt is unbuttoned at the neck. His whole manner is more brusque, more businesslike. He is deliberate.

He arranges the leaflets on the table and sits. He stares at me. He doesn't say anything. A long while goes by. He continues to stare at me. Then he takes a typed document from his briefcase. He puts it in front of me and without any preamble places a pen beside it. He asks me to sign the document. I shake my head. He takes the manuscript back and pages through it. He appears to read it. He asks me if I understand why my clothes have been taken. I say no. He tells me that they're being checked for explosive residue. He pushes the document along the table, towards me again and he holds the pen for me to take.

'Sign,' he says. 'You might as well.'

I shake my head again.

Another day, perhaps a week or so later, Ricardo and I are together again. Ricardo asks me if I am going with the people from the Centre to Wilson's Promontory – a camping trip is being planned. I say I am, that I've heard it's beautiful there. He agrees but then says, Australia is only a place in-between, Michael. One day you'll go back and what will you do? What would you do? I ask. It isn't as clear cut for me, he says. Why? I inquire. You don't know? he asks. I know of Chile, of what happened there. No… about me, he says. What is there to know? I gave names, Michael, names and faces that were never seen again.

Coughlan talks about the H-Block Campaign. He reads from the leaflet about Bobby Sands. He asks me to tell him what the 'Five Demands' are. What does 'Political Status' mean? Why should murderers be given political status? Answer me, he demands. I still won't say anything.

He asks me if I know a Jimmy Murnane? He describes him: red hair, glasses, a married man. I don't answer. Patricia Glavin, do I know her? I don't answer again. He wants to know why I won't talk. I say, why should I. He laughs.

He takes a beige-green folder from his briefcase. He opens it and looks through it. There are copies of letters inside: photocopies. They look familiar. He turns the folder around so that I can see better. The letters are letters that I've sent, some that I've received. One of the letters is from a Mr Jim Murnane letting me know about a bus trip that is being organised to Dublin for a march in support of the hunger strikes. Another is from the local section of the National H-Block and Armagh Committee. Patricia Glavin's name is at the bottom of this letter. There are others too, some are personal. He lifts the photocopies page-by-page. I stop looking. I hear him laugh.

'Michael,' he says, 'look at me.' I don't.

Before the funeral, Ricardo's body is taken to the Centre where there's a short non-religious ceremony. After the mourners leave, I ask to be left alone with him. In a room at the Centre, in a room I've heard him speak in, discuss in, debate in and laugh in, I cry. I go to him and unbutton his shirt. I slide my fingers underneath the cloth onto his skin. He is cold, colder than I expect. I move my fingers along his chest, over the stitches of his post-mortem cuts, on over his ribs to where he is marked. I feel those marks, the welts and tautened skin, the burn marks, and I rub them back and forth. I caress them and say, 'I'm sorry, Ricardo. If no one has ever said that to you, then I say it and I say it for them too. Sorry.'

The sullen, smaller detective comes into the room. His name is Mallin. He stands beside me but he doesn't say anything. Coughlan continues with the questions. He lists off an array of (political) organisations, and then more names. He asks me about my father. Why have I no brothers and sisters?

I don't answer these questions either. I look at Mallin. He sticks his tongue out at me. I look away. I'm shivering.

Coughlan asks, 'What's wrong?'

I tell him that I'm cold. Mallin walks to the pew-seat. There is silence in the room. Coughlan stares at me and then down the length of my body. An orange rolls across the floor, from Mallin. I watch as Coughlan picks it up. A second orange is also rolled along the floor. Coughlan picks this up as well. He holds the oranges in both hands. He smiles at me. Have I ever been asked to join any political organisations? I ask him again if I can have something to keep myself warm.

'You can fuckin' freeze for all we care,' he replies.

There is a nice Bed and Breakfast near Lough Inne, on the hill overlooking the lake. It is about two kilometres west of Coughlan's new home as the crow flies. This is where I base myself. It is a picturesque place, quite beautiful, and I tell the proprietors that I am here for the bird watching. I have the paraphernalia to prove it: a Pentax SLR, a four hundred millimetre telephoto lens, tripod and micro-binoculars, khaki pants, hat and trousers. I'm decked out as they say in these parts.

The proprietors of the Bed and Breakfast like my enthusiasm. They are a young couple, formerly economic emigrants to the United States. They returned to Ireland just a year ago. They have put all their savings into the Bed and Breakfast. They hope that I like it, but they worry about the tourism numbers and whether as many people are coming to Ireland anymore because of all the bombs up in the north of the country. After a time they ask me why I emigrated to Australia. I tell them that I had to go, that I feared for my life. They aren't prepared for this. Unfortunately it's a conversation stopper. After a long while they ask me a little bit more. They ask could the police not've helped?

Coughlan places the oranges on the table. He doesn't resume the questioning. He leaves the folder of letters open but he takes a notepad from his case. He begins to write in this.

A good length of time goes by again. No one says anything. I wonder at first what he's writing down but I have trouble concentrating. I feel very cold. I have my arms wrapped around me. During this, as he writes, I think I hear him ask, 'Do you like oranges?' I am not sure. His voice is barely audible and, in any case, the question seems odd. I don't say anything. After a few minutes he literally jumps from behind the table, at me, knocking it over completely. I move out of his way but this makes him worse. He shouts at me to stand. He points at the original spot, at where I had been. I go there.

I look instinctively to see where his hands are. He shouts, 'Do you like oranges?'

I reply, 'Yes', and look over at Mallin.

Coughlan's voice booms again, his face is red and flustered, 'Did I tell you to look at him?'

'No,' I say and look away. This seems to calm him.

I walk into a small supermarket on the Baltimore side of Skibbereen. I know Coughlan is inside – I've followed him. I don't buy anything but I walk along the busy aisles until I see him, at the meat counter. He is tanned and though older, this seems to suit him; it matches his remaining ginger hair. He is wearing a shirt with rolled-up sleeves – it is a fine day outside. The shirt is scuffed with dirt on one side as if he's coming from work. He banters with the woman who serves.

I stare at him and he notices this. He looks at me as one does in the normal course of events when one notices a stranger. He looks away immediately but then looks back again, sensing my stare. I don't smile but I look at him like I know him. He's confused – I see this. It dawns on him that he might know me – that there is a past, maybe. He turns back to the counter. The woman smiles, handing him a flat packet. I leave the shop immediately and stand into a nearby pub. Have I made a mistake in letting him see me? I don't know. But I'm sure now that he knows. And I want that, I realise. I want him to know – I'm here.

*

Coughlan goes to the formica table and sets it back on its feet. He is breathing heavily. He picks up his pen, the pad and the folder. One of the oranges has rolled into a corner. He gets this. Then he arranges everything as it was, meticulously, not paying any attention to me. He sits again and begins to write.

A long time goes by. I am very cold. I keep rubbing my arms with my hands to keep warm; neither of them pay any attention. Mallin stares from the side seat. Coughlan reads and makes notes. Eventually Coughlan stops. He gets up and walks over to the far side of the room opposite Mallin. Then he walks out of my field of vision, to the back. There is quiet again for a long time. The room is very still. No noise. I hear nothing until I feel him right behind me, against my buttocks. I stand as steady as I can, motionless.

'I'm sorry,' he says. His tone is soft, even apologetic. His breath is in my ear. 'About the oranges.'

I nod.

'It's nothing personal.'

I say I realise that. He laughs quietly behind me. I am very unsure. I think about what he might do. There are two of them and I am alone. The room also. I have heard no outside noises in the whole time that I've been in here. Who knows that I am here?

'You see, I won't be giving Detective Mallin one either,' he continues. I say nothing. I just feel him move against me, behind – the poke of his crotch. He asks me, do I understand. I say yes. I feel his hand move around my waist. It is near my belly button. He is beginning to enclose me, and press. His breathing is close.

'I don't think you do,' he says.

There is silence. Suddenly he turns me. An orange is put under my nose. Its skin is coarse and cracked and I can smell the essence when he squeezes it. It is fresh in the room.

'See now?'

I shake my head. I'm confused and cold and I don't understand why he is asking me about the orange.

He pushes it into my face, jerking my head backwards.

'It isn't an eating variety,' he says and laughs.

I drive into Cork on a busy Friday afternoon. I go immediately to the street on the north side of the town, to where the Garda Station is where I was held. The Station is at the end of the street on the corner and I see it immediately. The door and window frames have been painted but otherwise it seems exactly the same.

I park and walk up the steps to the door. The officer on duty is a Bangharda – a policewoman. She smiles and I say I want to report a lost wallet. She gets a form and asks me for my name. The address I give prompts her to ask me if I'm a visitor. I say, yes, from Australia. A lovely place I suppose, she says. Yes, I say, in a sense.

I look around as I reel off my lies about the content of the wallet. On the back wall is the same type duty-roster planner that was there all those years ago; there is the same cartoon about a blind motorist knocking down a dog; and there is that picture of the Sacred Heart above the door that leads to the back stairs. In the corner I see the same grey filing cabinet, the one that I had my head shoved into and banged closed on me.

It is all the same, I think, and I must answer: what am I going to do?

Coughlan walks over to where Mallin is sitting and indicates to me to follow. 'Come,' he says. He sits down and points to a spot in front of them both, 'Here.'

I walk over and stand in front of the two sitting men. I ask them again for something to keep me warm. Coughlan crosses his legs. 'You're very skinny,' he says. He turns to Mallin. 'Do you think that that's why he's involved in the hunger-strike campaign?'

Mallin looks at me. He considers this. He says that he had been under the impression that I was the martyr type, that I would die for Ireland. He looks me up and down. 'It has merit', he says, 'this skinniness theory.' He stares at me again. I stare back at him. Quite suddenly, Mallin breaks into laughter. Coughlan interrupts, 'Would you?' he asks. I don't understand, I say.

'Would you die for Ireland?'

Oifig an Ard-Cheannfoirt (Chief Superintendent's Office). Statement in relation to the case of Mr Michael McCarty, September 7, 1981:

Mr McCarty was arrested at 5.05 p.m. on Wednesday, May 13 under Section 30 of the Offences Against The State Act. He was taken to _____ St. Garda Station. After questioning, he was released later the same night, at approximately 11.35 p.m.. At no time was Mr McCarty held at any place outside of _____ St. Garda Station, other than at the time of his arrest.

There is a knock on the door. The young detective-driver comes in. He hands Coughlan a sheet of paper and stands beside me, waiting. Coughlan glances at the page. 'These results can be relied on?'

The young detective nods.

'And they've been double-checked?'

The detective nods again. Coughlan stands up. We are almost face to face. I back away a step.

'We weren't wrong, Michael,' he says.

He walks around me, over to the centre of the room. He pulls a long stocking from his trouser pocket – not as long as a woman's but long for a man's. He points to a spot about a metre away from the formica table. 'Kneel there,' he says.

Mallin pushes me. I walk but I am reluctant. Coughlan points again. I watch him stuff one of the oranges into the stocking. For the first time I think I know what is going to happen. I look around. Mallin is now standing as well, about to come in my direction; the younger detective is taking off his jacket. Coughlan has difficulty getting the second orange into the stocking, because of its size. He comes towards me, jostling it. The orange begins to drop along its length. He stops. He's about a metre away. He wraps the neck of the stocking around his palm. About fifty centimetres hang below his hand, the two large oranges bulge in the foot.

I say that they are wrong. I say that I have never been near explosives in my life. Coughlan tells me to kneel again. I don't for only a second. It goes through my mind that I will be vulnerable kneeling. I hesitate.

The first blow comes across my stomach. He shouts something like 'Kneel down' or 'Didn't I tell you to kneel down.' I feel my insides explode. I collapse. He keeps shouting at me to kneel. I'm not able to move. I feel a sharpness right across my centre as if all my insides are about to rise.

A letter arrives from Ireland in late December '89. Inside is an article about Coughlan clipped from an Irish newspaper. The article is by a Peadar Rinn, a security correspondent and it runs as follows:

Last night in an unexpected development Chief Superintendent John P. Coughlan announced his decision to retire from the Gardaí. Citing personal reasons the controversial police chief refused to be drawn on the timing of his announcement. Last month John Coughlan was at the centre of a row with the newly appointed Garda Commissioner, Jerry Brown. It is widely believed that Coughlan opposed the appointment.

Within Garda ranks there was surprise at last night's development. Though it was confirmed that John Coughlan's decision might well be unconnected with the recent controversy. There has been speculation for some time that Mr Coughlan was re-considering his position following his wife's death late last year after a long and unsuccessful fight against cancer. Colleagues in the force described Coughlan as being 'devastated' by his wife's death.

The former chief spoke briefly last night about aspects of his own controversial career, including the allegations that were made against him in 1981, and again in 1983, that he was involved in 'maverick' policework, alleged to be part of a covert anti-terrorist operation in the South.

At the time it was alleged by a number of individuals that the then Detective-Sergeant had engaged in 'brutal and degrading' behaviour to persons held in his custody. The internationally respected organisation, Amnesty International, concluded in a general assessment that 'behaviour and actions consistent with the practice of torture' had taken place over a three year period at least, at a number of locations in the Republic beginning in early 1981. In a subsequent development, in early 1984, the then Superintendent Coughlan won a substantial libel case against a national newspaper after he was named as one of five main offending officers. However he has always maintained, despite subsequent promotion that his reputation and motives were irreversibly damaged by the allegations and innuendo that arose during this period.

In a statement the Minister for Justice, __ _____, paid tribute to the former Chief Superintendent. It commended the 'very high standard of his work'. In 1986, John Coughlan was awarded a medal of honour for his effort in developing a 'Major Accident and Emergency Plan' for the harbour region. In 1988, he led a high profile team of senior detectives to Zimbabwe to help with the development of a modern police force there. He intends to retire to his native west Cork.

'Provo bastard,' I hear. I curl up. I shout at them to stop. One goes to either end of me. I am held outstretched, on my side. The blows begin again. The oranges are swung into my belly. They shorten the length: Coughlan holds the stocking at two points and aims the blows more. He beats me on my ribs and lower back. I feel sick and I smell orange juice. My legs are held apart and I'm hit repeatedly in the testicles. I feel very hot. I know I will pass out. I am pulled along the ground by the hair. My head feels light as they drag me. I feel an awful pain. Someone is holding me by my testicles and twisting. They take turns. All the time: admit it, admit it, admit that you're a Provo.

I show Ricardo the newspaper clipping from Ireland – the report about Coughlan. He reads it and says what will you do when you go back? I shrug my shoulders and say I don't think I can go back. You will I think, he says. What would you do? I ask. It's easier for me, he says. It's abstract – because I can't go back.

After a while, after we have eaten and have had some wine, Ricardo continues, I've often thought about the idea of going back, of what it would be like. What would I do? Would I want revenge? But even now I don't know. In Chile the rout was so deep – there are so many to seek revenge for. Is it a place to begin?

I am thinking about those words since I came home, since I came back here to Ireland. *Is revenge a place to begin?* What am I doing by doing anything to this older Coughlan – this retired, seemingly heart-broken man? Who is he or what is he now? Is he a dupe? Is he spent? Is anything to be gained by killing him? As the days pass in my Bed and Breakfast abode, I remain equivocal about what to do. I observe him but I'm unable to make up my mind.

*

We leave the station some hours later. It is late. I am put into the back seat of the car; the young detective gets in beside me. Coughlan is in the front passenger seat, away from me, something that I am glad of. Mallin drives.

We proceed from McCurtain Street, through St. Luke's and then out of the city by Dillon's Cross. From that point on I'm not sure of where we are. We travel on a busy road for a good length of time and then we leave it for a narrow, secondary road. It is dark but I am able to see the ditches on either side by the light of the head-lamps. We meet no traffic apart from a small hatchback car, very early on.

I don't feel well. I slump in the back to one side. After about thirty minutes, we turn off the secondary road onto what is probably a farm track, continuing along it for another while. The road gets progressively worse, though the car absorbs this. I can feel its solidity and power as we move quickly along.

St Patrick's Catholic Church in Skibbereen is a fine large building, cavernous inside, with a long central aisle leading up to a white marble altar. It is situated on a small hill off North Street on the Cork side of the town. On a Sunday morning I mingle with the throng that drifts sullenly into this place of worship. I know Coughlan is about because I've followed him.

It is darker inside than I expect and quite cold, but I find a seat on the left edge of the aisle, a few rows behind Coughlan, directly down from the altar railing. He is already sitting when I take my place. He is dressed smartly in a brown suit. He holds a small black prayerbook in his left hand.

When the priest enters I watch Coughlan stand. I stand as well. A hymn begins and I watch him sing, his eyes closing at one point, piously – former Chief Superintendent John P. Coughlan.

We pull in close to a verge. The doors of the car swing open. The young detective gets out. He drags me behind him. We mount an embankment. I find it difficult to see where I am going. I feel very tired, like I have no energy but I am ushered along.

We move steadily all the time. Mallin leads. Some distance along, the ground begins to level out. I see a railway track and we join this. I find it more difficult from then on. I have to jump from sleeper to sleeper to keep up. I slip and fall. I'm pulled up. I half fall again. I feel sick. I ask them to slow down but I am told to shut up. After a time I can make out a limestone bridge ahead. We walk out on to it.

That Sunday morning in St Patrick's Church, I watch Coughlan take his place in the queue for Communion. There is a steady bustle all around as others gather to receive the sacrament. Coughlan is fourth in line, behind another man, two women and a boy. He stands rigidly, concentrating in prayer. I watch. When his turn comes he approaches the priest and leans forward over the railing to take the Host.

He turns from the altar and comes down the aisle between the queues that have formed. His face is stiff. He holds the Host in his mouth and directs his eyes at the floor. He walks evenly with his hands clasped at the front. This is when he looks. He stops and our eyes meet. There is no expression on his face or to be more exact, none that I recognise. But I realise then that he knows who I am. Or has remembered. 'You're Michael McCarty,' I almost hear him say.

He takes his seat. I watch him kneel in prayer again, giving thanks. I sit there. I'm behind him. But I've begun to sweat. For the first time since I've come back I feel afraid. I stand up and as calmly as possible, I leave.

Halfway across the bridge, Mallin calls to the others to stop. He grabs me by the hair and pulls me over to the wall. It is low lying, only about crotch height and he shoves my head out over the parapet edge. There is a drop of some fifty metres.

From the time that they have beaten me I have only been addressed as 'Provo Bastard'. Mallin says now, as he holds me over the wall, 'This is your last chance, Provo Bastard.' The others join in: 'Are you going to talk, Provo Bastard?' 'You're a dead man, Provo Bastard.'

My head is held over the ledge. It is shoved there. I feel the sharp edge of the wall on my sore stomach. My head is forced down again and again. I can see a stream below, in between the bushes going underneath the bridge, and a clot of rocks at one side. Mallin pulls me back. He turns me around and sits me on the wall; he holds me. Coughlan comes closer. His face is almost against mine. I won't look at him but he catches me by the jaw and makes me. 'You're a fuckin' prick, McCarty,' he says. His spittle rolls into my eye. I cannot wipe it away.

'Throw him over,' I hear Coughlan say. No one moves. I sense their hesitation. I hear his order again, this time more definitely, 'Throw him over.'

Uphill from Coughlan's house by about fifty metres is a small clump of trees and bush. Ivy is everywhere and it is the perfect cover especially when you are wearing khaki. This is where I am and I'm sure. Everything is right. From the very moment I took up position, I have felt that this day will go well, that this will be my – our – day.

I begin reviewing everything again so as to be sure. Have I done things as I should have, as I planned? I believe my tracks are covered. I believe I can make good my escape. I believe in everything that I am doing – do I not? I do – though the surreptitiousness of it all is a special enjoyment that I hadn't planned for. I think about this and about my method, about the control that I am exerting over this, the final play – it is good. Here, under the canopy of ivy, I feel powerful about the past in a way that I have not felt before, as if Coughlan is already in my clutches. I think, is this what justice is about?

Mallin puts his two hands around my left ankle; the younger detective does the same to my right. I am crying and struggling with them, but it isn't any use; they are strong. I feel my body weaken as I go over the side of the bridge. My toilet runs down my back and stomach, some of it onto my face.

They hold me steady at first. I remain perfectly still. My head lies against the cold limestone block, and my back rests against the arch wall. Only then do I notice the brightness of the night and light of the moon on the fields. In the far off distance there is a house light, I think. It is faint and flickery. There is an ordinary stillness about and they too make no sounds. Minutes – it seems a lifetime – go by. Then the shaking begins.

'Provo Bastard, Provo Bastard,' they shout.

They swing me from side to side at first, then up and down. Coughlan says something, but I cannot make it out. They begin to count to ten, in unison.

I re-arrange the crate of oranges for the last time – I want them to look presentable. I point all the oval stickers saying 'Valencia' upwards, in the same direction. They are uniformly large oranges but the Styrofoam packing is damaged on one side. I hide this by placing some confetti paper around the edges.

I examine my place of hiding again. I account for my accoutrements one by one. I brush the mulch back into place and lift the ivy to one side. Carefully, I step out into the bright sunshine.

I make my way along the ditch at the side of Coughlan's house. The area remains quiet. I stop and stoop. There is no traffic on the boreen outside his house, right along its length, but I check with the binoculars back and forth to make sure. Further on, below, is Toe Head and more fields sweeping downwards like an inverted crescent towards the sea. The water is flatly calm, and the weather on this, his last day is fine. My view holds. I look out into the distance at the still sea water and think of death, the moment of death to be precise. It is like being out on the ocean on your own on a very calm day. The total silence. The aloneness. Nothing to excite the senses, nothing anywhere to avail of by way of a diversion. Floating. Everywhere, just the calm flat sea. Knowing that you will die. It is nearly ten years since it happened – my nightmare.

From time to time I still feel myself swinging from that bridge, being held by my two ankles at first and then by just one. Hearing their laughter, their abuse and their hatred of me. Now I do not panic. I measure and reason with what they did. I try to place my life apart from the actual episode and to see it in some context – I have time to thank for that, and the Centre and Ricardo too of course. I am struck again by his death, by his desperate lonely end. It has brought me on this long road home.

I take out a small newspaper clipping that I have carried with me since I left Australia. It is a short account of the opening in 1986 of the Torture Victims Rehabilitation Centre in Melbourne. There is a picture accompanying the article. In the picture Ricardo is standing outside the Centre on the day that it was opened. At one side is a banner made of white cloth. The writing in black says *Prisoner Without A Name – We Hear You*. My contribution. Ricardo described the Centre to me once: 'what I will leave behind'.

Before climbing the ditch, and making my way out onto the boreen in front of Coughlan's house, I change. The brown, delivery man coat barely fits but it will do. It says, 'Donovan's Fruit and Veg'. On the back is the happy reminder, 'We deliver'.

I lift the crate of Valencia oranges and place it under my arm. I walk up the gravel path to his lovely home. Coughlan's bike is by the door. I knock. Everything is as it should be. I feel completely confident. I have no feelings of unease, just a presentiment that what has long been wrong will now be put right – at least in part, in a small way. Mentally, I am clear about what I must do: that is what's important. I hear the door latch move inside. The door begins to open. My free hand holds the steel cosh while my foot slips towards the gap made by the opening door: this door will not re-close.

'Yes?' I hear him say, firmly. The first words that we have spoken in all these years.

'Special fruit delivery, Mr Coughlan. Oranges.'

Dead Man's Shoes

DAVID EVANS

WHEN THE news got round that Piet Bezuidenhout had broken his neck at the Pampoenfontein gymkhana, every bachelor, divorcé and widower in the district thought he might be just the one to fill the dead man's shoes.

After allowing the widow the briefest period of mourning consistent with decency, suitors came from far and wide – not only from dorps like Pampoenfontein, but even from Cathcart and Queenstown – on the thinnest of hopes.

It wasn't hard to see why. In our part of the Karoo, the summers are burning hot and bone dry and the winters shivering cold. The soil is poor, the work hard. The few farms are far from each other and a tank-emptying distance from towns of any size. These days not many women – white women, that is – want to put up with such conditions. Anne Bezuidenhout, though nearly forty and a bit skinny for some tastes, was pleasant-faced with wide green eyes and a voice which carried soft currents of her native Galway. She also had a flickering smile, charming and at the same time tantalising, hinting somehow at private amusement and undeclared opinions. She worked hard, though she had no need, running a spotless house and maintaining poultry, pigs and a large vegetable garden as profitable sidelines to the sheep and cattle farming for which Piet Bezuidenhout had been respected throughout the Cape Midlands.

Most important, she was rich.

None of us mentioned that. None of us talked about ten thousand *morgen* fully paid for, fruitful lands and the machines to plough and fertilize and harvest them, hills well grassed enough to feed sheep and cattle even in bad times, a stream deep enough for swimming curving sweetly through the middle of it all, and seven working boreholes as insurance against the worst drought. She and Piet had bought it together – she had saved some money of her own – and it had prospered through their happy though childless marriage. Now it was all hers, thanks to the big piebald gelding which had unexpectedly pitched poor Piet straight onto his head during the tentpegging.

None of us talked of the quality of the stock or the money everyone knew was piling up in the bank. None of us talked of the up-to-date equipment, the modernised dairy, the freshly white-washed *rondawels* for the labourers, or the brand new Saab cabriolet which stood beside the big Renault station wagon in the garage. None of us mentioned the original paintings in nearly every room, or the library full of imported books, or the unostentatiously expensive furniture and drapes. Nor did anyone mention the swimming pool or the resurfaced tennis court and the lawns which surrounded the house in a lake of smooth green you could have played bowls on.

Instead, we talked of her best interests – her financial welfare, her happiness and her safety. We did this, her well-wishers and suitors, in ones and twos and even threes and fours, such was our concern for her, visiting usually in the spacious *voorkamer* dominated by a huge Theunis de Jongh sunset and with an unrivalled view of the lands.

Anne, at first in her widow's black silk, then, as the months passed, the blouses and trousers which were her everyday wear, received everyone politely. Perhaps she hoped that in time her suitors would lose heart. Most did, but seven of us, friends, or at least close acquaintances of the couple, persisted.

You might say we were a motley rather than a magnificent seven. Harry Smith, the town's auctioneer, was the oldest and a bachelor, because, so people said, he had been too mean to share his money. Jamie Roy, a farmer and recently bereaved, was the youngest, just forty-five to Harry's sixty-five. Maritz Grootbek, Pampoenfontein's only lawyer, was reputedly the cleverest, though not clever enough to stop his pretty young wife running off with an agricultural machinery salesman. Japie van Os, another farmer, who had lost his wife in a terrible shooting accident in the worst years of the old South Africa, was the richest, though not as rich as Anne. Frank Sellars, a trader and like Harry a bachelor, though no one had ever worked out why, was the nicest, a man who remembered birthdays and anniversaries and was always the first on the doorstep with a little present. Hannes Snyman, the butcher, and many years widowed, was the biggest, a man built like one of the oxen he sometimes chopped up. Last and least me, a teacher, divorced by a wife who had found me, my profession and Pampoenfontein too dull for her: nonetheless I felt I had something to offer a woman of Anne's cultivation. After all, she had initially come to the district to teach at the school where I was headmaster.

Anne's situation, understandably caused anxiety. First there were rumours that she was going to sell the farm to the new government – avid to buy land for its supporters – and take herself and her wealth back to Ireland. Then, when we learnt to our relief that she was staying on, we discovered that she wasn't hiring a manager (though several candidates volunteered immediately) but taking charge of the staff herself.

Nobody disputed that it was a good staff with a reliable Black foreman, Samuel Pitso. His father had served Piet's father and he and Piet had practically grown up together. When Piet had sold the old, smaller farm in the next valley and bought Toekoms, Samuel had moved with him. Anne had taught him to read and write and to do simple sums. This bit of education hadn't spoiled him as it did so many. He knew his place: bossboy among the black workers, he was nonetheless respectful and quiet to the point of taciturnity with white people. His mother, Maisie, and his two young sisters, served in the house, a team which was the envy of many a farmer's wife.

But a good Black staff was one thing. A woman trying to manage it on her own was quite another.

We tried to point this out to Anne. Farming was hard, said Japie, waving a freckled hand at the lands, particularly in the Karoo where what droughts and deluges didn't destroy, locusts and meerkats did. Anne nodded agreement, but replied that she came from a long Irish peasant tradition and was used to hardship.

Jamie Roy tried another approach. Solitude could be a terrible thing, he remarked, his still boyish face glowing with concern, especially on the long winter nights, such as were beginning. Now that her period of mourning was well over it was surely time to consider the question of companionship before loneliness came like a jackal in the night to thieve her peace of mind.

Anne listened to him gravely. She had loved Piet and missed him terribly, she said, but as long as she had books and music and paintings and the faculties to enjoy them she would never be truly lonely. 'Besides,' she added, 'do I not have all you wonderful friends to rescue me from solitude and boredom?'

It was Maritz Grootbek, his large white brow corrugated with intellectual effort, who put what most of us thought was the clincher. We still lived, he rumbled, in dangerous times. This might be the new South Africa and our first Black president might be a good man bent on reconciling former enemies, but some of his followers couldn't be trusted. It hadn't been so long ago that we had all been frightened out of our wits by the unrest stirred up among our labourers by communistic troublemakers. And hadn't Japie van Os accidentally shot his old wife stone dead one terrible night in the panic of a false alert to the effect that guerillas were overruning his farm?

So we agreed with Maritz that it was asking for trouble for a woman to be on a farm alone without a man to protect her. And we envied him for being the one *slim* enough to make out a case bound to win the day.

But we had reckoned without Anne. 'I'm not alone,' she protested softly. 'And I do have a man.'

She treated the three of us who had trekked out to see her to that flickering smile of hers and gestured towards the lands where the big Xhosa could be seen driving the Bezuidenhouts' giant tractor. 'I have Sam to protect me.'

Only a foreigner like Anne could have got away with such a remark. Pampoenfontein may have accepted that all of us – whatever our colour – were equal citizens in the new South Africa, but we were all proud of our past and no white man there could be expected to tolerate any talk of a black being as good as a white, whatever the *koppe* might pretend in Cape Town or Pretoria. Sitting there, holding my cup of coffee, I could only admire Maritz's restraint, the only sign of his outrage being a deepening of the corrugations on his forehead.

'I meant someone man enough to fill Piet's shoes,' he said gruffly. 'A real man – a *Boer*.'

'Ah,' was all she said. Then.

But one day, many months later, she invited the seven of us suitors to the house. We arrived together in two cars – to cut transport costs, Harry said, but really, I suspect, because we wanted to watch each other. Surprisingly, Anne wasn't waiting for us at her front door as she usually did. But in the middle of the front stoep stood a pair of brown shoes, large and slightly muddy. Sitting comfortably on a *riempie* stool smoking a pipe, his hat on the back of his head, sat Samuel Pitso almost as if he was guarding the shoes.

'Where's the *Nkosikazi,* boy?' Jamie demanded roughly. 'Go and fetch her. Hurry!'

'Did you see that?' Japie van Os exclaimed after Samuel had risen unhurriedly and gone off into the house. 'Maritz was right. This place needs a man in charge. That used to be a good boy. Now he goes in the front and doesn't even take off his hat to white people.'

Most of us had tales of the new insolence which had come in with the new South Africa and more would have been said on this subject had Anne not appeared, apologising for keeping us waiting. 'I've decided, after much thought, to take a husband,' she said. 'And because I find it impossible to choose between you, all such excellent men, to be sure, I'm acting on an inspired suggestion from dear Maritz.' She pointed to the shoes and her rare smile flickered. 'Whoever fits those – but perfectly mind! – can have me and all that I own.'

In vain we protested that the idea was monstrous, absurd, mad, even for a woman from the land of leprechauns and fairies. It was the silly Cinderella story turned upside down. 'I'm a woman of instinct,' she replied, 'and I know this is right.'

Harry Smith left immediately, giving Maritz an ugly look and muttering that it was bad luck to try to step into the shoes of the dead. But the rest of us sat down right there on the stoep and somewhat sheepishly removed our shoes to reveal socks of varying pattern, newness and, shamingly, in my case, a potato or two.

Jamie Roy tried first, putting his left foot gingerly into the brown shoe as a fussy child might step into a muddy pool – and withdrawing it fast.

'I could have told him he was too small,' exulted Frank Sellars. 'It takes a man.'

It was Frank's turn to blush and shuffle away, when his foot slithered around inside the shoe.

'Who would have thought old Piet had such big hooves,' grumbled Hannes Snyman when even his considerable foot proved too narrow.

I shook my head miserably, knowing by now that my size eight stood no chance.

'You might as well give Sam here a go,' I said bitterly, indicating the headman who had appeared on the edge of the verandah and was standing there quietly, his hat in his hands.

Japie van Os gave a contemptuous cackle.

'I mean to,' Anne said, motioning the fellow forward. He seemed hesitant, then kicking off the Wellington boots he was wearing, slid first one and then the other bare black foot into the shoes.

We stared, we glared, we blinked in disbelief, then stared again.

'A perfect fit,' exclaimed Anne.

There was nothing we could do. In the old days Pitso would have been found floating face downwards in a furrow, but this is the new South Africa. Jamie did try threatening him but the Black man only laughed at him. There was a rumour that Maritz wanted to put out a contract on him but changed his mind when word got round that Samuel was distantly related to the family of the State president. We tried to dissuade Anne, but, stubborn woman that she always was, she simply smiled her flickering smile and got on with the arrangements for a quiet wedding.

In time we accepted the situation and some of us even visited Toekoms, which continued to prosper. But the once proud Maritz Grootbek was inconsolable, broken. 'To think,' he groaned, 'that I gave her the idea and that Piet's shoes should fit that *swartgoed*! It's like a bad miracle.'

I never had the heart to tell Maritz, but one day I had a few *dops* with Josiah Meintjies, an old Coloured cobbler from Cathcart. He wasn't a man I liked or normally bought drinks for, but he was the only person who ever repaired my hunting boots properly so I kept in with him. I mentioned what had come to be known as the Cinderfella story and he chuckled maliciously.

'Bad it might have been, but it wasn't no miracle that those shoes fitted,' he said, knocking back his cane spirit and coke. 'Because I made them for Sam Pitso. I made them in return for six pairs which had belonged to the late Mr Bezuidenhout and were too narrow for Sam.'

He swallowed some more of his drink, gurgling so much that I thought he would choke. '*Ja, meneer,* I can understand why you're looking like you want to *sjambok* someone. Those shoes you all tried on were Samuel's own. Live man's shoes – dead man's bed.'

Some Rain Must Fall

MICHEL FABER

FRANCES STRATHAIRN came home to find that her partner had cooked her a meal.

'First day at your new job,' he said. 'I thought you'd be exhausted.'

My relationship with this man is in crisis, Frances reminded herself, kissing him on the lips. *There is no doubt about it.*

But of course there was doubt. Exhausted, she collapsed on the sofa and ate her meal, which was excellent. Her own recipe, followed to perfection.

'So how are the kids?' he asked. It wasn't a question about any children belonging to him or her: they weren't that kind of couple. He was asking her about the pupils at Rotherey Primary School.

'It's too soon to tell,' she said.

The first thing she'd got them to do was tidy up. Wellies in neat rows. Coats on pegs. Story books arranged from largest to smallest. Every pencil sharp.

Neatness was not her own personal bugbear: she merely knew, as a professional, that it was what the children craved. She was their new teacher and had been imposed on them at short notice; a contract must be made. They needed to demonstrate their goodness, their usefulness; they needed her to demonstrate her authority. Most of all, they needed life to go on, with a maximum of fuss.

'Next: does every one of you have an eraser?'

The rustle and click of a dozen pencil cases being disembowelled.

'Anyone whose eraser is smaller than this, gets one of these,' she smiled, holding up one of the bagful of brand-new Faber-Castells she always brought along to new classes.

General wonderment as every child realized he or she qualified for one of these magnificent gifts.

Out of the corner of her eye, Frances observed one of the school's other teachers watching her from the doorway of the next room, wondering no doubt if Frances was really worth three times an ordinary teacher's salary.

'Now, I want every one of you to look through your project books and choose a page that you think has your very best handwriting on it. When you've chosen, I want you to lay your books open at that page, all together on the floor just here... No, not on top of one another – all showing fully. Edge to edge, like bricks in a wall. But with a little space in between. That's right... Give each other room. Good... Good...'

Frances squatted down, giving the children the hint that she could play with them at their level, while reminding them with her bigness and her spreading halo of skirt that she was something other. Though scarcely interested in their handwriting at this stage, she noted that nobody was conspicuously incompetent: Jenny MacShane, their teacher until last week, can't have been too bad.

On the morning of the second day, the two children who hadn't turned up on the first day presented themselves. That was a good sign: word of mouth amongst the mothers, perhaps. Frances read the absence notes: upset tummy for little Amy, doctor's appointment for little Sam. Fear, most likely, which could have grown unmanageable if they'd been allowed to stay away longer. She welcomed Amy and Sam back to their school, gave them their erasers. They were slower than the others to settle in, so Frances decided, among other things, to put off the essays until tomorrow.

Frances herself was slow to settle in to her new house on the hill above Rotherey village. Her last lodgings had been in a ramshackle apartment – dog's dinner decor, hastily convened furniture. She'd liked it there: it had once been the occupational therapy wing of a mental asylum, before Care in the Community had evicted the inmates. It still had some intriguing features: the odd mark on the wall, peculiar plastic things sealing some of the power outlets, a wicker clothes-basket woven by unsteady hand. This house in Rotherey was a council house, cosy and generic; a policeman and his wife had lived there, and respected all its prefab integrities. Not so much as a WANTED poster in the loo.

'The anonymity of this place gives me the shits,' she said to Nick, her partner.

'Well... Can I change anything for you?' he offered. 'I've got the time.'

Enjoying a sabbatical while he waited for his doctoral thesis to be assessed, he did indeed have the time, but there was nothing Frances could imagine him doing with this house. Rather, she wanted *him* to change.

'Let's go to bed,' she sighed.

The next night, though, she stayed up.

'How long, do you think?' he asked, just to sort out the sleeping arrangements.

'As long as it takes,' she replied.

As with everything, he was fine about having to sleep on his own; well-behaved, well-behaved, well-behaved. She wished he would haul her up to the bedroom and fuck her. It would be inconsiderate and inconvenient, God yes: she had no time for sex tonight because she had the children's essays to examine; eleven responses she must keep distinct in her mind, eleven plans of action she must conceive by the morning – as well as needing some sleep, of course. And yet she longed for him to knock her off course, or at least dare to try.

In her lap lay the children's essays: *About Me, My School, and My Teacher.* To each one she had clipped the best I.D. shot she'd been able to cull from the school's photographic montages of prizegiving nights, sports teams, Christmas concerts. This first one was Fiona Perry, the blonde-haired one with the tiny ears and the oversized T-shirts.

Our school is called Rotherey Primary School. It has three big rooms, the oldest kids are Primary 6 and 7 and that is the room I am in. We do the hard stuff. Next year I am going to Moss Bank Accademey. Our teacher says thats where the fun really begins. Our teacher isnt at the school any more. The last day I saw her she had to go home because she was crying. The next day was the day I was off sick with food poisning (the wrong kind of fish). But my best friend Rachel says our teacher just lost her head that day and now shes not coming back. We have a new teacher now who is you Mrs Strathiarn who is reading this essay!

Frances turned the sheet face down on the couch next to her. 'The wrong kind of fish' – she smiled sadly. The wrong kind of fish could make a child an absentee on a day which might have changed its life forever. Fiona Perry had missed a Wednesday presumably quite at random; by that evening her parents had been phoned to permit her, along with all her classmates, to stay home a bit longer while a replacement teacher was found. Clearly, little Fiona was turning on the charm for the newcomer without missing a beat; Mrs MacShane had simply disappeared from her young life as if rubbed out by that lovely new eraser.

My school is called Rotherey Primary, wrote Martin Duffy. *I am in the big grade, Primary 6. I use to live in Bolton when I was young. My mum says that what happened with Mrs Macshane has got nothing to do with me and I should forget about it. Lots of people have asked me about it about 1,000 times and some times I tell them and some times I dont. But every time I do tell I forget it worse and worse, because really as soon as Mrs Macshane started crying I got embarsed and covered my eyes and I didnt see much. So thats my story.*

As if to punctuate, a toilet flushed. Nick, coming down for one last pee before sleep.

Don't you realise our relationship is in crisis! she felt like yelling out to him, which was such an absurd impulse that she laughed out loud. He heard her laugh and came to her, his wrists still wet from hurried towelling.

'Something funny?' he wanted to know. His sense of humour was the best thing about him – one of the best things, anyway. He stood there, naked above the waist, a spray of glistening water-drops across his ribcage, a glow cast over his contours by her reading lamp. Her breath caught with the pain of soon not being with him anymore, because she would push him away, make sure he would never come back.

'Come here,' she murmured. He obeyed.

She would make love to him fast, here on the couch, then get on with her work. She speculated on what Martin Duffy had really seen through his ten little fingers, which were always tinged with the Marmite he had for breakfast. The covering of eyes was a social gesture, a message to one's peers asking for confirmation of the transgressive status of an event... She slid her rear over the edge of the couch to let Nick get inside her from where he was kneeling. So, did Martin Duffy really not see much? She doubted it. She might have to work on him, if there was evidence that his apparent robustness was a defence mechanism. Being new to the village made him vulnerable straight off, though on the other hand it would have prevented him getting too attached to Jenny MacShane. Right now she had to admit that her clitoris wasn't getting enough friction, especially with that damned condom, and her back was being repeatedly stabbed by a metal zip on one of the cushions.

'Let's go upstairs,' she said.

After orgasm, drunk with endomorphins, she drifted off to sleep, nestled against his back.

The school is fine and my old teacher is fine.

This was the entire text of Greg Barre's essay. Which one was he again? She couldn't picture him, even with the aid of the photograph – admittedly an out-of-focus shot.

'What does this kid make you think of?'

She handed Nick the photograph across the breakfast table. He checked his fingers for margarine and took hold of the tiny square of card by its edges.

'Shy,' he decided after a moment.

'Why?'

'In Christmas plays they always give the non-speaking shepherd parts to the shy ones. The girl in front is obviously the one who says 'We have followed a star', or whatever. This kid just has to tag along – maybe hand over a gift.'

She smiled at him as he handed back the photograph, a real eye-to-eye smile, the most genuinely intimate exchange they'd had for days. He was perceptive, all right. When it came to strangers.

'You'd make a good father,' she purred, still conscious of her flesh tingling with satisfaction and sleeplessness.

'Let's not start that again,' he advised her, tersely. Something flashed disconcertingly in her line of vision. It was the photo of little Greg. She hadn't accepted it yet, and Nick was irritated all of a sudden, waving the image at her as if she'd already lumbered him with a child he didn't want.

The school was walking distance from the house. A long drive in the passenger seat of someone's car would have given her a precious last chance to read the other essays. How could she have fallen asleep last night? She was like those men that women were always complaining about in advice columns.

'Good morning Mrs Strathairn!' chorused the children when she walked in.

She was 'Mrs' to them. She was always 'Mrs' to her classes, by professional decision. She felt that children trusted her more if they believed her to be a conventional spouse and mother, as if this made her an emissary from that storybook world where family equations were not negotiable. Open-minded, unconventional, coolly feminist among her peers, she was able to compromise instantly and enthusiastically when she saw the need for it. Perhaps this quality more than any other got her chosen ahead of colleagues in her field, at least in fiendishly delicate situations like this.

She'd figured out almost immediately which of the children were the touchy-feely ones, and she drew them to her as bait for the others. Her talent was to radiate safety and the restoration of order. It was a gift she had possessed well before all her years of training.

Already children were pressing themselves to her, whispering things into her ear just for the thrill of leaning against her soft shoulder. The ones she was most worried about weren't these, but they would help thaw the others out.

'Rachel? I'm told you know how to use the photocopier in the office. Can you make ten copies of this very important document, please?'

Rachel (*I don't play with many people at all I like doing work much more*) hurried away to the sacred machine, glowing with pride at the confidence shown in her as she prepared to step into an off-limits zone and tame the mysteries of technology.

Frances had a feel for the group as a whole, its tensions and safety valves, its flame-haired explosives, its doe-eyed emollients. The shock of their last day with Mrs MacShane was working its way through their systems at different rates; Frances guessed that either Jacqui Cox or Tommy Munro would be the first to crack, in some spectacular incident that would appear to have no connection with their old teacher. Jacqui (classic hot-house flower, very particular that her fellow pupils spell her name 'the proper way') had written in her essay:

I like my teacher very much and I wouldn't want another one, at least not permanently. She has all my old work and it was her that wrote my reports and she knows why she wrote what she wrote. So when she comes back she will be able to keep me straight.

Tommy Munro, an ill-coordinated, excitable boy with startlingly long eyelashes and a prem head, wrote much the same kind of essay to the best of his rather more limited abilities:

My old teacher is fine and everthing els is to.

But his old teacher wasn't fine, at all, and Tommy was struggling with the impossibly unfair challenges of ruling straight margins and glueing sheets of cardboard together, his emotions corkscrewed deep into his pigeon chest.

Miraculously, nothing unusual happened on the fourth day, at least nothing any ordinary teacher wasn't paid to deal with. Just a heated argument about who was supposed to bring the sports chairs inside now that it had started raining – class beauty Cathy Cotterill overwhelmed by responsibility. Red-faced, grimacing with a bee-stung mouth that would soon be grinning broadly again, she was one of life's intuitive survivors. Her essay had devoted two matter-of-fact lines to the circumstances of Mrs MacShane's departure, then went on to fill a page with *'I don't play football much I rather play hop scoch. On Monday I get Jim I am not very good at Jim'* and so on. Her anger had in-built transience and a limited scope: as an emotional firelighter she was, comparatively, a dud.

Exercising authority like a physical skill, Frances calmly took hold of the flailing ends of the dispute and wound them around her little finger. The yelling stopped, the threat of mayhem disappeared without a trace, and within ten minutes she had her entire class sitting at her feet, spellbound as she paraphrased text and showed photographs from a book about albinism. Frances had quite a number of these sorts of books: odd enough to promise children a frisson of the bizarre, informative enough to fill their heads with the crunchy cereal of fact, irrelevant enough to be unthreatening. The sight of white Aborigines with pink eyes was enough to keep even Tommy dumbstruck while the cleverer ones frowned over the finer points of genetics. As the rain dimmed the skies outside and the florescent strip light took over, the children looked a bit albino themselves, a phenomenon Frances pointed out to suppressed squeals of queasy delight. 'Maybe it's catching,' she teased.

At hometime it was raining so heavily that even those children who lived easy walking distance from the school were picked up by relatives or neighbours in cars. All except Harriet Fishlock and her tiny brother Spike from the tots' grade. (Frances found it hard to believe his name could really be Spike, but that was what everyone seemed to call him.)

'I don't know how I'm going to get Spike home,' sighed Harriet, fussing her pet-sized sibling into his greasy dufflecoat, 'without him getting totally soaked.' Harriet lived in a shabby caravan park on the edge of the village with her alcoholic mother and a stepfather who could get spare parts for cars if necessary. There were rumours of sexual abuse, and a social services file running into dozens of pages.

'I have an umbrella,' said Frances. 'A super-duper giant umbrella. I can walk with you as far as the petrol station.' She watched the flicker of calculation cross the girl's face: yes, the petrol station was not in view of the wretched caravans: yes, the answer was yes.

Together they walked through the streets of Rotherey, the pelting rain screening the shops and houses as if through frosted glass. Everything was an indistinct and luminous grey, a vast sea with a mirage of a village shimmering on the waves, through which car headlights cruised slowly like distant ships. To get the best cover from the umbrella, Spike and Harriet walked on either side of Frances, and after ten minutes or so Frances was surprised and delighted to feel Harriet fumbling to hold hands with her.

Near the edge of the village, a red light pulsed luridly through the gloom: a police car parked outside the MacShane house. They were there every day, apparently, though what they hoped to achieve at this late stage was hard to imagine. Perhaps they thought David MacShane would come back to pick up his mail or feed the dog.

The rain was thrashing down absurdly now, as if in fury, almost deafeningly noisy against the fabric of the umbrella. Luckily there was no wind, so Frances was able to hold their protecting canopy still as spouts of water clattered off the edges all around them.

'This is awful!' shouted Harriet.

'No it's not!' Frances called back. 'We're safe under here, and the rain won't last!'

They passed the petrol station; Frances said nothing. She understood she was crossing a Rubicon of trust and would soon glimpse the farther shore of caravan-land.

'This is where we live,' said Harriet when the park was in view. The rain, softening now, shimmered like television static all over the dismal junkyard of permanently stalled mobile homes. Frances knew that to accompany the children any further would be to push her luck.

Yet, as Harriet and her brother were leaving the canopy of their new teacher's umbrella, Harriet made a little speech, spoken at a gabble as if escaping under pressure.

'Mrs MacShane used to come here sometimes after school. To see a man who's moved away now. They made loud noises together inside his caravan for hours, then she'd go home to the village. It was sex – everyone knows that. That's why Mr MacShane got so angry. He must of found out.'

The secret relayed at last, Harriet grabbed her brother by the hand and hopped gingerly into the marshy filth of her home territory.

*

In Frances's home – or rather, the house she would live in for the duration of this assignment – all was not well. The wild weather (highest volume of rainfall in a single day since 1937, the radio would have told her if she'd known how to find the local station) had battered through the roof's defences, and there was water dripping in everywhere. Frances walked through the upstairs rooms, squinting up at the clammy ceilings. They seemed to be perspiring in terror or exertion. In the bedroom especially, the carpet sighed under her feet and the bed was drenched: Nick had brought the buckets in too late. Returning downstairs, Frances almost broke her neck on the slick fur of the carpeted steps; in a perverse sort of way, this actually knocked the edge off the contempt she felt for the house, as well as shaking her up badly.

'I did check all the windows were closed when the downpour started,' Nick told her a little defensively. 'I just didn't expect the place to leak, that's all.'

'I want a child with you, Nick,' she said, hearing herself talk as if through the din of a rainstorm, though the rain was unobtrusive now, and locked out.

He stared at her uncomprehendingly, as if her comment might, after all, decode itself into being about buckets or laundromats.

'We've talked about this before,' he said, warningly.

'I want it.' She wanted him to take her upstairs, smack her down on the sodden bedsheets, and start a little life that would grow up to walk under an umbrella with her one day.

'I've told you,' he reminded her. 'You could maybe adopt one, as a single parent, and I could see how I feel. No guarantees.'

'It's not the shared responsibility I'm worried about, you bastard,' she said. 'I want your baby and mine. From the beginning. Nothing on the slate except our genetics. A clean start. Adopted children bring their damage with them from the womb, from the day they leave the womb. Already in the cradle they're soaking up their parents' fuck-ups.'

'Oh! Well!' he exclaimed, gesticulating aggressively. 'What a pity the fucked-up human race has to keep bringing children into the world, instead of leaving it to experts like you!' Mesmerised by his violent display, she followed the sweep of his big hands, longing for him to hit her, batter her to the floor. But even in anger he was hopelessly, infuriatingly safe.

'Damn right!' she screamed in a misery of triumph.

'You know what you are?' he accused her, shoving his face right up to hers so she could see his lips forming the words with exaggerated clarity. 'A – con*trol* – freak.'

After they'd finished arguing, they stripped the bed, turned up the central heating and went out to Rotherey's only restaurant, a combination hotel and snooker hall which also did Indian.

Inevitably, the mother of one of the children from Jenny MacShane's class was there too, buying a carry-out, and she stumbled straight to Frances and Nick's table.

'I just want to thank you for what you're doing,' she told Frances blushingly. 'Last night, for the first time since... you know... the MacShane business... Tommy slept right through without having nightmares or wetting the bed.'

'That's good to hear,' smiled Frances.

'I just want to say that I don't care how much you're getting paid, you're worth every penny.'

'Thank you,' smiled Frances. Warmth came harder to her when it was parents or other teachers wanting it.

'I just wanted to know... Is there any chance of you staying on? As Tommy's permanent teacher?'

'No, I'm afraid not,' smiled Frances. Her lamb korma, already none too hot when it was served, had stopped steaming altogether. And she could tell that this woman was going to go away and tell the other mothers that Frances Strathairn wouldn't stoop to work at a teacher's wage.

'Much as I'd love to,' she sighed, making the effort, 'the powers that be wouldn't let me.'

The mother went away then, walking with a peculiar shambling gait and a posture which suggested congenital inferiority. Frances continued to stare at the door she had gone through, and picked at her food irritably. God, how she disliked herself for pleading impotence when that had nothing to do with why she must move on! This pretence of being the passive slave of higher authority – it was a deplorable lapse in dignity, an act of prostitution. And to top it all off, she was going to break up with her man.

'I've seen you like this before,' observed Nick quietly from the other side of the candles. 'You always get like this just before it's over. Those kids that survived the bus crash in Exeter, remember? A few days before you finished up there, we had almost the same argument–' he smirked, '–almost the same restaurant. And that time in Belfast...'

'Spare me the details,' she groaned, tossing her fork into the mound of rice and taking a deep swig of wine. 'Ask the proprietor if there are any rooms free for tonight. If so, book one.'

He stood up, then hesitated.

'For how many people?'

'Two,' she chided. 'Bastard.'

Next day, the children started breaking down at last, more or less as

Frances had been anticipating, with one or two exceptions. Tommy Munro had sidestepped the process, behaving with unusual maturity and poise for a brain-damaged kid; maybe, because he was so used to being confused and mistaken all the time, he'd come to believe that the incident with his old teacher must have happened in one of his nightmares.

Greg Barre, however, blew his crewcut top just after lunchtime, starting with a misunderstanding about which times table he was supposed to have learned, and climaxing with a shrieking fit. Mrs MacShane's name was thrown up in the ensuing hysteria and several children were soon weeping and accusing each other of causing what had happened or failing to stop it when they should have. Martin Duffy wailed his innocence with fists clenched against his day-glo sports shorts; Jacqui Cox wailed her guilt with arms wrapped tightly around her head. The teacher of the adjacent class rushed to the doorway, trembling with fear, her face twitching with a ghastly nervous smile like the ones sometimes seen on people about to be executed.

Frances motioned to her the signal for 'I'll handle this', and a nod of permission to shut the door. Then she moved forward and took control.

By the end of the day, she had them all quiet again, entranced by her own soothing murmur and the gentle patter of rain on the windows. She sat in the midst of them on a high stool, keeping the stories coming and the airwaves humming, hypnotizing herself to ignore the fact that her rear end was numb under the weight of Jacqui's body in her lap. Jacqui was going to be a big girl, at least physically. Emotionally, she was too small for life outside the womb, and she clung to her teacher's waist with marsupial tenacity, pressing her face hard into Frances's bosom. She had been weeping for hours, an infinitely sustainable whimper: nothing that half a lifetime of reassurance couldn't fix.

Greg Barre was playing quoits with Harriet Fishlock and Katie Rusek, happy as a lamb, wearing the same sackcloth pants he'd worn as a shepherd in the Christmas play. His own trousers were drying out on one of the radiators; he'd soiled them at the height of his frenzy. Frances had recognized she couldn't afford to leave the group to attend to him alone, and had chosen Katie to bear him off to the toilets and help him get changed; a risky choice, given the rigid gender divisions in this little world of Rotherey. But Frances judged it was the right one. Katie was mature and self-assured, Greg was afraid of her and secretly infatuated too. Most importantly, Katie was smart enough to perceive that the situation – half the class weeping and throwing hysterics, a boy with shit in his pants – was beyond the control of just one adult, and she caught the devolution of responsibility as if it were a basketball. In her essay she had written:

My name is Katie Rusek and I am in Grade 7 of Rotherey Village School. Something very bad happened here last week. Our teacher Mrs

MacShane was giving us a Maths lesson when her husband came in to the class room with a shot gun. He swore at Mrs MacShane and hit her until she was on the floor. She kept saying please not in front of the children but it didn't make any difference. Then her husband told her to put the end of his gun in to her mouth and suck on it. She did that for a few seconds and then he blew her head to bits. We were all so, so scared but he went away and now the police are looking for him. Every time I think about that day I feel sick. I ask myself, will I ever get over it?

From her perch, Frances watched Katie Rusek watching Greg Barre prepare to throw another quoit. Desperation to impress his guardian angel was making him suddenly awkward, a faltering of confidence which both Katie and Frances, from their different angles, noticed instantly.

'Let's play something else,' the girl whispered in his ear, before he'd even thrown.

Frances murmured on. She was telling the class about her squelchy house, her wet bed, how she'd spent the night in the Rotherey Hotel. She made up a story about how she and her husband had tried to sleep at home but the water had come up through the mattress and soaked their pyjamas. She described how she and her husband had balanced the mattress on its side near the heater and watched the steam begin to rise. She kept returning to the theme that her house was in chaos just now but that she could manage because she had people to help her, and soon everything would return to normal. All the while she pressed her cheek against Jacqui Cox's wispy skull, stroking her gently at key phrases.

She talked on and on, effortlessly, the words coming from a reassurance engine idling deep within her; her words and the rain maintaining a sussurating spell over the children. Most listened in silence, some played games, completed word puzzles or drew pictures. No drawings of guns or exploding heads yet: Tommy might do one of those for her next week sometime. In the days following that, she would smooth the new teacher in and then move on to God knows where.

Jacqui convulsed in her arms, jerked awake the instant after falling asleep, and repositioned her ear in the hollow of Frances's breast, reconnecting with the heartbeat.

'It'll be all right, angel,' Frances purred. 'Everything will be all right.'

■

Since winning an Ian St James Award...

Faith Addis, the author of five published books including *The Year Of The Cornflake* from Andre Deutsch, has recently seen a television option taken up on these books. A major comedy drama series is now in development. Initially, seven 50 minute episodes will be shown on BBC 1. Faith has also written a sixth book, as yet unpublished.

Alison Armstrong has had short stories published in a variety of publications. Recently, she took a three year writers' residency with Renfrewshire Libraries/ Scottish Arts Council. Much of her time involved encouraging children to write and this area of work has become Alison's particular concern. Since leaving the residency, she has taken children's groups on a weekend/evening basis, and juggles two 'proper' jobs in Adult Education. In the midst of all this activity, a novel is slowly, stealthily taking shape...

Kate Atkinson's first novel, *Behind The Scenes At The Museum*, which won the 1995 Whitbread Book of the Year Award, has now sold over 500,000 copies in the UK and was also a bestseller in the USA. It has been translated into twenty languages. Her second novel, *Human Croquet*, came out in 1997 and her third novel, *Emotionally Weird*, will be published in 1999. Kate is now working on the television screenplay of her first book.

Sylvia Baker has had three books published by Headline Review: *A Certain Seduction*, *The Loving Game*, *Falling In Deep*. She is now working on a fourth novel.

Dick Bayne lives in the Cotswolds and leads walking holidays in Italy when he is not writing. He now has an agent to represent his novel, a thriller set in central Africa. He is currently working on the sequel.

Jonathan Carr started out as a solicitor, following a degree in Law. He writes for the gay press including *Gay Times*, *The Pink Paper*, *Attitude* and has written and produced a short film. He is now working on his first novel.

Maria Caruso teaches literature and creative writing at Marylhurst College in Portland, Oregon. Her most recent publications have been in the literary quarterlies, *The Sonora Review* and the *Santa Monica Review*. She is currently at work on a mystery titled *The Hour of Lead*.

Francesca Clementis lives in London. After ten years in advertising, she is now a full-time writer. She is a regular contributor to Radio 4's *Weekending*, has written pilot sitcoms for television, short stories for numerous women's magazines including *New Woman* and *She*, and even the libretto for a musical comedy, *Dear Lonely Heart* (twice shortlisted for the Vivian Ellis Prize). Her first novel, *Big Girls Don't Cry*, is published this year by Piatkus.

Josephine Corcoran started writing while studying for an English degree at Chichester Institute. Her story, *Algebra*, was adapted for BBC Radio 4 and she has published work in *QWF* magazine and the 1997 UEA anthology, *Catapult*. Her stage play, *Jocasta*, was performed at the Chelsea Centre Theatre and, last year, as a finalist in the BBC/Arts Council competition Write Out Loud, she wrote and directed her first radio play, *The Songs That Houses Sing*.

Julia Darling is based in Newcastle upon Tyne. For some years she worked as a performance poet with The Poetry Virgins, an all female troupe of writers and actors. She has won several awards for her short stories which have been serialised on radio and published in anthologies, as well as in her own collection, *Bloodlines*. Her first novel, *Crocodile Soup*, was published last year by Anchor/Transworld. She has written a number of plays for theatre companies; her most recent full length stage play, *Eating The Elephant*, toured the country last autumn. She is currently writing her second novel.

Louise Doughty is a novelist, critic and broadcaster. In 1995, her first novel, *Crazy Paving*, was shortlisted for four awards and was followed by the critically acclaimed, *Dance With Me*. Her latest book is *Honey-*

Dew which she is adapting for film. All her books are published by Simon & Schuster. She has also won awards for short stories and radio plays.

Kevin Doyle is from Cork, where he now lives. His stories have been published in Ireland in *The Cúirt Journal* and in *Flaming Arrows*. At present he is working on a novel about an accident at a chemical plant, and on a play about the lost papers of the Irish anarchist, Jack White.

Alan Dunn lives in Cumbria. *French Kisses* was his first published story. Since then he has had success in other short story competitions. His first novel, *The Collier And His Mistress*, was published by Little, Brown in 1993. His second novel, *The English Dancing Master*, was published in 1995. He is currently finishing a novel on running; he counters this insanity by teaching creative writing, studying for a literature degree with the Open University, and playing in a folk-rock band.

David Evans was born in South Africa which he left after five years in prison for anti-apartheid activities. He now lives on Merseyside. *Dead Man's Shoes*, his second Ian St James Award-winning story, has also been broadcast on BBC Radio 4. Other publications include short stories and poetry and he has had plays on stage, radio and television. A new play has been accepted for production in Johannesburg and a novel – also set in South Africa – is nearing completion.

Stephanie Ellyne was born in New Orleans and worked as an actress in Oregon before moving to England. A winner of the London Writers Competition and the Ian St James Awards (twice), she had a short play broadcast on LBC as part of the New London Playwrights Festival, and is close to completing her first novel.

Michel Faber was born in Holland, grew up in Australia and, since 1993, has lived in the Scottish Highlands. His debut collection of short stories, *Some Rain Must Fall*, was published by Canongate last year. He has won the Macallan and Neil Gunn awards. The millennium bug in his PC has a cunning plan to obliterate several of his novels before anyone else can see them.

Lorna Fergusson was born and brought up in the North East of Scotland. She studied English at Aberdeen University and Merton College, Oxford. For fifteen years she has taught English in Oxford, where she lives with her husband and two sons. Her first novel, *The Chase*, set in the Perigord region of France, will be published by Bloomsbury this year. Her second novel is nearing completion.

Judy Forshaw has written scripts for *EastEnders* and *Byker Grove* on BBC TV. She was commissioned to write an original piece, *Da Gama's Last Stand* for Crucial Films, a comic tale on a Catholic theme. While continuing to write for television, she has worked consistently on her own scripts including *Vinegar Alley*, a four-part serial set in London during a sweltering summer.

Douglas Galbraith was born in Scotland and educated in Glasgow and St Andrews. His first novel, *The Rising Sun*, will be published next year by Picador.

Elizabeth Harris is the author of twelve novels, nine under her own name and three under pseudonyms. The majority of her work has been published by HarperCollins but she has recently signed a three-book contract with Hodder & Stoughton. She has also completed a course in archaeology with the University of Kent and travelled widely on research trips. She was married in 1997 and now spends much of the year in an ancient Breton cottage where the peaceful atmosphere is conducive to writing.

Tobias Hill was born in London and still lives there. His first collection of poetry, *Year of the Dog* (National Poetry Foundation), won an Eric Gregory award, the second, *Midnight in the City of Clocks* (OUP), was a Poetry Book Society Recommendation, and the third, *Zoo* (OUP), is a PBS Commendation. In 1996, he won the Cambridge University Harper-Wood Award for Literature, in 1997 he was a Wingate Scholar, and in 1998, he received an Arts Council Award. His first book of short stories, *Skin* (Faber & Faber), won the Pen-Macmillan Prize. His first novel, *Underground* (Faber & Faber), won a Betty Trask prize. Tobias Hill is London Zoo's inaugural Poet in Residence.

Jude Jones was trained as a classical singer at the Guildhall School of Music and worked professionally in scores of venues across Europe. She was a founding member of The New Music Theatre group and co-creator of Webb Foote Productions in the eighties. In addition to acting, singing and directing, she also wrote most of the material. In the nineties she concentrated on writing: short stories, poems, a play, a lengthy text contribution to the computer game 'First Encounter', and longer prose including a recently completed novel, *The Bandaged Man*.

Nick Kelly has recently achieved considerable recognition as a writer – but not in the field of literature. His songwriting ability earned him the accolade of Best Solo Male Artist at the annual Heineken/Hot Press Irish music critics awards for 1997; this following the eight years in his band, The Fat Lady Sings. He has also won several creative awards as a copywriter at one of Dublin's leading advertising agencies. Nevertheless, Nick remains committed to spending at least some of his life working with words which neither rhyme nor sell.

Juliet McCarthy was born in San Francisco but has spent most of her life since leaving university moving around the world with her husband and five children. Her abiding interest in people, combined with a love of medieval history, has sustained her ambition to write.

Mike McCormack's collection of short stories, *Getting It In The Head* (Jonathan Cape 1996), won the Rooney Prize for Literature. This was followed by a novel, *Crowe's Requiem*, also from Cape. Both books have also been published in America.

Anna McGrail has now had two novels published, *Blood Sisters* and *Mrs Einstein*. She has also written several non-fiction books, including *You And Your New Baby* which won an award from the British Medical Association, and continues to work as an editor and journalist in the field of health and social care.

Denis Sexton lives in County Kildare. His plays and short stories are broadcast on national radio. He also presents his own talks and stories on that medium. Last year, he was shortlisted for the Fingal Scribe, a national short story award. At present, he is reworking a novel before submitting to a publisher.

Hwee Hwee Tan currently lives in New York. Her first novel, *Foreign Bodies* (Michael Joseph), was published when she was 23. She received first class honours in English Literature at the University of East Anglia and was a graduate student at Oxford University. Her short stories have been broadcast by the BBC, including *Hungry Ghost* which won a best-of-the-year award. Her fiction has also been published in *Pen International*, *Critical Quarterly* and *New Writing 6*. In 1997, she received the New York Times Fellowship from New York University.

Phil Whitaker was born in Kent. He studied medicine at Nottingham and creative writing at the University of East Anglia. His debut novel, *Eclipse Of The Sun*, was shortlisted for the 1997 Whitbread First Novel Award, and won both the Mail on Sunday/John Llewellyn Rhys prize and a Betty Trask Award. Phil's second novel, *Triangulation*, is published by Phoenix House this year. He lives in Oxford with his wife Lynn and their two cats.

Carrie Worrall was born in Guisborough. After graduating in modern languages (Russian and French) from Cambridge, she taught in Hong Kong and travelled extensively in the Far East. She worked as an advertising copywriter and journalist living in London, Leeds and Manchester before embarking on the MA in creative writing at UEA. She now lives in Hertfordshire with her husband and son. *Grace*, her first novel, born on a train between Manchester and Norwich, is published by Piatkus.